Praise for Miran

'Oh my heart, this book! What
and bittersweet, and a spark o
Josie Silver, bestselling author of *One D...*

'An engrossing love story, beautifully written'
Sarah Morgan, *Sunday Times* bestselling author

'An exquisitely tender and breathtaking novel,
beautifully written. This is Miranda at her best'
Cathy Bramley, *Sunday Times* bestselling author

'Romantic, heartbreaking and emotional ... A magical
story about love, hope and forgiveness, and I am
envious of anyone who has yet to read it'
Cressida McLaughlin, author of *The Cornish Cream Tea Summer*

'A sweet, clever love story ... I adored this book'
Dorothy Koomson, *Sunday Times* bestselling author

'Tenderly written novel [that] is full of hope
and the joy of taking a second chance'
Daily Express

'A sparkling romance, packed with tenderness'
Woman's Weekly

'Emotional story ... full of both heart and soul'
Fabulous

'A love story we can all connect with'
Woman & Home

'This story will have you championing the pair all the way'
The Sun

Miranda is the author of eleven books, including six *Sunday Times* bestsellers. Her books have been translated into seven languages and have made the bestseller charts in four countries. She has been shortlisted twice for the RNA awards (for Novel of the Year in 2010 with *Fairytale of New York* and again in 2012 for Contemporary Novel of the Year for *It Started With a Kiss*). She has now sold over a million copies of her books worldwide. Miranda lives in the Black Country with her husband and daughter.

Also by Miranda Dickinson

The Day We Meet Again
Somewhere Beyond the Sea
Searching for a Silver Lining
A Parcel for Anna Browne
I'll Take New York
Take A Look at Me Now
When I Fall in Love
It Started With a Kiss
Welcome to My World
Fairytale of New York

Miranda
DICKINSON

our
story

ONE PLACE. MANY STORIES

HQ
An imprint of HarperCollins*Publishers* Ltd
1 London Bridge Street
London SE1 9GF

This edition 2020

1

First published in Great Britain by
HQ, an imprint of HarperCollins*Publishers* Ltd 2020

ISBN: 978-0-00-832324-0

MIX
Paper from
responsible sources
FSC™ C007454
www.fsc.org

This book is produced from independently certified FSC™ paper to ensure responsible forest management.

For more information visit: www.harpercollins.co.uk/green

This book is set in 11/15.5 pt. Caslon

Printed and bound in Great Britain by
CPI Group (UK) Ltd, Croydon, CR0 4YY

For Rachael, with my love.
Because she loved Otty and Joe first.

'When nothing is sure, everything is possible.'
MARGARET DRABBLE

Chapter One

OTTY

It's my last day.

I repeat it in my mind like a mantra as I go through the motions of the job I've done since I was twenty-one. Even though I have longed for this day to arrive, it's surreal to be living it.

Dad keeps glancing over when he thinks I'm not looking. I know what he's thinking. It's two hours until my final shift ends and I haven't had *the talk*. Yet. But I feel it in the air, the low rumble of approaching thunder.

'It won't be the same without you, bab,' Sheila says, setting another mug of tea next to my workbench. Where other people use words, Sheila Wright uses tea. This is easily the thirteenth mug she's brought me today, although, to be honest, I stopped counting around lunchtime.

'In a few weeks you won't even notice I'm not here,' I smile back, reaching for her hand when her eyes glisten. 'And I'll still see you at the cricket.'

She nods, dabbing her nose with a tissue she produces from her sleeve. When I was little, I used to imagine the inside of Sheila Wright's cardigan sleeves as endless winter landscapes of white.

She's as close to a real auntie as I've ever had. I'm going to miss her chats every day.

But it's time to go.

I turn my attention back to the bike frame propped up on the bench. There's something dodgy with its suspension and I'm determined to sort it before I hand in my RoadTrail staff badge. A clean slate for my next big adventure to begin.

An hour later, the inevitable happens.

'It's a good job, this.'

I smile but keep my attention on the suspension unit. 'It is, Dad.'

'I'm not looking for anyone else.'

'Well, you should. Steve and Jarvis can't manage the workshop on their own.'

'Oi,' Jarvis says, his head popping up from the bench on the other side of the workshop. One thing I definitely *won't* miss is never being able to conduct a private conversation in this place.

'I'm just saying you need an extra pair of hands here, Jarv.'

'If they come without a gob it'll be an improvement.' His grin is a balm to his barb. For Jarvis and Steve mickey-taking is a badge of belonging. If they mock you, you're in.

'You hope,' I grin back.

'This is a *proper* job,' Dad says. And there it is.

'So is my new one.'

'I mean a steady job. One you can rely on. People are always going to need their bikes fixing…'

'And they're always going to watch TV.'

'*Writing*,' Dad says, spitting the word out like a fly in his tea. 'That in't safe, bab. Six months and then what? You'll be out on your ear with moths in your wallet.'

I meet his frown. 'I'll be fine.'

I'll be more than fine. Writing is my dream. I've done the sensible thing for years, my full-time shifts in Dad's bike shop nothing compared with the endless unseen hours spent wrangling words onto the page. Tomorrow *that me* gets to step out into the light. I'm still expecting to arrive and find it's all a prank. I'm terrified of failing. But I can't wait to try.

'You can still change your mind.'

'I can't.' I glance over at my colleagues, lowering my voice. 'Russell Styles is expecting me.' *He wants me*, I want to add, but I don't. Dad doesn't understand what that sentence means to me. Out of the fifteen hundred scriptwriters who applied, a famous showrunner chose *me*. Even though it's my first experience as a staff writer, my first in a writers' room. My first of *anything*. Russell read my script and wanted me on his team.

'If you work with Jodie Comer tell her she needs a hunky bike mechanic in her life,' Steve says.

'Hunky? More like *chunky*, mate,' Jarvis shoots back.

Dad doesn't smile with them. 'Just think about it, our Otts. It's risky to rest your bills on a pipe dream.'

Nothing I say will change his mind. So I just hug him.

At the end of the day, we gather by the back door of the workshop. The sun is just beginning to dip over the warehouse roofs of the trading estate and starlings are bickering in the ash trees over the road. I fill my lungs for the last time with the scent of oil and metal, sawdust and leather. It's strange to think I won't smell it again, won't be followed home by it clinging to my clothes and hair.

Sheila is in tears, Steve has his arm around her and even Jarvis isn't cracking jokes. Dad stands beside me, a silent sentinel. For a moment, everything is calm. It only lasts as long as a slow intake

3

of breath, but I feel more expressed by the silence than by anything words could say.

'Right then,' I say, surprised to feel tears arriving. I hand Dad my badge and door pass and he takes it as solemnly as a war widow accepting colours from an officer. 'Thanks, guys. For everything.'

Jarvis gives my arm his usual punch, and then scoops me into an enormous hug. 'Knock 'em dead, Otty. You show 'em.'

I smile against his chest, the pull of Past Me suddenly strong. 'I will.'

Steve shakes my hand, which is the most physical contact I've had with him in all the years we've worked together. 'We'll be watching for your name on them telly credits.'

'Cheers, mate.'

I hug Sheila and Dad. 'See you soon, yeah?'

They nod and stand together as I walk from them across the car park to my car. When I open the driver's door, I turn back and take one last look. As one, the RoadTrail team raise their hands in salute.

I don't let myself cry until I've driven off the estate.

Tonight, I'm going to have a quiet one. Let it all finally sink in. I plan a takeaway from Diamond Balti across the street from my flat with one of their enormous Peshwari naans and a bottle of Chang beer, followed by a night of classic drama repeats on telly. Perfect. I'd say an early night, too, but I know my brain. It rarely switches off before midnight and tonight my nerves will probably push that much later. I'll sleep when it comes.

Monty, my yellow Fiat 500, creaks into the car park and when I kill the engine I sit in the stillness for a moment. Last time I'll make that journey. Last time I'll get home with the itch of not having written all day. Tomorrow, everything changes.

I consider going straight to Diamond Balti, but decide on a shower first. Leaving my car, I punch the entry number into the door lock and head inside. The three flights of stairs seem to take longer to climb this evening but everything feels significant today. I'm on the cusp of the next season of my life, my toes inching towards the edge, ready to leap...

Hang on. What's that?

There's an envelope drawing-pinned to my front door. That's odd. Why wasn't it posted through the letterbox? I pull the pin out, which takes more effort than I expect. Someone bashed it into the painted wood with considerable force. When I look at the brass dome of its head, I can see the pin is dented from whatever implement whoever put it there used. Poor thing. I pocket the pin and the envelope and unlock my front door.

It's not Birmingham's most spacious home, but I love my flat. I've rented it for seven years and it might as well be a palace for the security and comfort it gives me. That was another battle with Dad I stuck out and won. He wanted me to stay at home with him, but I needed my own space and somewhere I could write without having to justify it. I love Dad and I know he loves me, but I wish he wouldn't think he has to protect me from the world. I've stopped trying to argue the toss and instead just go with it, trusting that he'll see I made the right choice in time. This flat was the right choice for me: the first night I lived here, I wrote all night, going into the workshop the next day dizzy with exhaustion but buzzing.

I drop my rucksack by the kitchen counter and pull the envelope from my pocket. Inside is a single sheet of paper, typed.

Dear Miss Perry

NOTICE OF EVICTION
As landlord of Flat 6, Princess Building, West Park Road,
I hereby give notice of the termination of your tenancy
agreement, effective immediately. You must vacate the
property, including all furniture and personal effects, by
10 a.m. tomorrow. Failure to do this will result in legal
action being pursued against you.

Yours sincerely
Barrington Theopolis (Mr)
Landlord

What?

I stare at the paper as if the words might relent and rearrange
themselves into something else. The letter creases as my fingers
curl into fists around it. Eviction? Why? I have always paid my
rent on time, never missing a payment in seven years. I haven't
had any warning of this. He can't just evict me!

Shaking, I reach for my phone and dial Barry's number. I
swallow my panic and tears as I wait for him to answer. I won't
cry on the phone. I *won't*.

'Yes?'

'Barry – Mr Theopolis – it's Ottilie Perry. I just got your letter.'
You utter bastard, I add in my head, sucking in a lungful of air to
keep myself from screaming at him or bursting into tears.

'And?'

'You can't evict me. I've always paid my bills, I've never had a
complaint from you or anyone else in the building…'

'I have another tenant.'

'*I'm* your tenant, Barry. I've been your tenant for seven years.'

'She needs the flat tomorrow.'

I can't believe what I'm hearing. This can't happen, not tonight. My life is supposed to change tomorrow. And not like this. It can't be *this*.

'I need the flat *now*.' Deafening silence on the other end of the line sets my blood boiling. 'And anyway, you can't just evict me. I have rights.'

'That's not my problem.' There's no emotion in his voice, not even a hint of remorse or embarrassment at what he's doing. 'I will collect the keys at 10 a.m. tomorrow.'

'No you bloody won't,' I growl back, any pretence of calm abandoned now. He doesn't deserve civility. And I'm not going to beg him. If he wants me gone, it will be on my terms. 'I'm starting a new job tomorrow. So if you want the keys *you* will be here at 6 a.m. And I will require my deposit in full, in cash.'

'*Six?*'

'Six. Or else it will have to be late tomorrow evening. Your choice.'

A beat. I can hear his breathing rasp a little. 'Fine. 6 a.m., sharp.'

I hang up before he has the chance to do it first.

Anger fires through my body, tears and shock chasing its heels. My legs give way and now I'm on the floor, shaking, sobbing, gasping for breath. I should fight this, get legal advice, refuse to leave. But there's no time. I have a new job tomorrow and that's all that matters. I will not give Barry Theopolis the satisfaction of a fight. I will take my business elsewhere.

I just have no idea where.

I allow myself one moment to look around my home – now *not* my home for much longer – taking in the features so familiar

I don't see them anymore. The faded curtains, the stacks of books rising around the walls like the skyscrapers of the city because I've never had space for bookshelves, the sagging sofa that came with the flat and will be left here tomorrow when I'm no longer its tenant.

I can't believe I have to leave.

I sit up, drag my sleeves across my eyes to rid them of tears, will strength into my spine. I need to start packing. I'll work out the rest later.

Chapter Two

JOE

'Come over.'

'I can't.'

'Why not?'

'I have to work tonight.'

Her frustrated sigh slaps my ear where I hold my phone to it. 'Why don't you just shag Russell Styles and get it over with?'

'It's my job, Vic.'

'Yeah, right.'

'It *is*.'

'You know what, Joe? Forget it. You're not the only person I'm seeing.'

Wow.

I blink at the empty room. There's direct and then there's Victoria. I mean, I never imagined I was the only bloke in her life but I kind of thought she'd keep that to herself. 'Right, well. Have fun.'

I end the call.

'You off out, Joe?' Matt, my housemate, bobs his head around the door from the hall.

'Apparently not.' When Matt's expression clouds, I hold up my phone. 'I think I just got dumped.'

'You *think*? Who by?'

'Victoria.'

He chuckles and scratches his hair, which always looks like he's just rolled out of bed. Which he probably has. 'I thought you'd given up on her months ago.'

I grimace back. I should have, but I've been busy. And she has a habit of reappearing when I need distraction from work. 'Turns out she beat me to it.'

'Bummer, mate.' I expect him to mosey off to whatever it is he does most evenings, but he remains by the doorway. 'So – you're not out tonight?'

'Nope. Doesn't matter anyway. I have these sample episodes to get done and the agency sent over a script clean-up they want for the end of the week.'

'Man in demand, Joe.'

'Lucky me. You off out?'

A flicker of something passes across his face. 'Yeah. No. Not sure yet.'

He's working on a feature film script at the moment and is lost in his head most of the time. At least, that's what he *says* it is. Judging by the contents of the ashtray he regularly leaves in the kitchen – never quite making the bin – something else might be calling him to dreamland. 'Hey, but you should totally go out anyway.'

'Too busy. Like I said.'

'Joe. Stop wallowing.'

'I – er – I'm not?'

'That's what Victoria expects you to do, right? Hole yourself away, crying into your beer.'

Since when has Matt Evans ever worried about me? 'Actually, she expected me to be going out tonight. She dumped me because I wasn't.'

'Right.' He nods but his brow is still knotted. 'Even still, you should go out. At least get food or – something. I mean, when was the last time you ate?'

I'm about to dismiss this when I realise he's made a good point. I haven't eaten since a hastily grabbed bacon roll before my meeting with Russell this morning. On cue, my stomach protests its emptiness. I could go to that all-you-can-eat multi-ethnic buffet place in town where my friend works. I could eat enough so I don't have to worry about food again tonight and then work through till three or four-ish. Rumour is we have eight new writers arriving tomorrow and I need to be head and shoulders above them when Russell walks in.

'I might just dash out for food, actually,' I say, snapping my laptop shut and grabbing my keys from the kitchen counter. 'Do you want anything?'

'Nah, I'm good,' Matt says, noticeably brighter than a minute ago. 'Go. A break might be just what your brain needs.'

When he nods at my laptop I have a horrible feeling he saw the tellingly blank page on it before I closed the lid. I'm *not* stuck. I'm just… in a bit of an inspiration lull. Food will help.

Food *does* help. I don't want to admit Matt's right, but being away from the house does wonders for the script. It helps that my old schoolmate Nish works at the buffet place and doesn't care if I work while I eat. An hour turns into two and before I know it, it's almost one in the morning. Nish grins at me as I apologise on my way out.

By the time I get back to the house, sleep and a full belly are conspiring against me. Heading to bed with every intention of working there till the birds start singing, I crash out as soon as I get in.

Which is why, when I jump awake in brave sunlight and grab my phone, I'm sick to discover it's 6 a.m. I'd planned to get into Ensign Media early this morning to be there before the new intake arrives. Cursing, I throw on fresh clothes and drag my fingers through my hair in a lame attempt to tame it before I dash downstairs.

It's only when I'm waiting for my grumpy old filter coffee machine to do its stuff that I notice the note.

A bright pink sticky note, its edges curling, weighed down with a butter knife in the sea of crumbs on the breadboard.

Sorry, mate.
Moved out.
Matt

What?

I snatch the note from its crumby resting place and blink hard to clear sleep from my eyes. *Moved out?* When?

And then I let my gaze travel through the open kitchen door to the hallway. No shoes. No horrible shoe rack. *Matt's* wretched shoe rack he insisted on having there, stinking out the space. I walk through to the empty hall, turn left into the living room and see more evidence: the four empty shelves in the large bookcase where Matt's games and terrible sports biographies always lived. By the TV, no jumble of games console wires and controllers, no Xbox and Wii. I don't have to check his room to work out that the books and his desk will be missing from there, too.

He bloody moved out. A week before the rent is due.

Slowly, it hits me.

He owes me three weeks' rent. Money I don't have.

I can feel panic rising and make myself breathe against the assault. I still have a week. I need to regroup, work out a plan. Matt is an utter dick for doing this to me but I have more important things to do than waste any brain-time on it today – like making sure my boss sees me before everyone else.

Everything else can wait.

Chapter Three

OTTY

Sixteen boxes of books.

Sixteen.

And no furniture – unless you count the threadbare folding chair covered in flamingos I've had since university.

Clothes, yes. Shoes, not as many as people think a woman of my age should own. But the two suitcases in which they are currently hiding are barely visible beneath Mount Book Box.

'What am I supposed to do with them?' I ask my suddenly ex-landlord.

He shrugs and does that half-screwed-up expression of his that could mean anything from amusement to bemusement to agitation, but always looks like trapped wind. At least my eviction means I won't have to see his gurning anymore. Right now I'll take any silver lining I can get.

'I don't care what you do. Get them off my premises by 5 p.m. or I'm burning them.'

Never one for moderation, Barry Theopolis.

I won't argue with him. And I won't let him win. Today is the day my life changes and this nasty little man is not going to spoil it.

'Fine,' I say, my chin high.

He was halfway down the stairs anyway, but I see it register in a shake of his shoulders as he disappears back to his stupid big American car parked on the double-yellows outside. Why is there never a traffic warden around when you want one? He has parked illegally every time he's visited in the past eighteen months and not even a whisper of a parking ticket. How is that fair?

The slam of the front door reverberates through my shoes.

At least I have my deposit back. Grubby notes stuffed angrily into an envelope, shoved into my hands like I'd just demanded Barry's kidney. It will help me move on, even if right now all I want to do is curl up on the doormat that's no longer mine and sleep this all away.

I rub my eyes, the effects of my frantic, tearful all-night packing session setting in. Thank goodness the guys in Diamond Balti had a stack of empty boxes to give me when I hurried over there sobbing. If they hadn't, I don't know how I would have packed everything. I take one last longing look at the locked door of my flat, only now seeing the scuffs and scratches in its tired paintwork, the dark smudges around the Yale lock. Have those always been there? I don't know. But then how often do you closely inspect the outside of your front door when you have a key?

I *really* can't go back to Dad's. I won that argument – to go back would be to admit Dad was right. And if he's right about that, he'll think it makes him right about everything else, including my new job.

Because it isn't just working for Russell Styles that Dad disagreed with. There's another, bigger decision he still doesn't accept, over a year since I made it. I can't let him think for a moment that I was mistaken, then or now. I have to move on.

The thought twists my guts and my grumbling stomach reminds me it hasn't yet been fed. I check my watch. Just over an hour to spare. Is it enough? The book box mountain stares at me and I consider the three flights of stairs between here and the tiny car park. Sixteen journeys there and back are going to take a while. I consider knocking on my neighbour Stan's door at Flat 7, across the box-strewn landing. If he's up he might help me, but when I saw him yesterday he told me he was on nights again. It's barely 7.30 a.m.: I can't wake him.

Stuff it. I'll just have to shift them myself and pray that Monty's aged suspension is up to the task of carrying all my worldly goods. I grab the first box, whelp a little at its weight, and stagger down the stairs.

Forty minutes later, I'm squeezed into the minuscule amount of box-free space inside Monty, wishing I'd fallen for a bigger car eight years ago. A Fiat 500 seemed lovely back then, when I was still in my room at Dad's house and the dream of my own place seemed about as likely as me being headhunted by Disney. There must be some world record for the greatest number of boxes packed into a tiny yellow car. If so, I am the clear winner.

Monty creaks and groans around the roads on the way to West One, a brand-new skyscraper of offices and studios in the heart of the city. A dozen media and production companies have recently moved here, with more set to follow, boosting the city's bid to become the creative hub of the country outside London.

Russell Styles' production company is Ensign Media, on the eleventh floor of West One, as stated in the letter I have read and reread, which is currently lying open and slightly crumpled on the passenger seat, one corner crushed by my suitcase. The entry details to the building made my head spin. There's a barrier and a code and first-come-first-served parking – and that's before the coded entry and ID-swipe at reception, the airport-style metal detectors and the pass-operated lifts. What if I fail at the first hurdle and never reach the eleventh floor?

That's if I make it into the building at all. Car park security might take one look at me and think I'm a squatter trying to move in. Who arrives for the first day of their dream job with the entire contents of their home in their car?

And even if I do make the writers' room of Ensign Media, will they decide I'm too old to be there? Or too uncool? I imagine the writers' table populated entirely by twenty-three-year-olds – guys in cropped drainpipe chinos and striped tees with identical hipster beards, wafer-thin women in vintage print tunics over skinny jeans with huge scarves and expertly messy up-dos.

I have to stop this.

Positive panda, my nan used to say. 'If you're thinking it will be bad you'll be right. If you think it's going to be good, it just might be.'

I smile. Nan would be all over this if she were here. Striding into that room like a woman half her age, charming the socks right off Russell Styles. I wonder if she can see me today from wherever she is now. Is she cheering me on from the edge of her armchair, fists in the air and verbal Fs flying, like she used to while watching her beloved American wrestlers?

I score a parking space between two huge 4x4s, which even though it means a squeeze out of my door a contortionist would be proud of, is still one box ticked on today's list. I glance at my poor overloaded Monty as I walk towards the building that houses my dreams, praying security don't think he's a potential bomb threat. Would a terrorist cover their boxes in pink felt-tip-pen-drawn hearts, with bubble-letter labels like *Hunky Hardbacks* and *Lifesavers* and *Weepie Treats*? I don't think so.

At West One's imposing entrance I stop, letting my gaze rise with the steel and green-tinted glass twenty-two floors up to the leaden Birmingham sky. A single, brave shaft of sunlight is pushing through the stubborn clouds up there.

That's me, I think. Ottilie Perry, terrified new apprentice screenwriter, doing her best to shine.

I take a breath, shoulder my rucksack and walk in.

Chapter Four

JOE

'We don't need any more writers.'

Script co-ordinator Daphne gives me a look like I've just suggested oxygen should be optional, her eyebrows rising above the retro tortoiseshell rims of her glasses. A year ago that would have reduced me to a gibbering puddle of compliance, but not today. Today, I am *beyond* that.

'Scared they'll all be better than you?' she purrs.

'Of course not,' I snap back. 'Nobody's better than me.'

'Keep telling yourself that, Joseph.'

She reaches past me a little too close for comfort and smiles as she empties the last of the filter coffee into her eco-mug. I watch her sashay back to her desk. *Thanks for nothing, Daphne Davies.* I yank open a cupboard door in the 'office kitchen' – which is the biggest use of hyperbole in this place – and scrabble around for filters and ground coffee.

I'm not scared. I'm *not*.

But what if one of them is brilliant? Like, *Phoebe Waller-Bridge* brilliant?

Leaving the coffee machine complaining loudly as it brews a

fresh pot, I wander back to the windowless writers' room where the newly appointed scriptwriters will join the rest of us in an hour's time. Each place at the large, oval, beech-effect laminate table is marked by a blank pad of paper, a freshly printed series bible and a tented strip of whiteboard plastic, upon which each person will write their name. I think about how easily the dry-wipe-marker names can be removed and remember the scene last week when Russell fired half the team. Their names erased in one stroke, their seats ominously empty as the script meeting continued without them. In the pit of my stomach, a ball of nerves begins to roll.

Russell rates me, I remind myself. I was first on this team. But some of the writers he fired were *really* good. And now there's a whole new bunch to contend with.

I sneaked a look at the new intake's names on the sign-in sheet earlier. If I were casting them as characters in this unfolding drama, what personality traits would I assign them? Their names suggest mostly middle-class upbringings, the Charlottes and Jakes, the Jens and Joshes. But one sounds like she's coming straight from Swiss Finishing School – *Ottilie*, for crying out loud. Her last name reins it in a bit – Perry, a pretty common surname around here – but still. What kind of monster lumbers their kid with a name like that?

Are the new writers ambitious? Genius wordsmiths? Or are they the kind you find in any writers' room, the ones that keep their heads down and do the donkey-work? Sometimes it pays to be anonymous but consistent in this business.

I have no intention of hiding. This is *my* gig, my domain. And no *got-in-through-a-training-scheme* hustler is going to dethrone me.

'Mr Joe Carver, as I live and breathe!'

My professional smile snaps into place as I turn to see to my employer. 'Russ, hey.'

'Good to have you still on board, man.'

'Good to be here.'

Showrunner Russell Styles is a little flushed from his journey up. A heart scare at Christmas has him yomping up eleven floors-worth of stairs to get to work every day and he's very proud of it, even if he can't breathe well for a while afterwards. Not that it does much to counter the constant diet of high-fat, high-sugar crapness found in the writers' room, or the indulgent industry dinners he's a first-call guest for these days. But every little helps, I guess.

He slaps a comradely arm against my back and I'm drawn into a half-hug I wouldn't volunteer for. 'Now, don't worry about the new writers. That bright-eyed eight will likely be a stoic two by the end of the week.'

I remember the sudden sackings last week and swallow hard. 'Not worried, RS. I know you need me.'

His eyes twinkle. 'Always, Joe. Always. *So*, shall we prepare the bear pit?'

An hour later, the writers' room is a quivering mass of bravado and fear. My colleagues who survived the cut sit a little taller in their seats, but I know they're weighing up the newbies as much as I am. *Lots* of beards this time. All identical in shape, which is impressive if a little disconcerting. Beyond that, the standard cropped-chino-slash-brogues-without-socks ratio is strong here. Four women: two of the hair-flicking, oversized scarf-sporting variety; one rocking a buzz cut and impressive painted Doc Martens, who looks like she means business; and one – well – *surprisingly normal-looking* one. She has bright pink tips to her hair and rather lovely eyes, but beyond that she could be any person in any street. She looks scared to death. She should be.

The door opens and Russell strides in. As one, the writers rise and applaud. He feigns embarrassment but not convincingly. It's all part of the theatre of the writers' room: the scene of more drama than ever makes it to the screen.

'*People*,' he says, eventually signalling for the applause to end. There's an unholy concerto of scrapes as seats are resumed. 'Welcome. Before we begin, let me say this: every writer sitting here has earned their place in this room. There are no hangers-on. You are here because I believe in you.' The new intake blushes, gazing at Russell with even wider eyes. Those of us who survived Friday's cull aren't so comforted. 'Now, we have work to do. We're running this as a script-to-screen outfit. Three months to beat out at least a pilot and four episodes, preferably six, with a view to a full commission and a fast move to production.'

I see frowns being battled around the table by the newbies. It's new – the way a lot of emerging drama is happening in the US – and those of us with more experience are wary of it. More work, less time to do it in and significantly less money for doing it. But it's *Russell Styles*. And Ensign Media is one of the hottest properties in the business right now. I glance over at the girl with the pink-tipped hair. She looks like she might burst into tears.

Just then, her eyes flick to me. Before I can look away, she smiles. For a second I forget to listen to Russell. It's a tiny smile, barely there, but it seems to illuminate the space around her. I glance at the name she's written on the wipeable board: *Ottilie*. I was completely wrong in my assumption about her. She's lovely.

When I look back, she's staring at Russell again.

A little shaken, I pull my attention back to my boss.

No. That is *not* happening today…

Chapter Five

OTTY

I *know* him.

I make myself listen to Russell Styles, but it bugs me. Where have I seen that guy before? I should have looked at his name board, but I daren't take my eyes off my new boss again in case I miss anything. I've waited my whole life for this opportunity: I can't stuff it up now.

'Many of you have never worked like this, I appreciate, but trust me, this is the most efficient way to get our story to the screen,' he says. 'I want us to be a consistent, reliable unit, writing show after show. Multi-genre, multi-platform stuff. I'll need you to be flexible. You might be team writing; you might go it alone. I may pull some of you from this crew to another mini writers' room on a different project. What matters is that we make *magic*...'

Russell is an even bigger presence than I thought he'd be. Confident, comfortable at the epicentre of all our nervous energy, he has all the swagger of a man at the top of his game. His last series for BBC Studios won armfuls of awards and the leading actor is currently being mooted as the next Bond. He could pitch them a nursery rhyme right now and they'd probably commission it. But the success of his next project is down to us. To *me*. It's terrifying.

I'm spooked by the thought so I let my eyes stray to the names on the boards, slowly moving round the table until I reach the bloke I recognise.

Joe Carver.

Oh wow, that's *Joe Carver*! I'd forgotten he'd be here.

I read an interview with Russell Styles, while my application for this project was under consideration, and Russell mentioned Joe by name. *When you have the calibre of Joe Carver on the team, you know it's something special.*

I see Joe smile when Russell catches his eye, a nod of the head that tells all of us he and RS are buddies.

I watched the episode of *Southside* Joe wrote at least fifty times. He only ever did one, and I could never understand why. It was remarkable – taking the original book's story and deepening every theme for the screen without it ever affecting the pace. That's *hard*. Gabriel Marley won a Best Supporting Actor TV BAFTA for his role in that episode, but it was Joe's words that put him there.

And now I'm his colleague. My writing counted alongside his.

The thought brings beads of cold sweat across my palms.

We break for lunch at twelve and there's a dash to the food table. First-day buffet, Russell warns: we can't expect this every day. I stand back to avoid the crush and decide to move out to reception for a breath of fresh air. The windowless writers' room is a little oppressive and I need space. It's good to see light again, the city spreading out to the horizon.

I glance down to the car park eleven floors below. I keep thinking about poor Monty overloaded with all my worldly goods. What am I going to do? I'm over the moon about being here but where I'll go tonight after work tempers the thrill. Outside of this new job, I'm anchorless, a floating state of *me* in the middle of the city.

My head is too crammed with it all. I'll work out something later.

I sink into a leather armchair by the window and wish I could disappear into the cool darkness between its cushions. Hearing voices approaching, I shrink further down in the hope they won't see me.

'He did what?' A woman's voice drifts in, amusement playing in her tone.

'Moved out.' The man doesn't sound anywhere near as happy.

'When?'

'Last night.'

'And you had no warning?'

'Apart from the sticky note he left, no.'

'Dumped by Post-it? Poor baby.'

'Yeah, thanks for the sympathy, Daphne. What am I going to do?'

'Just advertise the room.'

'When, exactly? I have less than a week to find my own share of the rent and two pitches to sketch out for Russ.'

'So, ask your landlord for more time.'

I hear a long sigh before the man speaks again. 'Eric's wanted an excuse to get me out for months. One whiff of this and he'll have a professional couple in there like a shot. I can't lose the house, Daph. The light is perfect there. I can think there. It'd take me years to find somewhere else like that. It's… my *muse*.'

The woman laughs. 'You are such a diva, Joseph.'

Joseph? Is that…?

'What do I do?'

'For heaven's sake, Joe…' I hear the click of heels travelling to the reception desk, followed by the rustle of paper. '*Room available immediately. One month's rent in advance.* Now write your mobile number at the bottom and I'll stick it on the company noticeboard. There. Sorted.'

I wait until I hear them return to the writers' room, my heart thudding. When the door closes, I spring up from the chair and hurry out to Ensign Media's entrance, scanning the walls for a noticeboard. I spot it over by the water cooler.

ROOM AVAILABLE IMMEDIATELY.
ONE MONTH'S RENT IN ADVANCE.
NO SMOKERS. NO DIRECTORS. NO DIVAS.
ENQUIRIES: JOE CARVER

The rent amount he wants will leave a single crumpled tenner in the deposit envelope Barry gave me today. It's a risk I'll have to take. I don't even stop to take down Joe's number. Ripping the notice from the mocha felt of the board, I stuff it in my pocket, take a breath and march back into the writers' room.

Today is about taking chances. Making changes. This is a serendipity I can't ignore. Pushing through the huddled bodies of my new writing colleagues, I walk straight up to Joe Carver.

'I heard you were looking for someone,' I say a little too loudly.

The two writers with him stare at me.

'Ah, so you've heard the rumours already?' one chuckles.

I smile but keep my eyes on Joe. He's looking at me like Chewbacca just interrupted his lunch. Telltale nerves tremble in my hands and the temptation to leg it from the room surges inside me. But I can't back down now.

'I heard you were looking for someone,' I repeat, holding up the crumpled note. His eyes widen when he sees it.

'How did you...?'

'I'd like to apply.' He says nothing, so I press on. 'I'm Ottilie, Otty to everyone. I need to move from my flat – already have, actually. This morning. Wasn't my idea. I have everything in my car downstairs in the car park... The thing is, I have the money. Cash. Up front. And if you accept, I can move in this evening.' My lungs ache when I snatch breath into them, a swell of blood rising in my cheeks. 'Sorry. That came out fast.'

'It did.'

The other writers have edged away, leaving Joe and I staring at each other. His eyes are *really* blue. Up close I'm surprised by how young he looks. It makes me wonder if I look old to him. Not that it matters, but it might count against me. I was a little *creative* with my age on my application for this job, but now I'm here I can't bluff it.

'So...?' I ask, instantly wishing I hadn't because Joe doesn't reply.

He hates the idea.

I've said too much, blown my chance with the verbal torrent I just aimed at him. *This* is why I don't do this. Now he thinks I'm a pink-haired vagabond freak living in her car, trying to move into his space. Why did I think he'd even consider me?

'Yeah,' he says.

'Sorry?'

'You can see it after we finish here, if you like?'

'Really?'

28

'Mm-hmm.' He glances to the side as if seeking back-up.

'Yes,' I say quickly, before he thinks better of it. 'I'd like that.'

'Great. Thanks, Ottilie.'

He doesn't leave, like I expect him to. I don't know whether to say anything else or just grin inanely back. I don't want to risk this arrangement that feels as if it's balanced on fragile ice.

Then Joe Carver smiles at me.

It's warm and wide and inviting. And it's all for me.

Oh *crap*…

Chapter Six

JOE

I must be out of my mind.

Why did I agree to let her see the house? She's clearly strange. I mean, who carries all their stuff in their car? I don't know why she had to leave her last place, either. It could be something *really bad*. And in five minutes she'll know where I live.

Her smile is to blame. I thought the small glimpse of it was charming, but the full version blew me away.

Ugh. I never had this issue with Matt.

I move quickly around the house, shoving piles of dirty clothes under my bed and stuffing stacks of paper and notebooks into the nearest cupboard. My space is a bombsite when I'm working and I didn't expect to have a prospective housemate visit today. The bath is passable; a quick once-over with an antibac wipe makes the sink toothpaste- and beard-trimming-free. There's no time to vacuum, but stripped oak floorboards are thankfully forgiving in that regard; and at least I remembered to raid Ensign's fridge for fresh milk before I headed home. I give the liquid air freshener Mum brought the last time she visited a tentative sniff, but think better of spraying it around. According to the label, it's Dewy Roses. It smells like loo cleaner to me.

Ottilie might not like the house. I'm not sure that would be a bad thing.

But she has nice eyes. And a lovely smile. And *cash*.

Maybe a trial month is good idea. Test the arrangement – just to make sure she isn't a closet psycho or someone who wields vintage Samurai swords as a hobby. If it doesn't work out at least I'll have Eric off my back for a while and four weeks to find another housemate. By then Russell will have my sample scripts and I can think about everything else again.

I move the same ornament on the mantelpiece two inches to the left that I moved two inches to the right a minute ago. Groaning, I shove my hands into my jeans pockets to keep them still.

I don't know why I feel nervous.

Okay, maybe I do. Someone new means new rules, new rhythms, a whole new energy in the house. And she's a *girl*. I like girls, but I've never had one as a housemate. Most of my relationships with girls have been strictly your-place-or-mine deals. Lots of fun, but you both get to go home afterwards. No shared bathrooms, no arguments over the TV remote.

A knock at the door makes me jump and I grab a final look in the mirror before I go to answer it.

She's waiting on the doorstep like a rabbit about to scarper. When I offer my hand she grips it like a lifebuoy. A blush blooms across her cheeks and my nervous laugh mirrors hers. It feels like a first date, which is ridiculous.

'Hi,' she says, letting my hand go. 'Can I…?'

'Oh, sure. Sorry. Come in.'

I follow her into the hall and notice a layer of dust on the shelf under the mirror by the front door. I give it a surreptitious wipe as she pauses to inspect the Minton-tiled floor.

'That's gorgeous. Is it original?'

'Yes. My landlord Eric renovated the house about ten years ago and it was the first thing he restored. Nice, huh?'

'It's beautiful.' She straightens. 'Um, where do we go?'

'Just in there,' I say, pointing to the living room.

She unleashes that smile at me before she walks in.

I take a breath. *Cool and calm, Carver.*

The late-afternoon sun is streaming in through the large bay window and I silently thank the house for showing itself at its best. The way light fills the rooms is one of the things I love most about this place. Watching Ottilie now, the warm gold sunlight playing in her hair, I am struck by a sudden sense that she was always supposed to be here.

Steady on…

I shake the thought and launch into the tour.

Ottilie politely inspects every room, nodding and making encouraging noises. So far, so good. Finally, we reach what might be her room. I've left it until last for two reasons: firstly, that I wanted the rest of the house to win her over before she sees the bedroom, and secondly, because it's significantly smaller than my room. Matt didn't care but girls have opinions on this kind of thing. What if she prefers mine to hers? What if she'll only move in if we swap? Am I willing to surrender my sanctuary?

The answer to that is academic. I'll *have* to be.

She's very quiet. Standing with her back to me, facing the entire wall of empty bookshelves and small double bed. I can't tell what she's thinking. I don't want to say anything too soon, but her silence is unnerving.

And then I notice her shoulders start to shake.

Oh no. Anything but that…

'Is it—' I fumble my words. 'I mean, are you…?'

The shaking intensifies and a sob escapes. This is not good.

'Ottilie?'

'It's Otty.' She sinks to the bed, her back still to me.

'Otty – are you okay?'

'I'm sorry,' she says, wiping her eyes.

My heart hits the IKEA rug. 'Look, if you don't like it we could always discuss swapping…'

'No,' she says. It isn't the kind of no that's negotiable.

Well, that's that then.

'No problem. Let's just go back downstairs,' I begin. But then she turns. And she's smiling.

'It's *perfect.*'

'It is?'

She nods, her eyes glistening. '*So… many… shelves.*'

Eh?

'Shelves?'

'For my books. I have a lot of books.' She gives a loud sniff. 'My old place had no bookcases. I just had piles everywhere. Of *books*,' she adds quickly.

It's a little bit adorable and it breaks the ice.

Downstairs we talk turkey. That is, we agree she'll move in pretty much as soon as we've finished talking about it.

'Furniture,' I say, the thought suddenly occurring. Matt had little in the house apart from a desk in his room, a weird cast-iron

33

pan-stacking *thing* in the kitchen and that horrific shoe rack in the hall.

'I don't have any.'

'None at all?'

'One chair. With flamingos on it.' She giggles when she sees my confusion. 'You'll see. But no other furniture. Just books.'

She is a total surprise and the very last kind of person I imagined I'd share a home with. And she isn't kidding about the books: sixteen boxes of them. How she got them all into the yellow Fiat 500 parked outside is mindboggling.

Within an hour they're all in the house – *our* house now. Otty insists on buying pizza to celebrate and I don't argue. I find a bottle of wine Matt forgot in his hurry to leave and we open it. We talk for hours in the living room while ITV3 plays reruns of crime dramas on the TV in the corner – Morse and DCI Banks, Vera Stanhope and Hamish Macbeth all speaking words penned by so many screenwriters before us.

And just like that, Otty is in.

Chapter Seven

OTTY

Waking up in a new house is *weird*.

Especially when the Someone Else Who Lives There walks out of the bathroom wearing only a towel, just as you're heading in.

I was *not* prepared for that. To be fair, I don't think Joe was either.

I can't tell if the flush in his cheeks is from the shower or our meeting.

'So. Morning, then,' he grins.

'Morning.'

If I wasn't so mortified right now, I might enjoy this moment. I've felt like I'm at a disadvantage so far: moving into Joe's house, starting work at Joe's workplace. Even last night, when we laughed and chatted into the early hours, I was still aware that Joe was so familiar with everything in the house – which drawer the cutlery is in, where the wine glasses live, even which cushions belong on which chair in the living room. Now, in my thankfully modest nightwear, I finally have an advantage.

'Nice T-shirt,' he says, nodding at my Tom Walker tee.

'Cheers. Um, nice – *towel*?' I reply. That's the line that breaks the tension.

This is going to take some getting used to…

Half an hour later I come downstairs and find Joe in the kitchen, thankfully fully clothed. The coffee machine is working away, filling the space with its warmth and roastiness. Caffeine is definitely destined to be my saviour this morning. Even though we only had one bottle of wine between us last night, the combination of that and the huge adrenalin rush of yesterday has left my head decidedly the worse for wear. Joe doesn't seem to be in the same condition, amazingly fresh-faced considering the late night and our early start.

'Coffee's on,' he says, buttering toast on a breadboard that looks as old as the house. He looks up. 'You do like coffee, don't you?' Before I can reply he bats away the question with a wave of the butter knife. 'What am I saying? You're a writer: of course you do.'

Just like that. *You're a writer.* The first time it's been acknowledged in my everyday life. It isn't a jibe or a criticism: it's a fact. I feel tears threaten my eyes, which is completely daft, so I busy myself with finding a mug. Most of the kitchen stuff from my flat is still in a box in my room, but I brought my mugs downstairs last night and now they sit awkwardly in the cupboard next to Joe's far more upmarket ones.

'So, is it weird in the writers' room with us new writers coming in?'

'A bit.' He munches a triangle of toast. 'Doesn't make much difference to me. I just keep my head down, keep doing the job.'

'Some people yesterday were talking about the last intake getting fired. That must have been horrific, losing friends like that.'

'They weren't friends.'

'Oh.'

He waves the toast in apology. 'I mean, I don't usually do the making-friends-at-work thing.'

I glance at the slice of toast I've just picked up. I don't know whether I'm hungry now. 'Why?'

'Well, because…' Joe slides out a chair from the kitchen table and sits. 'Okay, the thing is, Russell is a bit impetuous. If people aren't working well in the writers' room, they go.'

Now I'm certain my appetite has gone.

'How long did the previous intake last?'

'I don't think you need to…'

'*How long?*'

'Less than a week.'

Winded, I sit heavily on a chair. The air around me becomes thick and I can't suck enough in to stop the burn in my lungs. 'No…'

'Hey, no, don't panic.'

'It's impossible not to. This whole thing is impossible…'

'Stop it. They weren't your lot, okay? They weren't *you*…' He's looking straight at me and I don't want him to see my fear, don't want him to know that about me. But it's too late and yet again I've revealed my inexperience. But suddenly his hand is on mine on the table and I don't know how to react. I look up at him. 'That is – I mean – you can do this. You can prove to Russ that you belong there.'

'How?'

'By believing you should be.' He shrugs, his fingers drifting back from mine like a gentle tide. 'Fake it till you make it. You know you're good enough – deep down. I mean, you had to believe that to even apply for this job.'

Do I believe I'm good enough? Right now I'm so scared I can't remember feeling anything but fear. I saw the advert on a screenwriting website and applied before I had time to think better of it. I sent my sample script – a twenty-five-minute drama pilot about a Midlands street not unlike the one I grew up on – and I honestly didn't think I'd hear anything from it. 'I just don't want to *not* be good enough, you know?'

Joe smiles. 'Do I know? Every day of my life, right there. Just tell yourself this: everyone is bricking it. Even the biggest, loudest mouths in that room. Even Russell. Each of us knows we're only as good as the next sentence we write.' He drains his coffee cup and stands. 'And if that doesn't work, just imagine everyone naked.'

'I read your script.'

I look up from the coffee station to see Rona, one of my fellow new writers, bearing down on me. She doesn't smile but I've already learned this isn't a bad sign. I'm surprised she's read my work, even though the last thing Russell told us yesterday was that he'd put everyone's sample scripts in the shared Dropbox file so we could familiarise ourselves with everyone's style. Or spy on the competition, according to Joe. I haven't looked at anyone else's yet. I need my nerves to calm down sufficiently before I do.

'Did you?'

'Yeah. *Amazing*, girl. Like, full-on authenticity.'

'Wow – um, thanks.'

'Happy to write with you if we have to pair up?' she says.

The compliment takes a moment to sink in. 'I'd love that. Thanks, Rona.'

She nods and heads to her seat.

The wild flinging open of the door sends us all scuttling to our chairs as Russell sweeps in. His handclap bounces around the room. 'Morning, team. Ready to work? Good.'

I watch him pacing the floor as he explains our brief for the first batch of scripts, remembering Joe's remark from breakfast. I can't believe anything scares Russell Styles. He oozes confidence, like it's sewn into the very fabric of his being. Then I recall Joe's *other* piece of advice and have to look down at my laptop to hide my smile.

We spend the morning going over Russell's vision for the series, the characters and themes we're going to adopt as our own and the style he believes will set this production apart from anything else currently on the market. The series bible is already twenty pages long: heaven only knows how big it will be once we all start writing.

I glance over at Joe, who is hunched over his laptop, typing like his life depends upon it. It's as if he's within an invisible box, oblivious to the rush of noise and energy around him. Contained, in every sense of the word. I admire his focus – I mean, that's obviously how he's got to where he is in his career.

I look down at the notes I'm making as I chat to my colleagues and I like what I see. I know it's early days and I know I'll need more than a few notes to impress Russell, but I like this strange new life of mine. Now I just have to work out how to make it successful.

Chapter Eight

JOE

Otty looks like she's been here for ever.

I watch her across the room, a smiling, chatting beacon in the group of writers that surround her. You would never know she was the same panicked housemate I had breakfast with this morning.

I'd like to think my pep talk made this happen. But the more I watch, the more I'm convinced this is all Otty.

She hasn't even been here two full days yet but she seems to know everybody already. As for me, I've tried my best *not* to notice them. Because knowing them means two things: first, you see their work and how good they are, which is never good for your head; and second, there's the whole *solidarity thing* that steps in between the job and the team. Both of them take your eyes off the ball – and that's dangerous. I don't want to be obliged to anyone but myself.

Otty didn't get the memo about this, apparently.

'Close your mouth, there's a train coming.' Daphne slides into the vacant seat by mine, pleased with her jibe.

'I wasn't…'

'Joseph, chill. It was a joke.' I see her following my line of sight and make sure I'm looking at one of the hair-flickers next to Otty. 'Ah, one of the Charlottes taken your fancy, hmm?'

'Nope.' Not that it's any of her business.

'Whatever. Look, I might have someone for your spare room.' She waits. When I don't respond her smile morphs into a frown. 'Okay, I thought that news must just have cracked your face.'

I bring my attention back to her. 'Thanks, but I have somebody.'

'What? When did this happen?'

'Yesterday. She moved in last night.'

Daphne folds her arms. '*She?*'

'I think it's going to work out,' I say, quickly adding: 'And if it doesn't, it gives me more time to find someone else.'

'And how did you find this – person? Telepathy?'

'Actually, she found *me*.' It feels good to say it and I don't know why. Other than the gift of disapproval oozing from my colleague, which I am enjoying more than I should.

Just then, Otty glances over and smiles at me. The game's up: Daphne clocks it immediately.

'You are *kidding* me.'

'Hey, it was your note that did it. Cheers for that, Daph.'

Even her perfect dewy foundation can't disguise the indignant flush that rises in her cheeks. 'What happened to "we don't need any more writers"? What happened to "I don't date colleagues"?'

'It isn't like that.'

'Isn't it?'

She's really rattled, isn't she? Having the upper hand with Daphne is a surprise development but it makes Otty even more of a brilliant decision. 'Otty needed a room and I needed a house-mate. It's the perfect solution. I don't have to explain my job to her; if the place is a tip because I'm on deadline she isn't going to moan at me because she'll likely be on deadline, too. We could even go for weeks without talking because we're wrapped up in our scripts and neither of us ever has to apologise.'

Daphne's eyes narrow. 'Or maybe you're letting your biggest competition into your inner sanctum. Giving her everything she needs to bring you down.'

'Yeah, Daph, because she's going to find so many of my deepest secrets hidden under the dirty plates in the sink.'

'Look at her, Joe! She's a player. Second day in this room and she already has that lot eating out of her hand. That whole "working-class chummery" act is a smokescreen. Russell said he's looking for team players, not lone wolves. If he sees Ottilie working her stuff with half the room and you not even bothering to learn their names, who do you think he's going to favour when the next cut comes?'

A small thought edges its way to the forefront of my mind: is this jealousy? I dismiss it. 'Otty isn't like that.'

'Which you presumably know because you've been aware of her existence for all of twenty-four hours? Trust me, she's trouble. The last thing you need is to be sleeping with the enemy.'

'I'm not sleeping with her…' I protest, but Daphne has already stalked away like a cheetah rounding on its prey. I shake off the irritation. Well, let her think I'm getting it on with Otty. About time she experienced being snubbed after all the months she's done it to me.

After sketching out the basic arc of the pilot and first three episodes, Russ suggests we pair off to flesh out the scenes. I'd rather work alone but Daphne's remark about our boss wanting team players sits uneasily within me. Just in case she's right, I'll show willing and do it this time.

'Hey, *pardner*,' the bearded hipster I'm paired with says in a woeful cowboy accent he's clearly proud of. He could be a Josh or a Jake or even a Bernard for all I know. It doesn't matter: ace this one and then I might get to do the rest alone.

My current writing partner bounces at my side and I have a horrible premonition that he might start like this and then transform into a bright-eyed psycho stalker, *Single White Female* style, only male. I think I hide my shudder well…

'Hey – um…?'

'Josh. Answer to J-Man, Joshy, whatever.'

'Right. I'm Joe – nice to meet you.'

Josh/J-Man/Joshy shakes my hand with far too enthusiastic a grip. 'Good to meet you, Joe. Fancy bashing out some words over food? I know a great sashimi place in the Jewellery Quarter.'

Spare me.

'Love to but I have another deadline tonight,' I shrug. His crestfallen face makes me feel like I just dropkicked a puppy. 'How about a breakfast meet? The place next door does great stuffed bagels.'

'Gluten-free?'

'Probably.'

'Great!' Bouncy Hipster juggles the laptop and pad in his arms to pull his phone from his back pocket. 'So ping us your number and I'll see you tomorrow bright and early, yeah?'

I'm exhausted by the time he's scampered off. This is going to be a long week.

'Joe.' Russell is striding over.

'Hey, boss.'

'A word in your ear?'

'Sure.'

He glances over his shoulder. 'Not in here. Walk with me.'

Instead of heading to his office, we pass through the entrance doors and commence a slow circuit of the eleventh floor. It's still early days for this building and a third of the offices are awaiting tenants. The opposite side of West One is an eerie, echoing vastness, the kind of place someone tours shortly before the strip lights splutter out and apocalyptic zombies lay siege to the building. I squirrel the idea away. Who knows when the undead might come in handy?

'How do you reckon the newbies are doing?'

I glance at Russell as he strides beside me. 'Good. I mean, probably too early to tell. But they seem to be getting on.'

'Hm.'

'What's on your mind?'

'I want to give them a few days to settle. Not like last time.' He gives me the kind of self-conscious grin more akin to apologising for nicking a parking space than cancelling eight writers' contracts in one fell swoop. We really are that expendable to him.

'I think it will serve the room best,' I say, careful to keep my tone steady.

'Mm. It helps that they have more about them than the last lot. More variety. I like the Brummie one.'

'Aren't they all…?'

'The working-class girl. Bit older. *Very* Brummie. Her script was gritty and urban and just what we need.'

'Ottilie Perry?'

'That's the one. Got to admit, she ticks a box the commissioners will like. Working-class, own-voice bollocks and all. I mean, look around the room, Joe: middle-class as far as the eye can see. But she has real potential. I like that. Keep an eye on her, will you? Report back regularly.'

This is awkward. 'The thing is, Russ…'

I'm silenced by the slap of his hand on my shoulder. 'My *wünderkind* and the workhouse apprentice. Practically a script in itself.' He chuckles at his own quip. 'All good, Joe? Excellent.'

As I watch him powering away my feet become lead weights on the newly laid office carpet. The last thing I want to do is babysit someone, especially my brand-new housemate. I gaze out across the carpeted emptiness to the wideness of the city beyond its windows. All I wanted was to focus on this job on my own. Fat chance of that.

Maybe if I can make it look like I'm mentoring Otty, Russell will be satisfied and leave me to get on with my own stuff. A point in my favour wouldn't hurt in that room. And as the least-experienced writer on the team, Otty's position is already perilous. The last cull took writers with five, ten years' more experience. She needs protecting – for both our sakes. I need her in that room and in our house, paying half the rent. Once Russ recognises her talent, I can back off.

I hope.

Whatever else, I need to read Otty's script. See what I'm really up against.

I'll do it tonight.

Chapter Nine

OTTY

Oh, this house. It's perfect!

While Joe and I are still sailing cautiously around each other, I feel like I've found my perfect space. What I overheard him say to Daphne Davies about this place being his muse makes sense now I'm here. The light is not what you'd expect to find inside when you view the house from the street. From outside it looks like a dark, imposing Edwardian villa, its ebony-painted window frames, white and black harlequin-tiled path and shiny black front door are imposing like many of the houses around here. But inside it's light and warm and welcoming.

There's still one person I know won't be won over yet, no matter how lyrical I wax about the light and the ambience here. I can't put it off any longer. Time to call home.

'Old houses,' Dad says, as if those two words carry a world of worry.

'You should see the cornicing and the original fireplaces, Dad. And the tiles in the hall are Minton…'

'Expensive, then, if anything gets broken.'

'Joe tells me the landlord is very understanding.'

I hear an indecipherable mutter, which I don't want to ask him to define. 'And that's another thing. Living with a fella…'

'His name is Joe, Dad. He's my colleague and my housemate.'

'He's a *bloke*, our Otts. There's only one thing his trousers will be interested in.'

I bite my cheek to stifle a laugh. 'Well, his trousers aren't interested in *me*.'

'You can't know that! He could be planning on jumping you as we speak.'

'Dad…'

'What do you know about him, eh? And how come his last housemate moved out? These are questions you should have asked before you moved in.'

'Joe is a decent guy, Dad. And you should trust me a bit more.'

'Don't start that with me, bab. We all know what decisions you make when it's left to you.'

I am not having this argument again. 'This is the right house for me. And when you see it, you'll agree.'

He has no answer for that. And I know it will irritate him. I imagine him pacing the car park outside RoadTrail, the hum of passing traffic and scuff of boots on concrete confirming my suspicion. And then he comes back with the only thing he can throw at me. 'It's times like these I wish you still talked to your mother.'

'If she'd left a forwarding address I could have.'

'Yeah, well.' He has to concede that. Fact is, when Mum left Dad she left everything – our home, the country, her interest in me. We don't talk now and I'm not sure we ever really did when she was at home. I don't feel I'm missing out, which is the saddest part. 'You could've found a place with a girl, is all I'm saying. Or another one on your own.'

'Not at such short notice. And not such a gorgeous place as this.'

'Right. And what am I supposed to tell Sheila?'

I screw my eyes tight shut and wait until the urge to give the answer I really want to subsides. Even though I knew this was coming, it doesn't make it any easier to hear when it does. I might have lived most of my life surrounded by opinions on it from everyone around me, but that stops now. I'm not working for Dad, I'm not living at home, I've made my decisions. And everyone else is just going to have to get used to it.

I take a breath: remind myself that they think they're doing what's best for me, even though they aren't. 'Tell Sheila I've found a lovely place to live. She doesn't need to know anything else.'

He'll come around, eventually. I hope, anyway. And even if he doesn't, this is *my* place. I don't need Dad or Sheila or half of the West Midlands to like it for me to be happy here.

'What's that?'

Rona puts the strange glass contraption on the scuffed scaffold-board desk beside me.

'That is an air-press for a coffee.'

'It looks like something from the Starship *Enterprise*.'

I sense the shadow of a smile. 'And *that's* what makes it cool.'

I arranged to meet my writing partner in the Custard Factory, in a hot-desking loft space her brother owns. It's industrial and achingly cool – the kind of place I couldn't have dreamed of working even six months ago. Everything is exposed brick and reclaimed steel and wood, the floorboards of the once busy factory space now polished and stained a deep cherry-brown. All around us people from across the creative industries are working together, air-pressed coffee steaming beside shiny laptops.

The beard ratio is strong here, too. I smile, remembering Joe's formula for spotting hipster venues. I dashed out of the house early this morning and yelled goodbye to him, but I don't think he heard me. He was in his invisible workbox again, at the kitchen table, his forehead furrowed into a deep frown. Come to think of it, he's been weird since he got back from Ensign yesterday. I saw him go out with Russell in the afternoon; when he returned twenty minutes later he seemed preoccupied and stayed like that all night.

I don't know if I should be worried or not. I don't know him well enough to spot the signs yet. At RoadTrail I'd become so used to my colleagues' emotional landscapes that I could decipher their mood by how they'd parked their cars outside the unit. It takes time, I remind myself, just like anything else. And whatever it is, it's Joe's business. I'm not the kind of person to instantly assume I'm responsible for someone else's mood. If Joe has a problem, it's his alone.

Besides, I have far more important things to focus on.

It's amazing to think that people across the world might one day watch actors speaking the words Rona and I are writing today.

Our first assignment is completing a scene where a secret is revealed. In the thriller we're working on, everyone is leading a double-life except for the central character, Laura Eye, who states at the beginning she has no life of her own beyond her work. This scene is the first glimpse viewers will get that Laura is lying.

Having somebody to spark ideas off creates a pace I haven't experienced before. And what surprises me most is that apart from our first ten awkward minutes writing together, I feel like Rona's equal. I never expected that. After four hours' work, we've achieved so much.

We arrange to meet tomorrow in the same place and I leave with a free coffee from her brother Jas and his phone number, which I might just use. Part of the new me. New house, new job, new life. I like that. I walk out of the building on pockets of air and around me the city beams.

I should go straight home, but I want to go into Ensign Media to pick up a spare copy of the series bible. I want to keep one at home that I can annotate as I go. I'm protective about the notes I take, probably because I have written in secret for so long. Everything in the writers' room is shared: it feels good to have something only I can see.

I'm in the lift to the eleventh floor before I realise I've parked, passed through the crazy entry system and navigated the security checks without even thinking. Another sign I'm more at home here now. I smile at my multi-reflections in the glass-lined elevator. *Less of a newbie now, Otts.*

The doors part and I step out with my head held high. I present my pass with a cavalier flourish to the panel on the wall and push open the door to Ensign's reception.

Molly looks up from her monitor at the welcome desk. She's probably not even twenty but she has a swagger like she's been in charge of reception for ten years. 'Ottilie, hi. The *Eye, Spy* team aren't in today…'

'It's okay, I know. I was just after another copy of the series bible?'

'There's a stack of them in the writers' room. Go on in.'

I thank her and head to the room. It's odd with nobody else here: almost as if it's lost without the bodies and noise inside it. I spot the stack of papers at the far end of the room and head towards it, my fingers tracing a trail around the edge of the writing table as I go.

'The team aren't in today.'

Startled, I turn back to the door. Daphne Davies is standing in the doorway. She isn't smiling.

'Hi, I know. I just needed another bible.'

'Destroy the last one, did you?' A smile appears but it doesn't soften her stare.

'You guessed it. Freak firestorm. Dragons. Usual occupational hazard.' It wrong-foots her for a second, giving me chance to breathe. I move to the stack of papers and slide one from the top. Fixing my bravest smile, I turn back and walk towards our script co-ordinator.

She steps into my path. 'So, I heard you're living with Joe now? Fast work.'

'It came up at the right time.'

'I'll bet.'

This is why I never worked in an office environment before. Why is everything a battle with some people? 'Anyway, I'd better be getting back.'

'Of course. Mustn't keep Mr Carver waiting.'

Okay, that's it. I am not leaving here with Daphne thinking she has licence to speak to me like that. 'I'm sorry, was there something you wanted to say?'

She does that mock-astonished look that bitchy characters do in Netflix teen movies. 'I don't know what you mean.'

I eyeball her. I can see my expression reflected in her expensive eyewear and I wonder if she even sees me. 'Right. If you'll excuse me…'

'Thing is about Joe Carver: he's a hustler. He likes to play the laid-back lad, all charm and nonchalance. He can make you feel like the only other person in the room. But he'd trample you to get where he wants to be.'

'Good job he just needs me to help pay his rent then, eh?'

Daphne sighs and holds up her hand. 'Ottilie, don't get me wrong. I'm not suggesting you're interested in him – although nobody would blame you if you were. He is not without his charms. Just be careful, okay? Because the man has an agenda. And you don't really know him, do you?'

I'm rattled as I drive home through the building traffic. I don't want to pay any attention to Daphne, but what she said has raised a question I can't escape. Dad said it too, didn't he? What do I know about Joe? I've seen how close to Russell he is and I know how focused he is on his work. And he *has* been weird with me lately. Closed off. Is that how he always is or is he having second thoughts about me moving in?

By the time I park outside the house, I'm a mess.

There's only one thing for it: I have to talk to Joe.

Chapter Ten

JOE

I read her script. And if I didn't like her so much already, I would hate her.

The thing is, the more I see Otty at work and spend time with her at home the more I'm convinced she doesn't realise how good she is. Her dialogue sparkles, the characters as real and rounded as if you'd watched them for years. I know she thinks she's flying blind, but she's *got* this.

Which presents me with a problem.

Two problems, actually.

First, Russell wants to know what I think. I want to be honest with him so he trusts me, and I don't want to sell Otty short. She's more than just one of Russell's boxes ticked for the writing team. Otty deserves to shine for her considerable talent alone, not where she's come from. But Russell has already noticed her talent: if I tell him how good she *really* is, will that make him forget me?

And second, it feels wrong to be spying on Otty. If the tables were turned I would hate to discover she'd been spying on me. I'd be furious.

I'm going to have to think about this.

'Joe.'

I jump and look up from my laptop. Otty is standing in the kitchen doorway. She doesn't look happy.

'Hey. Writing session go well?'

'Yup.'

'Great.' There's a pause that could split rock. She isn't smiling, and when I try to wear one I know I look deranged. I never had this with Matt. 'Josh and I did well too, for a first session. He's very… enthusiastic.'

'Enthusiastic is good. Even if you are judging him for his millennial facial hair.' It's a joke – I *think* – but delivered smileless it's a bit scary.

'Hang on, who said I was…?'

'Have I offended you?'

'Sorry?'

She takes a step into the kitchen. 'Because I've been going over it in my mind and I can't work out what's changed here.'

'Nothing's changed.'

Her arms fold across her body. 'You've hardly spoken to me this week. When I catch your eye at work, you look away.'

'Have I? I didn't mean to…' I may have been a bit careful around her while I work out what to do with Russell's request, but I haven't tried to avoid her. At least, I don't think I have…

'You're in your room as soon as I get home and either dashing out before me in the morning or trying to hide behind your laptop screen. If this isn't working…'

'No,' I say quickly – because the last thing I want is Otty moving out. 'It *is* working. I'm sorry. I've just had my head down.'

'Whenever I've been around. The thing is, I don't know you,

Joe. I don't know what you're thinking: when you're joking or when you just want to be left alone. And I just thought…'

She looks so lost and I want to hug her but she's right. I don't know her well enough, either.

'Right, come on.' I close my laptop, walk over to her and offer my hand.

She blinks at me like I'm speaking Russian. Or Martian.

'We need to get to know each other. Starting now. Shall we?'

Otty takes my hand like it might be an incendiary device and I lead her out into the hall. I risk giving her fingers a squeeze as I open the door and we walk out into the bright Birmingham sunlight.

The canalside bar is quiet considering it's a weekday. We find a table outside and take a seat, as homeward-bound business people and students scurry past. Otty is still glancing at me as if she expects me to turn into a werewolf any minute, but at least she agreed to come. I can work with that.

She sips her pear cider, the ice cubes clinking against the glass. I watch her, then realise I'm staring and turn my attention to the mother duck floating past on the dark canal water, and the five balls of fluffy feathers frantically paddling in her wake. I know how they feel.

'I'm sorry,' I say, not daring to look at her yet.

'Me too. I panicked.'

'I didn't exactly put your mind at rest.'

She traces a drop of condensation down the length of her glass. 'I haven't lived with anybody else for a long time. I'm still working out how to do it.'

'Well, I haven't lived with a girl before. Sorry, a woman.'

Otty gives a snort of laughter and almost chokes on her cider. 'Thanks for noticing.'

'That's not what I meant,' I say, but I'm laughing, too.

'For a scriptwriter you're rubbish with words sometimes.'

'Thanks for noticing.'

She's smiling when I look at her and it feels like a win. 'You're welcome.'

'You're right, though: we need to get to know each other. So, what do you want to know?'

'Favourite place in Brum?'

'Easy. Electric Cinema. You?'

'The Museum and Art Gallery. Pre-Raphaelite rooms.'

'Ah, bit of a Dante Gabriel Rossetti fan, are you?'

'More of a John Everett Millais groupie. Rossetti loved himself too much.'

'Fair point. Um, what's next?'

'Favourite place to eat?'

'Purnell's, of course. You?'

'Diamond Balti.' She laughs when she sees my reaction. 'It's a hidden gem. Best Jaipuri chicken in Birmingham and naan breads bigger than your head. I'll take you there some time.'

'Sounds like an experience. I'll look forward to that. Favourite football team? Villa or City?' *Don't say City, don't say City…*

'Neither.'

'Don't tell me you're a Baggies fan?'

Otty shakes her head. 'I'm not into football. Cricket's our family's game.'

'Worcestershire?'

'Get lost! I'm a Bear through and through. I'm a member of Warwickshire Cricket Club at Edgbaston.'

That's another surprise. Otty does not strike me as a cricket fan, let alone a member. As we talk, more surprises emerge: she's a former mountain bike mechanic, she's teaching herself Welsh for fun and her biggest ambition is to write a series of *Doctor Who*. None of which I would have guessed unless she'd told me.

Birmingham has its summer hat on, city workers settling outside canalside bars to bask in the warm late-afternoon sun. The Venetian clock at Brindleyplace chimes the hour and Otty insists on stopping to listen until its lovely chimes have finished. Three swans land noisily on the canal and pigeons dip and soar above our heads. On days like this, my adopted home city is the best in the world. I came here as a fresh-faced kid from Oxford, firstly to do my degree at the university and then my first scriptwriting job apprenticed to a unit Russell was leading. And although I followed his team down to London for a couple of years and then dallied with a production company in Manchester for nine months, I found myself drawn back to Brum when freelance work kicked off. This place fits me. That's all there is to it.

There's an unhurried air today, the day's work done and the promise of a light summery evening stretching ahead. Not that I work in an office, or have a workday that ends at 5 p.m. But for a while I can enjoy the atmosphere. And Otty's company.

Until we stop for chips on the way home and she asks me a question.

'What's Russell really like?'

Crap.

'He's a good guy. Can be a bit blinkered sometimes but successful people often are.'

Otty blows on her chips. 'It's just that you seem close to him.'

'He knows me, that's all.'

'I think it's more than that. He respects you, more than the rest of us. I mean, I haven't seen him take anyone else for a walk around the building.'

I didn't know she'd spotted that. I stuff a load of chips into my mouth and wince as their heat scalds my tongue.

'They're hot,' Otty says, looking at me like I've lost the plot. I probably have. Because I know the next question will be what Russell thinks of Otty and I don't think I can lie to her if she asks me.

I swallow the molten mouthful, imagining the blisters it's searing down my throat, and say the only thing I can think of that will change the subject:

'I read your script.'

The chip on the wooden fork halts between the paper and her lips, which drop open. I force my gaze back up to meet hers.

'Which script?' Her whispered question makes the steam dance above her chips.

'The one you sent with your application.'

She blinks. 'When?'

'This morning. Otty, it's really...'

'No!' She holds up her hand. 'Don't say *anything*.'

'But I thought it was...'

'Stop it!'

'But...'

'No, Joe! You can't just casually drop that on me, like it's a trivial thing. Like it doesn't matter.'

'Who said it doesn't matter?'

But now she's backing away from me and I'm not sure why.

'Don't tell me what you thought, okay? Not here.' She screws up her still half-full chip paper, throws it in the blue plastic bin outside the chippy and walks away from me.

I watch her leave, my own dinner no longer palatable. What just happened?

Chapter Eleven

OTTY

Why did I go off like that?

All he was doing was being kind, I'm sure. Before I started working on the writing team I would have killed to get any kind of feedback from Joe Carver. It was just unexpected when he offered it and I wasn't prepared.

And now I'm hiding in my room back at the house, too chicken to go downstairs and explain myself. *Great work, Otty Perry. Just brilliant.*

We didn't speak on the bus back from the city centre and as soon as we got in the house I fled upstairs. I can hear Joe crashing about in the kitchen beneath my room and I know he's annoyed. I owe him an apology and an explanation. But what would I say?

How do I say that the words on the page are like pieces I've torn from myself and stuck there? How do I explain that the thought of them not shining like I want them to is worse than death? I've never told anyone how I feel about my writing. I don't know if I will ever be able to express why I write, only that I *have* to. It's as if the words cram up inside my head and demand to be let loose on the page. But is that how every writer feels about their work? Or is it just me?

It makes no rational sense. They're *just words* – but they mean so much more than that. Until I sent that script to Ensign Media, I'd never shown my writing to another living soul. I'd never been on a training course, or met any other writers until the day I walked into the writers' room. I never expected to be successful with my script and now I'm being counted among some of the brightest writing talents in the country. It's terrifying, but the tiniest voice within me assures me I deserve to be here.

How do I say all of this to Joe?

The answer is simple: I don't. Not tonight.

Throwing the duvet over my head, I close my eyes and wish it all away.

Brrrhhhzz… Brrrhhhzz… Brrrhhhzz…

It takes me a while to decipher the muffled buzzing sound when I open them again. Daylight floods into my room from the curtains I didn't close last night and I groan as I see my crumpled clothes I've slept in. Eventually I pull back one corner of my duvet from where it's been kicked to the floor and discover my mobile angrily buzzing its alarm from within the folds.

A brief peer into the upstairs landing confirms the bathroom is free, so I dash in and bolt the door. If Joe is awake already, I don't want to bump into him on my way to the shower or – worse – on my way out of it. As soon as I'm done, I'm going to find him and apologise for last night. I just need to look less like an extra from *The Walking Dead* first.

Half an hour later, I dare to go downstairs. The sitting room is empty, the kitchen peaceful. Joe's laptop is gone from the table, his jacket missing from the back of the chair where it usually lives.

There's the faintest tang of coffee in the still air but the filter jug is cold. If he made a pot it must have been hours ago.

My heart sinks to my socks. What if he's avoiding me? Nobody would blame him if he were. I practically accused him of belittling me, after all. I am *such* a div.

I sit on the chair next to the one Joe normally sits on and let my hand rest lightly on the vacant seat. It's going to take some explaining when I do see him and I still don't know what to say. But I want to try. I like living here with Joe and I'm excited by the prospect of working with him. I don't want him treading on eggshells around me in case I take offence.

It's only then that I notice a sheet of paper propped up against the teapot in the middle of the table. Beside it is a new jar of jam and a grease-spotted white paper bag containing a flaky almond croissant. I reach over and take the note, surprised to find Joe's handwriting spilling across its surface.

> *Peace offering.*
> *Sorry I scared you. I didn't mean to.*
> *All I wanted to say was that I loved your script.*
> *Don't ever doubt you can do this. Your words*
> *are wonderful.*
> *Joe ☺*

The curls and loops of his hand shimmer and dance as saltwater floods my vision. These words – I think to myself as I read them again and again – these words will be my focus from now on. If Joe Carver believes in my writing, I should believe in it, too.

✳

Rona is grinning when I hurry into the loft workspace. Two large cups of coffee are already beside her and her brother gives me a cheeky salute as I pass him.

'Sorry I'm late,' I rush.

'You're not. I was early.' She lowers her voice. 'I knew I'd have to fend off *certain questions* before you arrived.'

Her nod towards her brother is anything but covert. I see Jas busy himself at the coffee counter. 'Subtle.'

'Little sister perks,' she chuckles. 'You have no idea how hard won they are.'

I have no brothers of my own but I've known Jarvis and Steve long enough to guess the deal. 'What questions?'

'Bribe me with cake and I just might tell you.'

'I'll pass for the moment,' I say, taking my laptop out of my bag. It's nice to think I was being asked about, regardless of what the questions were, and that together with Joe's note brings a broad smile to my face.

It helps that I love what we're writing, too. The characters seem easy to reach and bring to the page and being able to share ideas makes such a difference from writing alone. When Rona suggests a line and it's perfect, I feel a shot of excitement; when I see a potential twist we clap our hands and giggle like plotting school kids. It feels like a game – and even though our allotted group of scenes have to be ready for when the writers' room reconvenes next week, it doesn't scare me as much as I thought it would. By the early afternoon, it's written. We spend another hour going over it to make small tweaks, but it's as ready as it can be for everyone else to see it.

Jas ventures over to the table when he sees us packing up.

'All done?'

I smile at Rona. 'All done.'

'Good work. Don't suppose you fancy a drink to celebrate? I knock off in twenty minutes and there's a great bar down the street.' He glares at his sister who is making kissy noises. '*She's* not invited.'

'Charming. Wouldn't want to be a gooseberry anyway,' Rona snaps, giving my elbow a nudge.

'I'd love to, but I can't today. Next week, maybe?'

'How about Saturday?' He's far too cheeky for his own good but I like his style.

'Saturday would be good.'

'I'll pick you up about seven? Rona can get your address for me.' He grins and heads back to the counter.

'Oh, so I'm your secretary now, am I?' she yells after him, grinning back at me. 'Smooth move, Perry. Or should I call you *sis*?'

'Steady on! I'll see you at Ensign tomorrow, okay?'

'You certainly will. Great working with you.'

'You too.'

I stop by the craft bakery on the ground floor and the independent brewery around the corner to pick up supplies, before the slow drive home. I'm praying Joe will be there. I've been thinking about him all day, my mind still processing his note. I've underestimated him and what he thinks of me.

He's a hustler. He'd trample you to get where he wants to be…

I evict the rude interruption of Daphne's words from my thoughts. She's wrong. Joe Carver is my housemate – and my friend. If he wanted to step over me to get to his goal he wouldn't have written that note. Daphne Davies knows nothing.

I can hear the low burr of the television as soon as I stand on the porch. Taking a breath, I turn my key in the lock and open the door. Joe looks up from the sofa and gives me a thumbs-up.

'Hello, stranger.'

'Joe, I'm so sorry.'

'Forget it.' His eyes crinkle at the corners when he smiles, I notice. He looks tired.

'Thank you for your note. It meant a lot.' Not sure what else to say, I lift up the bag in my left hand. 'I come bearing cake. And beer.'

He sits up and pats the sofa cushion next to him. 'Then you are most welcome.'

And that's all the discussion we need. I join my surprising, rather lovely housemate on the old sagging sofa and the evening passes in a happy blur of conversation, beer, cake and TV.

Chapter Twelve

JOE

Tonight, Otty has a date.

I mean, I'm not surprised. I haven't expressly enquired about her love life and neither has she about mine, so we can both assume the other *is* dating. I just wasn't expecting to meet her date quite so soon into our house-sharing experience.

'Hi,' he smiles from the doorstep. He looks like Dev Patel and the porch light illuminates him like a film star. 'I'm here for Otty?'

Mustering what manners I still possess, I usher him into the sitting room and walk back into the hall. At the bottom of the stairs, I hesitate. Should I yell up or go and fetch her? If it were Matt up there, I'd yell. But Otty isn't Matt. And Matt never had dates arrive at the house to pick him up. Thinking better of shouting, I sprint up the stairs and knock on her door.

'One minute,' she calls from inside.

So now I'm stranded on the landing carpet, debating what to do with my hands like I've just been thrust on stage. I stuff them in my pockets and look up to the ceiling. This is crazy. It's almost like I'm the one waiting for my date.

And then the door opens. She's wearing a simple black tunic

and skinny jeans with silver flats, her pink-edged hair pulled up into a high ponytail. Tiny curls nestle at the nape of her neck and she wears a seaglass drop hung on a silver chain that rests on the line of her collarbone. She smells good, too…

I cough and take a step back. 'Your date's here.'

'Okay,' she grins, the slightest patter of pink on her cheeks. 'Thanks, Joe.'

We do a weirdly awkward *do-se-do* on the landing, both apologising when we move in the same direction. Laughing, she finally eases past me and skips down the stairs. I hear her voice dancing with her date's low tone and the click of the door latch being opened. Hurrying down, I reach the door just as it's closing, Otty's hazel eyes framed in the gap as I pull it back open.

'Have a good time,' I say, lifting my hand and instantly regretting it. Who am I, her dad? What's next? *Have her home by midnight?*

Ugh.

She's still giggling when I close the door and lean against it. I need *beer*…

I don't see Otty until next morning, which is largely due to me dashing back up the stairs last night when I heard voices in the porch at midnight. I didn't want to be sitting in the living room when they walked in. We're going to have to establish ground rules for dates in future, I think. The last thing either of us needs is to be tiptoeing around the other.

I'm sitting at the kitchen table in my usual spot, wrangling the last part of the scene I'm writing. The first bit flowed like a dream, but then I seemed to hit a roadblock and now every sentence is like dragging water from granite.

'Morning.'

'Hi.'

I watch Otty sashay into the kitchen. There's a definite spring in her step. Worrying. But she's fully dressed, so that's something. Only pouring one mug of coffee. Good sign. But three slices of toast in the toaster? What does *that* mean?

'I'm hungry,' she says, giving me a look like I'm judging her. Which I guess I am, but not in that way. Why *is* she that hungry, though? Did she not eat enough when she went out last night or did she expend a lot of energy…?

What am I doing?

I flash an apologetic smile at her and make myself stare back at the screen. Otty's sex life is absolutely none of my business. I am disgusted with myself. Even if I still want to know…

'How was the date?' I ask, keeping my eyes on my WIP. Better to just ask it, I reckon, and stop all this second-guessing.

'Lovely.'

'Oh. Mmm. Good.'

In my peripheral vision I see her shake her head at me and turn back to the toaster.

So. Lovely as in *lovely evening, shame about the date*, or lovely as in *my date was everything I dreamed he'd be and it was lovely*? It's impossible to tell. I don't know why it's getting to me, but it is and I don't like it. I knew living with a woman would be tricky.

The tap of my laptop keys meets the clunk of the toaster popping up, in the space where words are definitely not welcome. This is bound to get easier, I tell myself, bashing out any old words now just to keep typing and avert the wordless void. She'll probably experience this strangeness when I next have a date and then we can settle into an easy routine where we *never mention it again*.

I hit the keys a little harder than necessary.

Otty doesn't notice.

I never realised buttering toast could be so loud…

I keep typing.

'Do you want some?'

'No,' I reply. 'I'm good, thanks.'

The fridge door creaks when Otty puts the butter back. The cupboard door bangs closed when she's got her plate.

'He didn't stay, if that's the question you're not asking me.'

I look up and she's got her hands on her hips. I feel judged and seen and if I could shrink small enough to slip behind the loose E key of my laptop right now I would be doing it.

'I wasn't…'

'You were. It was a first date, Joe. So thanks for thinking he might have wanted to stay over, but also I am *not* like that.'

'Right.'

'Next time, just ask. Or don't. But let's not do this *not asking*, okay?'

'Okay. Sorry.'

She rolls her eyes but at least she's smiling. 'Good. He was a *great* kisser, though…'

And with that bombshell, she leaves me.

We work separately for the rest of the day, which is just as well considering I feel like a worm for how I acted at breakfast. At 7 p.m., I knock on her bedroom door and offer her dinner. Having finally won the battle with my dodgy scene, I am surprisingly hungry and I'm guessing she might be, too.

'As long as you're paying,' she says, shutting her laptop and picking up her jacket.

There's only one place we can head to. In the steamy warmth of Verne's Buffet my mate Nish finds us a table near the food stalls (less walking, more eating – he knows me well) and I laugh at how wide Otty's eyes grow when she sees the buffet run.

'This place is amazing! How many different types of food are there?'

'Chinese, Cantonese and Japanese on the middle island, then Jamaican, Thai, Indian and Creole around it.'

'I don't even know where to start.'

'Easy. The table nearest ours is starters of everything.'

We pile our plates high, Otty skipping from one serving platter to the next like a kid in a toyshop, and then we return to our table. I don't get another word out of my housemate for a full five minutes while she commences the onslaught on her starters. Finally, she looks up and chuckles as she wipes grease from her chin.

'Sorry. Hungry.'

'I guess it really was a good date last night then?'

'Not this again.'

I signal surrender with a spring roll. 'Sorry.'

'Can we just not talk about it?'

'Fine by me.'

'Because if you're going to be creepy-weird every time I have a date…'

'I won't.'

'Glad to hear it. So how's *your* love life, Joseph?'

I stuff two triangles of prawn toast into my mouth and shrug my apology at her loud protests. But it's good – *this* feels good. I like how we're bouncing back whenever a sticking point arises.

'Besides, I eat when I'm nervous,' Otty says, abandoning the subject of dates like the pile of empty pistachio shells on her plate.

Mouth too full to reply, I raise my eyebrows.

'The writers' room meeting tomorrow? Russell's had all weekend to read our scenes and what if he hates them? What if he's been planning which of our bony bums to kick out tomorrow? I mean, it's all right for you: you're *Joe Carver* and Russell adores you. But this is the first time he's seen my words on this project, and…' She finally pauses long enough to draw breath and down a mouthful of beer.

'You'll be fine,' I say, brushing crumbs off my T-shirt. Because she will be. Her writing is awesome, Rona's writing is great and bound to complement Otty's, and Russell is secretly a fan already. Although I can't tell her that. 'I'm nervous, too.'

'Yeah, *right*.'

'I am. Do you think my job is any more secure than yours? Or Russell's?'

Otty puts down her beer bottle with a clunk. 'No, you're not telling me that Russell Styles is struggling.'

'Not struggling, but not guaranteed success, either. Do you know he had three projects fail to be commissioned before this?'

'You're kidding me? But *Southside*, *Servant* and *Insiders* were such colossal hits.'

'They were, but TV commissioners are fickle. He needs *Eye, Spy* to be a hit, or future commissions will be harder to get.'

'Wow.' Otty falls silent as she takes this in; and in the gap before she next speaks I feel the weight of it, too. Then she slaps her hands on the table and stands up. 'I'm going to need more food.'

Chapter Thirteen

OTTY

If you can gauge the level of nerves in a room by the proportion of coffee consumed within the first ten minutes, then we are officially at Peak Fear.

Looking at the collection of dark-circled eyes and gaunt faces around the writers' room, I don't reckon any of us managed much sleep last night. I hope feedback meetings won't always be this scary. Even though I'm happy with the scenes Rona and I have written, today feels like we're about to be judged. What if Russell thinks our scripts stink?

Rona grimaces as she resumes her seat next to me. She's on her third large eco-mugful of filter coffee already. Joe and Josh/J-Man/Joshy are on their fourth. At this rate, we'll all be dancing the caffeine jig by lunchtime.

'Good morning, team!' Russell sweeps into the room, a stack of papers in his arms.

Everyone tenses.

This is worse than getting essays back at school.

Our leader is oblivious to the held breaths around the room

as he perches on the edge of the writers' table. 'So, first stabs at the pilot scenes…'

Someone's stomach gurgles. I see eyes trying not to open too wide.

Russell looks up after a gap so excruciating even Simon Cowell would call time on it. 'All good.'

Twelve pairs of lungs collectively exhale.

'I like them all. Some fine tuning here and there – I've indicated where this needs to happen on each team's notes – but overall, good work. I think we've nailed the feel of the series and the characters are emerging nicely.'

Across the table, Joe gives me a covert thumbs-up. I smile back. Next to him, Daphne gives me daggers. It makes me even prouder of our housemate-workmate thing. Daphne clearly hates it, but she doesn't matter. We are *winning*.

'But that's your last free pass.'

The room pales as one.

'Time is not on our side. If we're to get the green light for production after Christmas, we have to deliver this as early as possible. Two months at best, no more than three at worst.'

What? How is that even possible?

Shocked, we watch Russell stand and pace the floor. 'We can do it with this team. We have enough talent. But there is no room for hangers-on. If you aren't willing to write your arses off, you won't stay. I cannot afford for anyone to be taking it easy. So no time off. No slacking. I've given each pair a block of scenes to work on this week, deadline Friday. These run across the pilot and next three episodes. We just thump these out, as quickly as we can, regroup and move on to the next batch. So, let's hunker down now and run through the storyline for the first four eps and then you're on your own.'

✱

'So, Rona reckons you're writing the Next Big Thing in TV,' Jas says, reaching for the wine bottle and topping up our glasses. The hum of conversation in the soft-lit city-centre restaurant washes against my ears like a warm tide and it's so soothing I have to keep kicking myself under the table to stop drifting off.

'I hope so.'

'Been great for me because she's too busy to bug me,' he grins. 'Although it means I haven't seen you as much as I wanted.'

If I'm honest, this is more by design than circumstance. I like Jas, I do. It's just that working with him constantly two steps away is becoming a bit much. I've started to feel like I should be apologising for working, and I don't want that. So for the last week and a half, Rona has been coming to our house to write instead of the hot-desk loft. It works well, too: Joe and Josh/J-Man/Joshy in the kitchen, Rona and me on the sofa in the living room. Which means no admittedly handsome coffee-bar owners peering over my shoulder and trying to steer the conversation in the direction of dates…

I smile at Jas as he chats away, but a familiar sinking feeling is laying siege to my stomach. It has been for a while, if I'm honest. It could just be the pressure of my job, but I'm pretty sure it isn't.

Since the end of my last relationship over a year ago – and the fallout I'm still navigating with my family over it – I've been determined to get on with my life and date. Each one has been an act of defiance, a statement that the only person allowed to steer that part of my life is me. And Jas has been a perfect person to prove my point. But that's the problem: I can't see us going beyond that and I think he wants more. He's lovely, but he's not what I want.

I feel rotten. I'm not paying attention to what he's saying because I feel like he said it all the first time.

'Can I just say something?' I ask, when he stops talking long enough for me to get a word in.

'Sure.' He scoops a spoonful of risotto into his mouth.

'This is a great restaurant…'

'I knew you'd like it.' He chews and it's suddenly all I can see.

'And it's good to see you again, Jas…'

Tiny grains of arborio rice and bits of mushroom stud his teeth when he grins. 'You too, babe.'

'And you're a really lovely guy…'

The rice and the mushroom shards and the teeth vanish behind unsmiling lips. The fully loaded risotto spoon halts midway from the plate to its intended destination.

There's no going back now…

In the taxi on the way home I allow myself to breathe. I did the right thing. It might be a bit dodgy with Rona for a while, but it would've been worse to prolong it. Mostly, I feel relieved. Also, hungry. Next time I want to break up with someone, I'll wait until *after* dessert.

Which is why the smell of newly fried chips that greets me in the hall of our house is a heaven-sent perfume from the gods. I follow its golden potatoey aroma into the kitchen, where Joe looks up from the swanky deep fat fryer I didn't know we had.

'Hey, Otts. Want some?'

'I love you. Marry me.'

'Steady on…'

'I was talking to the chips.'

'Phew.' Joe wipes his brow in mock relief and grins at me as he grabs another potato from the bag on the chopping board.

I sit at the table and shrug off my jacket, feeling the weight of the evening finally leave. It's good to be home. And I love that he doesn't ask me what's happened. We're just here, waiting for food. Joe chops, I breathe and the chips fry. And though his back faces me, I know he's smiling, too.

Two weeks after the first scary feedback meeting, we reconvene in the writers' room at Ensign to find a surprise from Russell. The bubbles may be supermarket Prosecco and the champagne flutes might be plastic, but it's as huge a treat as the real thing. 'You lot are awesome,' Russell says, raising his glass. 'I'll be honest, I was nervous about it, but you've done Ensign proud.'

He slaps his hand on the large whiteboard that covers almost the entire wall behind him. The schedule of all six episodes now has more squares filled in and signed off than it has empty spaces and we applaud as Russell ceremonially signs off the last square in the pilot episode column.

'As a reward, you have exactly one hour to enjoy this complimentary alcohol at considerable expense to the company…'

'Cheers to Aldi's finest!' Joe pipes up, eliciting laughter from the room.

Russell's laugh booms over us all. 'Only the best for you, Mr Carver. So. One hour off, then back to it.'

We stand and gather in groups around the room, the sense of relief and celebration palpable. I see Joe and Russell walk out together and imagine our employer marching my housemate around the eleventh floor again like Martin Sheen and Rob Lowe in *The West Wing*. He insists Russell doesn't see him as any different to the rest of us, but I don't buy it. Lately they've been promenading frequently. Daphne tries to catch Russell's attention as they leave but he powers past as if she isn't there. I see her hand fall slowly back to her side. She looks after them and then the moment is gone: her killer smile is back and she's turned to command a conversation with Rona and the Charlottes.

'Bloody glad she's not talking to me.' Josh/J-Man/Joshy is grinning when I find him at my side. I must stop calling him that. It's been stuck in my mind since Joe confessed his nickname for his writing partner and if I'm not careful I'll say it out loud to him.

'Who?'

'Daphne. Scares the life out of me. I reckon she eats scriptwriters for breakfast.'

I grin back. 'Probably. So, Russell's happy with us.'

Josh raises his Prosecco. 'Long may it continue.'

'I'll drink to that.'

We clink glasses – which is more of a clunk than a clink given the plastic. And though the drink is cut-price and in an hour we'll all be back at the coalface, I let myself luxuriate in the moment. We've survived the first test. We've created something amazing. *I* did it.

My mobile buzzes in my pocket. I smile my apology at Josh as I move away to check the message.

And instantly wish I hadn't.

Hey Otty, how's life in good old Brum?
I have news. Be good to chat soon. Please.
I still miss you. Chris x

I stab my thumb against the screen to delete the text, looking up in time to see Joe walking back in, a steaming Ensign mug in his hand. I fix my smile back where it had slipped. Joe looks over, pulls a face and lifts his hand to his temple. He hit the beers a little too enthusiastically last night, so the switch from Prosecco to coffee doesn't surprise me. I manage a smile back but my whole body is shaking now. I thought I'd blocked his number. Why didn't I block it?

A prickle crosses my shoulders and I shake it off. I've left that part of my life behind. *All* of it. So why do I feel like it's refusing to leave?

I watch Joe amble over to Josh and repeat his *oh look I have coffee and not alcohol* routine, beaming a victor's smile when Josh laughs. I sip my drink; try to swallow the bite of cold dread.

I'm not going to talk to Chris. No going back. Being here is what matters.

Chapter Fourteen

JOE

We never saw it coming.

Russell loved our scenes and passed them all for the next stage of piecing the episodes together. He repeated his belief that we were the best team he'd ever assembled and we all believed him. The writing pairings worked, everyone was happy.

Then we arrived at the following weekly meeting to find empty seats.

Six writers gone. It's shocking.

At least Russell had the decency to do the firing away from the writers' room this time, although I don't imagine it was any less brutal an experience for the people he dispensed with.

It's scared all of us and now we're watching our boss like a hawk for any sign of bloodlust as he paces the room.

'I had a rethink last night,' he says. 'And I came to the conclusion we were carrying too much dead wood. The writers we've let go weren't contributing enough, in the right voice. We couldn't afford to piggyback them. To deliver this series, we need to be leaner, meaner…'

'Cheaper,' Daphne mutters next to me.

'But the good news is that I don't intend on ditching anyone else. We're taking no new writers on so you lot are *it*.'

I glance at my colleagues. Nobody looks particularly comforted by this.

'For the foreseeable,' he adds. Because of course he reserves the right to change his mind. It's no guarantee of safety for us. But at least we're still here.

My co-writer Josh is one of the casualties; one of the Jakes and both Charlottes are gone, too. Thankfully, Otty's writing partner Rona is still in the room, her eyes wide as she takes in the news. Otty mouths *What the…?* to me and I shrug. I had no more warning of this than she did.

It had all been going so well. Only last night Otty and I were saying how settled everything was in the room now the pilot is in the bag. Shows what we knew.

I'm an idiot for relaxing. Russ promised me he wouldn't cull any more writers after the last lot, but what did that promise mean in the end? If he's done it when things are going well, he'll do it further down the line, especially if we struggle to keep up the pace. To survive, we need to maximise our chances of staying in Russell's good books.

But losing such a significant number of writers is a blow. Everyone left in the writers' room feels it. How will we complete the series as fast as Russell wants it with such a small writing team?

If Russell has any such qualms, he doesn't show it. Already he's reassigning writers to new pairs like he hasn't just ripped the original ones to shreds, and he's halfway through doing it before I realise what's happening.

I glance up at the whiteboard to the list of writing pairs.

Rona – Jake
Otty – Tom
Joe – Reece

No, that won't work!

I like Reece, one of the oldest writers in the room, but he's fallen foul of Russ before and I don't reckon that makes him a strong candidate for staying. Tom's great, a real solid writer and the kind who keeps his head down and avoids confrontation. He could be good for Otty. But she blossomed when she wrote with Rona and that was largely down to her pushing herself. Rona could write Tom off the page and she might well do it.

I need to stay. Otty needs to stay. Russell is still obsessed with her as his 'working-class gem' – only the other day he took me off on an eleventh-floor walk to ask how she was getting on and rave about the scenes she'd written with Rona. Maybe if he thought the wrong pairing could dampen her passion for the project, he might change his mind.

I was going to call time on our round-the-building conferences, largely because I feel it's dishonest to Otty. But this is too important to ignore. I'm doing it for her – if she ever finds out I think she'll understand this.

I wait until Russell's announced all the pairings then follow him as he strides out of the room.

'Russ.'

He shakes his head. 'Don't say it, Joe, I know.'

'No, I think what you've done is brave,' I say, my toes squeaking in my shoes as they curl. I said I'd never brown-nose anyone to get ahead in this business. Some moral bastion I turned out to be. 'But I do have one suggestion to make the team even stronger.'

He stares at me.

I slap on my most earnest expression.

'Fine. Let's walk.'

He's speedier than normal and I struggle to summon enough breath to speak as we power around the building. I can't mess this up. There's too much riding on it.

'Let me work with Otty.'

'You? Why?'

'You saw what she did with Rona. The best writing comes when you have a team firing off one another's talent. Flint on flint. I can be that with Otty. You put her with someone who doesn't push hard, she'll be forced to back off, too.'

'You think Tom's a slacker?'

'No! No – Tom's great. He's a safe pair of hands and we need that to give this series weight, dependability. But Otty's a firebrand. She'll shine if she has the right tools.'

'Are you calling yourself a tool, Joe?'

I feel like a tool, scurrying after you like a yelping Yorkie. 'Maybe I am. Maybe I need a flint to spark off, too.'

Russell stops and I almost career into him. 'Maybe you do.'

It's the world's tiniest opening, but it's a way in. 'And you like Otty. You want to protect your authentic voice – you said it yourself, Russ. She's the one that'll silence the critics who say all drama is middle-class, middle-aged white-guy-led. She's my housemate, my workmate… Imagine if she were my partner, too. *Writing* partner,' I add quickly, realising how dodgy the previous sentence sounds.

'My *wünderkind* and my workhouse apprentice, together at last. Flint on flint. The ultimate meet-cute.'

'Well, I wouldn't term it exactly like that…'

'I like it! Good call, Carver. Let's go back in.'

So I watch as Russell relays the new plan to the surprised team and shrug my pretend surprise when Otty stares at me. I keep my expression steady, sit up in my chair like everyone else and pray nobody can see the way my heart is hammering inside me or the beads of perspiration peppering my palms.

It's a huge risk. If it goes wrong, it could cost me everything.

But it's done. We're as safe as we can be.

Now all we have to do is make this work.

Chapter Fifteen

OTTY

Something weird is going on.

Joe assures me it's all good, but I don't feel good about it.

Sharing a house with him is cool. Working in a team with him is great. But *writing* with him? That's a huge step.

And then there's the enormous fact that Russell just axed a chunk of our team and everyone is carrying on like it never happened. I know it isn't the first writers' room cull Joe and a few of the other original writers have seen, but it's my first and it was horrific. Brutal doesn't even begin to cover it.

I hang back as they all leave, unable to share the relief they all clearly feel at surviving Russell's cull. I told Joe I have a headache and I'm heading home, so he's right in the middle of them, laughing and talking too loud as they head for a bar in town. I don't feel like celebrating someone else's misfortune, which is how this feels. I just need a bath, a takeaway and a night in front of the blandest telly I can find.

'Otty.'

There's a figure by my car. I jolt as I see him, hood up, shoulders hunched against the chill of the evening.

'Josh?'

He slips off the hood. He looks terrible. 'Can we talk?'

My heart sinks. 'Actually, I was just on my way home…' I look over to where I last saw Joe, but he's gone. It's just Josh and me – and I can't get to Monty because he's blocking my way.

'I just need a minute,' he says. Hollow eyes bore into mine. 'Please?'

I know I should go. What can I possibly say to him? I have a job and he doesn't. It wasn't my decision but I still feel to blame.

I offer him my hand but Josh bypasses it completely and before I know where I am, I'm in the middle of a too-tight hug that lasts just a little too long. When he eventually breaks it, I step back and he flushes a little.

'How are you doing?' It's the most ridiculous question, but it's the only one I can think of.

'Crap,' he says, sorrowful grey eyes mooning over his ginger beard.

'What happened?'

'I got a message to call Russell, and when I did he told me I hadn't made the cut. No *thank you*, no *good luck for the future*. It just came out of nowhere.'

'We were shocked, too,' I say, adding, 'All of us,' in case he might be thinking otherwise.

'This just keeps happening, Otty. I don't know why. This was my last chance. My big break. I don't know how I'll pick myself up again.'

'You will.' *You'll have to. What choice do you have?*

'I mean, I thought my writing was good…'

'It was. It *is*.'

'Not good enough to impress King Russell though.'

I don't want to be here. I never volunteered to be the sole Ensign spokesperson. Why didn't Joe stay a bit longer?

'Then he's an idiot. You're great, Josh. Everyone thought so. Joe said…'

'Yeah, well, I haven't heard from Joe, have I? Which says a lot. I'm sorry, Otty, I know you live with him but seriously the guy is a snake.'

I'm so surprised I can't speak. Instead I stare, goldfish-mouthed, at him.

'He's so cosy with Russell all the time. And he's survived all the other writer culls. You can't tell me he didn't know it was coming.'

'He didn't.'

'I think Joe Carver knows exactly what's going on. I think him and Daphne are in it with Russell and he's as much a part of the decision process as they are.'

It gets worse. Josh starts to reel off every bad experience he's had in writing teams, identifying a *Joe Carver* in every one. The guy – it's always a guy, according to Josh – who's everyone's friend until it counts. The best mate of the showrunner, the one who'd sell his family to succeed. I heard this from Daphne, but it meant nothing then.

It means nothing *now*.

Josh is upset. He needs a target and he can't yell at Russell. All the same, I don't want to hear it. I don't want to doubt Joe, not for a second.

'I'm so sorry this has happened. There's something a million times better out there for you. I'm sure of it.'

I don't feel sure of anything. But Josh seems to take the hint.

'Cheers.'

'Take care, Josh.' I go in for a hug, Josh thinks he's kissing my cheek and we meet in an awful half-cheek-half-lips collision that sends both of us stepping back in horror. I need to get out of here.

'Sorry. We can keep in touch, yeah?'

'Sure,' I lie because I want to get away.

Josh nods and steps back from Monty. I've opened the door and am in the driver's seat before he can say anything else. But as I'm closing the door, his hand catches it and he leans in.

'Just be careful, Otty. With Joe? He's more involved with Russell than you think. You're too lovely to be sullied by someone like him.'

I'm shaking as I speed away.

I don't want to believe it. But even driving home, my brain is making connections I don't want it to. Joe *is* very close to Russell. Could he have known what was going to happen? They're always going off for private discussions – were they discussing this?

And even though I think Daphne talks out of her bum most of the time, what she said to me before about Joe refuses to go away. I'm angry that he didn't do the decent thing and contact Josh himself. No matter how innocent he is of all the other stuff, his silence is damning. And, while I know Joe couldn't have known Josh would show up at work this evening, I'm furious that Joe's insensitivity made me feel obliged to hear all this.

By the time I park outside the house, I'm ready for a fight.

'Oi, love, give us a smile,' Joe grins as I power into the kitchen.

And that's the only spark this powder keg needs.

'Get stuffed.'

Joe's eyebrows make a bid for the ceiling. 'It was a joke?'

Ignoring him, I switch on the kettle and chuck a teabag into a mug. After the day I've had, I need tea and then bed, not Joe Carver being a dick.

'Otts?'

'I don't feel like smiling, okay?'

'You should. There's plenty to be optimistic about. We're still on the team and Russell wants us working together. *And* the hipster beard and hair-flick ratios have significantly lowered in the writers' room.'

I stare at him. 'You are unbelievable.'

'Okay, do you have a problem with me?'

'Yes, I have a problem. Your writing partner just lost his job – along with several of our colleagues – and you're cracking jokes?'

'Oh, come on, Otts, that's not fair. You laugh or you die, that's how you survive this. How *we* survive this.'

'You worked with Josh. You wrote part of the *Eye, Spy* pilot with him. Did you even send a text to offer your condolences or thank him for the work he did?'

'Why would I do that?'

'Because it's decent, Joe! Because it's *human*.'

'It's the business we're in. Yes, it sucks, but it could just as easily be us next time.'

'And that makes it all okay?'

His groan echoes around the kitchen. 'I didn't say that. There's just no point in getting comfortable with anyone in that room because nothing lasts.'

'So I guess you and I shouldn't be friends then?'

I know I've pushed the point too far, but I'm horrified by Joe's attitude. As soon as the words leave me I can see I've lost the advantage.

'No, *I* think we should, Otty. But hey, if you reckon it would be a liability being friends with a heartless android like me, maybe we shouldn't bother.'

I grip the back of the chair and stare at the old grain in the kitchen table. I hope Joe will walk out but he doesn't move.

'And how do you know how Josh is, anyway? He might be fine. Furious with Russell, probably. But already applying for new writer jobs if he has any sense. It's what you do in this business.'

'He's devastated.'

'How do you know?'

'Because he was waiting by my car tonight.'

He stares at me. 'Oh, Otts, you didn't talk to him…'

'What else was I supposed to do? He's just lost his job and he is crushed by it. Panicking about how he'll pay his rent this month. Thinking his career is over. This isn't the first writing job he's been axed from. But I'm guessing you didn't know that because you don't believe in getting too attached…'

Joe snorts. 'Well, at least it saves me from kissing him better.'

'What is that supposed to mean?'

'Work it out.'

'I didn't kiss him better. I *listened* to him, like the rest of you should have done. It was the decent thing to do.'

'Why?'

'Because he just lost his job!'

'That wasn't your fault.'

'I know that. But nobody else appears to be bothered by it. We've just spent weeks working with him – I couldn't pretend that hadn't happened.'

'And why should you feel responsible? You didn't make the decision.'

'No, but he thinks you did.' That does it. I shouldn't have said it, but I am far too angry to back away.

'What?'

'He thinks you're in league with Russell. That you planned the whole thing.'

'How can he…?' Joe's expression stills. 'Is that what you think?'

'You go off with Russell all the time. He seems to consult you on everything else, so why not this?'

'Yes, he talks to me. Because I've known him the longest. But we don't discuss who he's going to fire. And if you think that about me, then I don't see how we can move forward.'

'I don't know what to think.'

We stare each other down. I can feel my anger ebbing and the approach of tears but I'm not letting Joe off the hook.

'Russell made the wrong decision, Joe.'

'Maybe he did. But that's his business. And if Josh wants to survive this gig, he's got to accept this stuff happens. No amount of sympathy is going to change that.'

'I did the right thing talking to Josh.'

'Fine.' He folds his arms. 'So, did it make you feel any better?'

I can't lie, even though every cell in my body wants me to. 'No.'

'Bloody hell, Otty.' He rubs the back of his neck. 'Do you need a drink?'

I shake my head.

'Do you want to talk about it?'

I don't, but then the words won't stop. 'It was horrible, Joe. Gut-wrenchingly horrible. How can Russell do that to someone and feel no remorse?'

'It's the business…'

'No, it isn't. And if it is, maybe I don't want to be a part of it.'

I see his eye-roll and wonder if he's ever gone through this. Has he always been so detached from his work? 'Otts, you can't save everyone. It's not your responsibility. Don't let this distract you from the brilliant job you're doing.'

'It doesn't sit right with me.'

'I know. But what matters is what you make of it. Words are all we ever have any power over. Everything else is bollocks.' He catches the smile that sneaks onto my lips before I can stop it. 'I have beer in the fridge. We can find a really bad TV movie to slag off?'

It's a lame offer and the weakest excuse for a white flag, but the blandness appeals.

I'm still not okay about this. I won't ever think Joe's approach was right. It's an uneasy truce, but we need to move on. Because tomorrow, we become writing partners – and we have to make it work.

Chapter Sixteen

JOE

Convincing Russell to let me write with Otty was the easy bit. Now I have to do it.

I woke up far too early this morning and abandoned any attempt to go back to sleep. There was no point. My head is like New Street Station at rush hour and rest is out of the question.

So I've been drinking coffee since six and there's still no sign of Otty. I was going to suggest we went out for breakfast before we begin, to ease ourselves in a bit, but first I need to check she's still speaking to me.

It doesn't help that we argued last night. Otty's a div for indulging Josh, but I can't fault her reasons. I just don't like her suggestion that I don't care enough – or that I was involved in the decision. I was as shocked as anyone when Russell sacked those writers. Maybe I should have called Josh, but what would I have said? *So sorry you lost your job, mate, but at least I still have mine?* There's no way that call would have appeared to be anything other than faux sympathy from a patronising git. Better to say nothing than insult him further.

All the same, I feel bad about it.

It's not a blinding start for our writing partnership. But I'll have to pick up the slack and run with it. We don't have time for arguments.

It's almost 8.30 a.m. when Otty appears and every muscle in my body is twitching from caffeine overload. My attempt at a friendly smile goes unnoticed as she heads for the coffee jug. I take a breath; steady myself.

'Morning.'

'Mm.'

That opening line needs work. 'Ready to write for your life?'

She turns slowly, dark-rimmed eyes accusing. 'Perhaps not the best choice of words.'

'And *that's* why we are going to make a great team. Me spouting banalities and you correcting them.'

It's the smallest smile in the history of positive facial expressions. But I can work with it.

'Idiot.'

'You're welcome. Fancy breakfast out first?'

Otty sighs and the frown eases. 'I thought you were never going to ask.'

Of course, we don't discuss the script when we're eating breakfast in the small independent Jewellery Quarter coffee shop. This is partly because the coffee and Harissa-spiced baked beans on sourdough toast are too good to interrupt with serious conversation, but mostly because the whole 'writing together' deal suddenly feels so *real*. And, frankly, terrifying. I hadn't expected that. One thing we've quickly established since Otty moved in is a delicious rhythm of banter that weaves through our conversations. It's as easy as breathing. Even when we argue, there's an energy I haven't experienced with anyone else. I just assumed that it would instantly transfer to our writing partnership. But it's startlingly absent. I wish I knew why.

'These beans are incredible.'

'Told you.'

'And you were right.' She observes me over her next forkful. 'Even if we are paying eight quid for basically beans on toast.'

'*Epic* beans on toast.'

Otty laughs. 'I never had you pegged as a hipster.'

'Ah, don't be fooled by my clean-cut, nerdy exterior. My heart has a beard and cut-off chinos.'

'I hope our words fly onto the page as easily as this.' I watch her smile fade as she lifts her large artisan coffee cup and takes a sip so long I wonder if she's trying to hide herself inside it.

'They will,' I say.

I hope they will. They *have* to.

Maybe it will be better when we get home…

```
FADE IN:
INT. THE KITCHEN OF A SURBURBAN
EDWARDIAN TERRACED HOUSE


Two screenwriters sit beside one another
at a kitchen table. Both have laptops.
Both are staring at blank pages on their
screens. JOE looks at OTTY. She is frown-
ing at her screen, biting her thumbnail.


                    JOE
        Why is this so flippin' difficult?
```

I nudge Otty and slide my laptop over the kitchen table to face her. She reads what I've just typed and groans. Then she reaches across and types a reply:

> OTTY
> Because we are clearly LOONS.

I feel the tension shift between us. It's a relief. We've been stuck like this for almost an hour since we came home and something has to give. I know I'm procrastinating, but the game calls to me and I can't resist. I type back:

> JOE
> Speak for yourself. I'm amazing.

She snorts and the game is *on*.

> OTTY
> You write the damn script then,
> Captain Amazing.

I make sure she sees my melodramatic eyes-to-heaven move, and then type:

> JOE
> I would, but my cape keeps
> snagging on the keys.

Her laughter is a gift.

OTTY
Title of your autobiography.

JOE
Sounds filthy.

OTTY
Everything sounds filthy to you.

JOE
Title of *your* angsty 90s album.

OTTY
We need to focus. Seriously.

JOE
This is much more fun.

OTTY
It is. But unless Laura from *Eye, Spy*
is likely to pose as a time-wasting
screenwriter, I don't think Russell
will rate this script.

She's right, of course. Bloody annoying, too.

'Fair enough,' I say. 'Although I reckon Russell would love to know our real-life story. *The true struggles of a house-sharing writing team* – it screams chart-topping Netflix documentary series, doesn't it?'

'We'd need significantly more car chases and explosions in it to interest Russell Styles.'

I laugh and accept defeat. 'Probably.' I slide my laptop back to my side of the table and resist the urge to add…

```
                          JOE
                  You'd be surprised.
```

… to the end of it before I delete all the text. Nerves roll in my stomach. What would Otty say if she knew I'm updating Russell on her progress? She'd be *livid*. Anyone would. I watch the words disappear from the screen, the brief after-image causing a shot of fear before they fade from my sight.

The action we're writing today is intercut between two scenes: one where Laura – the protagonist and spy of the title – is meeting with her boss to fight for her position, and the other where she is in a secret therapy session, revealing to her counsellor exactly how close to breaking point she is. But so far we've tried three different entry points and none of them work.

'Laura wouldn't start by confessing all to her therapist,' Otty says, twisting the pencil she doesn't need on the pad she doesn't need either. Tiny dots of graphite dust have been stabbed into the top page, miniature explosions of grey pushed into pristine white.

'I thought that's what therapists are for.'

'They are, but you don't just walk in and blurt it all out.'

'Don't you?'

'No.'

'How do you know?'

Her eyes flick to her screen. 'I – *don't*. I'm just saying that's not how it works.'

I don't believe her. Her reaction is too odd to ignore. But I can't push her on it because it's almost midday and we've written exactly nothing. I store it away for another time. 'So, where do we start?'

'Laura walks into both rooms. Symmetry from the beginning.'

'*Nnnnuurr!* Wrong answer.'

'What was that supposed to be?'

'Cliché buzzer. Seen it in every script since the dawn of time.'

'*Nnnnuurr!* Hyperbole alarm.'

She's too quick. Shame we aren't writing a comedy. 'Too much build-up. Russell would hack that to bits.'

'Not if we justify it in the script.'

I get where she's coming from, but I know Russell. I know what he likes. Straight to the action, no messing about on the way. I don't want to hold it over Otty because this is her script as much as it's mine, but we can't afford to muck up where Russell's concerned. Individuality is for spec scripts and solo projects, not collaborative screenplays.

'Trust me, Otty…' I begin, cringing at my own condescension.

'No, you know what, Joe? I'm in that room because Russell trusts my instincts. He loved the scenes I wrote with Rona, so he'll love the ones I'll write with you.'

'Not if we can't even agree how to start them.'

A scrape that sets my teeth on edge sounds as Otty pushes back her chair, snatching her laptop from the table. 'Fine.'

'What…? Where are you going?'

'To the other room,' she snaps, stuffing her notebook and pencil under one arm. 'I'll write the therapist scene, you write the MI6 meeting.'

Mouth agape, I watch her leave.

Chapter Seventeen

OTTY

Okay. So maybe storming out like that wasn't the best response.

Or the most professional.

But neither was Joe 'I'm chums with Russell Styles, dontcha know' Carver's. *Trust me, Otty* – like he was patting me on the head.

This isn't about Joe. He just pushed the wrong buttons at the worst time. Truth is, I've been a wreck since last night. First all the stuff with Josh, then my fight with Joe and then a night of broken sleep while my brain decided to stay up and replay it all. Stupid brain.

And also because, with that one sentence, Joe managed to morph into my dad.

Trust me, Otty…

I've lost count of the number of times I've heard that tone whenever my father decides to offer his wisdom. The condescension – always the weapon of choice for a man who wants to win an argument. I know Joe isn't Dad, but it felt the same as every conversation I've had with my father over the past year. Like they know what's best for you; like your own mind isn't strong enough to make the right decisions. Dad-chats are just not simple anymore: there's always an unspoken edge to every conversation we have. A silent elephant stubbornly wedged into the space between us. A Chris-shaped impasse. It's another complication in an already weird situation.

There have been no more texts from my ex but I've become wary of checking messages all the same. I'm hoping it's a one-off. I don't have the mental capacity to deal with that on top of writing.

And I'm not having my housemate think he can talk to me like Dad and Chris have.

I stretch my legs out along the small sofa in the living room until my heels meet the cushions on the far end of it. Every muscle feels one wrong move away from cramp. I know I hold my body in tension when I'm nervous but today the knots refuse to budge.

At least there are words on my screen now – real words this time, not fake script games with Joe. They need finessing, but the bones are there:

```
            DR MONTGOMERY
What would you like to talk about today?


                 LAURA
            I don't know.


            DR MONTGOMERY
  What made you decide to see me?


                 LAURA
          Do I need a reason?
```

                    DR MONTGOMERY
              Do you think you need one?

                       LAURA
              Do you always talk in riddles?

                    DR MONTGOMERY
              Do you always evade questions?

                       LAURA
                      (beat)
              I think my boss wants to fire me.

                    DR MONTGOMERY
              What makes you think that?

                       LAURA
              He's been watching me. Talking about
                        me.

                    DR MONTGOMERY
                 Isn't that his job?

                       LAURA
              It's more than that. I catch him staring
              at me across the room. Like he's waiting
                   for me to trip up.

                    DR MONTGOMERY
                 Trip up? In what way?

LAURA
Make a mistake. Say something out of
turn. Cry when I shouldn't.

DR MONTGOMERY
Do you cry often?

LAURA
Sometimes I'm scared I'll never stop.

I look back at my screen, take a breath and type words to fit the rhythm in my head. Little by little, Laura opens up, her therapist teasing each bit of information from her. The pace quickens, the verbal sparring turns into heartfelt honesty, and by the end of the scene the therapist is completely in Laura's confidence – something she will later regret…

When I'm finished, I look up at the clock on the mantelpiece and am shocked to discover it's almost 4 p.m. I can't hear any sound from the kitchen, but then Joe is the quietest typer I've ever heard. I hit my keys with increasing fervour as I enter into the pace of a scene – I know even a room away Joe will have heard every tap, shift and space hammered out on my battle-scarred laptop.

The adrenalin subsides and a gnawing hunger surges in its place, followed by a thud of guilt in my gut. I really need to make things right with Joe. This partnership won't work if we're forever yelling at each other and flouncing off.

I tiptoe into the kitchen. Joe is leaning back in his chair, head-phones on and eyes closed. I should let him know I'm here but there's something about his stillness that stops me. His eyebrows are slightly raised, as if he's just been surprised by a pleasant

thought, and the first hint of a smile rests on his lips. The calmness of his features is strange and new – like seeing the sea become smooth as glass after a storm. I watch the subtle rise and fall of his chest as he breathes and notice for the first time how long his eyelashes are along the line of his closed eyes. What is it with blokes and eyelashes? I wish mine were as long as that.

Something shifts inside me and I make myself move towards the kitchen units.

When I start opening cupboards in search of plates, I hear Joe stir.

'How's it going?'

'It's done. You?'

He stretches his arms above his head. 'Finished a while back. What time is it?'

'Later than you think,' I reply, smiling when he double-takes at his watch. 'Hungry?'

'Starving. What are you making?'

'Sandwich for now and then I thought I'd make us a pot of chilli?'

'Excellent plan.' He yanks the lead from his laptop and winds it around his earphones. 'I'm sorry. For being a moron.'

'Generally or just this afternoon?'

It takes him a moment to work out I'm joking. 'Specifically for this afternoon. I'll apologise for the rest as we go.'

I'm halfway into making dinner later when I realise that I haven't opened a wrong cupboard or had to search for pans and utensils. My body moves instinctively between fridge and worktop and hob, never missing a beat. The familiarity is comforting. When I first moved in, I never thought I'd be as at ease here as I was in my flat. It's such a relief to discover it again.

'What's up?' a newly showered Joe asks when he returns to the kitchen, rubbing his head with a towel as he accepts a glass of wine from me.

'Er, nothing. Why?'

'Oh. You look happy, is all I'm saying.'

'I am. I love this house.'

He looks around and I swear I see him give the kitchen worktop a surreptitious pat. 'Me too. It certainly makes writing easier. Well, it usually does.'

'Sorry. Again.'

He bats away my apology. 'Not your fault. But we do need to work out how the hell we're going to do this.'

He's right. Today was a first stab, but from now on we have to make it work. 'Any suggestions?'

'We split scenes where we can, write them separately and then bring it all together. I guess the more we do it, the easier it'll be.'

I nod. 'And we need to read each other's work. All the time. Check we're on the right track.'

He winces. 'More wine might be required to make that happen, but you're right.'

We swap laptops and sit at opposite ends of the table, reading in silence, the bubbling pot of chilli on the stove the only sound in the room. I like what Joe has written. It's pacy and on point and exactly what Russell will want to read. So why doesn't it thrill me like it should? I read it again, thinking I might be too distracted by the structure – but the same drop of disappointment pulls my gut.

'What?'

I stare at him, instantly guilty for not loving his work. 'It's good.'

His eyes narrow. 'No, it isn't.'

'I didn't say…'

'You didn't need to.'

'Joe, it's fine.'

'Right, ground rules. We have to be completely honest with each other if we have a hope of this working. We've got to say what we really think. No recriminations, no arguments if we don't like what we hear. Regardless of which pieces we write, we both have to own the whole of it as if every word is ours. We have to make sure every word is right.'

I feel sick, but it has to be done. 'Okay. Who's going first?'

Joe swallows hard. 'I will.'

Chapter Eighteen

JOE

This is *horrific*.

Once we'd got over the initial awkwardness of sharing a home, a job *and* a script, I'd assumed everything else would fall into place. I'm no stranger to criticism – either giving it or receiving it – but this is next-level terrifying.

She's going to hate what I'm going to say about her script. And I dread to think what horrors she's spotted in mine.

But I was the one who insisted on complete honesty. I can't back out now.

Putting off the inevitable, I suggest we move to the living room. Otty agrees. Once the cushions have been rearranged, I've poured more wine and we've danced around each other more than necessary, we run out of reasons to delay it.

We sit as if awaiting an executioner, laptops brandished like shields.

'Go on then,' Otty says, downing the last of her wine. 'Shoot.'

'Total honesty.'

'Yes.'

'And no recriminations?'

'Can't promise that will be easy, but I'll do my best.'

'Okay.' I rub sudden beads of sweat from my palms onto my knees, hoping Otty doesn't notice. 'This isn't a criticism of this scene as such, more a general observation.'

Two lines crease between Otty's eyebrows. 'Right…'

'It's just…' Now I'm here, the words *aren't*. 'Your writing is great. I totally get what you meant about the therapist scene having a slow build. But I look at what you've written and I look at you and the two don't always match.'

'I'm not a spy on the verge of collapse, Joe.'

'I know. Sorry, this isn't coming out well. I feel like the person you can be on here,' I tap the screen of her laptop, 'isn't the person you are in here.'

She watches the vague waving of my hand above my head. 'In the living room?'

'No. In the house, in this street, in the city.'

'I don't follow.'

'In life. You can be so brave on the page – breathtakingly so, when it happens. But I think how you see yourself in real life is hijacking that ability.'

'I thought we were talking about the script.'

'We were. We *are*. But I feel like you're pulling back in your writing in between these brave moments because you don't fully believe you can write like you do.'

I knew she wouldn't like it. And I'm making a total arse of myself trying to express it, which doesn't help.

What I mean is that in her script there are sections where her word choice is practically apologetic, always after a flash of brilliance. I just think if she can fully accept that she was born to write and embrace the potential of that, who knows what she could achieve?

That's what I want to say. But I don't get the chance.

'Right. Noted. Is it my turn now?'

Her abruptness cracks the air. That isn't a good sign. 'Um, be my guest.' I brace myself.

'Your scene is lacking something. Passion. Edge. It could be any conversation between a boss and employee, anywhere. Not the pivotal moment where Laura fights for her professional life by lying about her personal one.'

My hackles begin to rise. 'In what way?'

'When I read your *Southside* script…'

Oh *fantastic*, here we go. Like I haven't had this reference a thousand times before from every starry-eyed wannabe script-writer I've met in the last five years.

'This isn't *Southside*.'

'I know it isn't, but it's still you writing it.'

She's folded her arms now, chin raised. Like that, is it, Otty? That's the way you want to play this?

'*Southside* was a different thing entirely. A different time. Nobody has the licence to air a spec script like that anymore. It hardly ever happens.'

'I read that script, Joe, lots of times. I studied it. You were breathless and brilliant. You never dropped a beat. This scene is as crucial as any in that episode – more so when the twist is revealed.'

'Laura is clearly panicked and nervous and on the edge.' I'm stabbing at the back of my laptop now, as if the point I'm making will burst through the screen and hit Otty squarely in the face. 'I don't see how it could be any clearer.'

'You said no arguments, Joe.'

'I'm not arguing. I'm stating facts.'

'Well, I don't see it.'

How can she not see that in my script? The whole scene is Laura battling her nerves in the face of her boss. Is she being deliberately obtuse?

'It's *there*. I don't think you're even talking about what I've written.'

'Oh really? How do you figure that, Joe?'

'Because it makes no sense. I just think you're angry I called you out.'

I shouldn't have said it aloud. Otty snaps my laptop closed and throws her hands up. And I glare back – because even if she's right for one nanosecond, I'm not giving her the satisfaction of seeing it.

'No, I'm trying to do what you suggested.'

'So it's my fault?'

'Get over yourself, Joe! Go and nurse your dented male pride better, and come back when you're ready to write like an adult.'

'But we need to sort this scene.'

'We're *done* for tonight, don't you think?'

But I'm not done. Far from it. I don't know why I ever thought this could work. 'I write with passion, Otty. It's in every line I write. I'm bloody good at what I do. And Russell *headhunted* me because he wanted me on his team. I was first in. I didn't need an open call to beg for a place. So you'll forgive me if I don't feel the need to take advice from an entry-level writer with no experience.'

What the…? Where did *that* come from?

I've said too much. I don't want to see the wound I just inflicted. Disgusted with myself, I do the only decent thing I can. I get the hell out of there.

Up in my room, I slam my head against the pillow. Why did I do that? Why sabotage my own suggestion? Otty didn't deserve that and she doesn't deserve a writing partner who can't handle criticism. At least her criticism was about what I'd written. Why did I think full-on character assassination was the way to go?

Her scene is brilliant. So brilliant it scares me – because if Russell has another cull and it's a choice between Otty and me I'm not sure I'd win. I just wish she hadn't mentioned *Southside*. I didn't realise she knew I'd written that episode, or that she'd read it, let alone *studied* it. I should be flattered. But it's complicated.

I wrote that episode what feels like a lifetime ago and it almost broke me. And since its success I can't even look at it – because I know what I've lost.

I see Otty's hope and irrepressible belief in how writing should be and it makes me feel weary of the whole thing. She hasn't yet had the sting of rejection, or kicks of doubt when jobs don't go the way you'd hoped. And that should be celebrated and protected, but instead I can see it all lying in wait for her, a minefield she's about to wander into.

It's still no excuse for what I said. But I don't know how to fix it.

Chapter Nineteen

OTTY

I *am* brave in real life. I'm braver than Joe Carver, that's for sure.

He knows nothing about me.

And what kind of an idiot suggests complete honesty if he can't handle the truth? I've never seen someone so spectacularly miss the point as Joe just did. How on earth has he survived as long as he has in this industry if that's his reaction to constructive criticism? At least I was talking about the words on the page, not some completely unwarranted critique of my personal life.

Git.

I kick the leg of the nearest chair and immediately reach down to straighten it. It isn't the chair's fault.

'Sorry, house,' I say to its quiet walls. This should be our sanctuary, not our battleground.

I take a glass from the drainer on the sink and fill it with water. Then I drink it slowly, taking my time: a well-practised act I've repeated after every argument, every peak of tension in my life. Take a moment. Breathe. Focus on one simple thing.

And then I walk upstairs to Joe's room.

I knock but don't wait for an answer. This needs sorting now, not when he's sulked for hours. He looks startled when I walk in, scrambling upright on his bed as if I'm aiming a flamethrower at his head. I sit on the end of the bed and pull my legs up so my chin is resting on my knees. Joe watches every move with wary eyes.

'So, what was that about?'

He scratches his knee, the faded denim suddenly summoning his attention. 'Sorry.'

'Thanks for the apology. But that's not what I asked for.'

'I overreacted. It won't happen again.'

'Too right, it won't. It can't, Joe. We don't have time for it.'

He raises his gaze and I hold it, long and slow and steady. I think I see a hint of fear in the deep blue stare. 'I know.'

I thought this could work, but today has been horrendous. I know Joe thinks we can write together, but we're clearly incompatible. 'I think we should call Russell in the morning. Explain the situation and ask for his original pairings to be reinstated…'

'No, Otty…'

'I think we should. We tried to write together, but it didn't work. Let's just call it quits before we do any real damage. Because, I don't know about you, but I love living here. With you. I think we can be the best of friends and true allies in that writers' room. But writing together? It's too much for us. We should just accept defeat and move on.'

I wasn't expecting him to look so shocked. Anyone could see the disaster today's writing session became was a bad idea. Even the house seems to breathe a sigh of relief when I say it.

'Today was rubbish. Tomorrow will be better.'

'No, it won't. You said I should believe in myself, Joe: well, I *do*. Enough to know when something is dead on its feet.'

'I didn't mean…'

'It doesn't matter what you meant. The fact is, you don't know me. All you know is what you see on the page. Working together and fighting like we did will destroy us eventually. I don't want that to happen.'

Joe looks as though he's been punched in the gut. I haven't seen this version of him before and it sits strangely with the Joe Carver I've become accustomed to.

'Wait. I was out of line when I said that. Your writing is brilliant. It's honest and knowing and, yes, brave as hell. It scares me how good you are.'

'I really don't think…'

'No, listen. I couldn't handle the *Southside* comparison because I'm not that writer now. I poured my soul into that episode, did what Hemingway said and bled my words all over the page. I lived every word and fought for each one through all the revisions. And then the producers decided to hire somebody else to write the next two series. No *thank you*, no acknowledgement of my input, of how that episode shaped the rest of the show. I only discovered Gabriel Marley had won the BAFTA for my work when he mentioned it in an interview months afterwards. I wasn't even credited in the list of writers when the award was won.'

What a horrible experience. How do you come back from that? 'I had no idea.'

He shakes it off. 'Nobody does. But that's why you holding *that* episode as the benchmark for great writing is the worst thing for me to hear because I don't want that happening to you. Writing like that, at that level of intensity, it's just not sustainable. The guy they hired in my place was what they call a "safe pair of hands". Not passionate, not on the edge: solid and dependable. He writes what makes the producers and commissioners happy. Passion never comes into it.'

'So that's how you write now?'

'It's kept me in work and in demand for five years.'

'But does it make you happy?'

'Paying my rent makes me happy. Writing for a living makes me happy. Not being worried about being replaced makes me very happy.'

In that moment, I realise that Joe and I will never be alike. Without passion, without mining something hidden deep within me, I couldn't write. I know I'm new to this and I realise this is the first time I've risked my livelihood on the words I write, but I left a really safe job to do this. Passion is what drives me.

'I can't write like that.'

His eyes are still as he speaks. 'I know. But see, that's why we make a great team. Your passion, my experience. All bases covered. We can push each other, protect each other...'

'Or destroy each other.' Right now it feels like we're magnets with poles reversed, forcing us as far apart as it's possible to be.

'Not if we know exactly where we are. You're brave, I'm cautious. I'm experienced, you're just starting out. You have to see how that could work?'

I let it sink in. I came up to his room with every intention of pulling the plug on our writing partnership, but is Joe right? 'I don't know.'

He edges across the bed to me and offers his hand. 'Otty, if you trust me, I promise I won't let you down. No more fighting. Just words. Would you give us another go?'

My hand is in his before I can think better of it.

And then, we're hugging.

I'm not sure how it happens, or who initiated it, but it feels right. It lasts longer than either of us expect, so that when it ends we pull back, both a bit flushed.

'So how do we do this?' I ask because I'm still not certain it's even possible.

Joe grins. 'First, we eat. Then we start from the beginning – *together* this time.'

Chapter Twenty

JOE

We write. Late into the night. And I'm startled by how relieved I am that Otty agreed to this.

It starts slowly, awkwardly, each discussion tentative, both of us edging around the questions. It's like every word I say to Otty, or suggest for the page, is weighed and considered before I dare to voice it. But gradually the tension eases. As the page fills with words, our confidence grows.

I can't believe I flipped the way I did. Hours after the event, the memory still makes me squirm. More than that, I can't believe I told Otty everything about *Southside*.

Well, *almost* everything.

There was the small detail of my disastrous, short-lived affair with Carla, the supervising producer. I'm not proud of that – mainly because I should have seen the danger before I strolled headlong into it. Turned out I was a willing volunteer for her plan to make Ced Martin, executive producer, jealous. It worked like a dream – and probably ended mine.

'Joe?'

I realise Otty is waiting for me. 'Sorry.' I reach across and type the next line of dialogue. Our spy, Laura Eye, is leaving a message on her late mother's still-active voicemail, as she does every night before she sleeps. Nobody knows Laura made contact with her mum after years of estrangement, shortly before her death, so she feels it's a safe outlet for her grief and loneliness. Of course, it isn't, but our protagonist doesn't know that yet.

The voicemail was Otty's idea and it's brilliant. It reveals so much more of Laura's character and motivation than she would divulge to her therapist or the other members of her family – and it's heartbreaking that she's essentially pouring her heart out to a machine with her mother's voice.

'If you want to call it a night you can,' Otty says, stretching her arms above her head. She's been trying to disguise her yawns for the last hour and I can feel the drag of tiredness down my spine.

'What time is it?'

'Gone 3 a.m.'

'I didn't realise.' When I look at her I can see dark shadows hollowing out her cheeks. 'We probably should – if you want to?'

She grins at the screen. 'We've just sent Laura to bed, so maybe we should do the same.'

We save the file, power down my laptop and head upstairs. On the landing, Otty stops by her bedroom door.

'Night, then.'

'Goodnight. We did good.'

She smiles. 'We did.'

There's a moment when I think we might hug, a slight leaning towards each other. My breath catches – and then Otty pulls back. I don't know if I'm relieved or disappointed, but the smile we share instead is as close to an embrace as we could get without touching.

When I walk into my room, the mirror on the wardrobe reflects a version of me I haven't seen for a long time. He looks happy. I like him.

'Somebody's chirpy for a Monday.' Daphne clicks sweeteners into her coffee, the squeak of her acrylic nails against the plastic dispenser a teeth-grating intrusion.

'Morning, Daphne.'

'How's it going with the live-in writing partner?'

I pour coffee into my mug, ignoring the edge in her question. 'Good, thanks.'

'I imagine it must be intense, spending all that time together.'

'Not really.'

'Liar. Risky, though, putting all your eggs in one basket. One big row, one misunderstanding and – *pouf* – the party's over.'

'We work well together. And we're enjoying living together, too.'

That hit the target. I see the flicker in her expression before she regroups. 'Shag her yet?'

I don't even deign to answer that, raising an eyebrow at Daphne as I walk away. *Nope, you're not going to dent my mood,* I say to her in my head. *Not this morning.*

It's been the longest few days but I'm really proud of the script we sent to Russell yesterday afternoon. It has more depth than the scenes I wrote with Josh and I think even Otty would say it has deeper emotion than the writing she did with Rona.

Of course, Russell might *hate* it.

That's why I'm here at Ensign so early this morning. My guts have been in knots for hours and there was no way I was getting any sleep last night. I love our scenes, but for me they're a risk. Russell has only ever seen my work in its solid, dependable state.

I don't know if he'll agree with us inventing a dead mother and a risky device in Laura's voicemail messages. It isn't in his series bible and it didn't feature in any of our plot discussions within the writers' room. It feels right, but the last time I was so certain of something, I lost it all.

I hear voices in reception and make my way out of the writers' room. Otty has arrived and she and Rona are laughing together. Daphne is doing her best to look disinterested, but I know she'll be straining her ears to catch every word. And then Russell is suddenly among us.

He looks relaxed. Considering he's read everyone's submitted scripts this has to be a good sign. I see him pocket a *pain au chocolat* from the stash I brought in – my blinding plan to bribe my way past any potential script niggles – and check to make sure nobody's seen his blatant defiance of his doctor's advice. And then he spots me and walks over.

'Joseph! This your idea?'

'I thought it wouldn't hurt.'

He reaches into his pocket and puts a torn-off chunk of pastry into his mouth. 'You've got to give me the address of this bakery. Divine.' He brushes off the shower of pastry flakes from his shirt and clamps a hand on my shoulder. 'Walk with me.'

Uh-oh.

I push the shot of fear back down inside as we set off at Russell Styles' pace. It's fine. It will all be great. This is just his usual Otty-check, nothing more.

But what if he loved everyone else's scripts except ours? What if this is a kind intervention before we all go into the writers' room?

Breathe, Carver.

Russell is busy talking about the building – there's a plan for a digital production company to move into one of the vacant eleventh-floor office spaces in the next few months. I make positive noises at the right junctures, but we're getting close to the halfway point on his usual route: the place where he will stop and say what we've come here to discuss. My throat is suddenly dry.

He stops abruptly and I stop, too. I squirm behind a badly fitting smile.

'Your script, Joe…'

'Did it arrive okay?' I'm playing for time and the squeak at the end of my question betrays my raging nerves.

He laughs. 'Of course it did. And it was…' He waves a hand in the air as if trying to catch the right word.

Oh crap…

'… Inspired.'

'It – it was?'

'I have to admit, it was a risk pairing you with Otty. But what a pay-off! Fantastic, Joe. Just the kind of out-of-the-box thinking we need. Clearly she brings out the best in you.'

Relief almost buckles my knees. 'That's great, Russ. I mean, we knew it was a bit – *out there* – but it works, yeah?'

'Absolutely. And it's another weakness in Laura we can tease the audience with. Get 'em gasping and OMG-ing all over Twitter, eh?'

'Word-of-mouth power!' I say, cringing at my air punch as soon as I've thrown it. My hand falls like a rock to my side.

Russell doesn't seem to notice my transformation into an overexcited buzzword-utterer. This morning is a morning of small mercies. 'I love what you're doing with our workhouse apprentice. I see big things for your partnership if you keep producing work like this. Good job, Joe.'

I'm about to reply that Laura's voicemail messages were all

Otty's idea, when Russell grins and sets off back to the office. I'll tell him when we next talk. Accepting the praise for Otty's work just isn't right. But I can't deny the rush of exhilaration as I hurry after him.

We *did it*. The risk paid off.

In the writers' room we take our seats. I can feel the nerves rising like steam from my colleagues as they watch Russell walk in. They must all be battling the same doubts I did before my Russell-walk. I like the tiny advantage I have over them. But then I see Otty's expression and remember that she doesn't know we're in the clear.

Under the table I reach across and squeeze her hand where it rests in her lap. She jumps and looks at me.

'He loves it,' I mouth.

Her eyes grow wide and then it's like sunshine breaks out across her face. It's the loveliest thing.

'Thank you,' she mouths back.

Across the table, Daphne coughs.

'Your scripts all made the cut,' Russell announces, smiling as a tsunami of exhales and released laughter rings around the room. 'So we sign them off and we move on. I'm happy with these pairings so I'm going to keep them. Your writing partner is now your permanent co-writer. Congratulations, guys. I'm excited about the work we're doing.'

I smile at Otty. She smiles at me. This is going to work, isn't it?

Chapter Twenty-One

OTTY

'Pass us one of them scratchings, our Otts.'

I hand Dad the bag of pork scratchings, nicking one on the way. As he always does, Dad mock-gasps at my daughterly audacity and I bow my head and pretend to look guilty.

I've missed this.

It's a gorgeous day today, the sun washing across the green of Edgbaston Cricket Ground. The game has settled into a steady rhythm of warm willow cracks and single runs, gentle ripples of applause and the occasional peak of excitement. It's a county match, the mighty Warwickshire playing Yorkshire, and we're fielding right now.

Most of RoadTrail will be here soon, Jarvis and Steve are on their way over and Sheila is due to arrive after lunch. But for now, it's just Dad and me.

'We've got 'em on the rails, I reckon,' he says between munches. 'They had us last year but we in't about to roll over again.'

'It's a good team,' I reply, enjoying the sun on my shoulders as it reaches our side of the ground.

'It is.' He reaches for another handful of scratchings. 'So, how you getting on in that old house?'

'Nothing's broken yet.'

He nods. 'Give it time. And your chap?'

'Joe's not my chap.'

'Housemate, then. Is he treating you well?'

I have to laugh at the formality of the question. 'He hasn't broken me yet.'

'Ottilie!'

'Sorry. We're fine. We're writing together now.'

'Are you?' I can tell by the sudden drop of his bushy eyebrows over his blue eyes what Dad thinks of this.

'Russell put us together. It took us a while but it seems to be working.'

'Well, as long as you've still got a job.' He jumps to his feet, staring at the game. 'Catch it! *Catch it!*' His groan joins those of our fellow fans as he resumes his seat. 'What kind of a catch was that? Anyone'd think they'd buttered the ball.'

Dad's sudden emotional outbursts at cricket matches never cease to amuse me. It's a sign of home. This has been part of my life for as long as I can remember. Sitting in the same stand, in roughly the same seats (not too close to the exit, not too close to the front), in all weathers, sharing snacks, sandwiches and flasks of tea with Dad and any number of family members, friends and RoadTrail people. But the way I've always liked it best is like today: Dad and me.

'Any luck with finding my replacement?' I ask. Dad made some noises a while ago about looking, but I've heard nothing since.

'I told you, I'm not replacing you.'

'You need someone else in the workshop,' I begin, but Dad's tut stops me.

'Bab, you may need it. That job of yours might be peachy right now, but I've heard it's a fickle business and they're just as likely to drop you as take you on.'

'Russell loves what I'm writing with Joe. I think we're going to be there a long time.'

'Well, let's hope so.'

'You still need to get someone in.'

His stares at the bag of scratchings in his palm. 'I know.'

'Even if you want it to be a short-term thing.'

'I *know*, Otts. My life, you sound like Sheila.'

'Well, maybe we both have a point.'

He waves off my suggestion with all the irritation of a man frequently called out for his daft stubbornness. He'll get there in the end, I'm sure. He'll have to: I've risked too much to be working at Ensign and I'm not going back.

The Yorkshire batsman, who has been sitting pretty at the crease for the last half-hour, suddenly hits the ball awkwardly – and we're on our feet. I hold my breath as the ball sails out across the field, our team racing to meet it. And then it drops like a dream into the fielder's hand and the entire stand erupts. Dad and I hug and I swear the sun shines brighter than it did a moment ago. Grinning at the other Warwickshire fans around us, we retake our seats.

Dad mops his brow with an imaginary handkerchief and whistles. 'Got 'im! Better late than never, eh?' He smiles and pats my knee. 'Good to have you here, bab. Been too long.'

'I know. It's just so busy at work. I've hardly had time to think.'

'You work hard. Always have.' He takes another pork scratching from the bag and chews thoughtfully. 'You know, Sheila was asking how you were getting on.'

The compliment creaks beneath heavy emphasis. 'I'll see her

today, though,' I reply, my stomach knotting. I feel bad about not seeing Sheila since I left Dad's place. I love her – always will – but it's not straightforward to see her outside of RoadTrail anymore.

'You know, Chris is back in town.'

And *that's* why.

'I thought he was in Oxford?' Nerves lift the end of my question to an uncomfortable pitch and I cough to try to pull back control. The wording of his text returns to my mind: *I have news.* Was that what he wanted to tell me?

'He was.' Dad watches me carefully. 'But he reckons there was too much calling him home.'

The exhilaration from the catch fades as a cloud drifts across the sun. I watch a line of shadow sweep across the cricket ground, dulling everything.

'So where's he working now?'

'Oh, I don't know. Some sort of freelance consultancy blah-de-blah. That techy stuff of his is beyond me. Point is, he's back. And Sheila says he's practically a different man.'

I know where this is heading. I'd hoped to avoid the subject, seeing as we've been here for almost three hours without Dad mentioning it. But that was too optimistic, even for me. Of course it isn't over with. It might never be.

'Well, that's good for him. And nice for Sheila too, I imagine, having him closer.'

'Oh, she's over the moon. I am, too. Always loved the lad. Despite… you know.'

I hold my breath, willing something to happen on the pitch that steals his attention and robs his train of thought.

Yeah, like *that's* going to happen.

'Maybe… you could see him now he's back? Chat things over?'

'No.'

'Couldn't hurt.'

Muscles knot across my shoulders. My chest grows tight. I didn't want a fight today but I'm not going to back down on this. '*No*, Dad. It could hurt – a lot. We said all we had to a year ago.'

Dad's arms fold across his chest and I can feel lines being drawn between us. 'No, bab, *you* did. As I recall, poor Chris didn't get a look-in.'

Poor Chris. Here we go. 'You don't know what happened.'

'I know what he told me. And Sheila.'

'And what about what *I* told you?' I catch the stares of the group seated behind us and pull my voice back to an angry whisper. 'If Chris is getting on with his life then great, but there is nothing else for us to talk about.'

'You could be married by now. Maybe thinking of kids. Most girls your age already have them.'

It's pointless. Dad just isn't designed to accept that I could want anything other than marriage and kids. He married Mum the day after her nineteenth birthday and they had me when she was twenty-one. Even Mum divorcing him and shacking up with a tour rep half her age in Magaluf didn't shake his hope for Chris and me. We'd grown up together, after all, our families as close as if we were all blood-related. Chris asked me out at the school disco in our GCSE year, and from then on everyone assumed we were heading for the altar. Looking back, I have the worrying suspicion my dad and Sheila agreed our future together when Chris and I were still in nappies.

'I'm happy where I am, Dad.'

'But are you? Everyone gets cold feet, Otts. And I know us lot weren't much help. We were just excited for the wedding. We'd been excited about it for years…'

And that's the problem. Because I didn't just break up with Chris: I smashed both our families' dreams of us getting married. And though it was the right decision for me, I felt like I'd betrayed everyone by not conforming to their vision for my life. It haunted me like a belligerent ghost during the last twelve months I worked at RoadTrail, hanging mournfully in the shadows of every conversation, every day. Because how could I look at Sheila and not see her hurt? Or Dad without seeing his disappointment?

But I did the right thing.

I wasn't happy. If I'd stayed at RoadTrail, married Chris as we'd planned to do this Christmas, and started the much-longed-for family everyone wanted, I would have been a living, breathing lie.

I feel Dad's hand on my arm. 'He'd accept you doing the writing thing, however long you needed to do it. Now he's had time to think he'll have realised that's where he went wrong. He'd let you do it now.'

'*I've* let myself do it. And I'm happy.'

'Words aren't the same as family, Ottilie.'

No they aren't, I want to reply. *At least I can control words and delete them if they become unreasonable.* But there's no use arguing. Dad has his opinion and it won't change. This city will have to be big enough for Chris and me. I just hope I don't bump into him.

'Otty! Otty! Otty! Oi! Oi! Oi!'

The chants of my former workmates bring the most welcome release. I see Dad hunker in his seat as Jarvis and Steve stomp down the steps and edge along the row towards us. I hug Jarvis and high-five Steve, who holds his rucksack as a safety shield between us to ensure I don't hug him, too. I know there will be smuggled-in cans of Batham's bitter in that rucksack, secreted within the folds of his anorak and jumper along with four enamel mugs he will innocently decant the beer into as he hands it out. Steve's alcohol-smuggling skills are second to none.

'I wondered when the cavalry was arriving,' I grin, avoiding eye contact with Dad.

'More like the clowns,' he mutters.

'Miss any good stuff?'

'We just got their guy out after a long spell,' I reply, offering Jarvis the bag of pork scratchings. He takes a handful and stuffs them all in his mouth.

'Nice one,' he says, spraying crumbs. 'How's it going in TV world?'

'Good, thanks. Are you and Steve surviving without me?'

'Just about,' Steve grins, pouring dark amber bitter into a sneaky mug hidden between his knees. 'It's a laugh a minute with your dad.'

'Button your lip and pass us a beer,' Dad grumbles.

'Sheila coming?' Jarvis asks.

'Should be,' I reply before Dad can say anything.

'Has he told you your ex is back?'

Fabulous. 'Apparently I'm the last to know about it.'

'He'll be sniffing round you soon enough. Just kick him to the kerb when he does.' I appreciate Jarvis's gentle lean against my shoulder more than I'd tell him. Of all the RoadTrail employees, Jarvis is the closest to an ally I've had. He was the only one to tell me I'd done the right thing when I left Chris.

'Less of that,' Dad says, but it doesn't matter. At least I'll have one wingman on our stand today.

We watch the game and our conversation eases away from

Chris Wright. The sun warms us, the smuggled beer soothes and the rhythm returns. But the same edge of unease remains beneath it all for me, darker, uncertain water swirling around my feet.

I'm exhausted by the time I get home.

The house welcomes me with cool quietness, its rooms bathed in gentle late-afternoon light. Joe isn't there. I'm glad. My mind needs the stillness to recalibrate. Sheila never arrived, in the end. Her car had a slow puncture so she had to sort that instead. I feel like I've dodged a bullet.

At some point I'll have to face it. Probably Chris, too.

And I will.

Just not today.

Chapter Twenty-Two

JOE

The board in the writers' room is gradually filling up with Russell's signatures. We're halfway through the episodes now, all of us working at a pace unlike many of us have been asked to write before. I'm *knackered* – Otty is, too – surviving on caffeine and a totally rubbish diet that my body will surely kick me for later. But it's working. The more scenes we produce, the more confident we grow, and the happier Russell becomes, which is the main thing.

I just wish he wouldn't keep assuming all of our innovation comes from me, like Otty's idea that Laura now has a dead mother she leaves voicemail messages for. I felt Otty stiffen next to me as he praised it.

'It's quite frankly brilliant. It gives us another weakness for Laura, another secret someone else can abuse. I always knew Joe was good, but this is next-level…'

I corrected him then like I've corrected him so many times during our eleventh-floor power-walks, but I'm starting to wonder if he even hears it now. Maybe it's become subliminal – he's so used to me adding, 'That was Otty's idea… Otty wrote that', to every compliment he wrongly aims at me that perhaps his brain is still registering it when his ears aren't.

I hope so. I hate feeling like a double agent.

Something Otty wrote last night set alarm bells ringing. Laura Eye is talking with her therapist, and she says this:

LAURA

The duplicity is the hardest to take,
you know? Never trusting anyone. Always
assuming the other person is lying in
some way. Because I'm lying to them,
too, aren't I? I have to.

DR MONTGOMERY

Isn't that part of your job? Withholding
truth sometimes?

LAURA

Yes, I suppose so.

DR MONTGOMERY
(consults notes)

What concerns you about it now? Has
something changed?

LAURA
(looks out of the window)

I think someone close to me is lying.

DR MONTGOMERY
Why do you think that?

LAURA
Because he's holding something back. I
feel it when we're together. It's as if
he's taking orders from someone else…

I know that Laura Eye is talking about Gus Parkinson, the guy she's working alongside at the multinational corporation she's been assigned to protect. My head is well aware that Otty isn't writing it about me. But I've seen her expression whenever I return from talking with Russell and it worries me. I'm probably feeling guilty. No, I definitely am.

Does Otty know? She isn't letting on if she does. But that doesn't make me feel any easier about the whole thing. Maybe we're safe enough now. Russell likes our writing, so he'll keep us together regardless. Perhaps I'll have a word with him, suggest that Otty knows what she's doing and doesn't need a mentor anymore.

Mind you, even that sounds patronising.

At least other areas of my life are simpler. I have a new date for a start.

It's very new and only happened yesterday, but tonight I am going out with Molly for the first time. Molly Stephens is the receptionist at Ensign. She's beautiful and to be honest I noticed her ages ago. But when I started there I was still seeing Victoria on and off, so I wasn't looking for anyone else. Molly's lovely, a little shy but engaging, and I'm excited about getting to know her better.

Also, her dad is mates with Robert Plant from Led Zeppelin,

which is more than a bit cool. I hear they get together quite a bit so I'm hoping she'll invite me.

Shallow? Perhaps. But it's going to add an extra bit of spice to an already promising evening.

'Make sure you have her home by midnight,' my housemate and writing partner grins, wagging her finger at me like a failing-to-look-stern headmistress.

Otty is, of course, having the time of her life tonight. It's the first date I've been on since she moved in and she's relishing the chance to exact revenge on me for how I was the night of her first date with Rona's brother.

'Very funny,' I say, leaning down to tie my shoelaces.

'I will be scrutinising your breakfast choices in the morning for signs of *wanton shaggage*.'

She is enjoying this far too much.

'That's not a word.'

'Er, I think you'll find it is. "*Shaggage* – noun – the unexpected baggage that inevitably follows a bout of shagging. See also *bonkage* and *knobbage*."' She beams like a smug victor on a podium.

'They never taught me that in English lessons.'

'Maybe they should have, Joseph.'

I straighten and grab my jacket. 'You know, this gets old really quickly.'

Otty blesses me with a wry smile. 'Have a lovely time, Joe.'

'I will.'

'Be *good*,' she calls after me.

'I'll be *amazing*,' I call back.

'Ugh. Get out of my house immediately!'

I grin as I leave.

*

I've arranged to meet my date in a decent restaurant just off Chamberlain Square. Not knowing what she likes, I played safe and booked us a table at a small French bistro. French is good, right? I arrive first and wait at the table for her, suddenly feeling nervous. Which is daft, considering I'm hardly new to this. But now I'm at the table, trying not to demolish all the breadsticks before Molly arrives, I'm acutely aware of how many months have passed since my last date. It isn't that I haven't wanted to; I've just been busy.

I'm only here now because Otty and I agreed we needed a Saturday off.

I've seen her go on the odd date here and there, too, but nothing serious. I can't even remember their names because she maybe mentions them once and then they're gone. Work has been so all-consuming that it's no wonder we're both a bit lacklustre on the dating side.

All that could change for me tonight, though, if it goes well.

I check my watch: Molly is five minutes late.

That's okay, I assure myself. *We're just playing it cool on the first date.*

I raise my hand to summon a passing waiter and have just ordered a beer when Molly arrives.

She looks beautiful. Her blonde hair is loose and curls up where the ends meet her shoulders. She's wearing a white blouse and fitted black trousers and her belt has just a hint of glitter that shimmers as she walks. Remembering my manners, I scramble to my feet to greet her with a double-cheek kiss.

So far, so awkwardly good.

'Did you find this place okay?' I ask as the waiter pulls out a chair for her and I sit back down.

'Yeah, it was exactly where you said it would be.'

'Right.' We share timid smiles. 'Would you like some wine?'

She glances at my newly arrived beer. 'You already have a drink.'

'I know. But I can leave it if you wanted wine instead.'

What? One thing's for certain: I need to work on my first-date small talk because I *suck* at it tonight.

Molly lifts her hand and the waiter reappears. 'Beer for me too, please.'

'*Oui, mademoiselle.*'

She shrugs, her smile dazzling. 'I like beer.'

I resist the urge to laugh because at that moment, I like Molly.

As first dates go, it's surprisingly good. Dinner arrives and we both relax. By dessert, things are positively cosy.

'I was hoping you'd ask me out,' she admits, mid-tarte Tatin.

'Were you?'

She nods. 'For a long time. I even thought about asking *you* on a date. But I didn't know if you and Otty were a thing.'

'Ah. We're not.'

'I know that now. It's just you were always together at work. And then Daphne said you lived together.'

I bristle. 'Right…'

'She seemed to think there was more going on than just sharing a house?'

I've seen the dead-eyes Daphne's been firing our way in the writers' room. The woman is obsessed with us. I know Otty is wary of telling her anything now. 'Daphne sees drama everywhere. Don't listen to her. Otty and I work together and live together, that's all. She's dating, so am I.'

A small crease appears between Molly's perfectly groomed eyebrows. I'm not sure why – I mean, I've just explained everything, haven't I? 'Okay.'

'I'm having fun,' I say, although it sounds more apologetic than I intend.

'Me too.'

Molly plays with the last piece of apple on her plate, her spoon twisting left and right as if guiding an ice hockey puck across the cream-glazed base of her bowl. I follow it, mesmerised, her voice strangely far away when she speaks. 'We could have more fun next time if you wanted to come to mine?'

'That would be… Yes, great,' I manage, the bistro suddenly very warm indeed.

Outside, Molly pulls me in for a kiss that is as long as it is sweet and I promise to see her again soon outside work. We didn't talk about Robert Plant tonight, but I'm not disappointed. Judging by our goodnight kiss, there will be plenty of opportunity for that…

I half expect Otty to be waiting up to grill me when I get home, but I find the house in darkness. No doubt she's saving up her jibes for tomorrow. I might call her bluff – arrive in the kitchen in only my boxers and take two cups of coffee back upstairs with me. Or I might rock up in the clothes I've worn tonight, as though I've only just come home.

Smiling to myself, I grab a bottle of beer from the fridge and head up to my room to work.

'It's your turn to get the coffee.'

I look at Otty over the screen of my laptop. 'I got them last time.'

'No, I got these.'

'Did you?'

136

She laughs. 'Must have been some night for you and marvellous Molly. It's addled your brain.'

I pull a face but I'm enjoying the banter today. Otty beat me to the chase this morning by leaving a note in the kitchen inviting me to join her at this city café for a working brunch. All my clever schemes to wind her up about my date therefore failed – and by the time I arrived it seemed too late to try.

I haven't been here before, but I like it. Excellent coffee and laid-back service, all within a short walk of Birmingham Cathedral. In fact, the service is so laid-back it takes practically an hour for them to make your coffee. They seem to be enjoying themselves, though, and it's oddly calming to watch the baristas at work.

I'm glad Otty suggested working out here. I'm not a fan of Sunday writing but, with a deadline, every day is a writing day. If it had to be anywhere, it's best in a place like this. Stuck at home we'd never be this productive.

We have a breakdown of scenes we have to write and as we complete each one I mark another tick on the list. Mum used to mock me for my insistence on tick-boxes on every kind of list. But it makes me feel like I've achieved something – however small. It's the completionist in me. I like everything done and accounted for. Leaving stuff half-finished does not put me at ease.

I tick another box with a flourish and grin at Otty. 'Five down, five to go.'

She laughs. 'Ooh, we're at the midpoint twist!'

'Okay, here's one: Laura and Gus run out of coffee because one of them forgets whose turn it is to buy the next round?'

'Rubbish. That's not a twist to get people talking on Twitter.'

'It's unexpected. And everyone can identify with the horror of an empty cup…'

She shakes her head. '*Loon*. What we need is something…' She breaks off, her smile vanishing, her eyes wide.

'What?' I ask. It's not unlike Otty to stop mid-sentence because an amazing plot point has shocked her into silence. But then she ducks her head down behind her screen. That's not what usually happens.

'*Down here*,' she insists. When I don't respond, she grabs the collar of my shirt and pulls me down, until my face is an inch from hers.

'What are we doing?'

'Don't look.'

'Don't look where?'

'Over… by… the… *door*,' she hisses, which of course makes me try to see what I'm not supposed to be looking at. But there's just a random bloke standing there, scanning the room for a table.

'Otts, you're hurting me,' I yelp as she yanks my head down again.

'Just… Hang in there.'

'You're being weird. What's going on?'

Her sigh could cool everyone's coffee on the tables around us. 'I don't want to see *him*.'

'Who?'

'Don't look!'

'*Ow*, would you stop grabbing my neck?'

'Sorry. I just can't let him see me.'

'Who? The chap by the door?'

She gives me a look like I should have worked this out ages ago. 'He's my ex.'

'You had a date with him?'

Otty closes her eyes, her jaw tight. 'No. My *proper* ex. As in the guy I broke up with before I got this job?'

'Oh. Long-term?' She nods. 'How long-term?'

'I started going out with him when I was sixteen.'

'Bloody hell…'

'And every time I've seen him since it ended I've just broken up with somebody else. So Chris thinks I'm lying about dating other people. He thinks it's only a matter of time before I admit the truth and take him back.'

I stare at her. 'Would you take him back?'

'*No*. Were you even listening?'

My neck is beginning to ache from the unnatural angle Otty is holding it at. And this sudden revelation is messing with my already post-beer-hazed brain. 'You don't need to hide, Otts.'

'Yes, I do. The place is packed, he'll be gone in a moment.'

I raise my head and see that she's wrong. 'Well, actually…'

'Ottilie? Is that you?'

At close quarters to my housemate I can practically feel her heart sink. Slowly, she lifts her head and I follow.

'Chris. Hi.'

'I thought I saw you.'

'You did.' Her smile pulls her lips into a thin line.

'Glad I did.' His eyes make a super-creepy slow drop as he takes her in. Like he's eyeing up his next meal. It makes *me* feel sullied and I'm only sitting by its subject. 'You didn't reply to my text.'

'No, sorry. Work and stuff.'

He shrugs. 'I thought that was what it was. So, I guess you heard I'm back?'

'Dad told me. Birmingham won over Oxford, did it?'

'What's *in* Birmingham did.' He smiles a too-wide, too-white, definitely icky grin and I instantly dislike him. 'Also I got offered a great job with a tech agency start-up.'

'Great. Um, congratulations.'

'It's less money than I was on in Oxford, but with house prices cheaper here it's practically a raise.' The dark smudge of his shadow passes over my tick-box list of scenes as he leans in. 'Perfect job to build a home on – support a partner… and kids…'

'I'm happy for you.'

'I knew you would be. So, you seeing anyone?'

Otty cringes beside me. I'm offended for her. I mean, I'm a fan of directness when it's necessary but this bloke is off the scale. Was Otty really saddled to *that* for all those years? She's visibly shrunk into her chair now, a diminutive scrap of what I know her to be.

This is horrible. I can't just sit here and let my lovely friend and writing partner be subjected to Captain Creepy's subtle-as-a-brick leering. She doesn't deserve such blatant disrespect.

Otty is about to reply when I clear my throat and Creepy Chris's attention slides to me.

'Oh, I'm sorry, I didn't realise you had company.'

'We're working, actually,' Otty says, her smile the weariest I've seen. 'This is Joe, my…'

'Boyfriend,' I rush, before I have time to think it through.

Otty's mouth hangs open and I smile brightly at her, hoping my rapidly developing plan is instantly conveyed through my expression. For a horrible moment I think she's too shocked to understand, but then I see her cotton on. '*Yes*, he is… Chris, meet Joe Carver.'

Creepy Chris looks like he's swallowed a bucket of eels. 'Hey,' he manages, extending his hand. 'Chris Wright.'

'Hi.' I shake his hand warmly and then slip my arm around Otty in a move so smooth Daniel Craig's Bond would be in awe. I feel her shoulder tense briefly before she leans into my half-embrace. The line where our bodies meet becomes deliciously warm.

'I didn't know…' Chris splutters. 'I mean, when I spoke to your dad he told me you were single.'

'Your dad, always the joker,' I say, grinning a little too enthusiastically at Otty. Considering I've never met her father, will this look convincing?

'But he said…' Otty's creepy ex gives a laugh that's more his nerves leaking than the carefree sound he wants it to be. 'Oh right, I get it. Good joke, Otty. You almost had me there.'

Otty blinks at him. 'It's not a joke, Chris.'

'But he's…' His hand gives a vague wave as if we should all know what it means.

'Gorgeous?' Otty finishes.

Blimey.

I fix my smile.

'No – I mean, it's just a surprise. He's not the kind of bloke you usually go for, that's all.' He shifts from one foot to the other. 'So, how did you meet?'

'We're working together,' Otty says. 'On the TV drama I got the job writing?'

'Oh, so you did that?'

'I did.'

'Yeah, well it's okay if you're single. Not a career, though, is it? How much does it pay? I'm guessing not much. I mean, you're not Quentin Tarantino, are you?'

Okay, this guy is one sentence away from a punch. Thankfully, Otty replies before I can tell him where to shove his dumb assumptions.

'It's the best job in the world, actually. And totally a career choice – like I told you for years.'

Ouch. No wonder she kicked him to the kerb if he tried to

stop her writing. I squeeze her shoulder to let her know that she's smashing this.

'It's great, too, although a lot of work.'

'Probably for the best that you moved in then, darling,' I say, stroking her cheek with my other hand.

Otty's eyebrows lift so high they are practically in her hairline. 'Um, probably…'

Creepy Chris is paler than the whitewashed walls now. 'Moved *in*?'

'A couple of months ago,' Otty nods.

'Right…'

'It's perfect,' I carry on, enjoying the effect on Otty's smarmy ex far too much to consider where I'm going with it. 'Although sharing a house with this one can be pretty distracting…' I gaze deep into her eyes. 'It's too easy to forget work *entirely*…'

'Actually, we should probably be going,' Otty says, but it isn't panic I hear in her voice. It's a deep, breathy playfulness. Suddenly, it doesn't feel like we're joking…

'Yes, we should…' I force my eyes back to Otty's ex, who looks about ready to slip between the cracks in the reclaimed oak floorboards. 'Good to meet you, man. If you'll excuse us…'

Outside, a safe distance from the café, we finally collapse into helpless guffaws.

'My *boyfriend*? Where did that come from?'

I lean against the wall. 'It seemed like a good idea at the time.'

'You almost gave me heart failure,' she giggles. 'And then when you slipped your arm round me…'

'Smooth, huh?'

'So smooth.' Her face glows as she beams up at me. 'That was terrible acting, though.'

'Was it? I thought I was good.'

'Seriously, don't ever get carried away with your words and think you can perform them.'

'Hey, it convinced Creepy Chris.'

'Yeah, but what does he know?'

'It was worth my bad acting just to see his reaction,' I laugh. 'Did you see his face? I thought he was going to faint and…'

But I don't get to say any more because right then, Otty hugs me. And I'm so surprised the words freeze on my tongue.

She is holding my body to hers so tightly. I hesitate, not knowing what to do; my hands out at my sides as if touching her might make her disappear. But she presses in – and my arms instinctively fold around her. Otty's skin is warm; her hair dusted with the scent of the coffee shop.

She holds me for a long time.

I don't want to move.

'Thank you,' she says eventually, head against my chest.

'For what?'

Her sigh warms my skin beneath my shirt. 'For caring about me.'

And then, the hug is over.

We share pink-cheeked smiles and walk back towards the cathedral. She doesn't mention it again – neither do I. But something has shifted in the air between us, a micro-quake in the atoms that form our world.

Does Otty sense it, too?

Chapter Twenty-Three

OTTY

We are in the home straight with the first season of *Eye, Spy*. Nerves fizz like exposed live wires, all of us are one wrong word away from an argument and Russell is a brooding, prowling beast circling us all.

It hasn't helped that yesterday *The Sentinel* published a piece by well-known TV critic Nathan Byford-King, which suggested that iconic showrunners like Russell, Jed Mercurio, Chris Chibnall and even Queen Phoebe Waller-Bridge were ruining the quality of British drama:

> Instead of innovation we are subjected to endless parades of caricatured parody: the side-wink, kill-the-star, slit-throat 'event TV' culture we allegedly can't get enough of. But it's a diet empty of any benefit. Surely the time is right for these behemoths of popular drama to step aside, take their mammoth egos with them and allow better writers not so obsessed with personal brand-touting to tell the stories we need?

It was the kind of nasty, snobbish click-bait stuff designed to annoy everyone, and should have been ignored for the utter guff it was. But it worked. By lunchtime it had been shared and quoted hundreds of thousands of times across social media – sending Russell into a tailspin of rage. He's convinced himself that if even one sentence of *Eye, Spy* is off-target, it will fail. Even a long walk around the building with Joe didn't lighten his mood.

A dark cloud hangs over us today as we work. Russell's insisted that all the final scenes are written in-house, in this room. It's tough for everyone. Like writing inside a pressure cooker. And Russell is in here with us, all the time, watching our every move with the maniacal scrutiny of a black-suited vulture.

It feels like we're writing for our lives.

Joe grimaces when I look at him. I mirror his expression. Then we duck down behind our laptop screens and keep typing.

At least I have Joe. Writing in these conditions could be too much if I didn't feel I had support. But I know he's on my side.

We haven't talked about it, but what he did on Sunday blew me away. I just thought he'd sit there while Chris and I spoke – anyone else would have been embarrassed into silence. I still can't get over how he threw himself into it. I mean, I knew we were friends and recently we've grown closer. But that was next-level mate support. I'm still giggling about Chris's face when Joe did his boyfriend speech. Dreadfully delivered, utterly inspired. It doesn't take away any of the other rubbish clinging to our break-up, but for this small moment it feels like I've snatched back a little power. That feels good.

A nudge against my arm summons my attention back to the laptop screen, where a new line of script has mysteriously appeared:


```
                    LAURA
        Well, this is a bundle of laughs.
```

Checking Russell isn't looking at us, I lean casually over Joe's keyboard and type:

<pre>
                    GUS
         I feel like we're in an exam.
         Why are you writing as Laura?

                   LAURA
       Why not? I'd make a great Laura.
          You're just jealous, Gus.

                    GUS
       You wish. Is it going to be like this
            till the season is done?

                   LAURA
        R is v. stressed. I caught him scoffing
      handfuls of mini-doughnuts this morning.
                Not looking good.

                    GUS
           Who brought doughnuts in?

                   LAURA
      Tom. He knows what R's like just before
              deadline. Like this:
</pre>

Joe sticks his tongue out and crosses his eyes. I have to bite the inside of my cheek to stop myself laughing.

＊

At lunchtime, I grab a fresh coffee and a handful of fruit from Ensign's kitchen and commandeer a leather chair in reception. The door opens and a slightly flustered Daphne strides in. I look back out at the city, but she's already clocked me. Before I can move, she's taken the armchair opposite mine.

'Brutal in there today,' she says, spreading a large white napkin across her lap and producing the smallest box of sushi I've ever seen from a company logo-printed canvas bag. 'Haven't seen him this bad since *Insiders*. That was when he had his health scare and Miri put her foot down.'

'Miri?'

Daphne blesses me with a pitying look. 'His second wife? The one who's had him dashing up the stairs every morning?'

'Oh, I haven't met her.'

'Nor are you likely to. She won't come near this place.' She expertly picks up a *hosomaki* roll and delivers it to her mouth. 'So, Joe tells me the two of you are writing well.'

'I think we are.'

'It's so good that he's taking time to invest in you.'

What is she saying? 'It's good that we're investing in each other.'

'But only in the writing sense, yes?'

Not this again. 'As friends, too.'

'*Just* friends. I'm glad. I'll admit, I was concerned. Especially given how close Joe and I are becoming…' She leaves just enough of a pause for this to sink in, then rises elegantly from her chair. 'We'll be seeing so much more of each other soon, Otty. I hope you're okay with that.'

It's only when she walks away that I realise I don't know whether she meant seeing more of me, or seeing more of Joe.

147

It's almost 9 p.m. when we leave Ensign. My eyes ache so much I have to sit in Monty in the car park for a while until they adjust to the night view. When I blink, the ghost-image of my laptop screen reappears for a second, imprinted on my retina. Joe said he'd meet me at home – he's volunteered to get a takeaway tonight as neither of us has the energy to cook. At least writing the remaining scenes at Ensign this week means a night free from work. Not that I reckon Joe or I will be awake for long after we've eaten.

As I lean back into my seat, two figures emerge from the glass doors and walk slowly across the car park. I follow them absent-mindedly, blinking again to coax the life back into my vision. The couple skirts the edge of the parked cars, their bodies passing through alternating shafts of streetlight and dark pools of shadow. Then, under the nearest light to me, they stop and face each other. Slowly, they embrace. And it's only when they lean in to one another that the orange glow bathes their features.

I can't believe it.

Joe said he wasn't seeing anyone. Despite his two dates with Molly, I haven't heard him mention seeing her again. I thought it was just him losing interest – but is *this* why?

And how could he be seeing *her* after all the jokes he's made?

Has this been going on all along? And when was he going to tell me?

I feel sick, but I can't stop watching.

Daphne rests her chin on Joe's shoulder, his hands against her back. And if I didn't know my car was hidden in the shadows between two others so nobody can see, I would swear that Daphne looks straight at me – and smiles.

Chapter Twenty-Four

JOE

I don't know what got into Otty last night, but something was off.

I thought I'd done the right thing driving several miles out of my way so I could get her a takeaway from that Diamond Balti place she loves. I *think* she was pleased. She looked surprised. She just wasn't really in the room after that.

She's probably tired. We all are. And if Russ doesn't calm down, he'll send us all jumping over the edge with him like a pack of sleep-deprived, caffeine-crazed lemmings.

I tried talking with him again yesterday, but Daphne appeared and hijacked the conversation. She's been acting strange lately, too, but that's nothing new. She's also become more than a little tactile. Not sure how I feel about that. I mean, there are huggy people and arm's-length people and Daphne Davies was always firmly in the latter camp. She's the last person I expected to become one of life's huggers.

Irony is, a few months ago I would have been all over that like a rash. What is it people say about being careful of wishes? She insisted on walking to the car with me last night and the hug she gave me was… *unexpected*. She said it was a gesture of support from one writer to another, but I'm not sure. If I didn't know better, I'd say she was making a play for me.

Women are strange creatures.

I check my watch as I run along the path towards the park at the end of our road. 6.25 a.m. – enough time for a lap before heading back for a shower. Russell wants us in at eight thirty this morning and I have to be ready for whatever he throws at us. By rights I should still be in bed making the most of my rest before another voluntary incarceration in the writers' room, but I needed fresh air and the chance to blow off some steam.

The park is empty save for a gaggle of miffed-looking Canada geese and a couple of early-morning dog-walkers. The grass is damp and a thin layer of mist hangs low across the park. Every part of my body aches, but the run seems to stretch out knots in my shoulders, back and legs. I push on, following the path around the lake, over the bridge from the feeder stream and out across the wide green space.

Ten minutes later, I arrive back at the house to find Otty's yellow Fiat gone and a black Transit van in its spot, its bumper almost touching the dark blue paintwork of my Volkswagen Golf in the next space. I hope it isn't still here when she gets back: Ottilie Perry is highly territorial when it comes to parking spaces, I have discovered. Doing my stretches by our gate, I look at the name on the van, painted in silver-edged red letters:

ROADTRAIL
For all your two-wheeled needs

The name feels familiar, but I don't know why. Have I seen this van before? I can't remember, not that I'm going to try too hard.

It's far too early to attempt any kind of brain-wracking, so I leave it and open the gate.

When I'm putting my key in the front door lock, a cough behind summons my attention.

'Morning. Are you Joe?'

I survey the balding, short man, who I guess to be in his mid- to late sixties. He's wearing a black polo shirt, black trousers and boots, an identical logo to the one on the van emblazoned across his chest.

'I am.' I step back onto the path to meet him. 'Mr?'

'Perry. Michael Perry.' He offers his hand. 'Ottilie's dad.'

'*Oh*… Hello,' I manage, remembering to shake his hand just as he is frowning pointedly at it.

What is he doing here? And, more importantly, is it possible he could disintegrate me with his stare?

'Would you like to come in?'

Please say no, please say no… I might be feeling refreshed from my morning run but my brain is not ready to deal with this level of adulting this early.

'I will for a bit. I'm on my way into work, so I can't stop long.'

Ugh. 'Okay, this way.'

I usher Mr Perry into the hall and show him the living room, hoping he might take the hint and sit in there while I figure out what the heck I'm supposed to do in this situation. I've never met him before – I've always been out when he's visited Otty here. Judging by the way he is grimly inspecting every detail of the house and me, I don't think he's going to love either of us, or think us worthy for his daughter to choose to live with. Possibly the bright pink T-shirt and tight electric-blue shorts I chose for my morning run aren't helping matters, either.

I make some vague mumble about tea and head for the kitchen, my heart crashing to my trainers when the measured steps behind confirm Otty's dad is following me in.

Where is Otty? She surely hasn't gone to Ensign this early? I know she parked outside the house last night because I saw Monty's indicators flash when she checked she'd locked it using the key remote through the living-room window. What do I say when her dad asks me?

'I'm guessing she isn't in,' he says, inches from my shoulder. Not content with wielding a terrifying death-stare, is Mr Perry a mind-reader, too?

'I don't think so. Her car isn't outside.'

'Have a row, did you?'

'Eh? No, nothing like that. She might have gone into work early or maybe she's getting petrol before the morning rush on the roads. Would you like tea?'

The kettle bubbles into life and I let the familiarity of its sound calm me. I have to get a grip. Otty's mentioned things aren't always easy with her dad, but it's clear she loves him. I have to make the best impression I can, even though my dayglo running attire hasn't set me off to the best start.

'I thought it was a long shot, like. I was only planning on driving down our Otts' street, check she was there, you know? But then I saw the space so I parked. I thought it'd be good for the two of us to have a chat.'

He says 'chat' with all the menace of a Peaky Blinder.

Oh *great*.

'How do you take your tea?' I squeak.

'Milk and one sugar, thanks.' He slides a chair out from the table and sits. Watching me. Wordlessly. With his Brummie death-stare...

I make tea and hand him a mug. 'Hope it's okay.'

He observes me from under thickset brows. 'Tay's tay, lad.'

'Sure. Right.' I drop to a chair opposite his and now we're sitting like two rather genteel cowboys taking tea before High Noon. 'So – er – what did you want to talk about?'

'You. And our Otts.'

'What about us? I mean, *her*. And me?'

'She likes you. Trusts you. Told me you were great friends.'

'We are, I think.'

'But nothing else?'

A brief image of Otty hugging me after Creepy-Chrisgate flashes into my mind and for a horrible moment I'm scared her dad sees it. 'No. Nothing else. Apart from writing together. Which we are. And she's brilliant, Mr Perry, honestly. Gifted.'

'Call me Mike,' he says, unsmiling. 'And I appreciate the compliment. Otty's always worked hard for everything. She tells me this is her dream job.'

I nod and take a gulp of far-too-hot tea, styling out the pain as my tongue melts behind my tight-lipped smile. 'Her writing is excellent and I can tell how much she invests in it…'

'I want you to take care of her,' Mike says, so suddenly it winds me.

'Sorry?'

'Look after her. Look out for her. She'll never tell you, but that girl of mine's had more than her fair share of crap to deal with over the years. I don't want her to get hurt. Understand?'

'Of course.' I'm not sure I do. What exactly is he asking me to do? Does he really think Otty can't take care of herself? But then Mike's stare softens a little. A smile is still a stranger to his face, but I see the dad not the judge. I rest my mug on the table and look at him. 'Sir, your daughter is wonderful. She's become a real friend since she moved in and I would do anything to protect that. I promise I'll look out for her.'

He surveys me for a moment, then gives a small nod. 'Appreciate that, ta. So tell me about this writers' room: what goes on in there?'

'Hasn't Otty told you…?'

'*You* tell me, son.'

I explain how the team was set up and what Russell's plans are for us. Mike takes it all in, pausing occasionally to sip his tea. As I talk I feel the tension ease between us and it's only when Otty's father drains the last of his mug and stands that I realise we've talked for half an hour.

'Right, I should be going. Cheers for the tay and the chat, Joe. I appreciate the—'

'Dad? What are you doing here?'

Otty is standing in the kitchen doorway, her pink-tipped hair tied in a messy knot on the top of her head. She has a brown paper bag in one hand and a cup-carrier holding two takeaway coffees in the other. And she looks horrified.

'I nipped over but you weren't in,' Mike says and for the first time I see what a smile does to his stern features. 'So Joseph here kindly let me in and made us a brew. And now I'm off, or else Jarvis and Steve will be shivering on the doorstep.'

'Okay…' Otty is still taking this in when Mike plants a kiss on her cheek.

'I'll see you soon, bab.' He turns back. 'And you should come up the cricket with us, Joe.'

'Really?'

'You'd love it. You can meet everyone – put a face to the name and that.'

'I – er…' I begin, looking for confirmation from Otty, who appears to be seeking it from me. 'I'd love to.'

'Next weekend, then. Otts knows the time and the place. Take care, both. I'll see myself out.'

We watch him go and stare after him until the front door slams.

'What happened?' Otty asks, agog.

'He was just sitting outside in his van when I got back from my run. Where have you been?'

She raises the cups and bag. 'Getting these. I thought we deserved a breakfast at home, free of indigestion, rather than trying to eat at Ensign in all the pressure.'

'That's very kind.'

'It is, isn't it?' She smiles – and instantly my friend is back.

Whatever was on her mind last night is clearly not now – and that's a relief. Work might be crazy, I might have just had the scariest encounter of my life with her father, but Otty is here and she's smiling and we have breakfast together before we face the madness of the writers' room.

Also, I need her to give me a crash course in cricket…

Chapter Twenty-Five

OTTY

It's *done*.

The postcard lines on the board each have Russell's sign-off signature. Six episodes, including a pilot, complete.

We're reading through the final scene that Joe and I finished writing yesterday, every line of dialogue and direction spoken aloud by Russell. I have to sit on my hands to keep my nerves and excitement under control. The twist revealed in the very last scene was my idea – an initial red herring that began with Laura's voicemail messages she leaves for her dead mother and, when she tearfully confesses it to one key character, ended up changing the whole focus of Laura Eye's story, leaving the door wide open for a second series. I've seen how all of us have taken it and woven it into our own sections of the story. It's seamless and feels completely organic.

And it was *my* idea.

I don't think I'll ever get over that.

'Here we go, folks,' Russell beams, all trace of his week-long thunderous mood vanished. 'The final gut-punch.' He reads:

GUS

You did all you could, Laura. It's over.

The door opens and WILSON strides in.

WILSON
It's far from over.

LAURA and GUS turn, shocked. WILSON is
grim-faced.

WILSON
The operative you apprehended was not
Kingpin.

LAURA
What? How do you…? Did he…?

WILSON
Richardson was a foot soldier, not a
general. Just following orders.

We see this shock sink in as WILSON
continues.

WILSON
He is refusing to give specifics, but
he's told us enough. A second agent ran
the operation. A person who significantly
outranks him.

                    GUS
      He could be lying. Saving his skin.

                   WILSON
      We don't think so. What he told us was
      enough to identify a potential suspect.

      GUS looks at LAURA. She turns to WILSON.

                   WILSON
      We know little about her, or her recent
      activities. But we believe her to be a
        skilled deep-cover agent. A clear and
                 very present danger.

      WILSON clicks a remote and a passport
      picture appears on screen. It is DR
      MONTGOMERY. We see LAURA'S shock. The
      camera remains on her throughout.

                 WILSON (O.S.)
      Her name is Anya Soren. Recent aliases
      include Elizabeth Price, Amy Parks and
      Maura Campbell. Has anybody seen this
                      woman?

      LAURA shakes her head, but we can see
      she is lying.

                    WILSON (O.S.)
Last confirmed sighting was a month ago,
at a medical conference in Oxford. After
that, nothing. But Richardson suggests
 she is in possession of intelligence
that could compromise everything we have
                 worked to gain.

LAURA'S breath is visibly harder. She is
battling fear.

                    WILSON (O.S.)
She could be anywhere. And whatever she
     knows, she's taken it with her.

The camera moves closer until LAURA'S
terrified eyes fill the shot. All other
sound becomes muted as her intense
breathing grows louder and louder. At
the crescendo, the screen suddenly…
                              FADES TO BLACK.
             END OF SEASON ONE.

A beat after the last line, the writers' room erupts in applause.
It's elation, extreme fatigue, relief and pride all jumbled together
and I don't think I've ever felt anything like it in my life. Russell
applauds us, for the first time real emotion breaking out. In that
moment, I understand what it means to him. Why he's been
so awful during the past week. This is his reputation, his future
commissions, his career balanced on the potential of this series.

He basks in the celebration for a while, before raising his hands for order. As we settle back down, Joe's hand squeezes mine.

'We did it,' he whispers.

I mirror his daft grin.

'Okay, guys, listen – amazing work. Truly. I look at how far we've come in, let's face it, an obscenely short amount of time…' he greets our rueful laughter with a salute, 'for which I will not apologise. But we did it. From here, *Eye, Spy* goes to the commissioners. Provided they give the green light, it's then the tangled business of securing a production company – all of which, you will be glad to know, is my headache, not yours.'

I can't even begin to imagine what it would be like to see actors on screen speaking my words. But I know this series could be amazing. We just have to believe it's possible.

'And now, we celebrate. Whatever the fate of our beautiful show, we've created something incredible. So I have booked us into Purnell's tomorrow for lunch on me. We'll meet here at ten and then head over. For now, get out of my writers' room and go home!'

Chairs are pushed back, laptops and notebooks scooped up and the Ensign writers' room team bustle out into the fresher air of reception.

Joe hugs me first, then goes over to Russell who embraces him like a prodigal son. Rona appears and we hug, too.

'Can't believe it's over,' she says. 'I thought that last week would finish us.'

'I know. Are you doing anything tonight? You're welcome at ours if you fancy pizza and beer.'

She grins. 'Love to, but the only date I'm after this evening involves a long hot bath, a bottle of wine and crashing out in front of Netflix.'

'Sounds perfect to me.'

'But how about tomorrow? After Purnell's? We could go for a drink or something?'

'Let's do it.' I smile at my friend, remembering how much she terrified me when I first met her and how I'd worried about offending her when I dumped her brother – needlessly, as it turned out. So much has changed and I like it all.

I scan the room to find Joe – only to see him and Daphne embracing in practically a carbon copy of what I saw the other night.

Well, maybe I don't like *every* change…

'A toast!' Russell yells over the clamour of the restaurant. 'To us!'

Joe and I raise our glasses. 'To us!'

The writing team laughs and clinks glasses, all of us a little brighter-eyed than yesterday, thanks to many hours of sleep. Almost everyone did what I did, it seems, even those who'd talked about heading straight to the pub or hitting the town when Russell dismissed us. I reckon none of us were awake past 5 p.m.

Purnell's is like a restaurant from a Hollywood movie, all polished glasses, precise service and food so beautifully presented we don't know whether to eat it or photograph it as art. Joe is in his element here: it's his favourite place even though he's rarely afforded to eat here. Today we have the most expensive meal on the menu – the Purnell's Journey – a five-course culinary spectacular. It's amazing and completely not what any of us are used to. There's champagne, too.

'I hope someone commissions the show,' Rona says. 'Imagine how foul Russell's mood will be if he's blown all this money on us and the show doesn't sell.'

Joe leans over, grinning like the kid that got all the birthday cake. 'Business expense,' he says. 'Won't cost him a thing.'

'We need photos!' Rona yells, brandishing her mobile. 'Everyone hutch in!'

We squeeze together, a giggling, undignified huddle, as Rona takes the picture. Then more phones appear and suddenly we're posing in every direction.

When our spontaneous photoshoot is over, we flop back into our seats at the large circular table and a delighted Russell orders more champagne.

Joe digs his spoon into the meadowsweet ice cream and almond dessert that has just arrived and closes his eyes in reverent awe as he savours it. 'This is heaven, Otts.'

'Pudding's okay, is it?'

'I would marry it if I could.' He leans down to his plate. 'Are you single?' He pretends to listen, then slaps a hand to his heart. 'She says she's not the marrying kind but she's up for a torrid affair.'

'Better not tell Daphne that,' I say, champagne bubbles summoning the words before I can stop them.

He frowns. 'Why?'

'Come on, Team O-Joe,' Rona says, leaning in between us. 'I want a photo of the two of you.' When we protest, she pushes us together. Joe looks at me for a moment, then smiles for the camera.

'Rubbish. You look like you're side by side in church. Put some passion into it, Carver!'

Joe groans and flings his arms around me and I grab him back, our cheeks pressed against one another as we diva-grin for the camera.

'That's more like it!' Rona reviews the image and beams. 'Look at that!' When she turns the screen to us, we laugh. We look hilarious. But we look happy.

'That's so cool,' Joe laughs. 'And will probably be mortifying when the champagne wears off.'

'It's a moment in time. We'll need to remember this when we get back to work. I'll print a load out tonight and give you copies if you like?'

I smile. 'That'd be great, thanks.'

'Order! Order!' Russell is tapping a champagne flute with a fork.

The chatter subsides as we look at our leader.

'I just want to say thank you. For your commitment and brilliance and skill. And for not shopping me to the press for being a grumpy sod! I think we've built a great team here and I don't want to lose momentum. I want to keep the writing partnerships we've established because I know they work. And when – note, *when*, not *if* – the show gets green-lit, we'll write another team show, just like we've done with *Eye, Spy*. Consider yourselves hired for the long term.'

I'm in shock. Surprised, delighted, and completely gobsmacked. We'd been told our contracts were on a project-by-project basis, but Russell's announcement means this is now, as Dad would say, a *proper job*.

And tomorrow at the cricket match, I'll tell him.

Chapter Twenty-Six

JOE

I will never understand cricket.

Thankfully, Otty does and she's told me enough to help me wing it today.

From what I can make out, it's a big deal to score an invite to a Perry family-and-friends Edgbaston meet. So I can't stuff this up. I don't want to stuff this up, partly because Mike Perry could burn out my eyeballs with his death-stare if I did. But mostly because I don't want to let Otty down.

She's been on a sleepy-eyed high since Russell formally employed us. Today, she's sparkling as much as someone catching up on a three-month sleep deficit can.

'Here we go, Joe!' she yells as she and her dad jump up. I follow them and the rest of the crowd around us. Something exciting seems to be happening on the – *pitch? green? field?* I can't remember which – and lots of players are running towards one corner. After quite a long time of not much going on, this is a nice change. But then there's a groan and everyone sits down again, followed by a patter of applause that sounds like rain bouncing off leaves.

Of course, I'm last to sit down, a little bewildered but grateful I haven't offended anybody.

Otty slips her arm through mine and gives it a squeeze. 'Don't worry, you'll get the hang of it soon.'

'Hope so.' I'm not convinced. Thirty-four years of existence haven't unveiled the mysteries of this game to me so I don't see how a couple of hours in an overcast cricket – *stadium? ground?* – will do the job. Nevertheless, I'm glad I came. It means a lot to Otty and, actually, it means a lot to me. Mike didn't have to invite me. This is A Significant Event, and I'm going to be the best clueless cricket student I can possibly be.

'Not a fan, I take it?' Mike *almost* manages a smile.

If I were writing a script set at a cricket – *tournament*, maybe? – I would have a cheat sheet of terms beside me so I could always refer to it. I can't do that here, though. Maybe I could jot them down on my palm with a biro when Mike's not looking…

'Relax,' Otty whispers to me.

'Yeah. Sorry.'

'Hey Dad, Joe and I get to write something new next week.'

Her dad keeps his eyes on the match but his eyebrows rise. 'Oh yeah? What?'

'We find out on Monday,' I say.

'Exciting, then.'

'It will be. And a relief that Russell's keeping us on.'

Mike turns. 'How long for?'

I love the way Otty blossoms when she's happy about something. I swear she grows an inch taller. 'For the long-term. Permanent positions, he said. So it's now a *proper* job.'

I don't know what Mike was expecting to hear about Otty's writing career, but I'm pretty sure this wasn't it. For a moment he doesn't seem able to reply, his mouth gaping a little. Otty keeps on beaming between us.

'Well. That's good.' Mike nods, his attention drifting back to the cricket players.

Something strange hangs over the resulting pause. In my peripheral vision, Otty's shoulders drop.

'Is your mum coming today?' I ask, keen to plug the awkwardness with words and sound. Otty's spoken of her family quite a bit but she's never been very specific about her mother.

I see Otty and Mike tense in tandem.

'Not on the scene.'

I could kick myself. Why did I think now was a good time to ask?

'Oh. Sorry…'

The warmth of Otty's smile is welcome. 'Don't worry, she's not dead. She moved to Spain years ago. We don't talk but it's okay.'

Mike shakes his head. 'Got enough from the rest of our lot to keep us busy, eh bab?'

From what Otty's mentioned about her family before – and the extended network of non-related aunties, uncles and friends she counts amongst them – she's from a different world to me. They are her roots: where she comes from and where she returns to reconnect. My family are supportive from a distance. I know they love me, they know I love them, but we don't need to be together to prove it. They're happy in Oxford, and Mum occasionally drops in if she's guest-lecturing at Birmingham University. And that's fine by me.

Half an hour later more of the Perry Cricket Posse arrive: two of her former colleagues from the bike-repair shop Mike owns (Jarvis and Steve – I learned their names at least), and her auntie-who-isn't-really-an-auntie Sheila, who fusses around Otty like she's a puppy. It's loud and bustling and very Brummie – and I don't know how you'd ever find stillness or calm in the middle of it all. But I like their energy. At the centre of the commotion, Otty shines.

'So you're the guy our Otts is shacked up with,' Jarvis says. It's a statement, not a question, and I'm not sure what he thinks of me.

'We're housemates. And we write together.'

'So you say.'

Otty rolls her eyes. '*Jarv...*'

Beside him, Steve glowers. 'He'd better be a gentleman, Otts...'

'Pay no attention to them, both of you,' Sheila says. She seems lovely, one of life's true sweethearts. But the glare she gives Jarvis and Steve could cut steel. 'It's about time Otty had a good friend.' She smiles at me.

Otty shifts a little beside me and I wonder if this is the usual level of scrutiny applied to her life, or just for my benefit.

'Button it, boys,' Mike barks, and I'm convinced all the cricketers far below our stand jump as we do. 'I've had a chat with Joe and he's a good lad. Now simmer down and watch the match.'

And just like that, I'm *in*.

I grin at Otty and she winks back. Test passed. Death-stares avoided.

And then it's late afternoon and the match ends to good-natured applause. We rise and walk as a group towards the exit. At the top of the stairs to the ground floor, Sheila suddenly starts to wave.

'Over here!'

She's facing the steps, her back to us. Beside me, Otty tenses. And then I see why.

Creepy Chris emerges from the departing crowd. Otty looks at me and is about to say something when Sheila and Chris come back towards us. So they know each other? Odd…

'Better late than never,' Sheila says, linking her arm with The Creepmeister's. But he isn't looking at her. I hear Otty swear under her breath as he makes a beeline for her.

'Hi, Otty. I didn't know you were coming.'

'Dad invited us.' Her voice sounds strained.

If her dad weren't next to me I would repeat my super-smooth arm-around-the-shoulder move and send Chris packing again. But I can't. All I can do is flash a comradely smile at Otty so she knows she's not alone.

'I see you brought the new boyfriend,' Chris says.

Jarvis snorts. 'Too late, mate, we already tried that one.'

Chris frowns. 'But – he *is*. She told me…'

'When?' Mike is death-staring right at me.

'Week or so ago? I met them in town. Couldn't keep their hands off each other.'

I hear a tiny noise like air escaping from the neck of a balloon and realise it's coming from my housemate.

And then, everything shifts into slow motion. Mike's expression thunderous, Jarvis and Steve's open-mouthed delight, Sheila reaching for a tissue from her sleeve, her eyes reddening, Creepy Chris looking from Otty to me and back to Otty, as if he's watching a tennis champion flounder at match point.

And my wonderful friend, crumpling slowly in the middle of it all.

I can't let this happen to her.

Not considering the ramifications, or trying to work out exactly what's going on, all I can think of is getting Otty out of there.

I can't remember what I say – something vaguely unoriginal along the lines of, *Goodness, is that the time? We must be going* – and then I grab Otty's hand and guide her through the crowd up to the stand entrance and down the stairs to the main exit.

I don't head for the bus stop, instead leading her across the busy road outside Edgbaston Cricket Ground to the lush greenness of Cannon Hill Park. We weave in and out of the departing crowd, skirting the ice-cream vans and a troupe of circus performers entertaining a gaggle of kids, and keep walking until we clear the main drag. We don't speak as I guide Otty up the grass bank past ripening cherry trees, softly bowing green willows and russet-leaved maples, towards the old bandstand I used to go and sit in when university hangovers were crushing my brain.

I allow myself a moment to breathe when I see it's empty. Gently, I lead Otty up the steps and over to the wooden bench that runs around its circumference. We sit, side by side, almost together but not quite.

Otty is breathing hard, but I don't think the walk here is responsible. I wait for her to speak – but she hangs her head and says nothing.

We are two people who write words for a living. So why can neither of us find the right ones now?

Chapter Twenty-Seven

OTTY

It's a *disaster*.

Dad thinks I lied to him. Steve and Jarvis, too. They think I'm *with* Joe. Sheila looked like I'd punched her in the heart. And if Chris has half a brain cell he'll work out that the lie was to him, not to everyone else. Today was supposed to be me proving to them I was right, to show them the life I fought to live on my own terms is pretty bloody perfect. Now I just look like a liar.

'Otts?'

I can't look at Joe yet. I *can't*. I just used his kindness to kick my family. Some friend I am.

'Otty – look at me.'

Stupid tears! Don't turn up now! I try to shove the emotion away, which only makes it surge back stronger.

Joe's voice is soft as the autumn breeze, warm and low near my ear. 'I'm just going to guess-talk this, okay? See if I've got it right. So… Creepy Chris is Sheila's son?'

I nod. A tear escapes and runs down my nose. It leaves an almost perfect circle when it drops on the knee of my jeans.

'And the long-term relationship you left, that was something your family wanted to happen?'

My head bows lower.

'O-kay.'

I sniff. 'I'm sorry I didn't tell you.'

'Kind of an important plot point, that.' A glimmer of humour plays in his voice.

'Mm.'

'The reviewers on Rotten Tomatoes would not be impressed.'

When I dare to glance at him, one side of his mouth lifts in a half grin.

'5/10 – disappointing,' I say, mimicking a disgruntled cinemagoer.

'3.75/10 – Oh-Em-Gee why didn't they *tell* us?'

More tears chase the first escapee when I laugh. I wipe my eyes with the sleeve of my denim jacket. Joe's attempt at a Californian accent is worse than his acting ability in the coffee shop, but I love that he's even trying to make me feel better.

'We got together so young,' I say. 'Looking back, the hints were always there with our families, you know? Sheila was Mum's best friend – they grew up next door to each other. When Mum left, Sheila stepped into the breach. I think her and Dad saw Chris and me as the next generation of their friendship.'

'Like they planned you both into it?'

I stare at him. I've never thought of it in those terms, but it's exactly what it felt like. 'It's all the unspoken stuff, over the years. It builds into something insurmountable. The expectation. And the implied threat it carries: like stepping off that path would mortally wound them. Like you'd betray them if you didn't do it. Especially once Mum wasn't on the scene. We were the great hope for the

Perrys and Wrights. So I went along with it for years because I wanted to make everyone happy. But it was suffocating – and as soon as Chris proposed, it got worse.'

My heart contracts and I have to wait until the pain subsides enough to breathe again. In the moment when Chris asked me to marry him, it seemed right to accept. But I still remember the panic when Sheila appeared at my family home the next day carrying an armful of bridal magazines – the paralysing horror of watching my father and future mother-in-law planning me into a day, a marriage, a *life* I didn't want.

'You did the right thing, though. Calling it off.'

'It didn't feel like that when I did it. It felt like I'd detonated a bomb beneath my family.'

There's a long pause then. A pattering of birdsong, and the distant hum of cars on the main road beyond the park, rush in to surround us. I'm suddenly aware of Joe's breathing.

Then his hand closes over mine on the weathered wood between us. 'What we need,' he says, the hint of conspiracy dancing in his tone, 'is wine. Lots of it.'

'Yes, please.'

He smiles. 'Come on, then. Let's go home.'

I have never been happier to hear those words…

When we get back, the house is filled with the warm spiciness of the beef and ginger stew we prepared for the slow cooker this morning softly bubbling away. Bless Joe Carver and his large shiny kitchen gadgets. I've ribbed him before about the kitchen resembling a QVC cooking-appliance segment – all chrome shininess and dubious necessity – but this evening the slow cooker is our saviour.

I'm not hungry, but I intend on consuming a considerable amount of wine tonight and I need something to line my stomach first. And actually, when we're tucking into bowls of very spicy stew in the living room, sitting side by side on the sofa in our comfy clothes, it's the perfect meal.

'How much ginger did you put in this?' Joe asks, his cheeks flushed.

'Quite a bit. With allspice and cardamom.'

'It's good,' Joe says, but I can see beads of sweat glisten along his brow. 'I might have chucked in a handful of chilli flakes, too.'

That explains the heat. 'I don't think we'll get colds for the foreseeable.'

'Excellent,' Joe squeaks as he coughs, sending us both giggling. He wipes his eyes on his sleeve. 'It may be painful but at least we're in this together.'

When he looks at me I'm suddenly not sure if he's still talking about the stew. I stuff the question away. Right now I just need to have fun.

We eat for a while without talking, Film4 playing an indie movie we missed the start of, so that it appears we're casually spying on someone else's life from the comfort of our sofa.

If someone were watching Joe and me, what would they see?

I'm still shaken by what happened this afternoon, as much by Joe's response to it as by the whole boyfriendgate situation with everybody else. He properly rescued me. Taking my hand like that and spiriting me away. I don't think I've been rescued before – usually it's me saving everyone else. I've always thought the whole bloke-rescuing-a-woman thing was a bit of macho positioning, as if every woman is expected to automatically reset to 'helpless' whenever a man decides to take over. But it wasn't like that with

Joe. I don't think he even thought about it before he moved. The spontaneity surprised me. I think it surprised him as well.

Of course, the mess hasn't gone away: it will still be waiting for me. I'll have to work out how to deal with it soon. But not tonight. I don't want to think about it tonight.

'You are not drinking fast enough, Ms Perry,' Joe says when he leans over to refill my wine glass and finds it still half-full. 'Pathetic effort.'

'Sorry.' I reach over and down the remaining wine in one swallow, holding the empty glass out to my startled housemate. 'There you go.'

'That's one way to do it…'

We watch new red wine tumble from bottle into glass as Joe pours it. The moment is inexplicably, remarkably intimate. He swaps the bottle for his own glass and clinks it against mine.

'To forgetting,' he says.

'To forgetting.'

We drink.

And I wonder. What does Joe really think? Is he embarrassed? Amused? Does he regret his part in it? I want to know, but I can't bring myself to ask. And the whole 'I'm Otty's boyfriend' thing: did he do that because he felt sorry for me? Is he wishing he hadn't bothered now?

Another bottle soon sits empty on the coffee table. Joe shuffles into the kitchen to find more. I rest my head back against the sofa cushions and close my eyes. I can hear my housemate crashing about, banging cupboard doors and voraciously singing out of tune. My mind swims in today's tide: cricket and family and Chris and Sheila and tears in the Cannon Hill bandstand, all swirling in the alcoholic blur, carrying me far out…

'Crisps!' Joe yells triumphantly and I open my dizzy eyes to see him plonk three large bags of them on the table, followed by two wine bottles from under his arm.

'Result!' I yell back, the room spinning a little now.

He flops down beside me, bag of crisps in hand, and rests his head on my shoulder. 'You're ace, you are.'

I snigger. '*Ace?* What decade did you just drop in from?'

'Ace… Groovy… Fab… Splendid… Top notch… Spiffing… Look at me, Otts, I'm going back in time in superlatives!' His voice trails away and he waves his hands above his head as if falling through time and space.

'Nutter.'

'You called?' He sits up and rips open the packet, sending a shower of artisan potato crisps across us both. Breathless with laughter, we wipe them away. As we do, our hands brush against each other's – and in the tipsy clumsiness there's endearing warmth.

There's something I should say now – I feel it teetering on my tongue. I take a breath…

Then Joe stuffs his mouth with crisps and starts doing a Don Corleone impression from *The Godfather*, causing a fit of helpless laughter. It steals the words from me and the moment to say them is gone.

Chapter Twenty-Eight

JOE

A university mate once told me there are seven stages you pass through on a drunken night out. He called them The Seven Dwarves of Drunkenness:

Happy

Tipsy

Rowdy

Forgetful

Hilarious

Maudlin

and Comatose.

I thought he was kidding, until I encountered each and every one of them during my three-year degree. Some lasted as long as a single round, others arrived together, but all of the blighters showed up eventually.

Otty and I are currently entertaining Hilarious, although I fear Maudlin might be waiting in the wings. I've lost count of the glasses of wine we've drunk. Two of the three bags of crisps are empty save for crumbs and salt dust. I don't even know what time it is – I don't have my watch on and it's hours since I last looked at my phone. Several films have passed by on television and because neither of us has been paying attention they've merged into one strange, multi-genre, incomprehensible screenplay.

But right now, *everything* is funny.

At one point *Robin Hood: Prince of Thieves* came on and I did my best Bryan Adams impression singing '(Everything I Do) I Do It For You'. Otty laughed so hard she fell off the sofa and cracked her head on the edge of the coffee table. I rushed over to her but by the time I got there she'd passed through shock and was laughing at the pain. Then she started quoting lines from the Mel Brooks' spoof, *Robin Hood: Men in Tights* – which, once you watch it, will guarantee you can never take the Kevin Costner film seriously ever again – and it sent us both gasping for air somewhere between the floor and the sofa.

The urge to laugh still clings to everything we say, but I can feel its grip loosening a little. We're back in a sensible seating position now and I've fetched us two pint glasses of water in a vain attempt to lessen what are bound to be kamikaze hangovers in the morning.

We needed this after the events at Edgbaston. I'm not sure we've fully addressed what happened but tonight I don't care. It's been a hell of a couple of weeks and this is the blowout we deserve.

I look at Otty now, sleepily content amid the cushions, the rise and fall of her breath soft and every line of worry smoothed from her skin, and I'm in awe. I can't imagine the years she endured, trapped between her family's expectations and the pull of her own heart. I don't know how she found strength to leave Chris. Knowing what it would do to the people she loved most. And then having to work with them all for a year, their pain and disapproval at close quarters.

She's braver than me. And even more remarkable than I thought.

I always wanted to write, so I did. The only barriers I faced in chasing my dream profession were my own doubt and fear. My family wouldn't have cared what I did or whom I was with: that's not a bad thing, either. They would have been okay with whatever decision I made. It's only now I see what an easy ride that gave me.

The empty wine glass in Otty's hand is beginning to tip, so I reach out to rescue it. As her fingers let go of its stem, she wakes, turning her head to look at me.

'Hi, Joe.'

'Hi. You were dropping off then. Want to go to bed?'

A sleepy smile spreads across her face. 'I don't think my dad would be happy with that.'

A wine-soaked blush stings my face. 'I didn't mean…'

'Joe, don't panic! I was joking.'

I know she was – of course I do – but laughter suddenly seems harder to summon.

Otty struggles upright and takes the pint glass from the table. I watch her drink, a cool stillness settling inside me. Hilarious gently slips out of the room. When Otty looks back at me, I sense Maudlin slither in.

'My dad won't be happy unless I'm with Chris,' she says. 'Or alone.'

'You don't know that. Your dad's a good man, Otts. He cares about you. He might come round.'

She shakes her head.

'He *might*.'

'It was always Chris. That was the deal. Dad and Sheila wanted…'

'What about what you want?'

'What about it?'

I'm tired now. I can feel its weight pulling my shoulders, my head too heavy for my neck. I want to close my eyes and sleep, but I can't leave Otty hosting Maudlin alone. We started this together: I'm determined to see it through to the end.

'You get to choose, Otts. Stuff what anyone else thinks.'

She curls back up on the sofa, a cushion cradled in her lap. 'So, what's the story with you?'

'Me?'

'Yeah. I thought Molly-on-Reception was the latest flame. But you haven't mentioned her for ages.'

I'd kind of hoped she hadn't noticed, but of course I underestimated my housemate's ability for biding her time. 'I saw her twice. First time it was all coy innuendo and come-back-to-mine eyes. Second time...'

'You went back to hers?'

I remember standing in Molly's living room, pouring wine, excited by the promise of the evening. And then we'd eaten a meal she'd ordered in, during which time something changed.

'*Joe*,' Molly had barked.

The sharpness of her tone had snapped me from my thoughts. 'What?'

'You're not in the room.'

'Sorry. Work's crazy at the moment and Russell's being a nightmare. Otty and I have to...'

And that's when I'd clocked the problem. Or rather, Molly had clocked it for me.

'Otty again. You know, maybe next time you should just bring her with you. She's practically been with us since you arrived tonight.'

I can't tell Otty that. It was just Molly reading stuff into it that was never there. Sure, I talked about Otty but I was talking about work, and that includes her. And the house – which includes her, too…

Why can't a guy have a really close female friend without the world assuming they're in love?

'I went back to Molly's and we had dinner and then she asked me to leave.'

Otty blinks. 'Harsh.'

I let my sigh carry the weariness from my body as I slouch back. 'Want to know the worst thing? I wasn't bothered. Pride not even dented.' When I look at Otty, I can't read her expression. So I press on, aware this is the first time I've admitted how I feel about relationships right now. 'I can't find the enthusiasm for it, you know? Dating. Not like I used to.'

Her eyes remain on me.

'It's probably the work. I don't have the capacity to accommodate someone else when everything is focused on the script.'

'Except Daphne,' she says. It's so quiet I almost miss it. She looks away.

'Daphne?'

'You have space for her.'

What? 'Where did you get that idea?'

'She told me. It's okay, Joe, you're allowed a private life.'

'I'm not with Daphne.'

'Yeah, yeah, okay.'

'I'm *not*.'

Maudlin pushes between us on the sofa, seeping its bleakness into every exchange. I don't want to give it room, but we're already succumbing. When Otty looks back at me, her eyes glisten.

'I saw you with her. The other night, when we left Ensign late. And then she said…'

'What did she say?'

'That she was with you.' She screws up her eyes. 'No – not *with* you, but that she would be soon.'

'You don't believe that, do you?'

Her shoulders lift and drop. 'You can do what you want, Joe.'

'I'm not seeing Daphne, whatever she says. And for the record, she hugged me. Okay?'

Surprised, Otty stares at me. 'Okay. Sorry.'

I'm stung, but I don't know why. 'Anyway, you date.'

'I haven't for a while.'

'How come?'

She picks at a stray thread on her sleeve. 'Same as you, I guess. Too busy. Not into it. And the whole Chris thing…'

'Doesn't mean you can't find someone.'

'Easy for you to say. You have half of Ensign lusting after you.'

I laugh because my housemate is clearly deluded. 'Not Molly. Not Daphne…'

'Er, *yes* Daphne. And Rona.'

I stare at her. 'Now you're just making stuff up.'

'She asked me if you were single last week.'

'That's… *terrifying*.'

Otty laughs then – a real laugh – and it's such a gift in the strange atmosphere we're in that I laugh, too. 'She'd eat you for a snack.'

'Man, she would. Nothing left of me but still-quaking bones…'

Otty leans her head against the sofa's back and I do the same, both of us gazing up at the corniced ceiling as if the stars were visible beyond it. As if the universe were slowly turning in the sky above our heads. The ceiling *is* rotating a little, but that's just alcohol spinning my brain. We fall silent for a while, an unfamiliar air between us.

And then I hear Otty's sigh.

'It's a disaster.'

'What?'

'All of it. Chris and my family and… I don't know, maybe I should just call it a day.'

'Call what a day? Not your job?'

'*No*,' she laughs, as if I've just suggested she gives up breathing. 'The love thing. Maybe I should just accept defeat, get three cats and become a mad spinster cat-lady. I'd save myself years of heartache.'

'Don't be daft.'

'I don't think it is. Love doesn't work for everybody. Why push myself into something that's only going to fail?'

'Bollocks, Otts. You just haven't found the right person…'

'No. *No*. Don't spin that "he's out there if you keep looking" line. You might have options, but I don't. And I don't want to waste my life chasing a mirage. If the only person who wants me is Chris bloody Wright then I hereby choose the three-cat single life.'

She isn't joking now, is she? Indignation wells up within me. She *can't* think like that. She has no idea how wonderful she is. And tonight I might just be drunk enough to say it.

'Chris is not the only person who wants you.'

'Shut up.'

'I mean it.'

'Oh and you know this because…?'

I twist a little so I'm facing her, every nerve firing within me.

'Because *I* do.'

182

It's a sucker-punch of emotion, a sudden sobering revelation that shakes me. I feel the room drawing in around us, a dolly shot pulling the entire world towards two lonely souls on the sofa.

Otty is looking at me now.

Is she smiling? I can't tell. I don't want to see but I need to know…

And then, she kisses me.

It's there before I know it – and over before I can respond.

Otty pulls back, shock and surprise and horror and amusement passing across her face in alternate waves. She makes to speak – but I've already made up my mind.

I want this.

I stop thinking. My hands find her face, my fingers tracing the curve of her cheek to the contour of her jaw. Her eyes search mine as I edge towards her. It's new and startling but as old and certain as time. I feel the warmth of her skin as her hands rest on my arms and move, slow as a sleeping breath, up to my shoulders. My heart crashes in my ears, Otty's breath hot on my lips in the delicious pause before we meet…

In that moment, I am exactly where I want to be. And I don't ever want to leave. The die is cast, the decision made.

We stop fighting.

And we give in.

Chapter Twenty-Nine

OTTY

The first thing I see is light.

Just a white blur at first, shifting and dancing through water as I blink. I feel like I'm emerging from a frenetic tumble of movement and noise into stillness. I blink again.

The next thing I see is that nothing is where it should be.

The window isn't at the foot of my bed; it's to my left. The sheets are different. The space doesn't seem to be *my* space.

I turn my head and see clothes that aren't mine draped across the back of a chair, a pile of books I don't own on the desk that doesn't belong to me, either. I try to sit up, but that's when the pain hits.

The crushing ache sends my head back into a pillow far lower down than I'm used to. I can't think past the pain, or reach round to drag the fragments of consciousness together to make sense of it all. With one hand clamped to my forehead, I reach out the other to anchor myself to the expanse of mattress beside me. My fingers find the ridges of the fitted sheet, the slight indentation cool where the duvet has been thrown back. As if someone was there until a little while ago…

Joe.

Joe's bed.

This is *Joe's* bed.

I sit bolt upright, suddenly numb to the screaming pain in my head. The books are Joe's, the clothes his, too. I glance down at the side of the bed and recognise one piece of clothing he definitely doesn't wear.

I snap my eyes shut. I don't need to see any more.

How did I end up in Joe's bed?

My mind is a stubborn blank, my hangover too fierce to salvage any memory that might remain.

Think, Otty!

Okay.

My eyes fall on the corner of the duvet pulled back in the space beside me. If Joe had tucked me in, he wouldn't have left it like that. And it's the wrong side for me to have thrown it back myself. I let my gaze travel from the duvet to the space where the fitted sheet is crumpled, up to the single pillow. The indentation in it makes my heart drop.

Right.

So maybe we crashed out together, Joe too tired to think of doing the gentlemanly thing and taking my bed when I was in his. Perfectly understandable. Completely innocent and sensible.

Except that doesn't explain the *item* on the bedroom floor. Or the lack of items I'm wearing…

Who am I kidding? It's obvious what happened.

Why can't I remember it?

Tears flood my vision and I turn my head into the pillow to sob soundlessly. I don't know how I got here and I don't know what happens now. And if Joe isn't here, where is he? Did he wake before me, realise what we'd done and get himself as far away from me as he could? We had such a good thing here, in this house, living and working together. How did we throw that all away?

It hits me then, wave upon wave of revelation. What if we don't survive this? What if we can't write together? What if I lose the home I love? What if I lose Joe? Whatever else has happened, he's my best friend. What if this ends us?

I don't know how long I stay there, paralysed by fear and pain. I can't hear Joe and I'm pretty certain I'm alone. Which makes everything better and worse at once.

And then I see the photograph.

It's identical to the one stuck to the fridge in the kitchen with a *Blame It On The Writer* magnet. We're in Purnell's on the day of the season one completion lunch, crazy-posing for Rona's camera. Cheeks pressed together, locked in a wild embrace, wearing identically idiotic grins. I didn't know Joe had another copy. It's propped up on his desk against the stack of thesauruses and dictionaries I've never seen him use, right next to the spot where his laptop lies. We look so happy…

A memory arrives unannounced, startlingly bright in my mind. Lying in darkness, a single trail of moonlight seeping from the gap in the curtains illuminating my hand where it lies against Joe's naked chest. I feel the warm brush of his breath on the top of my head, the gentle stroke of his fingers on my hair, the soft, sure pad of his heart against my ear.

I stare at the photo, trying to match that image with the newly arrived memory. Is it possible…?

My breath stalls. What if this isn't the disaster it might be? What if Joe wants this?

The way he stepped in when Chris came back, and how he spirited me away from the aftermath of my family's row at the cricket yesterday – were those the actions of a friend or…?

And before that, all the weirdness when I dated Jas. Was it the awkwardness of the situation or the beginnings of something else?

And all the hours we've worked and lived and argued and cried and laughed together; every easy silence between the words; every moment we've settled into the familiarity of being Otty and Joe, here, in this house of light and welcome. Has every moment been leading us to this?

Otty and Joe grin back at me from the photo, eyes bright.

I want to draw them close to me and never let go.

But until I see Joe, I won't know what happens next.

A hot shower will clear my head, I hope.

Once safely there, I stand in the stinging flow of water, the steam obliterating my view. When it's done I go back to my room, my still-made bed accusing as I pull on a T-shirt, jumper and jeans and rub a towel against my head as I walk barefoot down the stairs. I'm stepping onto the cold hall tiles when a sound makes me freeze.

A drawer banging shut. The clink of a teaspoon in a mug. A muted buzz of music from the radio.

Joe's here.

I steel myself, surprised to feel a shot of excitement. This could work. I already love Joe as a friend – could I *love* him as more? I drape my towel on the elegant carved newel post at the foot of the stairs and run a hand through my hair. The single memory of last night sparkles again in my mind. It almost takes my feet from under me.

That's when I decide: I'm going to tell him I want this; that I think I might be falling in love.

It's shocking, but it's real. We could be great together. Maybe that's why I've lost my enthusiasm for dating: maybe it wasn't that I was short of potential dates, but just that none of them were Joe.

The revelation is so crazy I could laugh out loud, but my hangover dismisses that option as soon as it arrives.

I'm ready as I'll ever be.

Joe is by the coffee machine, his back to me. Without his T-shirt I can see the subtle changes in his musculature when he moves, the tension and release as he scoops fresh coffee into the filter and snaps it into place. He brushes coffee from his hands and I see the gentle dance of his shoulder blades. I feel as if I know them, although empty blanks hang where memories should be.

I *could* love him…

And then he turns. He stops dead, eyes wide.

'Hi.'

A smile plays on my lips. 'Hi.'

'I… um… I'm making coffee.'

'So I see.'

Say it.

'How's the head?'

'Not my best friend.'

He pulls a face. 'Mine either.'

Please say it.

'Sit down. I'll get you some tablets.' He bumbles to the cupboards, opening the wrong door first before finding the cupboard where pills and first aid stuff is bundled in with rolls of bin bags and the packets of dishcloths and air fresheners he told me his mum brings on the rare times she visits. 'Er… ibuprofen or paracetamol?'

I hide my smile. 'Whatever's nearest.'

He grabs a packet, half-slams the cupboard door and fumbles with the foil-backed blister pack, swearing under his breath when it refuses to yield.

'Give it to me if you like.'

'Sure.' He slides the packet across the kitchen table like a Wild West saloon barkeep despatching whiskey shots.

'Thanks.' I take two tablets, jumping when Joe bumps a glass of water on the table next to my hand.

Say it now.

Joe remains silent.

I take the tablets and drink, taking my time to be calm. It was always going to be awkward seeing each other after last night. Whatever happened, Joe must have woken up next to me and gone through the same tumble of thoughts as I did.

'Joe,' I say, my hammering heart making the dizziness worse. 'Talk to me.'

I see the muscles across his back tense. Then he slowly moves to the table and takes the seat next to mine. Our hands are inches apart on the weathered wood. I look up and meet his gaze.

'Morning-after mortification,' he says, with the ghost of a grin. 'Never thought I'd have that with you.'

I smile back. 'Me neither.'

'So, about last night…' He shakes his head at the old-worn phrase.

'It was unexpected,' I begin. 'A shock, at first. But the thing is…' *I remember the way you held me, stroking my hair…* 'I had time to think this morning and…' *I looked at that photo of us in your room and we look so happy…* 'I think I might…'

'Otts…'

I want to be happy with you…

'The thing is, Joe, I think…'

I might be falling for you…

'It was a mistake,' he says.

My thoughts career headlong off a cliff, suspended in the air for a second. In limbo there, I struggle to get my bearings, but then I'm tumbling after them. 'What?'

'Biggest mistake, eh?' His laugh is strange, more a shot of sound than a release of humour. 'It's so obvious. Working together, sharing this place, the high of the job, all that confusion at the cricket yesterday. And alcohol… We drank a *lot* last night…'

I stare at my fingers and watch Joe withdraw his, curling them into his palm. I'm slipping, his words clashing with the imagined conversation that's still playing in my head.

'I… I guess we did…'

'Hey, it's okay. I don't regret it.'

'Me neither.'

He folds his arms. 'Not that I remember much.' I see a flash of uncertainty. 'Do you?'

I was deluded to think this was anything more than a drunken mistake. I'm shattered but I'm damned if I'll let him see it. Self-preservation is what matters now, the instinct that's always saved me in the past. I will not let Joe Carver break my heart, wreck my career or take my home.

'Total blank,' I say, shoving a bright smile centre-stage. 'I'm guessing I was amazing.'

Joe's expression is oddly taut. 'I'm guessing I was, too. So – we forget it happened?'

'I think we should.' My heart hurts. 'I love you as a friend, Joe. I don't want to change that.'

'I – I care about you, too. I'm sorry.'

I keep my chin high. 'Nothing to be sorry for.'

He nods and returns to making coffee.

I bite my lip hard to keep the tears from my eyes.

Chapter Thirty

JOE

I'm glad I said it first.

Before she had chance to drop the bomb.

Damage limitation, they call it. Except it doesn't stop the damage. Right now it hurts like hell. I saw what she was going to say before she said it, so I got my punch in early. It doesn't feel like I won.

How can it not have meant anything to her? It meant *everything* to me.

I don't know what I expected her to do. I'd left her sleeping in my bed so soundly I thought she'd stay there until I returned with fresh coffee and gentle kisses to wake her. The breakfast of lovers – or some other sentimental crap my brain decided it would be. I thought I'd join her and we would stay in bed all day. I thought she'd want to make up for all the time we've spent dancing around each other, when we should have recognised what was right in front of us.

But she was never going to do that, was she?

I knew it the moment she arrived in the kitchen, showered and dressed. I felt grubby and dishevelled next to her. I knew she didn't want me.

How can she *not* remember last night? My own memory may be hazy but I remember what matters: I remember *her*. Is she lying? I don't want to think she might be because that would make it a million times worse. But if she remembers and still doesn't want me… I don't think I could bear that.

'I think I might go back to bed,' she says, resting her hand against her forehead presumably to avoid any further misunderstandings. 'Sleep this off.'

'Yeah. Good idea.'

She stands and waits. I hate the hope that rises in me, willing her to change her mind and tell me she remembers everything and wants me after all. I don't want to hold my breath but I do, releasing it in a long, slow exhale when she walks out.

I keep my smile steady until she's gone.

The coldness of the kitchen seeps into my limbs as I sit. I've never felt alone in this house, not even when Matt moved out. But today the ache is raw in my chest. She's here but she's not. Our friendship is a soulless body, its heart ripped away. Things will never be the same.

I could go back to bed but I couldn't escape her there. I could rest on the sofa, but the memory of our kiss lingers on its cushions. Even in the kitchen the ghosts of a hundred happy exchanges gather. On the fridge door, an Otty and Joe I no longer recognise smug-grin at me, oblivious to my pain.

I need to get out of here.

The city is cloaked in grey when I walk through it, the sunlight that summoned me from my bed this morning long gone. Suits me just fine. I don't want to feel hopeful now. Bright sunshine would be cruel, in the circumstances.

I caught a bus into the city centre and now I'm skirting the new development at Paradise that links the Museum and Art Gallery in Victoria Square with the new library and the Symphony Hall. I think I'm heading towards the canals at Brindleyplace, but I'm not really monitoring my route. I just want to walk.

Will we ever get past this?

Otty seems well on the way to it, of course. But I'm far behind. What about when we start to write again? Tomorrow we'll discover the next project Russell has for us and we'll be expected to pick up where we left off. Can I sit with her for hours, be that close to her, knowing what I know – what we did – and still function as we did before?

A chatter of angry geese crash-lands on the canal as I emerge from the concourse between the Symphony Hall and the Convention Centre. The noise jars me. I shake it off. I'm jumpy and I don't like it, my senses on high alert. It isn't my hangover. It's *her*.

I catch my reflection in the windows of the canalside restaurant. I look away. I don't want to see the pain in his face, the haunted eyes of someone who just made the worst mistake of his life.

My feet stab against the blue brick steps up to the bridge that crosses the canal, far harder than they need to. I want to walk Otty out of my system, kick the memory of her kisses, her skin, the scent of her hair with each step. I want to forget, like she apparently has.

I have to forget last night – we both do – and find a way to work together.

It's just going to take time…

Chapter Thirty-One

OTTY

It's only been a few days since we celebrated finishing *Eye, Spy*, but returning to Ensign Media feels like I've been absent for months. We're both here, Joe and me, doing our best impression of the happy writing team we were before. But I feel like a shell.

I hid in my room all day and night yesterday. I just couldn't face seeing Joe again, knowing the mistake I almost made. As it is, he's none the wiser, thinking I'm as embarrassed about spending the night with him as he is. So we met in the kitchen at breakfast this morning, our well-worn double act clicking back into place, if a little dented.

It will get better, eventually. I just need to keep smiling until it does.

Russell is on top form, at least. He swaggers into the writers' room wearing an enormous grin and I half-expect him to start high-fiving us all like a coach in a sports movie after a big win.

'Everyone caught up on sleep? Or drinking?' He smiles at the ripple of laughter that travels around the room. 'Excellent. Well, team, I have news.' He performs one of his now infamous pauses, then holds up a sheet of paper. 'Official green light. Production company on board, casting begins this week. Commissioners are moving fast on this one. They want it on screen in six months' time.'

We are lifted by the surge of delight that takes us all with it. Hugs break out across the room. I hug Rona and reach across the table to grasp hands with Reece and Tom. Then I turn, just as Joe does – and the air is cut from our sails. We half-hug to maintain our carefully choreographed performance, but it's more of a confused, hot-flushed mismatch of arms. Over Joe's shoulder, I see Daphne's eyes narrow.

'Everyone's excited about it. Plans to show a single episode per week, no box set on streaming services until the entire series has been broadcast. "*Event TV*", kids, so Nathan Byford-King at *The Sentinel* can go and choke on that. I might invite him to a press screening and sit right next to him with the popcorn…' He rubs his hands together and laughs. 'But I'm getting ahead of myself. I always said I was setting up this team to be Ensign's powerhouse – more than a single-series operation. It's a new way of working. A dependable, consistent source of primetime hit shows. Well, congratulations: you're it. I want to cover a range of stuff, from digital shorts and single-episode dramas right up to full-series and feature-length productions.'

It's the dream. It should be exciting. It *is* exciting, but it isn't how I thought it would be.

'Bagsy the film,' Joe mutters under his breath, loud enough for me to hear and I look at him without thinking. He risks a tiny smile. I send one back. It's a stolen second of solidarity, but it's the biggest step we've made since *that* night.

I'm not sure it's even a truce, but it helps.

The plan for the next month is to work on pilot scripts based upon pitches Russell has written, the most viable of which will be taken forward. If this is successful, we repeat it until we have a bank of scripts for potential development.

'We'll keep the same writing teams,' he says. 'No point in reinventing the wheel. So today we plan and then you're off.'

An air of excitement fills the room as Russell talks us through his ideas and we all pitch in with suggestions. As the time passes, I feel Joe relax a little beside me. I do the same. It's not perfect and we still have to work out how to navigate being at home together, but it's better than I feared it might be.

At lunchtime I'm waiting for coffee when I feel a soft pressure on my shoulder. I turn to meet Joe's hesitant smile.

'Otts, can we talk?'

'I'm just getting a drink.'

'Won't be long.'

I glance over his shoulder towards the door. 'You taking me on a Russell walk?'

His eyes flicker. 'Sure, why not.'

We slip out of the room, my pulse thudding so loud I expect to hear it reverberating around the empty corridors. I haven't done the eleventh-floor circuit before and I'm acutely aware of Joe watching me as we walk. It's far bigger than I've imagined, West One's still-to-be-let interiors eerily imposing.

'Are we supposed to be talking?' I ask after we've walked a few minutes in uneasy silence.

Joe stops walking. 'Yes. Sorry.' He stands a safe distance away from me.

I stay where I am and hug my arms to my body. It's cold here, but I don't know if that's the building or the company. 'Is this going to get easier, with us? Because it's horrible.' I hear the quake in my voice and hate it.

'I hope it will. It has to.'

'What if it doesn't? Maybe we should just tell Russell…' I see Joe's horror at what that sounds like and quickly add, 'that we'd like different partners.'

'No.'

'We have to do something…' I don't want to cry. I don't want another row. I want *us* back.

'I know. How do we fix this?'

I shake my head, my mouth empty of words. So Joe speaks instead.

'I don't want to lose you. *Us*. We made a mistake. We have to live with it – and each other.'

It's incredibly bleak, put like that. But he's right. 'I don't want to lose us either.'

I watch Joe as he stares at the ceiling, hands on his hips, like he does when we've hit a block in a scene. If only this were as simple as unravelling an unruly section of dialogue…

'What would Laura and Gus do?' I say.

Joe's eyes flick back to me. 'What?'

'If this were Laura and Gus from *Eye, Spy*, not me and you, how would we write them out of it?' The idea blooms in my mind as I give it voice.

'Well, Gus would be trying to be practical. Not letting Laura see she was breaking his heart.'

I wince a little. Joe's words have an edge I'm not sure how to take. 'Laura would be trying to outrank him. Hiding her own pain until she can tell Dr Montgomery in therapy.'

'That's just them marking their positions. It doesn't solve the problem.'

'So what would?'

He thinks for a while, leaning against a solitary partition in the vast empty space. 'They would make it an open joke.'

'Sorry?'

'Their enemies would expect them to conceal any involvement. So they joke about it. Openly. No attempt to hide their mistake. Nobody can exploit a secret everyone knows.'

'They joke about sleeping together?' Is that what he's suggesting?

'What's the alternative? They're doing so well – *undercover*, I mean. They have a good thing going. The joke would unite them, not divide them.'

'But they're still hurting...' I pull back, knowing I'm not talking about our characters now. 'How can that be something they are okay with?'

He looks at me for a long time. 'It hurts now. But if they share this, maybe it will get easier.'

I don't like it at all. It's bad enough to dismiss what we shared as a mistake, but to invite others to laugh at us? How does that make it any better? 'So they just tell everyone?'

'No. I'm not suggesting that. They joke about it between themselves. And then, if it leaks out – if someone else works out what's going on – they have the perfect cover. *Oh that? We just laugh about that now...*' He spreads out his hands like he's just completed a magic trick. 'See?'

I don't know how that protects their hearts. But maybe if they share an approach, it's a touch point that could unite them. I hate the idea of the joke but I want to find common ground with Joe. 'Can you do that? Can *they*?'

'I think they can.' He moves a little closer. 'I think we can.'

That's it, then. Block removed. Strategy written.

So why does it feel like a lie?

Chapter Thirty-Two

JOE

Hide behind humour. Isn't that what every self-respecting male protagonist resorts to? So much for being original with my coping strategy.

But, against the odds, it seems to be working.

It's been two weeks since Otty and I decided on the joke and it's starting to feel part of our everyday patter. I still sense a hesitancy when it's about to happen – a brief flash of concern before we leap – but we're getting better at it.

'Ugh, put it away,' Otty says as I lean around her, bare-chested from my morning shower, to steal a slice of toast she's just buttered. 'Nobody wants to see *that* this early in the morning.'

'Seem to recall you did once,' I grin, pushing the stab of guilt away.

'Emphasis on the *once*,' Otty retorts, fast as a gunshot. She even risks a swift appraisal of my towel-wrapped waist before she turns back to the breadboard. It's a strange flirtation and uncomfortably affecting. I see the tension in Otty's shoulders and turn away. It's far from easy. But we're trying.

Russell's called the writing team in early this morning – and he wants to see Otty and me first. Not sure what to make of that yet. He phoned us at home yesterday evening to invite us, which is definitely out of character for the man who even resents having to send group emails to the team.

'What do you think it is?' Otty asks me as we drive into West One's car park.

I don't know why she's asking me. I'm as clueless as anybody. 'Search me.'

A familiar song starts playing on the radio and my housemate instantly brightens. 'Hold on, Tom's here.'

I laugh, but Otty is already singing along to the song, tapping the steering wheel. I've heard it before at home, when she's cooking with the radio on or listening to music as we work. I remember the title as she reaches the chorus: 'Just You and I'.

'Lovely song, Tom,' I say to the radio.

'We're going to be okay, Joe. Tom Walker will sort it. This song's like a talisman for me.'

'Let's hope so.'

At the barrier to West One's car park, she stops singing and looks at me. 'You don't think Russell knows? About us?'

'Not unless he's bugged our house,' I laugh. She's frowning when I look at her. I soften my voice. 'Hey. Don't worry. Laura and Gus have it covered.'

It's lame, but at least I get a smile in return.

I won't show Otty, but I'm nervous, too. We've worked well, our stuff is strong – the strongest in the writers' room, I'd say – but since *that night* there's a stubborn disconnect that all our brave words and hesitant jokes have failed to repair. Has Russell seen it?

We run the gauntlet of West One's elaborate security systems and make the lift with ten minutes to spare. In it, we stand at opposite sides as it ascends. As far apart as we can be… I shake the thought away. That's not fair on either of us.

When the floor counter flicks to eleven, I move next to Otty, daring to catch her little finger with mine as our arms hang side by side. She squeezes back. One tiny assurance. Our hands part as the steel doors open and we walk in silence to Ensign's door.

'Team O-Joe!' Russell's baritone booms as soon as we enter. He's adopted that name for us from Rona and it's stuck. You can hear how delighted with himself he is whenever he says it. I guess it's endearing – even if this morning it does little to ease our nerves. Safe behind matching bright smiles, Otty and I walk into Russell's office.

'Sit,' he commands – and we do, comically in time. On any other day it would be funny. 'I'm getting breakfast rolls in for us all and some kind of freaky veggie concoction for Rona and Reece.' He rolls his eyes. 'I'm sure they'll be over the moon.'

He waits for us to respond, but when neither of us does, he pushes a thermal jug of coffee across his desk to us.

'Thought we'd get the good stuff in first. Reward for being so bloody early. Go on – help yourselves! I persuaded the ground-floor coffee shop to open at six so they could fill this baby for me. Smart plan, huh?'

'Thank you,' Otty says. 'So, you wanted to see us?'

'I did. Can you both stop looking like I'm about to decapitate you, please?'

We make an effort to relax, which isn't all that successful.

'Joe, Otty, I'm not going to beat around the bush here. You are my best writers. Both of you. The work you did on Laura's development in *Eye, Spy* was inspired. It's what's made everyone so excited about the show – commissioners, production, even some of the cast we've got coming on board already. The buzz is all over the trade press. I can't stress enough how vital this has been to getting that green light. I owe you.'

I hear Otty's sharp intake of breath beside me. I'm holding mine.

'Thank you,' we say together, allowing ourselves a smile at our subconscious synchronicity.

'There's already an appetite for a second season.' Russell leans towards us as if the office might betray his secret. 'Keep that to yourselves, though. I want you to know, if we get another series, you two are my lead writers.'

It's not just a promise of work. It's *immense*. Being lead writer on a series of the magnitude we hope *Eye, Spy* will be is career-defining, life-changing stuff.

'Seriously?' I say, cringing at the squeak in my voice.

Russell nods. 'Good news?'

'Great news.'

'We'll still team write, but the three of us will bash out the bones of the story beforehand. I want you both in from the very beginning. *Four* of us, actually.'

Who else?

'Daphne?' Otty asks, reading my mind.

'No…' Russell pulls a face. 'I mean, can you imagine? No, I'm bringing in someone new. Hence the early-morning team briefing today.'

'Who?'

'Fraser Langham.' When it's clear neither Otty nor I know who he is, Russell frowns. 'Well, you *should* have heard of him. He's just back from working in the States with Shonda Rhimes. I was lucky to get him. Great guy. Visionary, versatile – he's as at ease on US writer-room dramas as he is with the traditional set-ups in the UK. And everyone wants him. The four of us will be leads on *Eye, Spy 2*, if we get it.'

I'm not sure how I feel about a new guy joining us. From her thinly veiled frown I can see Otty feels the same. We've come through so much as a team – survived the sackings and the writing partnership changes – and we're so much stronger for that. It's a mix that *works*. Why shake it up now, when we're on the cusp of enormous success?

Russell is peering at us over steepled fingers. 'Problem?'

'Not at all,' Otty replies quickly. 'When do we meet him?'

'He's arriving in an hour.'

Fraser Langham is a try-hard. The moment he enters the writers' room, it's obvious. Too warm, too confident, too cloyingly self-deprecating when he thinks he's losing a point. All he needs is a Nineties' floppy haircut and he would be a young Hugh Grant wannabe straight out of a Richard Curtis movie. Except that he's Scottish – a killer touch, he hopes. I notice the vowels lengthen, the tone drop to deep Caledonian velvet, whenever he's addressing the female contingent of our writing team.

It's *pathetic*. And if he thinks it's going to win him allies in here, he'd better think again.

We are a team. A unit. And no smooth-talking Scot is going to spoil it.

I catch Tom and Reece exchanging amused glances as they watch Langham smarm his way into the room. Good. I have them on my side. *Try and Sean-Connery your way out of that, mister.*

'It's an honour to join Ensign,' Langham says. *Is the patriotic hand-pat to the heart really necessary? Is it?* 'I'm excited about what you're all doing here. And working with this awesome team. Russ let me see your work on *Eye, Spy* and I've got to tell you, it shook me up.'

Who is he, Elvis?

I catch Otty glancing my way and I curl my upper lip in a blink-and-you'll-miss-it homage to The King. She hides her smile behind her sweater sleeve. At least we're united in thinking our new script executive is a bit of a tit.

Small victories.

We're forced to listen to Langham drone on incessantly about working in America, all the famous showrunners he's 'helped steer' – can you credit the guy? – and how he wants to be in at the beginning with Ensign to 'shake the industry up'.

I'll say this for him: he's a serious fan of *shaking*…

My fellow writers appear to be just as nonplussed by him as I am, which makes me feel so much better. Daphne definitely isn't a fan. I get the feeling she thinks she's been overlooked while Russell hauled his chum into the company.

I wanted something to unite Otty and me.

I think we might just have found it.

Chapter Thirty-Three

OTTY

'That guy is a *god*!' Rona exclaims, adding another coat of lipstick to the two she's just applied.

I don't think I've seen Rona wear lipstick at all in the months we've worked here. Something tells me the arrival of our new script executive and the sudden appearance of Rona's lipstick *might* be linked.

'I take it you're a fan?'

'I was starting to think we'd never get any decent men in that room.'

We are in the Ladies' loo at Ensign Media, having nipped out when the writers' room meeting broke for coffee. It's a serious cliché to be discussing men with my female friend in a glossy corporate washroom, but we chose our venue out of necessity. If I'd thought it was impossible to hold a private conversation at Dad's place, it's downright risky to do it at Ensign. Because here it isn't just gossipy bike mechanics looking for titbits to broadcast to whoever will listen, it's a group of highly skilled wordsmiths who know exactly how to embellish it beyond all recognition.

'We don't know he is decent yet,' I say. 'What was Russell

thinking bringing someone new in just as this team is working so well?'

'Divide and conquer,' Rona says, a suggestive eyebrow raised.

'Why does that sound filthy when you say it?' I laugh.

She hops off the sink unit. 'It's a gift. Also, because there's a hot Scot out there with my name all over him.'

Fraser Langham is… I'm not sure what he is yet. He's certainly divided opinion in the team. Joe hates him – that much is obvious. Maybe it's because he's threatened by how chummy Fraser and Russell are. Joe's been unchallenged in his role as Russell's bezzie mate up until now, so this must be a shock. Reece keeps eyeing Fraser suspiciously over the top of his designer specs, as if Fraser might jump him at any moment, Jake wears a frown that could slice cheese, and Tom is just disinterested in everything. Rona wants to shag Fraser on the spot. Which is understandable, given that he's built like an extra from *Outlander* – moody grey-green eyes like a storm-cloud, tousled red-blond hair and muscles visible beneath his shirt that Rona is going to end up licking if she keeps staring at them like she is.

And me? I'm still making up my mind.

He's trying a bit too hard to impress us, but I guess that could just be nerves. I won't lie: he's lovely to look at. But I have a sneaky suspicion he knows that. It's fun seeing how much he's winding up Joe, though.

'So what's going on with you and Joe?' Rona asks as we're walking back to the writers' room.

'Keep your voice down!'

'So there *is* something?'

'No… No, we're good.'

'I don't believe you,' Rona begins, but a certain script executive from north of the border commands her attention as he strides past into the room.

Fraser Langham: one point.

During the break, he's been looking at the pitches we've already made a start on developing and is now ready to give us his initial thoughts. Joe, Reece and Jake sit like three defensive monkeys – only instead of each one covering their eyes, ears or mouth, all three adopt the same arms-crossed position.

This should be interesting.

'Talk us through your thoughts, Fraser,' Russell invites. I feel the room prickle.

'Sure. You have great stuff here, guys. Excellent material for when we start to write.'

Start to write? Some of these ideas are well on the way to completion. Does Fraser know how fast we've been working?

'So, I think we should brainstorm…'

Frowns flash around the table. 'We've already done that,' Rona tells him. 'We're developing the pitches now.'

'Ah, well that's where I'm going to stop you. Some of these pitches are okay, but most need work. Back-to-the-drawing-board work – or executive whiteboard,' he smiles broadly at his own joke.

None of us follow.

Russell shifts a little and clears his throat. 'We've developed a way of working quickly…'

Fraser looks over his shoulder. 'And, no offence, Russ, it shows.'

Uh-oh.

Russell's mouth gapes a little. Daphne stares. The Three Angry Monkeys square up for a fight. Even Rona, who until Fraser started speaking was unashamedly measuring him for her bed, isn't smiling now.

'With respect,' Joe says, 'those pitches are a testing ground. Sketches that capture the essence of the idea. Nobody expects them to be production-ready.'

'Well, *Joe*,' Fraser says, making a point of reading the tented whiteboard in front of Joe, 'with respect, every piece of work produced here should be production-ready. We can't build a bank of credible, fleshed-out ideas if every one is just a crude sketch.'

'So what do you suggest we do?' Reece asks, arms still folded.

'Do better from the beginning.' The silence that follows bristles with fury. Fraser holds up his hands. 'Look, guys, Russ hired me to say it like it is. You're good – some of the most promising I've met in this kind of writers' room set-up since I got back from LA. But you're not the best. If you build in mistakes and misfires at the beginning, you have a greater chance of failing.'

'We have no intention of failing,' Tom snaps.

I watch Fraser's weary sigh and wonder how many other writing teams he's insulted within the first hour of working with them. 'Nobody's saying you are. But the fact is, Ensign needs to lead the market. And that means all product – in whatever form we make it – *has* to be strong.' He holds out his hands, his voice dipping to low, soft Scottish persuasion. 'Here's what I suggest, okay? We start again, but before we write a single line, we work out exactly what we're aiming to achieve, collectively.'

I see Rona is back on board. That accent of his is something he seems to use as a tool, a hook, even a weapon. It's fascinating.

'Now, I know you have established pairings and those will not change. But for the purposes of this exercise, I want to temporarily reassign you. I suggest Reece and Joe, you work with Rona, then Tom and Jake, you have Ottilie. That way, guys, you can help the girls to really get under the skin of this…'

What did he just say?

Eyebrows rise around the room. Even Russell looks shocked.

'*Help* the girls?' I ask, my pulse kicking. 'Why would we need help?'

'I think what Fraser meant…' Russell begins, but it's too late. I feel the writers closing ranks, a united battalion against this at best clumsy and at worst downright misogynistic interloper.

Fraser Langham's composure slips. Even that gorgeous accent can't save him now. This may prove to be Ensign Media's shortest ever appointment.

'I wasn't suggesting…'

'I think you were,' Rona counters. 'I don't know what you've seen in other writers' rooms, Fraser, but in this one we're equal. *That's* what makes Ensign an industry leader.'

The session is fast escaping from Fraser and everyone knows it. He's only saved when Russell steps in to prevent us hitting stalemate.

'Okay, let's call time here. Take a break, everyone. I'll order pizza and then we can thrash this out—' he casts a definite glance at Rona and me, '*together*.'

There's a scramble to leave the room and Russell pauses to slap a hand on Fraser's shoulder before following everyone else out.

I should follow them and leave our newest colleague to consider his stupid remark. But I hang back. I'm not sure why.

Across the room is a crumpled version of the man Fraser was when we were introduced. Gone is his swagger, his unwavering self-belief. It's a very different view and I wonder how much of his performance is a shield to who he really is. He doesn't realise I'm here, his head bowed over his mobile phone, his fingers making angry stabs at the screen. I almost feel sorry for him.

No, I *do* feel sorry for him. Not because of what he said, but because of his reaction now.

Beyond the closed writers' room door I can hear animated voices and too-loud laughter – mostly from Joe, it has to be said. I don't need to guess what the subject of their mirth is. In the still-ness of this room, I see Fraser Langham's shoulders droop lower.

Quietly, I get up and walk to the thermal coffee carafes on the table at the front of the room. I fetch two mugs from the stack, a couple of sachets of sugar and a teaspoon.

'Coffee?' I ask, pouring mine already.

Fraser starts and looks up. 'Hi – I didn't realise you were here, um…' He scans the name boards around the room, trying to work out where he's seen me sitting.

I decide I'm going to help him. 'Ottilie,' I finish. 'But please, call me Otty.'

'Otty.' The gentle beginning of a smile appears. Without the bravado, it's a soft, welcoming sight. 'Coffee would be good, thanks. Black, one sugar.'

I nod and slide his mug beneath the carafe spout, aware of him watching me.

'That's very kind.'

I smile as I stir in the sugar. 'It's just coffee.'

'Right. Don't suppose you have any Valium you could put in it?'

'Fresh out, sorry. You might want to bring your own in tomorrow.'

He gives a rueful laugh. 'Reckon I'll need it.'

I hand him his coffee and he smiles.

'Thanks. Look, I hope you know I didn't mean what I…'

'I *don't* know,' I say. I could let him off the hook now, laugh off his remark, but he needs to understand the gravity of it. 'That's the point. I'm assuming you're a decent guy and don't think women need to be assigned to men to be shown how to think.'

His eyes widen. 'Hell no…'

'Just a bit of advice, then: don't insult your female colleagues on the first day. We have very long memories.'

'Right. Sorry.' He closes his eyes. 'I am *horrified* with myself. What a rubbish start.'

'An apology will be fine. And *not* saying anything as stupid as that ever again.'

Fraser grimaces. 'Noted. Thanks.'

'Good.' I collect my laptop and head for the door.

'Otty?'

'Yes?'

I feel like he's debating how to phrase what he wants to say, but I see him mentally pack it away behind a smile. 'Thanks again.'

'My pleasure,' I reply, the pull to be with my colleagues suddenly strong.

Out in Ensign's reception, I join my friends.

'Well done for sorting him out, Otts. What a *dick*,' Joe grins, pulling a face at the untouched mug I've brought with me from the writers' room and exchanging it for a newly delivered coffee from the ground-floor coffee shop. 'Have this one, it isn't tainted by an opinionated, misogynistic git.'

'Cheers. I don't think he meant to insult us, though.'

'But he did. I give him a week. If he's lucky.' He winks at me and it's so good to see that I forget Fraser Langham's motives and his terrible word choice and concentrate on rebuilding bridges with Joe.

Chapter Thirty-Four

JOE

*P*illock.

Langham may have avoided any more *faux pas*, but he's trouble. Not content with having us rewrite all of the initial pitches we'd developed as a team with Russell, he now has us reporting to him for feedback on what we produce. *Quality control*, he calls it. *Being an interfering git*, more like.

We work till 3 p.m., thrashing out new possibilities for Russell's one-line elevator pitches. I don't think we've come up with anything to match our original ideas, but if Langham needs proof that our collective gut feeling is better than his ridiculous process, so be it.

'This is a total waste of time,' Reece groans, completing another index card and chucking it onto the pile we've created. 'Dare me to work a killer shark into the next one?'

We share conspiratorial smirks.

'Do it.'

'Rethinking your plan to bed the bloke, Rona?' I ask.

She shrugs. 'Had to. I've not got the time to deal with *that*.'

'Probably for the best, Ro. You'd have to develop eight different approaches on index cards for his approval before anything happened,' I chuckle. 'Fraser Langham is the only guy in the world who sees feedback as foreplay.'

'Ugh, can you not?' Reece shudders. 'Puts me right off my pizza.'

I like that nobody is defending Langham. Otty totally owned him earlier – and rightly so. I look over to the other group of writers, who are as uniformly miffed as we are. Otty is in the middle, between Jake and Tom, deep in conversation. I watch the way she uses her hands to explain a point – frenetic swoops and staccato beats that punctuate her speech. Things *have* been easier with her and me since Langham arrived. I'd rather be angry with Langham than Otty.

Russ and Langham return, Fraser noticeably less Tiggerish than before. I wonder what's been said in private. I hope Russ read him the riot act. It's hard enough for women in this industry without some privileged middle-class white dude mansplaining their role. Of all the mistakes he could have made, Langham picked the worst.

He takes his seat and looks straight over at Otty's team. I see the brief smile she sends back to him. My hackles rise. Of course, she's the sweetest person and it's typical of her to be kind, but it's stretching even her loveliness to bless that guy.

Russell is pacing now, picking up index cards and making a show of his approval. He must be regretting ever bringing Fraser Langham into this room. He knows how good we are: we don't need babysitting.

'All right, boss?' I say when he reaches us.

'Yeah,' he replies, turning his back on Langham as he grimaces. We all see it and I feel Rona and Reece bloom beside me. 'Fraser's suggested one-on-one feedback sessions later today, maybe running into tomorrow. You all okay with that?'

I shrug. 'Bring it on.'

Perhaps in a bid to lessen the impact, Russell suggests Langham use his office to meet each writer, while the remainder stays in here to continue work on the pitches. We break for coffee and as I'm walking to the kitchen to seek out much-needed biscuits, I notice Langham beckon Otty into Russell's office.

Good luck with *that*, Fraser.

A moment later, the door flies open and Otty storms out. She walks straight into the writers' room and by the time I get in there she's working again, head bowed, stabbing furious words with a sharpie onto a stack of index cards. What happened there?

I don't manage to catch her attention for the rest of the afternoon, but I see no trace of a smile whenever I check.

'Dude.'

I feel a hand on my shoulder and look up. Jake looks ready to punch someone, so I'm guessing he's just had his meeting with Langham.

'Good sir. How goes it?'

'Don't ask. You're up.' He slaps his hand on my back as if I'm leaving for the Western Front.

Perfect. I am going to enjoy this…

Langham is looking far too comfortable in Russell's chair and I notice the vacant seat waiting for me has been strategically moved a small distance away from the desk. Seriously? This is a feedback meeting about a few words on index cards, not an audition for a Hollywood film.

'*Hey, Joe*,' he says, laughing at his own joke. 'Ah, love a Hendrix reference. I bet you get that a lot.'

'Good job my mum hated the name *Jude*, hey?' I say, grabbing the back of my chair and swinging it right up to the desk to sit. His flinch is my reward.

'Yeah, please sit down,' he says pointedly as I smile a beatific smile and cross my legs.

He takes his time laying out the index cards I've submitted for his learned opinion, each one deliberately placed. As he does so, there's just the slightest hint of raised eyebrow.

So, that's how you're playing it, is it? Fine. Do your worst.

Unfortunately for this dude, he's met me at my arsiest. I need a target and he's just swaggered right into line.

And I'm pretty certain he just upset the woman I... *care* about. I don't need any more reason to fight him.

'I've heard a lot about you from Russ. Impressive CV, too,' he says.

'Thank you.'

'Stalled a bit after *Southside*, mind...'

'Realigning my career. I see it as a sign of a mature writer.'

'Hm.' He picks up a card and flicks it absent-mindedly between his fingers.

Got no answer for that, have you? Point to me, I think.

'I'm not going to lie, Joe, your work is excellent. It stands out in that room.'

I wait. He smiles.

What's this, Langham? No final barb? No last-minute kicker?

'Thanks,' I say. And the nod of his head confirms he thinks he won that round. *Ugh.* 'So, any particular feedback?'

'No. These are all good.' He moves a dismissive hand over my pitch ideas. 'I'd say eight out of the ten are stronger, but for a sample in the time we've had, good work.'

We engage in a nonchalant-smile-off. Just as it's getting uncomfortable, he stands and offers his hand. I hurry to my feet.

'I think we may have got off on the wrong foot, Joe,' he says, his voice dropping to deepest, sincerest Scot. 'I'm well aware what everyone in that room is thinking. They look to Russell – and to you – for their cues. I'm not asking for allies, just professionals. I hope I can count on you.'

Walking from his office, I'm rattled. He denied me the fight I was expecting and that kicks more than any punch he could have thrown. *Clever bastard.*

Long game it is, then.

Otty catches my eye when I return to the writers' room. I mouth, *OK?* and she gives the slightest shake of her head. That settles it: Langham and I are still at war.

It's an age until 6 p.m. when our session ends. We're a subdued troop when we file out – no laughter, no hanging back to chat. If that's what Langham was after, he's achieved it. Russell looks concerned and that gives me hope that this is a passing issue. A six-feet-tall, muscle-bound, strawberry-blond *but basically ginger* issue.

Otty walks beside me and doesn't speak until we're in the lift on our way down. I nudge her arm.

'Hey.'

'I'll tell you later,' she hisses under her breath.

Wow. She really is upset.

When we reach the ground floor, I notice the new coffee place is still open. 'Tell me now,' I say.

She lets me steer her into the bright warmth of the concession and I leave her sitting on a large wingback armchair while I fetch coffee. As I wait in line, I watch her. She's staring blankly out of the window at the bank of straggly lavender edging West One's car park. Her chin rests on one hand, her elbow propped on the arm of the chair. She has no spark. No lightness. Nothing of the Otty I know.

It's a knife to me.

Is she angry with Langham, or *me* still?

Whatever else has happened between us, I never want to make Otty sad. I wish I could scoop her into my arms for a hug, like I used to. But I don't know if we'll ever return to that. The helplessness burns.

She still hasn't moved when I deliver her drink.

'I got you a creamy syrupy thing with gold sprinkles,' I offer.

'Is that the official title?'

'It's the working title for one of my pitches today,' I say. That elicits a smile. Good. 'What did he say to you?'

She studies me for a moment, and then digs her spoon into the dollop of gold-dusted cream. 'Who?'

'*Who?* Scottish bloke. Name like an estate agents'. Built like a brick sh—'

'Okay, okay.'

Now *that's* a proper smile.

'He wanted to see me first, so I thought great, get it over with. I wasn't worried or anything. Not really. I know Russell likes my work and he's the one paying my wages.'

'What happened?'

'Right, get this: Fraser waited until I was in the office and then he told me he didn't want to talk about it then. He said he needed to see everyone else first and was just letting me know.'

'What? Did he want you to sweat or something?'

'I couldn't work it out.' Now she's sparkling with it: the gossip, the build-up to the killer punchline when she reveals what Langham said to make her storm out. It's like I've got my Otty back. Not *my* Otty – the Otty she was before. 'He said, "Don't sit down" and then he perched on the edge of Russell's desk – like he owned it – and told me he didn't want to see me this afternoon. Weird, huh?'

'Totally. What did you say?'

'What could I say? I just gave him a look like the one you're wearing now.'

I know we haven't reached the end of the story, but I want to prolong it – us, being *us*, not two friends reeling from a disaster. So I won't give her the chance to deliver the punchline yet. 'He's definitely odd,' I say. 'When I went in, do you know what he'd done?'

Amusement dances in Otty's eyes. I love that I've helped it be there. 'Tell me.'

'He'd pulled the chair out to practically the middle of the floor. Like I was going to sit in front of a row of judges or something. What was that for? So he could see me swinging my feet like a kid?'

'At least he let you sit down.' She eats the spoonful of cream and scoops another. 'He left me standing there like a right prat.'

'Maybe he has a thing about chairs.'

She giggles, wiping cream from her lips. 'A chair thing?'

I pretend to be serious, but it's hard not to smile when the game is this good – and this wanted. 'A *chair* thing. It's all about control. Of wood. He decides if the chair deserves you or not. You either stand next to it or sit on it in the middle of the room where he can see *every leg…*'

'Argh! Stop it!' Otty squeaks, helpless with laughter.

'Not even remotely sorry.'

'Gross, Joe!'

'You're welcome.'

'Anyway, I asked him why we couldn't just do the appraisal there. Do you know what he said? He said he thought I'd get a greater benefit from his thoughts if we did my appraisal *over dinner*.'

'Oh...'

'I know! I mean, how utterly disrespectful is that? So it's okay for him to talk to everyone else, but I have to have some patronising *special time* where he can bestow his wisdom on me?'

I try to maintain my smile, but I've lost the urge to laugh.

Otty carries on, oblivious. 'And that coming after telling Tom and Jake they could "have" me in their group. Not "include" me, "*have*" me, like I was someone's annoying kid sister who had to tag along. Does he think I need babysitting? Or bribing with food?'

'What a *dick*...' There's far more venom in my reply than I intend.

'Thank you! I knew you'd understand.' She mixes the remaining cream into her coffee with increasingly violent stabs of her spoon. 'I was furious. I told him, in no uncertain terms, that I was a professional and, as such, if he wanted to talk to me about my work, he could do it in a proper manner, over coffee, during office hours.'

She's so proud of her stance that I can't bear to tell her. 'Well – good for you.'

'Honestly, Joe, I couldn't believe it. Refusing to see me as equal with the rest of the team – treating me like some little woman who needs everything mansplaining over dinner...' Her voice trails away, realisation finally dawning. '*Oh*...'

My expression must be yelling it, too, because she pales.

'He was asking me out to dinner, wasn't he?'

'Yeah.'

She screws up her eyes. 'Oh *bollocks*.'

'But still, highly unprofessional,' I offer.

'There's no way I would have gone.'

'Of course.'

'Probably a lucky escape,' she says.

I fake a laugh because I don't want her to see we aren't still having fun. 'Yeah, can you imagine?'

'Mmm…'

'And considering his terrible choice of words this morning, I dread to think what his killer chat-up line would be.'

She turns the handle of her mug so it rotates on the table between us. 'It would be awful, wouldn't it?'

'I bet.'

She's a little stunned from the revelation, but I don't think she's taking a brighter view of Langham. That's a good sign. I allow myself a little more fun.

'You look like a woman who needs my help…' I say, in a booming Scottish accent that could hail from just about anywhere from Dumfries to Thurso. 'Got any *shhexshy* chairshh?'

'Joe!'

'Come on, admit it: you want to know how Fraser Langham gets down and dirty…'

She glares at me and I realise I've taken it too far. About a hundred miles too far, given what happened with us not so long ago. I hold my hands up in apology. Otty goes back to her slightly scary stirring. I look down at my mug of tea, stewed now because, in all the fun of tearing strips off Fraser Langham, I forgot to remove the teabag.

'Fancy popping to Verne's?' I ask.

Otty smiles. 'I think we've earned it.'

I think we both just had a lucky escape.

Fraser Langham: 0 – Otty and Joe: 1

Chapter Thirty-Five

OTTY

I feel awful.

Fraser was trying to ask me out and there I was, too busy being offended for the entire female race. Which I stand by, *had* he been using food as a method of patriarchal control. Instead of just dinner.

That aside, it's a bit of a shock he even asked me.

I wouldn't consider it. Even if he is gorgeous… No. He has too many questionable features. His horrific choice of words yesterday, for one thing. The way he's clearly plaguing Joe, for another. And let's face it, the ham-fisted way he tried to ask me out. Who thinks a work appraisal is the appropriate place for a proposition?

He has lovely eyes, though. And that voice…

I look down at the two pairs of shoes I've pulled out as possibles to wear today. My trusty old black ballerina flats bought from a supermarket five years ago, comfy as anything and still going strong; or my large black biker boots I bought at the Custard Factory flea market last summer and haven't worn yet. They scream strength and a no-messing attitude, while secretly being as soft as slippers on the inside.

Bit like me, I think.

I pull a face. Not like me at all, actually.

My thoughts are all over the place this morning, hence my inability to choose shoes. For a brief moment when Joe and I were in the café yesterday, it was like I had him back. I've missed it. I didn't realise how much. I've been so concerned with keeping my head above water that I'd forgotten what I loved most about being Joe's friend: the fun we had.

I know Joe doesn't want me. But does he miss us?

And even though I'm pretty sure I won't accept Fraser's offer of a date, I can't escape the thought that he asked me within hours of us meeting, while I share my home, my job and my life with someone who knows me so well but backed away the moment we had the chance to be together.

I stare back at my choice. Old and predictable, or unexpected and sure?

Boots it is.

Joe was right about one thing yesterday: Fraser looks terrified when we meet in the West One coffee shop, as arranged, for our appraisal. I should put him out of his misery, but maybe not until I've discovered what he thinks of my writing. It's a little safeguard for me, a little more of a gift I can tell Joe about later. Maybe if we can get back the fun, like we did yesterday, we have a hope of surviving the rest...

The large yellow cups rattle in their saucers when Fraser sets them down. I went for black coffee because I thought it seemed the most apt to a professional meeting, even though I'm regretting what I said yesterday.

'I didn't know if you took sugar or not,' he says, a shower of brown and white packets dropping from his hand into a mini-mountain in the middle of the table. He stares at them as he sits.

'Thanks,' I reply. 'I don't.'

'Ah.'

'But we can take these up to the kitchen. Sugar is always in short supply, especially when the stress levels rise.'

'Stress seemed to be a feature yesterday.' Nervous Fraser Langham is a very different animal to the swaggery version I've already seen.

'It's always a feature. You know writers.'

He risks a longer look at me. 'I thought I did.'

'So, my work. Your thoughts?'

'Uh – sure.' He scrambles into action, fetching my index-card pitches from the pocket of his jacket and spreading them across the table like a croupier preparing to deal. I have to hide my smile because this version of our script executive is becoming more endearing with every new bumble.

I keep my spine straight, braced against the knot of anxiety in my stomach. Fraser may have had a less-than-perfect start yesterday, but it matters to me what he thinks of my work. I want to keep pushing myself, keep growing, so I stand the best possible chance of a long career.

He considers the cards for a while. Just as I'm wondering if this is a ploy – like pulling Joe's chair uncomfortably far from the desk – he looks up at me. 'They're great.'

I wait for a '*but*'. Fraser sips his coffee, sets his cup down carefully and says nothing.

Is this another of his mind games?

'Anything else?'

'No.'

Joe told me about this. It's a game to knock the wind out of my sails, a sudden lack of fuel to the fire. It irks me. 'Mind if I give you some feedback, then?'

'Um… go ahead.' He wasn't expecting that.

'*They're great* isn't really feedback.'

'But I think your work is great.'

'That's very kind, but I can't do anything with that.'

'They're just pitches. You produced a good number of consistently great ones. Brief fulfilled.'

If Fraser is playing a game, he looks awfully earnest.

'Fraser, can I ask you a question?'

'Of course.'

'Yesterday, when you suggested meeting over dinner, that wasn't about feedback, was it?'

I watch his shoulders tense. 'Otty, if I've overstepped the mark…'

'You kind of did. It wasn't really appropriate, given you were meant to be talking to everyone. Unless you're taking them all out to dinner as well?'

'I'm sorry.'

'And it could have been seen as a lack of respect for your female colleagues. Which, after your earlier mistake, might not have looked particularly good.'

He gives a heavy sigh. 'Right. Sorry – *again.*'

Maybe if Joe and the others could see Fraser like this they would be less inclined to hate him. I wonder what else he hides behind his professional veneer. It's enough to make up my mind.

'But – if you'd like to ask now, in a personal capacity…'

His eyes narrow a little as if he's scouting the ground for landmines.

'I would.'

My skin prickles. 'So ask me.'

Joe's not going to be happy. He's expecting me to return triumphant, with Fraser trailing in my wake. As it is, we're travelling back up to the eleventh floor, slightly flushed and trading smiles, our hands tantalisingly close as we stand in the lift.

It's unexpected. But I'm excited. It's so good to feel that again. This is my decision, my invitation to spend time with a man I would like to get to know better. A small return of control after what happened with Joe.

And he wanted to be with me. Joe didn't. It's as simple – and brutal – as that. Maybe it won't amount to anything. Maybe it's just the ego boost I need. I won't know unless I try, will I?

We're going to dinner tomorrow night. I just won't tell Joe.

As we leave the lift and walk towards Ensign Media, Fraser slows. 'Back to our professional selves, then.'

I smile up at him. 'As you were, Mr Langham.'

If he looks at me like that tomorrow night, we could be in trouble…

The moment I take my seat next to Joe, he's leaning in. 'What have you done with him? Did you leave him, bruised and bleeding, sobbing into his flat white?'

'He was very apologetic.'

'When you had him in a headlock? Or were threatening to smash every patriarchal bone in his body?'

I laugh. 'You seriously overestimate my abilities.'

'That's what superheroes always say.' He grins and my heart contracts. I don't like lying to him. We're on such uncertain ground still – I don't want to do anything to make it crumble.

'*Shh*. I need to protect my secret identity.'

Joe leans closer. 'Your secret's safe with me.'

Under the table, my brand-new boots pinch a little. I can do this. It's just dinner with a lovely guy. If Joe doesn't know, it can't hurt him. And if he doesn't know, he'll keep trying as hard as he is to get us back to how we were before. And I want that more than anything.

Chapter Thirty-Six

JOE

'Where are you going?'

'Just out.'

'Want some company?'

'Nah, I'll be fine.'

I follow Otty into the hall.

'Nice boots.'

'Thanks.'

Where *is* she going? Otty's been preoccupied all afternoon and now, with no warning, she's suddenly going out. Looking incredible. The kind of incredible that takes time and effort. Something's off here, I know it.

It couldn't be Langham, could it?

No. He's looked terrified whenever he's seen her. If they were planning a date he would have been lording it up in the writers' room today, rubbing my nose in it.

'Are you meeting someone?'

'I'm just going out with a friend, okay?'

'You don't dress like that for a friend.'

'I'm not. I'm dressing like that for me.'

Too defensive. It's definitely a date. 'Well, whoever it's for, you look – beautiful…'

What the actual hell, Joe?

Otty reddens.

Why did I pick that superlative? *Great, lovely, good* – any of these would have been acceptable. But *beautiful*? There's no way you can spin that. It's a word straight from the heart.

'Thanks,' she says, turning away. 'No creepy-weirdo-questioning tomorrow morning, okay?'

'So it *is* a date.'

Her groan echoes in the hall. 'No, Joe. Although apparently you've already made up your mind that it is. I might be late back, that's all. I might not see you before I go to bed.' The mention of the 'B' word sends both our eyes inspecting the tiles.

I step aside to let her fetch her coat.

'Well, you know where I am if you need anything.'

Midway into her sleeve, she stops to observe me. 'I'll be okay.'

'I know.'

'And you will be, too.' Her hand rests on my arm, just for a second. I don't know what to say.

I could kick myself.

The house is too quiet when she's gone. Restless. I flick through the films on Sky but can't find one that appeals. Nothing on Netflix, either. Probably for the best. Picking plot holes in movies on my own isn't fun. I think back to similar nights in this room, Otty and me on the sofa ripping strips off bad scripts and calling out lazy continuity. Laughing until we ache, Otty wiping tears from her eyes.

Us.

Like we used to be.

Our joke almost leaked out this morning. Rona has clocked the shift in tension between us and was trying to dig for details. She cornered Otty and me at lunchtime in the West One café queue.

'I have a pitch idea for Langham,' she said.

'Does it involve a basement dungeon?' I asked, ducking her swipe.

'Not every idea I have is about sex, thank you, Carver.'

'Probably just most of them,' Otty said.

'It's simpler than that. Two friends sharing – a house, let's say. And something happens…'

'Meteor strike,' Otty said, whip-fast, eyes twinkling at me – and instantly we were in a new game.

'Zombie apocalypse.'

'Psycho landlord.'

'Robot invasion.'

'Fig roll shortage!'

I clutched at my heart. 'No! The fear is real!'

It was so good, such an instinctive thing, and I could see my own thrill reflected in her expression. And then, the beat of sadness that inevitably follows everything since *that night*.

'Er, I'm still here?' Rona said.

'Sorry.'

'So these friends – this couple – have a great thing going. They're close and comfortable. It's sweet. And then, something changes.' She held up her hand. 'And no: not a dragon plague, or the arrival of an alien race, before you both start again. Something simpler.'

Her scrutiny of us was discomforting. Maybe that's why we made the mistake.

'Not *sex*?' I asked.

Otty's eyes shot to mine.

Rona studied us. 'You tell me.'

'If they did, it would only be once,' Otty said.

And that's when I should have kept my mouth shut. But I didn't.

'Once would be enough.'

I shift on the sofa now, remembering the pause, the burn, the cold-drain of realisation. And Rona between us, eyes like saucers...

Rona's said nothing yet, but it hangs over us now: a storm waiting to break.

No wonder Otty wanted to get away tonight.

I'm selling us short. We'll style it out. I have to believe that facing it together will unite us, even if it's mostly in mortification. The glimpses of the old Otty and Joe I've seen in recent weeks give me hope. If it was too much to take, I don't think we'd still be here.

A sudden, uninvited memory of Otty kissing me forces me to my feet, moving away from the sofa as if staying there will bring everything back. I take shelter in the safety of an armchair, reeling from it. Our brave banter and careful jokes may be holding strong, but how can I forget *this*?

I've tried to forget. I've thrown myself into everything else as a distraction; I've stumbled into a war of wills with Fraser Langham and when I've had the chance to build on what Otty and I still have, I've taken it. But the night we spent together haunts me. It waits, out of sight, until I'm alone and my defences have dropped.

It will be better when we have an actual project to get our teeth into. Russ reckons next week we'll all be assigned single dramas and shorts to start writing. Not working in a team with Otty these past few days hasn't helped, either. It's weird to sit opposite her and make decisions she isn't part of. It also doesn't help that our new script executive has us devoting precious hours to his pointless exercise. I think Russ knows it's damaging the team. With any luck, he'll keep us too busy to indulge Langham again. Maybe next week Otty and I will rediscover our rhythm and I won't have time to think about anything else.

And hopefully, Fraser Langham won't stuff everything up.

A thought appears. I dismiss it immediately.

No. Otty's not out with Langham tonight.

Chapter Thirty-Seven

OTTY

I feel bad about lying to Joe. But this is *lovely*.

Fraser is waiting for me outside the restaurant, as we'd arranged, his original suggestion of picking me up at home swiftly side-stepped. I am not ready to run that particular gauntlet yet, not for anyone.

'Hey. You came.'

'Did you think I wouldn't?'

'I wasn't sure you'd be willing to risk it. After I successfully managed to offend you *twice*.'

'I'm glad I proved you wrong.'

'Me too.' He leans in to give my cheek the lightest brush of a kiss.

And of course, he smells good. There's a fraction of a second before he moves back. I breathe him in.

'Shall we?'

Fraser holds the door open for me and we go inside, shown to our table by a waiter. I'm a little nervous and I think he is, too. Which is exactly what should happen on a first date.

I didn't even get a first date with Joe...

Annoyed with myself, I shake the thought away. Tonight is not about Joe. Tonight is about me – and my date.

Here, away from work and all the tension that's surrounded the writers' room since his arrival, Fraser looks calm and happy. And – *handsome*. I've been trying to think of another word to describe him – because, *hello*, Netflix movie – but handsome is the only one that fits.

He looks comfortable and cool in a dark grey T-shirt, brown leather jacket and blue jeans, his hair just a little tousled. But what I notice most is his slightly self-conscious smile, the fun that sparkles cautiously in those stunning eyes of his. It's disarming: so different from the Fraser Langham he shows everyone else. I have that sense again that I'm being granted a rare view.

'You look amazing,' he says, adding, 'if you don't mind me saying so.'

Beautiful, Joe said…

'So do you,' I say, determined to kick away thoughts of anyone else. 'And I don't mind at all.'

Once we've ordered food and wine, we both begin to relax. He's careful not to joke too much about Ensign, which is very wise. In return, I don't mention Joe. The night stretches long and unhurried ahead of us and I want to enjoy all of it.

'So how long were you in LA?' I ask, nodding my thanks to the sommelier who has just filled my wine glass.

'Almost two years, on and off. I was very lucky with work. Stars aligning and all of that.'

'You weren't tempted to stay?'

'A little. I mean, the place was fantastic, the people great, but it was crazy out there. The pace they work, the stress everyone's under, it wasn't sustainable. And I'm a born and bred Scot, so I melted in the heat.' He raises his glass. 'So, what will we drink to?'

I lift my glass in reply. 'To feedback?'

He shakes his head. 'I get the feeling I'm never going to live that down.'

'It's best you realise it now.'

'Okay. Let's drink to honesty.'

'Why honesty?'

His expression stills – another glimpse behind the scenes. 'Because you blew me away with yours.'

Did I? I've been trying to work out why Fraser wanted to see me outside of work, when all I've done is haul him over the coals for his mistakes.

'Thank you,' I say. 'To honesty, then.' Our glasses touch with a bell-chime of crystal. 'I'm not usually so direct.'

'You did the right thing. I was out of line. And you had the decency to tell me to my face. There aren't many people in that room who'd do the same.'

He's certainly got the measure of everyone.

'It's hard coming into an established team, no matter what you do for a living,' I say. 'I think nerves play a big part in misunderstandings.'

'I didn't think I was nervous but seeing how you all work together – how close you are – that's daunting for an incomer.'

'I know. When I joined the team it was already half-established. I felt completely out of my depth for a while. It took kindness and patience from them to help me feel I belonged there.'

It took Joe – encouraging me, supporting me…

Right, that's the last time I'm thinking of him tonight. I turn my attention fully to the beautiful man sitting opposite, who wants to spend the evening with me.

I don't really want to be talking shop all night, but there's one more thing I want to say. 'Here's the thing, Fraser. We're a great team at Ensign. I think you need to believe in us more. We've just delivered a first-season show with the potential to be a major hit – we know what we're doing.'

Fraser studies me for a while. Have I just blown our first date within the first ten minutes?

'There it is again. You wield honesty like a warrior wields a sword.'

I'm not certain that's a compliment. But I can't be anyone other than myself. 'I don't want to tell you your job. But I think you'll enjoy working with the team far more if you believe we're capable of being the best.'

'And I'm guessing you'll enjoy this evening more if we don't fill it with work stuff. This *isn't* an appraisal, remember?'

'Nice comeback, Mr Langham.'

'I'm glad you liked it.'

So we steer clear of work and talk about everything else – what we like and dislike, what got us into writing, what we do to relax. All pretty standard stuff, but with Fraser I feel I'm being given a personal guided tour.

'I was born in a small village called Nethy Bridge, in Strathspey. My folks worked at an outdoor centre in the Abernethy Forest, nearby. Cairngorms on my doorstep, lochs and purple-headed mountains – the entire Scottish idyll,' he says. 'A little different from Birmingham.'

'Which is a beautiful city,' I counter.

'Very beautiful, in some areas.'

Flirty. I like it. 'I was born here. My parents worked at

Longbridge in the car plant until that closed and they got divorced. Then Dad opened a bike-repair shop in Moseley.'

'What kind of bikes?'

'Mountain bikes and road cycles mostly, although he'll fix anything. That's where I worked until I started at Ensign.'

I like the way surprise lifts his features. 'You worked in a bike shop?'

'I'm a qualified suspension specialist, thank you very much. Studied Engineering at university, went to work for Dad when I graduated.'

'Okay. That's a plot twist. I figured you'd written for a living before.'

I laugh. 'Nobody knew I wrote until a year ago. Ensign is my first professional posting.'

'You're joking.' Fraser sits back, head on one side as he takes this in. I haven't mentioned what I did before to many people, my lack of experience a cause of embarrassment to me. But seeing the effect it has on Fraser is a revelation. 'I can't believe you've not done this before. Your writing is affecting, engaging, accomplished.'

'I think the term you're looking for is *great*,' I say, resisting the urge to giggle when I see his rueful grin.

When the meal is over, we pay and walk out into the mild night. It's a clear sky that glows a bright indigo blue above the city. I don't want to say goodbye yet, don't want my time with Fraser to be over.

He shuffles his feet on the pavement, hands planted in the pockets of his leather jacket. 'It's been a good evening.'

'It has. Thank you.'

There's a pause as we share hesitant smiles. Should I kiss him? I feel like I want to and we're standing so close that it could happen in a heartbeat. I see his gaze dance from my eyes to my lips and wonder if he's considering it, too.

Then he gives a self-conscious laugh and the moment passes. 'It's still early. Would you take a walk with me?'

I feel my heart expand. 'I would love to.'

He offers his arm – how cute is *that*? – and the leather of his jacket is cool against my skin as I loop my arm through his. He leans a little to bump against me. 'You'll have to lead the way, I'm afraid. I'm still getting to grips with this city.'

I know exactly where to head.

The lights of The Wharf ripple in the dark waters of the canal as we emerge from The Mailbox and follow the path towards the bridge. There's a slight chill in the air tonight, but I'm acutely aware of warmth from Fraser's body as we walk. Occasionally he touches my hand where it rests on his arm, his fingers lingering a moment longer each time. It makes the hairs on my forearms rise beneath the cotton of my jacket.

I love my city at night: the coolness of its canals, the bright lights of its buildings and the sound – music and laughter, traffic and life. People who've never lived here often mock it, the ones who have only seen terrible 1970s public information films portraying Birmingham as a grey sea of concrete. But I think it's beautiful. We have history and innovation, the cradle of industry and the heartbeat of an ever-changing, ever-evolving future.

I doubt Fraser's ever been here before. When I catch him looking at me it's a jolt of joy, the electricity between us magnified by the landscape we're travelling through.

'I never knew this was here,' he says, his eyes filled with the lights around Gas Street Basin. 'It's gorgeous.'

'Told you. It's one of my favourite parts of the city.' I point up to one of the waterside apartments. 'My friend Wren from university lives there. We've had many a drunken night along this towpath.'

'I'll bet.' He looks down at me. 'Can I ask you something?'

'Of course.'

'You and Joe Carver – what's the story?'

My heart plummets like a rock in the Worcester and Birmingham Canal. 'We share a house and we write together.'

'I just wondered because you seem close.'

We've reached the tunnel beneath the Worcester Bar bridge where two canals meet. It's impossible to walk two abreast on the narrow towpath through it, but I don't want to answer Fraser's question if we're moving in single file. So I stop and dare to look up at him. I am going to be as honest as I can, without telling him everything.

'We are close – as friends. I care about him. But that's all.' My eyes prickle. I blink the sensation away.

Fraser's arm unfurls from mine and we're standing apart. 'Then—' his hand takes mine, our fingers slowly lacing together, 'there's no one in our way?'

'No,' I say, pushing away the feeling that I'm lying to him. 'Nobody in our way.'

'You'd better come here, then.'

He pulls me close and I lean into him, his lips soft and his embrace unhurried. His arms circle me, warm hands resting at the small of my back as we kiss. It's gentle and warm and wonderful.

When we break apart, he strokes my face. 'I wanted that to happen since the day we met.'

I gaze up into his grey-green eyes, the lights of the city reflected there. 'And now it has?'

'I want it to happen again.'

Fraser's lovely face fills my vision as I close my eyes.

There are no lights on in the house when I park outside. I sit for a moment in Monty, trying to steady my breath. I'm buzzing from Fraser's kisses but the dread about seeing Joe has built steadily all the way home. I have no idea how we're going to navigate this.

He hates Fraser. Really, properly hates him. I don't know why exactly, but this is going to make everything a thousand times worse. I shouldn't have to consider what Joe thinks – he didn't want me, after all. But my heart is torn.

I don't know what I was expecting from tonight, but it turns out I want to know Fraser more. It's not just an act of defiance against Joe, although I suspect that impulse is part of it. I like Fraser. I want to see him again. Joe's just going to have to deal with it.

At least I won't have that battle tonight. I get out and lock my car, patting Monty's brave yellow paintwork. It's rusting a little along the edge of the roof but that only makes me love him more. The chill of the night whispers around me as I walk up the path to the house. On the doorstep, my heart contracts. I take a moment before I go in.

It's quiet, just the distant hum of the fridge and the soft contrapuntal ticks of the clocks in the kitchen, living room and hall. I could stay up for a while, let everything sink in, but I'm tired, so I head upstairs.

It's only when I'm on the landing that I see the light coming from Joe's room. His door is wide open. I have to pass it on my way to the bathroom. Is he asleep? Could I make the journey there and back unnoticed?

'Otts?'

Crap.

I could duck into my room, or dash downstairs, but I can't pretend I'm not here. If he's awake he will have heard the rattle of my keys at the front door, my footsteps on the stairs. I don't want to do this now, but he needs to know. Heart heavy, I peer inside.

Joe is sitting up in bed, a wash of blue light from the screen of his open laptop illuminating the contours of his naked chest. He leans over the edge of the mattress to retrieve a crumpled T-shirt from the floor, putting it on in that weird way of his: arms in first, head through last. 'Hey. How'd it go?'

I lean against the doorframe. 'Good, thanks.'

'You look tired.'

'I am. Crazy few days.'

He smiles back but I can feel he's steeling himself for more.

'What are you writing?' I ask.

'Thought I'd jot down some ideas for *Eye, Spy 2*. Nothing like a bit of optimism, right?' He looks at me. 'And I couldn't sleep.'

I'm not certain I'll be able to sleep tonight, either. Not after the conversation we are headed towards. I think Joe knows it's coming. 'Can we talk?'

'Sure.' He pats the bed. 'Come here.'

Of course it will happen there. The slamming of one door; the uncertain light from the next. Part of me doesn't want to see his reaction so close. It's going to hurt like hell. But if we're ever going to survive this, Joe needs to know.

I edge into the room, feeling the news swirl around my feet, ushering it into Joe's space. I'm a harbinger of doom, a messenger bringing shadow in her wake. As soon as I sit next to him, the memory of our night returns. If I could go back to that moment in the moonlight, suspend time long enough to rest my head against Joe and feel that safety, that peace, I would do it now. Just for a little while.

Instead, I put myself at the nearest edge of a safe distance from him, resting my hand on the duvet as close to his body as I dare.

'I lied, earlier. I wasn't meeting a friend.'

Tension flicks in his jaw. In the screen light, his eyes are deep and soulful.

'I met Fraser.' A wave of emotion swells within me.

Joe says nothing. Just a single, slow blink and jaw set firm.

Tears build. I breathe against the tide. 'It was a date. I should have told you.'

'You don't have to tell me anything.' His gaze slips.

'I really like him. But I wanted you to know first.'

'Why?'

'Because it matters to me what you think.'

His single, smileless laugh pulls his body further into his pillow. On the bed his hand retreats across the sheets, the empty indentation it leaves still close enough for my fingers to touch. 'Really.'

Already we're changing, close enough to feel each other's breath on our skin, too far apart to bridge the distance. I won't take it back, or wish I hadn't come here. I have to move on and Joe does, too. If he cares about me, he'll come back from this. If not…

I blink and a tear escapes. I can't look at him as it falls.

'I'm sorry I lied.'

I can't say any more. The bomb has dropped, shattering everything. I need to get out of here…

And then I feel his hand on mine.

'I don't understand,' he says. 'And I'm never going to like him. But you should be happy. You matter to me.'

I dare to look into his eyes. His fingers give a single, gentle squeeze.

'Get some sleep,' he says, his voice low. 'We're okay, Otty.'

It doesn't feel like we are.

Chapter Thirty-Eight

JOE

Of course I'm not okay.

But Otty and I need each other – and Langham isn't taking that from me.

It stung last night; I'm not going to lie. I didn't sleep for hours, replaying the conversation we'd had on my bed, where not so long ago she'd been mine. But when I woke this morning, I made a decision: I'm going to play the long game. Pretty sure Fraser Langham won't be at Ensign for ever – people like him never are. Right now it appeals to him because of the buzz surrounding Russell's writing team. But sooner or later, he'll be headhunted again or go off chasing greater glory. And there's no way he'd take Otty with him.

So, I'll stick it out. Show him he can't have her all to himself.

She keeps stealing glances at me as we work today. She's done it since we met in the kitchen for breakfast this morning. I make sure I smile whenever I catch her looking. We're waiting for Langham, who is in a meeting with Russell. I'm not looking forward to the moment he comes in and sees her.

'We're not going to say anything at work,' she told me as we were driving here. 'I mean, it's really early days.'

'I think that's wise,' I'd replied.

Is Fraser Langham capable of wisdom? I guess we'll find out.

Rona groans beside me. 'They'd better not be planning more of these.' She picks up a stack of index cards and drops them with disgust. 'Fraser may look like a god but I'm fast becoming agnostic.'

I glance at Otty, who is deep in conversation with Jake and Tom. 'Have you spoken to Otty today?'

Rona folds her arms. 'About what, Joseph?'

'Er, general stuff?'

'You can always talk to me, you know,' she says, which throws me a little. Rona Basu is the last person I'd consider a confidante. Largely because she scares me. 'If there's anything going on…'

Not this again. I'd hoped she would forget, but I reckoned without Tenacious-B muscling in. I half-wonder if I should tell her and then swear her to secrecy to make sure the news travels no further. But I'm not altogether sure Rona has fully discarded her lust for Langham, so best to just let Otty deliver that bombshell.

'You might want to talk to her,' I say because despite everything else, Rona shouldn't have to find out Otty and Fraser are together when the rest of the room does.

Otty and Fraser. That's going to kick for a while.

'Okay, bitches – pitches!' Russell strides in, Langham sailing in his slipstream. He's unapologetic when the entire writers' room team observe him, incredulously. 'Hey, it works for some showrunners. Thought I'd give it a go.'

'Not when you come from Rotherham, Guv,' Reece quips and laughter erupts.

'Fair enough. Okay, Fraser and I have gone through the pitches you've all been working on and we've chosen ones we want to adapt. Full treatments first, please, then we'll ask for a thirty-minute sample. And I know you will all be very happy when I say this: original partnerships, please.'

Relief washes around the room. We've been at Langham's whim for far too long. As chairs scrape back and teams reassemble, I look at our script executive. His smile is tight, arms drawn across his body like armour. I bet Russell pulled rank on him. He smiles at Otty and then I swear he makes a point of smiling at me.

Git.

'Joseph.'

I jump to find Russell beside me. 'Yes?'

'Walk with me.'

Not now… 'Yeah, sure.'

I don't want to leave the room, particularly when Langham rises from his chair and moves to Otty, checking to make sure I see it.

'Joe.'

'Right there, Russ.'

As I walk out of the room, I catch Otty's eye. Her smile gives me hope and crushes it all at once. Today I feel even guiltier about discussing her with Russ. Maybe I'll just tell him now. I think her job's as safe here as any of ours. Yes, I'm going to tell him. None of her work is down to me. That should be easy enough to say, right?

To my surprise, Russell doesn't head for the entrance for our usual circuit, instead turning left past Daphne's desk to his office at the far end. That's thrown me. I scurry after him, trying to remain calm.

Daphne lifts her head as I pass, biting coyly on the end of her biro. I train my eyes back on Russell. It is *way* too early for that.

It's a relief when the door closes. Otty and Langham and Rona and Daphne and any other nutter who might arrive with fresh chaos – they can all stay on the other side of the oak for as long as possible. My head is awash. I should have just gone to bed last night, hours before Otty came home, instead of staying up and deliberately leaving my door open. I thought she would tell me it was some other bloke, not Fraser. I could have dealt with that.

'Have a seat,' Russell says, reaching down to open a drawer and slapping a large box on his desk. 'Cronut?'

'Sorry?'

'I got them from the craft bakery in Digbeth this morning,' he beams. 'Pure rebellion in pastry form. Likely to stop my heart, but what a way to go, eh?' He throws a square napkin at me and takes one for himself, using it to lift a round, very sugary pastry filled with a pale green cream. 'Look at that. Clogged arteries in one handy package. Don't tell Miri.'

I hold up my hands. 'Wouldn't dream of it.'

'Good boy.' He stretches back in his seat and savours his first bite of pastry. 'Not going to lie, I'll be glad to get back to normal today. Team O-Joe back where they belong.'

Now's my chance. 'Actually, Russ, about Otty…'

'Yep, that's why I wanted a word.'

'The thing is, she doesn't need any more…'

'Pitches? Tell me about it,' Russell's words cancel out mine as they crash across them. 'So, Fraser's handing out projects in there but you and Otty don't have one.'

Concern ripples through me. 'How come?'

'Don't give me that frown, Joseph. It's good news.'

'Is it?'

'It is.' He narrows his eyes. 'Everything okay?'

'Absolutely.'

'And Otty?'

I stare at him. What does he know? What has he seen? 'Fine, as far as I know.'

'It can be hard in that room – at such close quarters. Easy to get attached.'

'We're fine. I just want to say…'

Russell nods. 'Good, then. I'm taking you both out of there so we can start work on *Eye, Spy 2*.'

All thoughts of what I was about to say vanish. 'We got the commission?'

When Russell laughs it's like sitting in the direct path of a sonic boom.

'I like your faith in us, Joe. No green light yet, but Fraser agrees with me that we need to be ready when it comes. No wasting time. So we'll meet to thrash out a treatment between the four of us and then I want you and Otty to write episode one. No team credit: you and Otty as named writers.'

Shit. That's huge.

'Wow…'

'I think the two of you are perfect. Your scripts, I mean.' He exhales and leans just a little closer over his desk. 'They have something none of the others do: connection. Can't manufacture that. Apart, you're great; together, you're awesome. A solid outfit. I will protect that, if it's what you need.'

My sleep-weary mind snaps to attention. What is Russell really saying?

'I have no intention of letting her go,' I reply, not certain what I mean, either.

'That's what I like to hear!' Russell slaps his desk, sending a shower of sugar granules dancing across the surface. 'We'll begin this afternoon, in the media suite.'

Chapter Thirty-Nine

OTTY

Fraser Langham is a *tart*.

I thought we'd agreed last night that we'd keep everything quiet for the time being, give ourselves time to get used to the change and enjoy discovering each other away from the scrutiny of the writers' room.

Fraser, it seems, is intent on us being discovered at every opportunity. His hand brushes the nape of my neck as he leans down to talk to Rona and me. His eyes flick to mine at the end of every sentence. And when I nip out at mid-morning break to get my laptop lead from my car, he follows and pulls me into a vacant office next to the lift to kiss me.

'Stop,' I giggle, but he kisses me more. 'Whatever happened to *we won't do anything at work?*'

'*You* happened,' he growls, his lips on my neck. 'I can't wait till this evening.'

At lunch, I see Joe talking to Daphne. She's mooning up at him, all false eyelashes and lingering looks. Just as I'm contemplating leaving, he jogs over.

'Hey. We've got a gig.'

'What?'

'This way.' Joe leads me by the arm to the media suite, checking we aren't being followed before he closes the door. 'I reckon we have five minutes before your boyfriend misses you.'

'If you brought me in here just to have a go…'

'No. I just spoke to Russell. We're starting *Eye, Spy* season two – now.'

I can't believe what I'm hearing. 'Has it been commissioned?'

'Not yet. But Russ wants to be ready when it does. And get this: we get billing for episode one.'

My mouth goes dry.

Joe's eyes are alive. '*Episode One by Joe Carver and Ottilie Perry.* Not the team. Us. Right at the start after a groundbreaking successful first season. Imagine it, Otts! First one of the hotly anticipated new series – and it's ours!'

And then it hits me like a thousand fireworks detonating at once. I let out a squeal and Joe grabs my hands. Before I know it, we're jumping and dancing together in the dimly lit edit room. It ends with a messy, spinning, gangly-armed embrace.

'Er, guys? Russell's looking for you.'

We jump apart and turn to see Jake in the doorway, staring at us as if we're possessed.

'Yeah, great, cheers,' Joe says, hurrying out.

'Nutters,' Jake shakes his head as I edge past.

I stuff my smile away when I see my colleagues, but I'm excited. This is the biggest break of my career – Joe's too.

But the moment it's time for the meeting, he starts acting weird.

And he isn't alone…

It begins when we're walking from the writers' room to the

media suite. Fraser and Joe flank me on either side, apparently engaged in a silent game of stares. Then Joe touches my arm.

'Hey, Otts, remember that chilli you made us the first night we wrote together?'

I frown. 'The one I make for us most Wednesdays?'

His eyes sparkle. 'Mm, Wednesday chilli. The first time you made it for me it blew my mind.'

'It did?'

'Don't be so modest! It was amazing. I wasn't expecting the intensity. So, *so* hot…'

'Okay…'

'Fan of chilli, Fraser?' Joe asks

Beside me, Fraser shifts. 'Uh, sure.'

'I'm sure you'll get to taste it soon. Otty and I have it all the time…'

I feel Fraser's hand rest gently on the small of my back. 'I look forward to it. Although I don't expect Otty to cook. I prefer to provide the feast…'

Oh, for heaven's sake.

'Maybe the two of you should get dinner together, seeing as you're both such culinary fans,' I say, moving away from them and opening the media suite door.

Now we're inside and working, but I can feel them both gearing up for the next round. What the hell is wrong with them?

We're gathered around the conference table, which is really a smaller version of the one in the writers' room. Joe and I on one side, Fraser and Russell on the other. On the wall a board is already prepared for the index cards we will write to plot out the second season of a show that hasn't even wrapped filming yet. I don't know whether that's blind faith or bloody-mindedness.

'We need an overarching theme,' Russell says, 'beyond the cases that Laura Eye is pursuing. Joe, Otty, the fake-therapist plot was inspired. So what's next?'

Joe looks at me. 'She goes after Dr Montgomery aka Anya Soren?'

'I think so,' I say.

Joe smiles.

'Too obvious.' We turn to Fraser, who I'm convinced is aiming his words straight at Joe.

Russell taps the table with his pen. 'How so?'

'It's what everyone expects. Laura Eye is mortified, on the back foot at work and unable to explain what she knows because it will majorly incriminate her. She gets assigned to find Anya Soren, knowing full well that if she succeeds, Soren can blow the case wide open and destroy her.'

'Sounds good to me.'

'Okay. But the thing is, Russ: that approach has to end season two with success for Laura. Unless you kill her off, which, you know, is always a possibility. But then what's going to hook viewers into a third season?'

'In the final battle Laura kills Soren but is mortally wounded herself,' Russell says. 'We think she's dead but at the end of the credits we cut to a single shot that suggests she isn't?'

Fraser shakes his head. 'Too obvious. We need a longer arc that takes viewers over two seasons.'

'We're not guaranteed a second season, let alone a third,' Joe argues. 'Leave it hanging at the end of season two and you may well end up with a cancelled story two-thirds in. Think *Farscape*. Or *Merlin*. Or even *Sense8*. It's too risky.'

Fraser bristles opposite me. 'Some of us are brave enough to take a risk, Joe. But I see your point.'

Russell is watching their exchange with quiet interest. 'Otty? What do you think?'

Talk about being put on the spot! I feel the weight of Fraser and Joe's stares. How did I end up as No Man's Land in their personal vendetta?

I think as I speak, praying something coherent will appear. 'I think either approach would work…'

My housemate and my date each nod their acceptance of a point scored. It's an added tension I don't need and when our session is over today I'm going to put them both straight. This is my opportunity and I am not going to let either of them derail me.

'But whatever else we do, Laura has to be the focus,' I say. 'I think we need to see her broken by the revelation at the end of season one and her journey to regain control.'

Russell sits back. 'Go on.'

Time to think on my feet.

'Hunted to hunter,' I say. 'We split the season: first half is Laura reeling, terrified that she might destroy the institution she's pledged her allegiance to – but also lost because whoever Dr Montgomery really was, she had become Laura's sanctuary, her strength. You often hear therapists, psychologists, trainers and so on saying they run the risk of clients becoming obsessed with them because they see the professional as responsible for their happiness. Laura could have developed a dependency on Dr Montgomery – and like an addict, she has to fight her addiction.'

'A split season might be a headache for commissioning more,' Fraser argues.

'It might. Or it might encourage commissioners to invest.' When they all look at me, I press on. 'First half, Laura is reeling. She's in a dark place and torn between her emotional need for

Soren and keeping her head above water in the organisation. But then Soren and her operatives start to target members of Laura's family. Soren is goading Laura to come after her. The stakes rise. So the midpoint is when Laura makes the switch. She has no choice but to protect the people and organisation she loves – risking everything in the process. If we only get two seasons, there's a satisfying conclusion when Laura kills Soren in a fight to the death. If we get three, we develop it further with Laura uncovering more, at a higher level within the organisation, making her a double agent within her own jurisdiction.'

'Yes!' Russell slaps the table. 'Bloody yes! We go with that.' He beams at me. 'Brilliant, Otty.'

I did it! I'm going to take this and run with it. Joe and I will make the best version of the story we can. And then, who knows what we could write?

Three hours later, exhausted but happy, I collect my things as we stand to leave.

'Great work, guys,' Russell says. 'We'll meet in a week with Otty and Joe's initial pitch and take it from there. Now, go home!'

'Heading back to ours?' I ask Joe as Russell leaves.

I notice his eyes flick to Fraser before he answers. 'Yep. We need beer and balti and bollocks on TV.'

Fraser weaves between us, his warm arm sliding easily around my shoulders. 'Actually, I was kind of hoping I could cook you dinner tonight. At mine?'

Joe looks away.

'Well, I…'

'Good – well, have fun,' Joe says, and he's out of the room before I can stop him.

Fraser kicks the door closed with his foot as he pulls me into his arms. 'See? All sorted. Now, where were we…?'

They've both been ridiculous this afternoon. But Fraser's kiss is sweet and his body warm and, right now, that's all I want to think about.

Chapter Forty

JOE

FADE IN:
EXT. A NARROW CITY ALLEY, LATE AT NIGHT
A man edges along the wall. He is sweat-
ing, terrified. As he reaches the dead-end
of the alley, a figure steps into the
streetlight beam at the entrance. A shadow
looms long down the alley. The identity of
the figure is concealed, until she speaks:

                    WOMAN
          Why are you running?

The MAN scrabbles against the wall. He
is trapped.

                    WOMAN
          You can't run from this.

                    MAN
          Tell me what I've done!

```
You were a smarmy git. You thought you'd
    won. But now, Fraser, you will pay…


The WOMAN signals to her right. The
whites of The MAN's eyes catch the light
and his screams fill the alley as a giant
index card falls and crushes him…
                            FADE OUT.
```

'Joe.'

I snap my laptop shut. 'What?'

Daphne folds her arms. 'I thought you and Otty wrote together.'

'We do.'

'So what are you writing there?'

I lay a protective hand on the aluminium lid. 'Just sketching out ideas. For *our* episode.'

That hit its target. Daphne shuffles the papers in the crook of her arm and pulls one out. 'What a good boy. Russell will be delighted. Not sure Fraser will be as impressed, but then his attention is rather fully focussed elsewhere…'

I guess I deserved that.

It still stings, though.

I didn't think Otty and Fraser would last this long. Okay, I hoped they wouldn't. But it's been a month and they are as loved-up as ever. And fighting him all the time is exhausting. Not that I have any plans to stop, of course.

'Anyway, this just came through. I thought you might like to see it before everyone else.'

She hands me the sheet of paper. It's a press release:

**BBC Studios announces cast and
broadcast details for EYE, SPY**

Eye, Spy, a six-part, one-hour drama set around the world of
corporate corruption is currently in production for BBC Studios
in association with Tempest Pictures and Ensign Media. Maya
Marple (*Insiders*) leads the cast as industrial spy Laura Eye,
joined by Mac Finan (*Empires End*) as corporate lawyer-
turned whistleblower Gus. Supporting cast includes Gabriel
Marley, Talli Paul, Emma Spurgin Hussey and Rory Wilton.
Created by Russell Styles (*Southside, Servant, Insiders*), the
six-week 'event TV' drama will be simulcast on BBC One
and BBC America in March next year. A deal has also been
signed with Netflix for subsequent world distribution.

We knew season one had started filming but until now the identity
of the cast has remained a closely guarded secret. Seeing the
full list in black and white is the biggest thrill. That's *our* drama,
performed by actors I love – and the actual date when the world
gets to hear *our* words. 'That cast is incredible. And a March
broadcast date is brilliant.'

'Thought you'd be pleased.' She takes back the paper. 'Better
go and share this with the writers' room ruffians. Congratulations,
Joe.'

I smile, waiting for her to leave before I open my laptop again.
I don't want her to see my latest dream-plot for ridding the world
– and Otty – of Langham. Immature? Probably. But it makes me
feel power where I have none and that keeps me fighting.

Daphne doesn't move. 'Must be tough, having Fraser Langham
popping over to yours. Has he stayed yet?'

I swallow the obscenity I'm tempted to chuck back. 'No. They don't – he hasn't. Prefers his own environment, apparently.' *Under a rock, most likely.*

'Are you lonely, Joe?' Her voice is suddenly very close, very low, by my ear. 'Because you don't have to be.'

I freeze. 'I'm – fine.'

But the hesitation was there and she knows. A year ago, this would have been a result. Could it be now?

Her breath meets my ear in warm bursts as she laughs. 'I guess it depends on what you want. Personally, I don't see anything wrong with a bit of fun.' Her hand rests on my shoulder, her index finger brushing the space where my neck meets my collar. 'If you're interested, you know where I am.'

Shaken, I watch her leave. I should dismiss it immediately; tell her where to get off. But she knows the deal and when she puts it like that, why shouldn't it be possible?

I am lonely. I hate that word, but I loathe the reality more. Otty has Fraser. She isn't thinking about me. And lately the loneliest I am is when I'm writing by her side. Maybe a mindless fling would work. At least I wouldn't feel alone in a room of lovers.

But could I really go there?

'You know what we need,' Otty says the next day when we're trying to write the treatment document for season two.

'New brains.'

'No...'

'Superhero typing ability.'

'Joe...'

'Sentient robots. Ghost-writing monkeys. Fifteen-fingered aliens...'

Her sigh flutters the lime-green Post-it note that's stuck to the top of her laptop screen. I don't know if it's coincidental, but since we started writing about spies Otty has become obsessed with sticky-notes covering the cameras on her laptop, mobile and iPad. They have her enthusiastic bubble writing on them, too, like the script she'd scrawled across her mountain of book boxes when she moved in: motivational lines, quotes from Jed Mercurio and Lin-Manuel Miranda, or – like today's offering – mini-messages to us:

We rock!
#BAFTA4Us

'You aren't taking this seriously, are you?' she says.

'I'm deadly serious. We have a full treatment to write by Monday – exactly four days away – and we're nowhere near on track. Right now, a multi-dextrous extra-terrestrial would be flippin' handy.'

Otty raises her eyes to the copper lampshade in the ceiling above the kitchen table. 'We need a miracle.'

'Nah, come on. That kind of talk doesn't achieve anything.'

She props an elbow on the table and rubs her eyes. She's wearing black nail varnish today and I've been winding her up with Goth jokes since breakfast. 'Sorry. I'm just a bit freaked after seeing the press release.'

'Me too. That cast, eh?'

She turns to me. 'Oh my gosh, I know! Laura and Gus are perfectly cast. But it's *nuts*, because I follow both actors on Instagram and next March they're going to be acting out my storyline, saying our words. And Emma Spurgin Hussey as Dr Montgomery is *inspired*.' She blows out a long breath, almost dislodging the sticky note this time.

'Proves we knew what we were doing,' I say, the squeak in my voice all the proof Otty needs that this means everything to me, too. 'Excellent scripts attract the best casts.'

'And Gabriel Marley, eh?'

'I know.'

She nudges my arm. 'Know what I reckon? He saw your name on the script header and he was like, "That guy got me a BAFTA. Where do I sign?"'

'Yeah, thanks, but I don't think my name was even on it. And it might have had more to do with the fact that Russell's name *was*.'

Otty will not be moved on this, it seems. I'm then treated to what can only be described as a five-minute MarleyFest – my housemate's dubious impression of Gabriel Marley speaking lines from *Southside*. She makes me laugh, but when that subsides, I realise: 'Those lines are all from the episode I wrote.'

'Of course.'

'And you just did them verbatim.'

She shrugs. 'I told you, I watched that episode on repeat for months.'

'Because of Gabriel Marley.'

A small frown creases her brow. 'Because of you.'

What am I supposed to say to that? I can't say anything because my throat is suddenly tight with emotion.

So I don't.

I just turn to Otty and hug her.

She relaxes into my arms and it's only when we've been there a while I realise this is the first time I've held her properly since *that* night. It feels like we've salvaged a fragment of what we lost. Maybe, if we can save more…

Reluctantly I release her and we sit back. She observes me for just a second, the gentlest hint of colour across her cheeks. '*That* is not getting *this* written,' she says, pointing at the screen.

'Back to it, then?'

'Immediately.'

'Yes, boss.'

We return to the document growing far too slowly on the screen between us. But when I sneak a look back at Otty, she's smiling.

Chapter Forty-One

OTTY

I am not expecting a message from Chris. But when his text arrives, I decide I can't ignore it. I'm in Cannon Hill Park, taking a rare break from writing to enjoy the seasonal colour and let myself breathe. The text jars the equilibrium I've been feeling, but I don't hesitate in calling back.

The shock in his voice when he answers my call is palpable.

'I thought you might just text me back…'

'We need to talk,' I say.

I've been thinking about what I'd say to Chris if he contacted me again since that awful meeting in the cricket ground. Secretly, I was hoping he'd taken the hint and that would be the end of it, especially as I've heard nothing until now. But I need to draw a line here, leave him in no doubt.

'Mum was devastated,' he rushes. 'She still is.' It stings but I expected it to.

'I will always love your mum. But she can't dictate our lives.'

'What if I want her to?'

I stare down at the piles of newly fallen autumn leaves at my feet and watch them lift and shiver in the breeze. 'You don't want that, Chris. I know you don't.'

So much has happened since that day. I look up and realise I've absent-mindedly wandered towards the bandstand where Joe and I hid back in the summer. The memory of what happened, both before and after we visited it, is raw.

A robin hops across the concrete base of the bandstand and eyes me in the pause that follows. I wonder if he expected an audience this morning. Finally, I hear Chris sigh, a long, slow exhale of resignation.

'You don't want us, do you? You don't want me.'

'No.'

'And there's no way back?'

'I'm sorry.'

'Because of Joe.'

I close my eyes. 'No, because of me.'

'I just think you need time, Otty. Get this writing thing out of your system and then you can focus on us.'

I keep my breath steady and my words civil. 'I will never get writing out of my system, Chris. It's who I am. And I need to be with someone that respects that.'

'Well, maybe I need someone who'll respect *me*.'

It's meant as a dig, of course, but it's the truth. 'Yes, you do. And you'll find her. She's just not me.'

There's a shorter, more staccato rush of breath on the other end of the call. 'Your loss. I don't suppose you've told your father this?'

The robin's head flicks to one side when I open my eyes. We have spoken, very carefully policed chats on subjects that don't include Chris, Joe or any of the lumbering elephants passing between us. I don't think I've been any more willing to break that than he has. But we haven't spoken about what happened. 'Not yet.'

When Chris ends the call, I know what I have to do.

I climb the steps and sit in the spot where Joe held my hand, reaching into the pocket of my coat to fetch my mobile. It's just chilly enough to see my breath and when I find Dad's number, a ghostly cloud of white partially obscures his picture on the screen just before I select it.

'Bab?'

'Hey, Dad.'

'What's up?'

I inhale to steady myself. Sad enough that Dad now only thinks I contact him when a disaster has occurred. 'Nothing, I'm okay. Can we meet? Today?'

'Where?'

'The Tea Room in Cannon Hill Park?'

'Give me an hour and I'll meet you there.'

The Garden Tea Rooms at one edge of the park is a bit of an institution and just happens to be one of Dad's favourite places. It's a whitewashed, boxy 1930s-designed single-storey building and serves the kind of food I remember from cafés as a kid. Ham, egg and chips, jacket potato and cheese and enormous full English breakfasts, all served on the kind of pale green and pale pink plates Nan used in her little flat. It's one of those places that's part of my childhood.

I'm hoping that the nostalgia softens his mood. My life has moved on significantly since the day at the cricket and Dad needs to see it.

He arrives exactly one hour after I spoke to him, even though he lives less than twenty minutes away and the autumn Saturday traffic is light. I wonder if he's been sitting out the wait in his car, watching the dial on the old Bakelite watch his first foreman at Rover gave him as a present when he graduated from his apprenticeship. Biding his time.

'I bought us tea and a sticky bun,' I say, pushing a mug and plate to his side of the table.

'Ta, Otts.' He sits and takes an enormous gulp of tea. 'Was beginning to think you'd forgotten how to use your phone.'

'Sorry. Work's been crazy.'

'Hm.'

I try a different approach. 'They've just announced the cast for that drama Joe and I have been writing.'

He's midway into a bite of the white-icing-smothered cinnamon swirl, so he just nods.

'Really great actors,' I press on. 'It's going to be amazing.'

'On that Netflix thing, is it? Or the one where you talk into your telly?'

'Terrestrial. BBC One.'

Dad stops eating. 'You're pulling my leg. BBC? The proper BBC?'

I nod, a swell of pride within.

'Well. That's something.'

'I'm so excited. We both are…'

Instantly, Dad's face darkens. 'Joe. Would this be your colleague, housemate, *just-a-friend* or boyfriend?'

I wish I knew.

'Just Joe. I'm not with him, Dad. He was trying to help.'

'By hoodwinking your family? Some help.'

'He told Chris he was my boyfriend so Chris would leave me

alone. I didn't ask him to, but yes, when it happened, it was the perfect – the *easiest* solution.'

'You loved Chris,' Dad says, as if I've forgotten.

'I did. Once.'

'You were happy. You told all of us that you two were happy.'

I stare at my untouched Chelsea bun. The syrup on the glacé cherry sparkles stickily in the bright light. 'I wasn't happy for a long time. I tried really hard to be.'

Dad pushes his empty plate away. 'Well, you made a damn good show of it.'

There is no answer to that. 'I'm not getting back together with Chris. I need you to hear that.'

'Sheila's beside herself.'

'She needs to accept it, too. I'm sorry, Dad, I'm not proud of how it all played out with Joe, but I can't apologise for trying to dissuade Chris. He can't make me happy. I'd make him miserable in time, too.'

My dad is quiet then. I wonder if he is taking in what I've said or preparing his next volley. The day I told him that I'd called off the engagement and left Chris, he told me it was just nerves and that it would all be fine in the morning. And that was his stance for months. Sheila carried on as though Chris and I were still together. She stopped bringing wedding magazines over, but that was her only concession. I couldn't be angry with her because I love her as much as if I were her blood niece. And it was always there when I was working with them over the next year – their quiet assumption that I'd come to my senses soon.

'This writing – it's what you want?'

'It is.'

'And you're certain you've not made a mistake with Chris?'

'Yes.'

Dad twists his mug on the brown puddle of tea that's spilled onto the table. 'Then you've got to do what you think is best. We might not like it – and I don't know why you can't just be happy with Chris – but it's your choice, bab. Your life.'

At that moment, I could hug him. It's a big step forward. 'Thank you.'

He shakes his head and his eyes fix on me. 'And if Joe makes you happy—'

So near and yet…

'Dad. I'm not with Joe.'

He stares at me. 'Why not?'

No point delaying what I was going to tell him. 'Because I'm seeing someone else…'

I wasn't planning to see Fraser today, but the conversation with Dad makes up my mind. I still don't think he got it, even after an hour of explaining.

But what about Joe?

Over and over.

I work with Joe. I live with Joe. But I'm seeing Fraser.

It would have been comical, if it didn't hurt every time he asked.

Even now, as I'm standing outside Fraser's apartment building, pressing the intercom, Dad's question is still playing in my head.

But what about Joe?

'He-*llo*?' Fraser's greeting makes me smile. In his accent, every word sounds musical.

'Hi, it's me,' I say, the door buzzer sounding before I finish speaking.

But what about Joe?

He meets me as the lift doors part, his arms strong and his kisses warm. I give in to the familiarity of his embrace, pushing every other thought away as we move into his apartment.

'It's so good to see you,' he murmurs, between kisses. 'I've missed you all day.'

'Me too,' I reply, wanting to say more but losing the words in the rush of emotion that follows. Fraser wants me without me having to prove anything or persuade him. He doesn't care what anyone else thinks – all he sees is me. It's powerful and real and right now everything I need.

'Stay,' he whispers, his words warm against my neck.'

'Yes,' I say, my mind made up.

I don't want to think about it anymore. I'm not with Joe. I'm with Fraser. It's time I started making the most of what I have.

Chapter Forty-Two

JOE

Otty didn't come home last night.

She *always* comes home.

Her bed isn't slept in. No sign of her car. And now I feel like a crazed stalker in my own home.

It shouldn't bother me but it does. And *that* bothers me. Even coffee isn't helping this morning. I stare at the dark screen of my phone where it sits on the kitchen table. Should I text her? As a concerned mate just checking she's okay? My finger hovers over the screen.

Ugh. My phone clatters back to the table.

Who am I kidding? There's only one reason I would text: to let her know that I'm here. To make her feel guilty for not coming home, for being with Fraser, right now, doing whatever they are doing. When did I become that person?

There are four slices in the toaster going cold. I put them in an hour ago and haven't left my chair since. Besides, I'm not hungry. I don't want to think about it, but I've just spent most of the morning doing exactly that.

She doesn't want me. I have to let her go.

269

I pick up my stone-cold coffee and shift myself upright to make a fresh jug. Everything aches today. I should probably go out – find some lunch, do some exercise – anything to stop me going over this.

I pull the glass jug from underneath the percolator and move it to the sink to fill it. As I do, something small, square and bright orange flutters to the floor. Bending down, I find it's one of Otty's daft motivational sticky notes. I turn it over to read the bouncy bubble script:

**We are such stuff
as dreams are made on.
The Tempest, Act IV Scene 1**

She's mentioned that before. It's her favourite quote from a Shakespeare play. Strange to think that the thing we've been tearing our hair out over for the past two weeks with this treatment is actually the stuff of our dreams. You have to love it or else you wouldn't put yourself through it. If we stop and really take it in, it's still a dream come true.

I have another dream, it turns out. It began the other day when we ended up hugging. It's set a spark burning in me again, like it did before. Possibility is a dangerous drug. It started me thinking that perhaps there was a way back for us. I wish I hadn't listened to it now.

It's gone 3 p.m. by the time Otty rocks up and I'm annoyed. We were supposed to be spending most of the day sketching out the first episode of *Eye, Spy* season two after Russell and Langham accepted our series treatment. But I'm not about to do that without her. It's our gig, our script. She *knows* this. So why stay out? I've had no text, no call, nothing to tell me where she is or what time I should expect her.

I meet her in the hall, a shadow-Joe, waiting to raise hell.

'Hey,' she says, passing me to hang her coat on the banister. She's still in the same clothes she was wearing yesterday, which makes her staying with Fraser an unplanned, *spontaneous* thing. And that makes it worse on so many levels.

'I thought you were coming back this morning.'

'I was just… later than I expected.' She's pulling off her boots, pocketing her phone and dumping her bag at the bottom of the stairs.

'It's after 3 p.m.'

'I know, sorry.'

'So, where have you been?'

Otty straightens, instantly frowning. 'I stayed at Fraser's.'

'Spur-of-the-moment thing, was it? Or do you like wearing the same clothes two days in a row?'

Too far, Joe.

But also, too late to stop what's coming. 'No, Joe, say what you really think.'

She shoulders past me into the kitchen. I hear the thud of cupboard doors and crockery being slammed onto worktops. I should let her bash and crash her way through it before I attempt to go in there. But I am in no mood for blatant common sense. I follow her in.

'What I *really* think is that you should have called me if you knew you weren't going to be back till later. We're supposed to be working.'

'I'm back now,' she snaps, her back to me.

'You could have called me. Sent a text. *Sorry, Joe, stayed at Fraser's.* Or *Back at 3 p.m....*.' She's ignoring me now, isn't she? I fix my eyes on her and add,

'Or *Gone shagging. Back later.*'

Otty says nothing, the teaspoon crashing into the sink when she's stirred her tea.

I fold my arms and wait. She moves from the sink, walks straight past me as if I'm not there and sits at the kitchen table. A little thrown, I stay where I am. She fetches her laptop from the centre of the table, unzipping its protective sleeve and setting it before her, screen open. And I'm still there, like a bodyguard, definitely not moving now because this has become a battle of wills and Otty is *not* going to win. She sips her tea, unwinds the scarf from her neck, pulls an elastic band from her wrist and twists her hair up into a messy bun on the top of her head. I quietly fume as I watch her carefully place a notebook, pen and mobile phone beside her laptop, drink her tea and metaphorically dig in.

Finally, she turns her head slowly to look at me. 'Well?'

'Well, *what?*'

'Are we working or not?'

I glare at her, considering my options. What I want to do is storm out. Yell. Cause a scene. All of which would have been options, had I not just been standing here like a plank for five long minutes.

If I wasn't so angry with her, I might be impressed.

So I take my seat beside Otty like a chastened kid, hating that it looks like I'm backing down.

We work. Words are written. But it's not fun. Or the *stuff that dreams are made on.* It's a long, frustrating, side-glance-heavy, bitten-back-fury slog.

At 8 p.m. we reach a natural break and grudgingly agree to call it a night. Otty closes her laptop and turns to me.

'Have we got everything we need for tomorrow?'

'For what?'

Her sigh is the heaviest she's heaved today – and that's saying something. 'For the party?'

Bollocks.

I'd completely forgotten. Back when Russ and Langham accepted the treatment, we decided to invite our fellow writers to ours for a laid-back party. Sort of a housewarming-meets-almost-Christmas-meets-treatment-completion celebration, although we're not formally calling it anything other than a gathering at our house. Some housewarming: if things between us remain as they are it'll practically be the Arctic in here.

'I'll grab stuff in the morning. Um, write me a list, yeah?'

'Right.' I can't tell if this is another mark against me. To be honest, I've lost count. 'Fraser's coming, by the way.'

Okay, *that's* not happening. 'He isn't.'

'Yes, he is.'

'He's *not*, for two reasons: firstly, we promised everyone it would be writers only, not management; secondly, Fraser doesn't know about the party.'

Otty squares up to me and I hold my ground. Round three? Four? Eighty-seven? 'Firstly, I never made that promise and secondly, he asked me if he could come, so someone's told him about it.'

I want to hit back, throw something into the fray that will stop

Otty in her tracks. She's already made me look like an idiot once today: I won't give her another chance.

And then the solution arrives. 'Well, Daphne's coming, too.'

Direct hit. 'No, she isn't.'

'She is. Because while you were loving it up with Langham, I was getting together with her.'

As soon as the words leave me, I hate myself. Otty's been sensitive about Daphne since the beginning and it was the perfect weapon. But I'm stunned by my own heartlessness. Not least because it now means I have to go through with it.

She seems to shrink a little, her eyes defiant, trained on me.

'Really?'

'Yes.'

'So when you told me there was nothing going on with you…?'

'There wasn't then. There is now. She's been chasing me for a while. Guess it was just time to… give in.' My resolve drains with each syllable but it's too late. It's said. And I've just inflicted a wound on my best friend. What kind of self-serving bastard am I?

Otty just stares and for a minute I'm worried she'll cry. I don't think I could cope with that. But then the resolve I've seen her draw from so many times before comes back. Chin lifting, shoulders strengthening, jaw set. 'Good. We can all have a great time.' There is no joy in her voice.

She keeps her eyes trained on me as she pulls in a breath. And then she walks out. I hear the kick of her heels against the stairs, the deliberate soft click of her bedroom door.

Not a slam. I could have dealt with yelling and door slamming. But her stillness and control is the starkest, sharpest retaliation.

The room echoes with her absence.

I can't back down or admit I lied. I have no choice but to see it through. So I find Daphne's number, type a text and send it before I have chance to rethink.

You said you wanted fun. I'm up for it if you still are. Joe xx

Chapter Forty-Three

OTTY

The last thing I want to be doing is hosting a party. Looking at Joe's face, I reckon he feels the same.

But we promised everyone. And Rona has been buzzing about it for weeks. So, here we are, pretending we didn't just knock seven bells out of each other, setting out the house for our guests, who will be arriving in less than three hours.

Including Daphne.

I can't believe I didn't see that coming. I mean, she's been all over him for weeks. I just thought – I just *hoped* Joe wasn't interested. Not that I have any right to tell him what to do in his private life. I have Fraser – and when Joe had the opportunity, he didn't want me.

The house is filled with the smell of two types of slow-cooked chilli on the hob and trays of mini beef Wellingtons and veggie sausage rolls baking in the oven. It should be perfect, but it isn't.

I can't do tonight with us barely talking. One of us has to attempt to be an adult.

I slip into the kitchen and switch Joe's coffee machine on. Then I take a couple of veggie rolls, blowing on my fingers as I liberate them from the baking sheet. I pour coffee, pile the rolls on a plate and head into the living room, where Joe is moving furniture.

'Peace offering?' I say.

He looks up and I'm relieved to see his features soften. 'Go on then.'

'They're hot. Be careful.'

He takes a veggie roll and juggles it between his fingers. 'Noted.'

'Can we just forget that row happened, please? I can't be here, smiling for everyone tonight, pretending we're okay if we're not.'

Joe nods, crumbs falling all over the place as he fails to eat gracefully. Then his face creases and his laughter fills the space. 'Sorry.'

I try not to laugh, but it's impossible. It feels unfamiliar but so very missed.

'I'm sorry, Otts.'

'Me too. Can I tell you why I didn't come home?'

'I think I can guess why you didn't come home.'

'No – not that. I saw Dad.'

Joe looks at me. 'When?'

'Saturday lunchtime.'

'How did that go?'

'It was the best chat we've had in a while and I think he finally got that I wasn't getting back with Chris. But then he got it into his head that you and me really were together, which is, you know, insane.'

'Bit harsh.'

'You know what I mean.'

'Told you I was a better actor than you give me credit for.' He risks resting a hand against my arm. 'At least he's got the message about Chris. Your dad's a good bloke. Just give him time with the other stuff.'

'Thanks.'

'And you've always got me as a mate, yeah? I know it's been rough lately, but look at us, Otts: we always bounce back. And we're still here.' He kicks a kink in the rug to flatten it. 'I've never had anyone in my life as reliable as that. That's why this—' he points a finger from me to him, 'works. So, we'll have a great party and show everyone that, okay?'

'Okay.'

'Good. Now, bump it out…'

He offers his fist in some kind of strange Nineties cool-kid move and, laughing, I fist-bump it as earnestly as I can manage.

An hour later the first writers have arrived. Jake and Tom are in the kitchen with Joe, Reece has taken up residence by the stereo and has assumed unofficial DJ duties, while I've just brought bottles of cider from the cooler for Rona and me. The house hums and everyone is in the best mood – such a contrast to the increasingly tense writers' room.

'This is great,' Rona says, helping herself to a handful of pretzels from the bowls Joe and I set up on the coffee table. 'All of us kicking back, not an index card or script in sight. And no bosses watching us.'

I drop my head. 'Actually, Fraser's coming.'

Rona lowers her bottle and gives me a stare that could slice steel. 'You're joking? Why?'

'He's my boyfriend. He wanted to come.'

'I'll bet he did.'

'And Joe's invited Daphne.'

'What? Did he have a lobotomy at lunchtime? Bloody hell, Otts, what is wrong with the pair of you?'

'Nothing's wrong. We're just two grown adults with relationships.'

'I beg to differ. You are two frightened kids in total denial.'

'About what?'

She shakes her head. 'Really? You really think I don't know what happened with the two of you?'

I swallow hard. 'You don't know…'

Rona grabs my elbow and frogmarches me to the bay window where there's a little space away from keen ears. 'Then let me make an educated guess: you and Joe slept together.'

'Keep your voice down!'

'I knew it!'

'Rona, you can't tell another living soul, do you understand? It was a mistake, we both owned it and we're working our way through it…'

'Oh, is that what you call it? I just thought you were two hurting souls ripping each other to shreds. My mistake.'

I have no answer for that. Is it really that obvious?

'It was nothing. We were drunk. I… I don't remember any of it.'

She's not buying any of this. 'But your heart does.'

'Please, leave it alone. There are no answers. Believe me, I've looked.'

'Oh, *mate*…'

I blink back tears. 'Can we talk about something else?'

Her arm goes around me. 'Sure. Sure, we can. I didn't mean to upset you. What time is your hunky Scotsman getting here?'

'Soon,' I sniff.

'Well, there you are then. You can lust after him to your heart's content. Annoying though he is, he could still take my mind off most things.' She grins and gives me a squeeze. 'Does he have a brother?'

Our friends are making themselves comfortable, bringing life and colour and laughter into our home. The house seems to swell with it, the joy of company making its rooms brighter, wider, even more welcoming. At least I still have this, I think. I catch Joe looking at me from the hall. I send him a smile and he raises his hand. But he feels a lifetime away.

An hour later, I've served food and every available space is filled with friends huddled over bowls. Rona and Reece declare the vegetarian chilli and veggie rolls a success. Conversation ebbs and flows like a gentle summer ocean and everything is calm.

I feel easier, too, now that we're here and everyone is having a good time. And what's strange is that Rona knowing the truth makes it a little lighter to carry. I hope she doesn't let Joe know though. He seems happy enough, chatting animatedly with Jake and Tom on beanbags by the fireplace.

The doorbell rings and I jump up to answer it, gesturing to Joe to stay where he is when he attempts to escape the beanbag's clutches.

'Better late than never,' Fraser grins on the doorstep. I'm glad he's here. His skin is warm when I stroke his face and his kiss ready and familiar.

'Now that's a welcome,' he grins. 'How about we skip the party and just go to see your room?'

'Behave,' I say, patting his chest. 'Plenty of time for that later.'

'I will hold you to that, Ottilie.' He peers into the living room. 'So, the gang's all here, are they?'

'They are. Look – before we go in – you're here as my boyfriend, not their boss.'

He nuzzles into my neck. 'Boyfriend? I like the sound of that…'

'Fraser, I'm serious. This is supposed to be us kicking back after the treatment going in for season two. We're just hanging out, having some food, and chilling. Okay?'

He chuckles and holds out his hands. 'Loud and clear.'

It's only when I see my colleagues tense as Fraser walks in that I understand why I shouldn't have let this happen. Everyone is polite and friendly, but the atmosphere mutes a little. I trail after him for the first ten minutes, ready to stamp out any fires he unwittingly starts, but after a while people seem more relaxed and I thankfully let him go.

'He seems happy enough.' Joe is by my side with two bottles. 'Another one?'

I accept it. 'Thanks. What time is Daphne getting here?'

'Any minute. I've made her promise to behave.'

That'll be a first if she does, I think. 'I've said the same to Fraser. So far, he seems to be playing ball.'

Joe takes a large swig of beer and looks at me. 'The thing is, Otts, Daphne and me...'

The trill of the doorbell summons his attention.

'Sorry – I'd better...'

I deliberately turn away from the door. I don't want to see the moment they meet. As it transpires, it doesn't make a difference. Surprised cat-calls sound from my friends.

'Go, Joe!' Jake calls, while Tom applauds.

Reece takes one look and grimaces. 'I'm going to need more beer.'

'I'll get you one,' I rush. Because I don't want to be there when Joe and Daphne walk in.

We've finished one coolbox-load of bottles already, so I go out into the small, original pantry just off the side of the kitchen to fetch more.

'It's *gross*,' Rona says behind me. 'You'd think they'd leave that until they're alone.'

My heart plummets to the red terracotta tiles beneath my feet.

'Here, hand us some bottles,' she says. 'Otty?'

'Yes, sorry.'

I scramble myself together and pass an armful of bottles to her. Between us, we tip fresh ice into the cool box and replenish the stock of beer and cider.

'There is a lot of drinking going on in there,' Rona chuckles. 'I hope you're prepared for serious sleepovers happening tonight.' Shock paints her expression. 'Not Daphne – I didn't mean her.'

I kick the cool box a little too forcefully into position beside the kitchen table. 'Don't worry about it.'

'Hun…'

'Honestly, don't.'

But Rona is not one to give up. Right now I wish she were. 'You're in love with him, aren't you?'

In the relative stillness of the kitchen, her question waits.

'I don't think…'

'Hey. I'm not blind, Otts.'

'I don't love him.'

'Okay. Now try saying that to my face like you actually believe it.'

I look at her, just as Joe and Daphne walk in. Daphne is draped around Joe's shoulders, one perfectly manicured hand jealously guarding his chest.

'Otty! Great party!' she drawls. 'And the house is *perfect*.'

I feel Rona watching me as I smile back.

No point saying anything now.

282

Chapter Forty-Four

JOE

It's too cold to be in the garden without a jacket. That doesn't seem to worry Daphne, who is energetically kissing me. I mean, it's nice, but it's like we're both trying too hard. That shouldn't be how it feels.

I push the critical voice away and throw myself into our kiss. Daphne murmurs between us and wraps her arms around my neck, her fingers pushing up into my hair.

Last year, whenever I imagined this moment – which, admittedly, was quite a lot – I didn't picture it being like this.

I finally manage to pull back. 'Come on, it's freezing out here. Let's get inside.'

'Are you cold, Joseph? I think I can find a few ways to warm you up.' She peers over the top of her glasses at me.

'I bet,' I smile back. *I bet?* Hardly the language of love, is it? 'But we should eat something first, don't you think?'

Daphne considers this. I'm starting to lose the feeling in my toes and I'm wishing again that I'd realised we were going to the garden when Daphne took my hand, so I could have brought another layer to wear.

Otty's expression when Daphne pulled me out of the room – it should have made me feel better about Langham. But it was like a wrecking ball to my stomach. She looked so lost…

'One more kiss before we go,' Daphne says and I oblige, more to distract my mind from the snapshot of Otty plastered front and centre there.

It's a relief to get back inside. My fingers are still blue as I scoop chilli into a bowl for Daphne. She wanders off to the living room and I take the opportunity to force air into my lungs.

'Someone's happy with their date.'

I bristle. 'You had chilli yet, Fraser?'

'Just coming to get some. I've been told I must try the veggie one. Otty was insistent.'

I nod at the second pan on the hob. 'Help yourself.'

Langham positions himself next to me and slowly stirs the pan. 'I take my hat off to you, Joe. That treatment for season two is brilliant.'

'We worked hard on it.'

'You did. Great job.'

To my horror, Langham holds his hand out over the bubbling saucepans.

'Congratulations. Would you shake my hand?'

I can hardly refuse, can I? We share the swiftest handshake in history and go back to serving our chilli.

'I know things haven't been easy between the two of us, Joe. But I hope you know I have considerable professional respect for your work. And I respect you for the friend you are to Otty. She depends on you, I think. And I realise as her friend you might not think me worthy of her, but I promise you, I will be.'

Go away, you smooth-talking git… 'Appreciate that, thanks. I'm just looking out for her.'

'I can tell how close you are. That's great. Bit daunting for the chap coming in between you, I'll admit.'

There's just a hint of vulnerability about him and this time it isn't the fake humility he uses for effect. It's real. I think the guy really is in love with Otty.

And that only makes me less willing to play ball.

'I can imagine. Otts and I are very close. I don't think I've ever had a friendship like it.'

He hesitates and I sense a question he doesn't want to ask yet.

An advantage is what I've wanted. 'I mean, it would be easy to misinterpret that kind of closeness…'

Fraser stops stirring the pan. Eyes trained ahead, he lets the question fly. 'But you've never…?'

I feign surprise. 'What? Oh… That would be awkward, wouldn't it?'

'Yeah. Good job she's not that kind of woman.'

And just like that, we reach a point of advantage. He clearly thinks it's possible even if now he's doing his best to convince himself he's wrong. And right then, I hate him. I hate that he is so convinced he has the measure of me, that he doesn't think Otty would want to be with me. *Shows what you know, Langham.*

'I mean, it only happened once.'

'What?'

'Just once. I think it took us both by surprise. It's behind us now, of course,' I add, my tone suggesting it's anything but the case.

I can see his breathing increase, the flush of red claim his neck. He looks straight at me, a storm-cloud-grey stare threatening thunder. 'You slept with her?'

'It was one time. Ancient history.' *It could happen again*, I will into my voice. *It could happen when you least expect it and you won't know because she's here with me and you aren't…*

It's out before I can think better of it, the game spiralling as soon as it's released.

He shrugs it off, of course. Pretends he thinks I've played a cruel joke at his expense. But when I leave the kitchen, I sense the damage smouldering in my wake.

It doesn't feel like the victory it was supposed to be.

But it's said.

By 1 a.m. only three stragglers remain – Daphne, Langham and Rona. We really need to call time and get to bed. Trust Otty and me to organise a party the first night of a working week. Saturday next time, I think. Or Friday, just to be on the safe side. I knew my writers' room colleagues could drink, but the amount they've put away is staggering. Russell better not be in the mood for yelling tomorrow.

'Want me to stay?' Daphne purrs next to me.

'Better not tonight,' I say, pulling her to me to kiss her brow. 'Work tomorrow.'

'Next weekend at mine, then?'

'Sure. Try stopping me.' I wish I didn't sound like I do when my mum suggests getting our disparate and very strange family together at Christmas. I can't very well complain about being lonely and then pass up the chance of a night with the woman I'm dating. I just can't do it tonight. Other things are clouding my mind.

Langham *seems* okay. He was with Otty on the sofa within a minute of my leaving the kitchen and they certainly looked cosy together. Now I can see Otty nodding a little, nestled into the crook of Langham's arm.

Is he staying over?

My stomach tightens.

Hopefully not.

I'm still watching Langham, though. I shouldn't have said what I did. I would have been incandescent if a bloke had done that to me about my new girlfriend. But he's a bigger man than I am.

Rona yawns and puts her empty beer bottle on the hearth. 'Right, dudes, that's me.'

'You off?' Otty pushes herself stiffly upright, pausing to plant a soft kiss on Langham's lips. 'Thanks for coming.'

Rona grins. 'Night, lovebirds. Joe, see you in the morning.'

'Back in the room!' I raise my almost drained bottle.

'Back in the rooooooom,' she replies, stomping out to the hall after Otty like a slow-motion Arnie in *Terminator*.

Over on the sofa, Langham looks from his departing girlfriend to me. His nod of acknowledgement comes a second too late. He's probably annoyed. I don't blame him. Just as long as he keeps it directed at me and not Otty.

'Joe,' Daphne nudges me.

'Hey.'

'Are you sure I can't tempt you?'

'Next weekend. I'll make it up to you.'

'I'll hold you to that.' She moves off the arm of the chair and holds out her hand. 'Walk me to the door.'

'See you tomorrow, Daphne,' Langham says as we pass.

'You will. Now you behave if you're staying, Mr Langham.'

'I'm not tonight. But thanks for the advice.' His eyes slide to me.

I usher Daphne out of the room. In the hall we meet Otty and there's a little awkward dance as she skirts us to go back to Langham. It's all still new, I tell myself. It won't always be like this.

As I kiss Daphne goodnight the living-room door closes softly.

It takes longer for her to leave than I want, but eventually I'm standing on the doorstep, my arm raised as her taxi pulls away. The beginning of a frost sparkles across the street. My breath rises in unhurried swirls. I should probably give Otty and Langham space, go straight upstairs and crash.

I shut the night out and stand in the hall. My phone is in the living room. I don't need it and it doesn't matter if it stays resting on the mantelpiece till morning.

I should probably leave it.

But I'm not going to.

Maybe it's my conscience kicking in, about two hours too late, but I need to check Langham's all right. It's very quiet in there. That's a good sign, right?

I open the door – and freeze.

They're kissing.

Not just the kind of show-kissing I've been doing with Daphne all night. *Real*, heart-stopping, body, mind and soul kissing.

I'm out and up the stairs before they even notice. In the safety of my room I get straight into bed, sticking my headphones in and my music on. He said he wasn't staying but given what I've just witnessed, Otty may well be changing his mind.

I put any remaining questions to rest as my head hits the pillow. I don't need to worry about Langham: he's doing just fine.

Chapter Forty-Five

OTTY

Last night, I made a decision: I've chosen Fraser.

I've wasted so much time letting my heart get battered by Joe. But it's unfair to give Fraser anything less than 100 per cent. That's what he's given me from our first date. Last night I realised, I've never had somebody so certain about me.

Joe will always be in my life. I know he will. The glimpses of the old us I've enjoyed in the last few weeks give me hope that, when all else is done, our friendship will stand.

In that respect, I am blessed.

Nan was a blessings-counter. She loved that old Bing Crosby song from the film *White Christmas* that he sings to Rosemary Clooney late at night, over liverwurst sandwiches and glasses of buttermilk. Neither can sleep, so Bing sings his remedy – counting blessings instead of sheep. Nan used to sing it in that tremulous soprano voice of hers, swaying in her bobble-slippers and second-best skirt that she wore around the house. She kept an old empty Hellman's mayonnaise jar on top of her fridge, a cross-stitched band fixed around it. Surrounded by faded flowers, looping stems and tiny hearts, a verse read:

-: OUT WITH DARKNESS :-
-: OUT WITH FEAR :-
-: COUNT YOUR BLESSINGS :-
-: KEEP THEM HERE :-

Nan carried a small notebook and tiny pencil in the pocket of her cardigan and I'd often see her stop, tear out a piece of paper and scribble something down, then head to the kitchen and post it into the jar. At the end of each month, she would spend an hour sitting at the square table in her sheltered-housing flat, taking out each blessing and reading it.

'They give me hope that more are waiting to be found,' she'd tell me. 'A promise of future treasure. Keeps me moving forward, looking for the next one, you see. You can't be a treasure hunter if you walk backwards.'

I feel lighter, as if a weight I've dragged unnecessarily around with me for months has finally gone. And I can't wait to see Fraser to show him who I am.

His Otty.

He isn't at Ensign yet, but Joe and I came in early because the script meetings begin today for *Eye, Spy* season two. Another reason why having a party last night probably wasn't the wisest choice.

Despite delicate heads, there's a real buzz around the writers' room table. Advertisements for the first season of *Eye, Spy* are appearing across the city, on huge billboards on the flyover and lining the section of the M6 that links to Spaghetti Junction; on the city streets and carried on the side of the city's buses. BBC One is running the first teaser trailers in amongst the seasonal programmes, even though two of the episodes are still being filmed and the rest are in post-production. It's thrilling and unbelievably scary all at once. *Eye, Spy* is already being billed as one of the must-see television events of next year.

'My team!' Russell says, walking in. 'We all good? Excellent. So. It begins. Again. Joe, Otty, do you want to run us through the overall pitch for this season and then we'll move to your treatment.'

'Shouldn't we wait for Fraser?' I ask.

'He's running late, so we'll make a start.'

As everyone consults the series pitch, Joe and I move to the head of the table to prepare.

'You okay?' Joe whispers.

'Yeah. You?'

'We'll walk it,' he smiles.

I'm proud of the work we've done. And as we talk everyone through the elements that will make this season even better than the first, I'm struck by how far I've come since the first time we studied a pitch. I have achieved far beyond anything I thought I might.

Tom, Reece, Rona and Jake nod along, Russell watching us all from his usual seat. We're a team now, not a motley crew of writers living in fear of Russell's culls.

But where is Fraser?

We break for coffee at 11 a.m. and I duck out into the empty side of the eleventh floor to call him.

'*Hi, this is Fraser Langham. I'm unable to take your call at the moment, but please leave a message…*'

I know he drank quite a bit last night but could that have delayed him? I can't imagine a hangover stopping Fraser from doing anything. Might last night's chilli have disagreed with him? Not sure how I'd navigate giving him food poisoning. That would be embarrassing…

Aware I don't have much time, I compose a text, sending it as I walk back to Ensign.

Are you okay? Missing you xx

'Any sign?' Rona asks when I return.

'None. And his phone's going to voicemail.'

'Hangover? Dodgy belly?'

I shrug. 'Possibly.'

'I wouldn't worry, hun. He's probably got the mother of all hangovers and he's sleeping it off. He looked tired last night.'

He did. I'd half-wondered if he'd ask to stay but he'd said he needed to sleep. I'm glad, actually. I was exhausted after all the weirdness with Joe and the last thing any of us needed was sharing an awkward breakfast together this morning.

Placated, I go back into the writers' room.

But by the end of the day, there's still no sign of him. No answer to my messages, all calls reaching the same voicemail message.

'Don't worry,' Joe says when we're driving home.

But I am worried.

Since we started seeing each other, Fraser has been the one who texts, the one who calls first. He was like an excited puppy and I'll admit that it was overwhelming in the beginning. But I think that's another outward sign of his confidence in us. And it's only now, in the absence of it, that I realise how much a part of my every day that's become.

And so the mind games begin.

He'll call at 6 p.m. when he knows I'm home.

6 p.m.: no call.

He tends to work late if he's at home. I'll text while he's working.

Number of texts sent: 4. Number received: 0.

He'll be in bed by 10 p.m., 11 p.m. at the latest. He'll call me then.

No call. No text. No change in the message when I call instead.

I carry my phone around with me, a poor excuse for a talisman, convinced that if I set it down for even a minute, I'll miss Fraser's call. But I'm starting to panic.

'Otty, sit down.' Joe is watching me from the sofa, my unplanned floorshow apparently amusing him.

'I can't.'

'You're going to wear a hole in that carpet if you carry on.'

'I'm okay, just let me be.'

'He'll be in bed now. If we did happen to poison him yesterday he's probably only just stopped barfing.'

'*Joe.* You're not helping.'

Joe's sigh meets the creak of the sofa frame as he stands. 'And you need to come with me.' He meets me mid-pace and firmly but gently leads me to one of the armchairs. Reluctantly, I sit. Joe crouches down in front of me, so that his face is at my eye level.

'Stop worrying. Fraser is big enough and ugly enough – okay not even remotely ugly, the lucky git – to take care of himself. As soon as he's better, he'll call.'

But he doesn't.

By 11 a.m. next day it's all I can think about. It's just so unlike him. I need to focus on the scripts we're all developing and this is threatening to steal my focus completely. It's time to bite the bullet.

While my colleagues buzz around the coffee machine I slip past them and head for Russell's office.

'Yes?'

I peer around the door. 'Hi. Can I ask you something?'

'Of course! Come in. Take a seat and a load off. It's going well in there, Otty. You and Joe should be proud.'

I sit in the chair nearest the desk. 'Thanks, we are.'

'Good. Now, what's up?'

'Do you know where Fraser is?'

There's a pause before he answers. Pauses are never good.

'He has a project we've been talking about for a while. He asked me if he could take a couple of days to work on it. I figured you and Joe are handling everything with the team so I agreed.'

'Is that why he's not answering his phone?'

'I would hazard a guess.'

'Is he at home?'

'To the best of my knowledge.'

'Okay. Thank you.' I start to stand.

'Try not to worry,' Russell says. 'I've known Fraser for a long time. He sometimes needs his own space.'

It's meant to reassure me, but it has the opposite effect.

I return to the writers' room and we begin the process of plotting out each episode, discussing the best way to tell the story Joe, Russell, Fraser and I have devised. Everyone is upbeat today, but I'm adrift in their midst. By the time we leave at 6 p.m., I've made up my mind.

If he won't answer my calls and texts, I'm going to see him.

'Otts, some of us are heading to the pub,' Rona says as I'm on my way out. 'Russell's coming too. You up for it?'

'Sorry, I have to be somewhere.'

Rona frowns. 'Are you okay?'

'I'm fine. Family stuff,' I say because nobody is likely to question that, least of all Rona, who jokes about her chaotic family all the time.

She grimaces. 'Well, if you require beer afterwards just give us a call.'

Pulling up outside Fraser's apartment building it's a relief to see his car parked in its usual space. It's a clear night, and already the late-November temperature is dropping. My fingers sting with cold when I press the button for his apartment. It rings three times – my heart contracting with each one. If he's here and still doesn't answer, what does that mean?

Finally, after the fifth ring, there's a click and a haze of static. 'Otty.'

'Let me in.'

I'm past asking politely.

The buzzer sounds and I yank open the door, hurrying inside. The lift takes an age to reach his floor. When the doors open an empty hall waits. No warm embrace to pull me in, no hasty kisses to greet me. His front door is open, but the absence of him hits me like a blast of cold air.

When I go in, Fraser is sitting in his armchair, looking out of the floor-to-ceiling window at the spread of darkened city. His elbows rest on his knees, chin on his folded hands as if he's keeping words prisoner behind his fingers. Slowly, his eyes move to me. In the half-light they look dark, endless.

'I've been worried about you.'

He stares back.

'Russell said you were working on something.'

A slow blink.

Fear and irritation spike my chest. 'Did you get my texts? Or my messages?'

His eyes flicker at that. But he still doesn't speak.

'Okay, I'm not leaving until you tell me what's going on.'

'You tell me.' I've never heard his voice sound like that. Low, heavy with insinuation. Alien.

I am tired and scared and I've had twenty-four hours of worry. That is not an acceptable answer and I am more than ready for a fight, if that's what he wants.

'*Talk* to me. What's going on?'

'When were you planning on letting me know that you slept with your housemate?'

All of the air sucks out of the room.

'What?' I can't hide the guilt in my whisper.

'Honesty. That's what I thought you were all about. That's what made me want to be with you. Turns out you are as much of a liar as anyone.'

'I didn't lie.'

'You didn't tell me the truth. It's the same thing.'

'You never asked me…'

He straightens and I sense the storm building. 'You never *told* me.'

I can't believe I'm hearing this. How does he know? Who told him? This isn't my fault and suddenly I'm angry. I'm angry and scared and not about to let him talk to me like that because I have done nothing wrong. 'And you haven't told me everyone you've slept with before you met me. Because that's not what people do when they're just starting out.'

'Joe Carver isn't ancient history, Otty. He's very much in your life. His bed is a wall away from yours.'

'What are you saying? That I'm shagging Joe behind your back?'

'I don't know. Are you?'

There is no coming back from that. 'Is that what you think of me?'

'It's what Joe thinks of you.'

'*What?*'

Fraser stands and walks towards me. I can't move.

'Joe told me you were in his bed. He seemed to think it could happen again.'

'When did he say that?'

'At the party. I have to admit, it made a lot of sense. You're always with him, locked in your closed little world, all the in-jokes and laughter. You see me but then you scurry home to him. At work, at home. Must be hard to resist when it's so close, all of the time.'

Hot tears sting my eyes. How dare he say that? And how dare Joe?

'All I have ever been is be honest with you. And not that what I did before I met you is any of your business, but what happened with Joe was a mistake I made, before I even knew you existed.'

'So it's happened before?'

'No. *No*, Fraser. If you knew me at all, you would know that. But clearly, you've made up your mind. So I guess we're done.'

He falters a little, but I don't want to see it. He can't chuck all of that at me and then retreat.

'Just tell me what happened.'

I want to go, but he needs to know how wrong he is.

'We got drunk. I'd had an enormous row with my family and I needed to kick back. It wasn't planned. I don't remember it. It was one bloody mistake and it happened before I knew you.' My tears are falling freely now. Fraser needs to see them. 'And for the record, I wanted to see you to let you know that I'm all in with us.

That I believe in you.' My voice falters but I'm not done. 'I thought you saw me for who I really am. More fool me, eh?'

His shoulders sag a little. He runs a hand through his hair. 'I don't know what to think anymore.'

Slam the door. Walk away.

'Then that's my answer.'

I hold his gaze for one last moment, haunted ghosts of regret, pain and hurt all staring out at me as our world collapses around us.

And then I leave.

Chapter Forty-Six

JOE

I am *buzzing*.

Even now I'm home, an hour after hearing the news, I can't believe it. It's beyond what any of us expected. And Russ just casually lobbed it into the middle of the conversation in the pub and sat back to enjoy the explosion, a great smiling northern ninja.

I just wish Otty had been there to hear it. Rona said she'd gone to see family, but that's news to me. Last I heard on that score she'd left her dad trying to get his head around her being with Fraser, not me. She should have been there tonight. But at least I get to tell her alone. I still remember the rush of joy I witnessed when I told her about our *Eye, Spy* episode. This is far beyond that. I can't wait to see her face.

I'm upstairs when she gets back, the slam of the front door summoning my attention as I'm dressing after my shower. I chuck on a sweater over my jeans and hurry barefoot down to see her. She is going to be blown away by what I have to tell her.

Her coat is on the banister, her bag on the floor below, boots nearby. A big pile of *Ottiness* making our home complete. This place just isn't the same without her in it.

'Hey, hey, have I got some news for you,' I say, ducking my head into the living room to find it empty, so jogging along to the kitchen instead. She's filling the kettle at the sink when I get there, snapping on the lid and flicking the switch. It makes me smile. Otty and tea is a match made in heaven. Even on the days she's been her most weary after work, the kettle going on is a non-negotiable.

'Oh?' She's fiddling with teabags and mugs and doesn't turn.

'Russ dropped a bombshell when we were out.' I pause, but when she doesn't take the bait, I press on. It's too exciting to wait. 'Ensign is merging with Tempest Pictures so we're becoming a full production company. Script to screen, the whole nine yards. And Russ wants us all in on it from the beginning.'

The kettle splutters into life. I wonder if she heard me because I was pretty sure this was the moment she'd spin round, shriek and jump about like a kid at a trampoline party.

'So we get to see whole projects through… Be part of the whole process? Otts?'

'Yeah, it's great.'

'O-kay… There's more, though: Russell is asking us all to submit a single-authored spec script. We have six months to write them and he will commission the best as the first Ensign-Tempest project.' I wait, but still no reaction. 'It means we'll be in competition for that, but it's an awesome opportunity for us. Don't you think?'

There's a click as the kettle boils. Otty pours water into the mugs.

This is *weird*.

'I thought you might be a bit more excited,' I prompt. What is wrong with her?

'I am. It's great.'

It clearly isn't. I skirt the kitchen table and stand beside her, leaning on the worktop to peer up at her. 'You okay?'

Her face is set like flint, eyes trained away from me. She isn't smiling. Did she go and see her dad? Or is she still fretting about Langham being incommunicado?

'Anything I can do?' I rest my hand on hers.

Otty looks slowly down, as if she's never seen my hand before. 'I just have one question.'

'Ask away,' I say gently.

When she lifts her head her eyes are red-rimmed, a stark contrast to the light hazel of her irises. 'When you told Fraser that we slept together…' the pause is deliberate, the accusation hanging like a noose, 'What was that about, exactly?'

No…

'Was it bravado? Jealousy? A bit of banter between lads?' Her voice shakes, her stare digging deep as daggers. 'Did you want to score a point? Or just make me look *cheap*…?' The crack in her tone slices my heart.

'I didn't mean…'

'Oh, I think you did, Joe. I think you knew exactly what you were doing.'

Panic rises, my pulse slamming hard. 'No, Otty…'

'Do you hate him so much that you would throw me under a bus to get a win?'

'No, I—'

'Do you hate me?'

'*No…*' How can she think that? After everything?

'So, what? You don't want me but you don't want anyone else to have me? Is that it?'

I stare at her, my mouth redundant.

'I am *lonely*, Joe. I am sick of being on my own. Fraser made me feel loved. *Wanted*. I haven't felt like that since—' her gaze shifts from me, 'I don't know when. But this – us – it's all supposed to be a joke, isn't it? *Laugh it off, Otty, make others laugh about it, too*. Except Fraser isn't laughing. I just left him thinking I lied. Thinking I'm cheating on him. When I have done *nothing wrong*.'

'Shit, Otty, I never meant to…'

Her hand escapes mine. 'Save it. I don't want to know.'

I hate that she's crying. That I'm the cause. 'Please, listen to me.' I reach out, but she backs away.

'I lost him, Joe. You got what you wanted.'

'I'll talk to Fraser. Put things right.'

'You've done enough.'

She abandons the tea and pushes past me. Panic gives way to real fear, prowling around us both. I see murder in its eyes. I hurry after her, slipping past and blocking her path, my arms out as a barrier between the wall and the stairs. I have to make her hear me. She has to know I made a mistake.

'No. Listen. I don't know why I said it. He just winds me up and…' I can see I'm losing her, so I haul it back. 'I was jealous, okay? He just turns up and wins you and rubs my nose in it… Not that any of that is your fault. Why wouldn't he want to be with you? You're amazing. And beautiful. You don't back down when life kicks you…'

She shakes her head, her feet impatient to escape, arms a tight shield across her heart.

'Tell me what to do to make this better.'

She's so close to me. I could close the distance in a breath. I could…

'I'm done, Joe,' she says.

'What does that mean?' Fear chimes in my voice.

The hazel stare looks through me. 'I will write with you. I will work with you. But I don't want to be here with you.'

I can't breathe. 'Don't leave.'

She blinks and tears run. My own loom large.

'Please don't leave me, Otty.'

She closes her eyes. 'I'm going to bed.'

Her body makes a sudden move and meets mine, but not in the way I want. Her shoulder forces into my chest, pushing me back against the wall. I watch her walk up the stairs – not a run, but steady, deliberate steps.

Above me a door closes. Silence rushes in like a tide. And the house watches me as I sink to the floor.

I've lost her, haven't I?

Chapter Forty-Seven

OTTY

I don't want to leave. But what choice do I have?

I haven't spoken to Joe outside of work for a week. The house mournfully observes our careful dance around one another. If he walks into the room where I am, I leave. I eat my meals in my bedroom. I wait until he's left in the morning before I go down to the kitchen for breakfast. When we have to write, we work methodically, mechanically, without speaking. Side by side. Worlds apart.

I *hate* this.

At work we force ill-fitting smiles onto our faces and carry on.

Fraser does the same. To the rest of the world, we're a united team. Behind the mask, we're empty shells.

I have to carry on. I'm not sacrificing my career and all I've achieved for anything. Everything I do is powered by a bloody-minded determination to hold my ground.

But every day another piece of me slowly dies.

Please don't leave me, Otty.

How can you leave someone who's already pushed you away?

I've lost him, Joe.

Fraser has the best poker face of us all, a consummate professional at all times. But every now and again, I catch a stolen glance, a moment of regret. I want to reach out to him, make things right. But I have nothing to apologise for. So the stalemate remains.

At least the second season of *Eye, Spy* is coming together. One by one the cards on Russell's board are being marked, the episodes growing scene by scene. Rona and Jake develop an entire subplot with Gus, the whistleblower Laura worked to protect in the first series who she is now romantically involved with, so that right until the final act of the last episode viewers won't know if he is part of the plot to bring Laura down or her closest ally. It's brilliant – but the irony of Laura's plight in the light of mine is not lost on me.

I think Laura and I would have interesting notes to share.

I'm reading the latest segment of their story now, sitting in the West One café, under the watchful eye of Rona. She's squirming a little as I read and I know exactly what she's going through.

'Relax,' I say over the top of the pages.

'I am relaxed.'

I have to smile. 'You're not. This is great.'

She frowns. 'But?'

'No *but*. It's brilliant. My guess is that Gus is going to be a viewer favourite in season one, so this tips everything on its head.'

'Especially with the actor playing him,' Rona grins. 'Bloody gorgeous. *Scottish*, too…' Her eyes grow wide. 'Sorry, I didn't mean…'

'No, I agree with you. He's perfect. Not all Scotsmen are prickly thistles.'

I realise what I've said as soon as the words leave me. Rona descends into giggles, taking me with her. 'Stick that on a fridge magnet, someone!'

'Whole new line of *Eye, Spy* merchandise, right there. We'll be quids in.'

My friend sits back in the armchair. 'Man, this place looks like Liberace threw up.'

I follow the line of her gaze to the ceiling, which is currently groaning under the weight of the tinsel and fairy lights attached to it.

Christmas is three weeks away. The famous Frankfurt Christmas Market in the centre of Birmingham is already in full swing and festive lights illuminate every street. I love this season in my city but this year I'm removed from it. The Christmas Market will be packed with couples and families, the streets and cafés full of friends kicking back and enjoying the spectacle. I don't fit there.

'It's *festive*,' I offer.

'There's festive and there's serious tinsel addiction. Even Hallmark movies would call this overkill.' She looks at me. 'So, how are you doing? And don't give me that manic pixie *I'm fine* routine. It might work upstairs for everyone else, but it doesn't work for me.'

I love her for not letting me off the hook. 'Nothing to report. It's as horrible as ever.'

'Are you still thinking about moving out?'

I smooth the edge of the script where the pages have folded over the staple. 'Not sure.'

'You love that house.'

'I do. But it's not the same on my own.'

'But Joe's there... *ah*.'

'Exactly.'

Rona claps her hands. 'Let's change the subject. Have you started writing your spec script yet?'

'I've made some notes, done a bit of planning. You?'

My friend gives a wry smile. 'Might have written a first draft already.'

'You're amazing. Scarily fast and prodigiously talented, though. Are you sure you're human?'

Rona adopts a glassy-eyed look. 'My creator informs me this is so.'

At least I have Rona. In all the mess she's been stubbornly reliable, taking me out when she can, instigating cinema trips to The Electric or meals out and only ever referring to Fraser or Joe if I mention them first. It helps that she knows the truth. Not having to explain it every time is a relief.

'We should do the Christmas Market on Friday.'

'I don't think…'

'Er, I'm sorry, Otty, did you think you had a choice in that statement? No, you don't. You've been cooped up writing for too long. You need ridiculously long hotdogs and *Glühwein* in those tiny cups, and carousel rides and clapping your chops round *Knobby-Brot*,' she grins at her comical mispronunciation of *Knoblauchbrot*, the German for garlic bread. 'Come on, Otts, you need some fun.'

Put like that, it's difficult to refuse.

When I get home, the house is empty. It's a relief. Any amount of time not having to avoid Joe is a gift right now. I overheard Jake and Tom talking about taking him out for beers earlier, so I hope that's where he is. Being taken care of, like Rona has been doing for me.

I put the Diamond Balti takeaway bag on the coffee table and head into the kitchen for a plate and cutlery. As I'm turning to go back, I see the photograph stuck to the fridge. Me and Joe at Purnell's. We look like different people. Suddenly, the loss of it hits me. All the fun, all the bright hope and potential those two fledgling friends had, lost to a stupid mistake and a great big lie. What a waste.

I leave the happy Otty and Joe grinning away in the kitchen

and return to my waiting dinner. Beside the bag, my laptop glows. I click a file icon and my spec script opens.

```
FADE IN:
EXT. A CITY PARK
LIZZIE sits on a bench, alone. She holds
a photograph.

                    LIZZIE
  This is where we met. Do you remember?
  Your shoelace broke. If it hadn't, you
 would have run straight past me. I think
  about that sometimes. Where we would be
  if one thing had been different. We met
          because something failed.


LIZZIE closes her eyes. There is the
sound of running feet. DAN runs along
the path, appears to trip and comes to a
halt. He looks down, picks up the broken
shoelace, looks around for somewhere to
go, heads for the bench.


                    DAN
          Bloody typical.


                    LIZZIE
            Sorry?
```

                    DAN
    You would think, with all the advances
    in scientific innovation, that somebody
    would have invented a shoelace that
                doesn't break.

    DAN sees LIZZIE, who is watching him
    with sweet sadness.

                    DAN
            Was that what I said?

                    LIZZIE
      I think there were more 'F' words.
                DAN sits.

                    DAN
              Yeah, probably.
                  (beat)
                Hi, you.

                    LIZZIE
            Hi, lovely you.

    DAN reaches his hand across the bench.
    LIZZIE does the same. Their fingers don't
    quite meet.

                    LIZZIE
          I was just remembering.

                    DAN
          Is that why I'm back?

                        LIZZIE
                 Of course. Always…
                        (beat)
            No. I need you to do something.

                         DAN
                 Anything for my Lizzie.

                        LIZZIE
         I need you to help me find the man who
                    murdered you.

I stare at the screen. It's a good start. But it's taken me for ever to get this far. I don't know if a supernatural crime-thriller is even in Ensign-Tempest's wish list. Russell might laugh me out of town. But this is the idea that won't go away, so I'm going to give it my best shot. At the very least, it will prove I'm capable of thinking outside the box.

I'm not going to write any more tonight. I need to eat and rest and hope Joe doesn't come home yet. I save the file, shut down my laptop, serve the Jaipuri chicken and rice and help myself to a chunk of giant Peshwari naan. Finding a box set of *Detectorists* on Netflix, I settle down to the sweet bumbling familiarity of Lance and Andy, searching for dubious treasure in their perennially golden Essex landscape. The words soothe me; the sweeping countryside vistas calm my burning eyes. I kick off my shoes, pile two cushions to rest my head on and curl up on the sofa.

As sleep calls me the sounds and sights on the screen mingle with the memory of stolen kisses where I now lie, and two friends becoming something new. Broken things changing the world by chance…

We met because something failed…

Chapter Forty-Eight

JOE

She's fast asleep when I find her. Curled up on the sofa, shifting blue and gold lights from the TV dancing across her face and body. Every line smoothed, every tension gone. She's beautiful when she sleeps.

Like the night she slept next to me.

I stand in the doorway and I can hardly breathe.

Oh, Otty. How did we end up here?

She still won't tell me if she's going to move out. Kind of hard to do when she isn't talking to me. I should ask, but I don't want to push her to make a decision in case it's the worst one. I don't want to lose her. But it feels like I lost her a week ago.

It hurts to be so close to her. It would end me to be further away.

If this were a script we were writing, I would take the blanket that *Movie-Otty-and-Joe* inexplicably keep draped over the back of the couch for such occasions, and lovingly cover her as she sleeps. But the only thing currently draped over the back of our sofa is a tea towel Otty must have used to protect her hands when she opened the metal foil trays for her dinner. No point using that to cover her, however lovingly it may be.

I should leave her. I should go to bed and pretend I didn't

know she was here. That would be the wise choice. Enjoy this moment, and leave.

But maybe I should turn the television off first.

As softly as I can, I edge into the room. The remote control rests on the arm of the sofa nearest her head. I consider my options: take the route in front of the sofa but risk the very small gap between Otty's makeshift bed and the coffee table piled with potential foil missiles I might knock over, or go around the back of the sofa. I opt for the latter. I can't help my gaze moving slowly along her curled body as I pass. First obstacle shakily navigated, I drop to my knees beside the arm of the sofa and carefully liberate the remote from its resting place.

I hear the soft tide of her breath as I point the remote at the television, tensing when the sound and picture click to silence and darkness. I turn back to push myself upright but my fingers touch strands of Otty's hair that have fallen across the arm of the sofa where it meets the cushions. The sensation stops me in my tracks.

Her skin is within reach. Cool as silk, soft as satin. And before I know it, my fingers are gliding across her forehead, pushing the wayward pink strands to join the rest across the cushion.

What am I doing?

My hand jolts back as if bitten by electricity.

Otty sleeps on, oblivious to me.

And everything becomes clear. I've failed her, as a friend, as a lover, as anything else I hoped I could be. If I don't do something, I could lose her for good.

I have to repair the damage I caused with Fraser.

It means telling one more lie.

And it will break my heart.

'Christmas market, this Friday after work,' Rona says, handing me a takeaway coffee cup covered with polar bears and scarf-wrapped penguins.

'What about it?'

'You're coming.'

'Not really my scene, sorry.'

Rona is undeterred. 'I wasn't asking. Everyone is going to be there. Reece, Tom, Jake, *Otty*. Fraser, too.'

I wish I hadn't made that decision last night but now I'm bound to it. If Fraser's going, maybe I can get him alone long enough to talk. I meet Rona's stare.

'Okay, then.'

She grins. 'Excellent! Glad you're as much of a pushover as everyone else, Carver. I don't know how I'd cope if anyone actually said *no*.'

I have a feeling I've just been played. I turn back to my laptop, at the frustratingly blank screen that's supposed to be my winning spec script. So far I've abandoned three attempts of varying length. Until I put things right with Otty, it's pointless trying. We've all been offered a single, one-hour consultation with Russell, to be taken at a time of our choosing, during the writing process. Reece and Jake have had theirs already; Tom is waiting until the script is written. I was going to wait, too, but maybe I should see him now. It might kick-start my script.

I leave the writers' room, careful to avoid Otty's glances. She made her own way in this morning and has maintained her silence most of the day. Quickly, I walk to Russell's office.

'Joseph! To what do I owe this honour?' He's in a fine mood behind his desk.

'I was thinking I'd book my spec script consultation with you.'

Russell raises an eyebrow. 'You have a draft already?'

'Not exactly.' When he waits for more, I add, 'Not yet.'

When he's calm enough, Russell has a way of looking at you, like he's seeing reams of backstory you've carefully edited from yourself. As if he can see the tracked changes, the discarded lines, the compromises. 'Sit, Joe.'

'Thanks.' I take a seat.

'Talk me through where you're at,' Russell says.

Not sure I can, but here goes… 'I have a sense of the story, but I can't find a way in.'

'Genre?'

'Human interest.'

'Vague. Narrow it down for me.'

'Lies. Words we use to protect ourselves that can become weapons.'

'Good. Go on.'

'I feel there are stakes, pace, some kind of peril, but at the heart it's a story of how we justify actions that make us feel safe.'

'Aaand back to vague.'

Was it? I thought that sounded good… 'Oh. Um…'

'Lies is a good theme. Who's telling them? Who are they? Why do they need the lie? What are they running from? Does someone else know the lie is there? What damage could the truth do?'

And that's why he's where he is. As soon as he says it, I kick myself for not identifying those questions. They are so simple, but I've missed them for days. 'See, that's why I need the consultation now.'

Russell shakes his head. 'No.'

'Sorry?'

'I want to see a draft before I give you your hour. You don't need me to hold your hand, Joseph. You are beyond that.'

How is that helpful? I stuff my irritation behind my smile. 'Right.'

'I believe in you. Look at what you've achieved with *Eye, Spy*. Look at Otty.'

Thrown by this, I stare back.

'She had raw talent when she arrived here, but you moulded her into a serious contender. Your influence, Joe. Your inspiration.'

'Otty was always a contender. She just didn't realise it.'

'Exactly. You made that happen.'

He isn't going to change his mind, is he? There's no point arguing. Otty's work speaks for itself – he'll discover that when he reads her script, when the words are hers alone and couldn't possibly be influenced by me.

'So, I guess I'd better start writing.'

'Yes. Go and write, Mr Carver.'

I smile my weary thanks and start to leave.

'Joe?'

'Yes?'

'Word of advice. Find a story worth telling. One that's worth your time. Too good an opportunity to miss.'

Is that a vote of confidence in my favour? It's only when I'm back in the writers' room that it occurs to me that this conversation could count as a consultation but Russell is offering me more later. Does he think I'm a contender?

Friday begins with me biting the bullet with Daphne.

She's been talking about a weekend away and so far I've managed to dodge her suggestions, but I can't fob her off for ever. I can't date her, however much fun it could have been. There's no point: my heart's not in it.

'I can't do this, Daphne.'

'The weekend?'

'Us.'

'Oh.' She raises her eyebrows. 'Can't say I didn't see that coming.'

'I'm sorry. I'm just not in the right place for it. Totally my issue.'

'Of course it is. I was amazing – I always am.' She sighs. 'You were boring me anyway, Joe. Plenty of real men out there ripe for the picking.' She turns on her brightest smile as Jake passes, making a point of leaning around me to watch his backside disappear into the writers' room.

I wonder if I should warn him he might be next on Daphne's list…

Otty is still avoiding me, but knowing I have a plan to fix that makes it easier to bear. When we finish work at 6 p.m., we climb into the minibus taxi Rona has booked and head through the heavy traffic into the city centre. There's a definite schools-out/ weekend vibe in the taxi. The laughter is raucous, the jokes close to the bone. Fraser sits up front with the driver, Otty on the back seat behind me, the only passengers not vociferously entering into the party spirit.

Birmingham's Frankfurt Christmas Market is heaving when we arrive, the bars packed with city workers, the food stalls swarmed around by hungry crowds. I might have told Rona earlier this wasn't my thing, but actually I love its noise and colour and life that batter you into festive submission. It's familiar and warm. I need that for what I've planned to do.

'Beer!' Rona yells and we trail after her, dodging bodies and sharp-edged shopping bags. The bar we choose is next to the council offices in Victoria Square. A large wooden angel chime rotates on its roof, ice maidens, angels and *Weihnachtsmann* figures dancing beneath the large propeller. We're served half pints of strong German beer and small gaudily decorated mugs of spicy sweet *Glühwein* as we huddle on thin wooden benches.

I see Fraser gazing over at Otty when he thinks she isn't looking. He looks about as terrible as I feel. I'm not proud of that.

Fraser made me feel loved. Wanted.

Otty's pain when she told me that. It was horrific. I never wanted to make her feel that way.

The beers flow and an hour later our merry band moves to a single table where we can finally yell conversations above the Christmas Market din. I see Fraser on the periphery, checking his watch. Now's my opportunity.

Leaving Jake and Tom singing dodgy versions of Christmas songs, I slip from the table and skirt the surrounding groups of drinkers to reach Fraser. He's surprised when I clap a hand to his back, his expression instantly darkening when he sees me.

'I need a word,' I say, loud as I dare to make him hear me.

He stares back and for a horrible moment I think he'll tell me to sod off. But he relents and nods in the direction of the side of the Council House. We walk a small way from the group, who thankfully don't notice us leave, towards the Starbucks branch and the small alley that separates it from the grand council building. There's a pocket of space here untouched by festive garishness. It's the perfect place to do this.

'What do you want?'

'A moment of your time.'

'Yeah? What for?'

'To apologise – for being a heartless bastard.'

That almost raises a smile. 'Go on.'

I take a breath, focus on what I'll lose if I stuff this up. 'What I said, about Otty and me, it wasn't true.'

His brow furrows.

'Well, we did get drunk and end up in bed once. But if I gave you the impression it was anything other than a mistake, I'm sorry. That's all it was. We've been trying to deal with it ever since. It was before you arrived, long before Otty fell for you.'

Fraser's eyes are still. I can't work out if he believes me. I hate every word queuing on my tongue like the lines at the food stalls beside us. Because once they're voiced, there's no going back.

'She's devastated. She thinks you hate her.'

'I don't…'

'She did nothing wrong. It was all me. All Otty has ever tried to do is love people. Make them happy. She is a good person, a brave, beautiful soul. And she needs to be cherished because believe me, Fraser, you won't find another woman like her.'

'But the night you spent with her?'

This is it. The moment I let her go.

'It was a mistake. It meant nothing.'

I can't say we return to the bar as friends, but there's a truce at least. I rejoin the guys and down the fresh beer they offer me in one, raising my hand for another.

I don't see when Fraser moves to Otty and spirits her away. I stare at the ground when speculation runs rife around the table about where they've gone. I trail the group past the Town Hall and the Museum and Art Gallery Otty loves so much, on through the new development at Paradise towards the Library of Birmingham and the lights of the Symphony Hall, my frozen breath rising steadily into the indigo sky.

I smile when I'm supposed to. I wait in line for bread pretzels and bratwurst rolls and yet more beer. I act like a man who hasn't just ripped out his heart with his own hands and stamped it to the ground.

And when I finally see them, illuminated by the star-cloud of tiny white lights beneath the library's black canopy, dancing slowly to the music of a busking band, I force myself to look. Otty's head is against his chest, his hand cradling her to his body. She looks at peace. He looks like the luckiest bastard in the world.

It's done.

Chapter Forty-Nine

OTTY

'Otty.'

That voice, warm against my ear. And when I turn, the storm-cloud eyes have me at their centre. Fraser Langham looks scared to death. But he's *here*.

'Can we talk?'

He steps back, an invitation. I don't even check to see if our friends are watching. I just stand up and follow him.

What does he want? And why choose tonight to speak to me when all he's done is pretend I don't exist? I don't know whether to be surprised or annoyed that it's taken him this long to acknowledge me.

It's too loud in the crush of the Christmas Market, the ground too packed with jostling bodies to even hear ourselves think. So I lead Fraser past the entrance to the Museum and Art Gallery and down into Edmund Street at its side.

In the shadow beneath the the Museum's Bridge Gallery that spans Edmund Street, Fraser's features seem as carved as the stone above us. I look up and I'm surprised by what I see. Instead of hurt or judgement, his eyes are earnest, searching. All day in the writers' room, he couldn't even look at me. What's changed?

'I'm sorry,' he says.

I don't reply.

'I didn't know what to think when I found out. I thought you lied to me…' He shakes his head. 'I made a mistake. I should never have accused you like I did.'

'I never lied,' I say.

'I know.'

'You should have known it straight away. Or talked to me, instead of just vanishing.'

His eyes close. 'Yeah, I know.'

I'm torn. He's made my life so hard these last days – refusing to listen, shutting me out with no way of reaching him. I've hardly slept. I've had to force myself to keep going, to put myself daily in that room where I'm so close to him but denied any access.

But I've missed his smile, his kisses. I've missed being loved by someone. With him gone and the stalemate between Joe and me at home, my world has been a cold, empty place where I don't want to stay.

I feel the sting of night air on my skin, the heartbeat of the market muted here. It feels like I'm on the edge of a new season. All I have to do is leap…

'Can you forgive me, Ottilie?' Fraser's voice is low, emotion-heavy.

I look up at him, aware that I'm holding my breath.

'I just want to stop fighting.' My voice is weary when I speak.

Fraser's hand is warm when it closes around mine. 'I just want you.'

I let his kiss take me, the shock of returning to his arms slowly setting in. We stay beneath the bridge for a long time, unhurried now. I don't think about my friends back at the German bar, or Joe, or all of the challenges waiting for me at Ensign next year. This moment is mine.

Fraser's smile is the most sparkling sight in the city tonight. He wears it as we rejoin the crowds, moving towards the Symphony Hall and the bars of Brindleyplace and Broad Street beyond. His arm is back around my shoulders and I lean into him as we walk. I'm dog-tired from emotion but this feels right. I don't know what made him change his mind, but I'm so happy he did.

Beneath the black canopy of the gorgeous Library of Birmingham, a quartet of busking musicians is entertaining the milling crowds. I'm surrounded by smiles and laughter; everyone is here for a party.

Fraser kisses me, then offers his hand. 'Dance with me?'

'Here?'

'Why not?'

'People are watching.'

He shrugs as he pulls me to him. 'So let them watch.'

The band begins to play a slow, acoustic version of 'I'll Be Home for Christmas'. Laughing, I let Fraser lead me to the space in front of them, blushing when I see the musicians' smiles. He gathers me into his arms, my head resting near his heart, and we gently move. I close my eyes and let the music carry us. This is as close to perfect as I could have imagined. I am loved, held close and most of all, believed. Everything I could have wished for.

'Happy?' Fraser murmurs into my hair.

'Yes.' I pull my head back to look up into his lovely face. 'What changed your mind?'

'Does it matter?'

'Yes, to me.'

He kisses me. 'I came to my senses.'

'Just like that?'

'Okay, I may have had some help.' I feel him draw me even closer. 'Joe told me the truth.'

Joe? What did he have to do with this? 'What did he say?'

'That he was wrong making me think it was still going on.'

'Well, he was.'

Fraser smiles. 'He's a good friend for you, Otty. Bit of a git for misleading me like he did, but he cares about you.'

The news sits uncomfortably within me. 'At least he apologised.'

'And was honest, too. Takes a lot for a guy to admit he was wrong. He said it was a mistake, that it meant nothing to him. That's what changed my mind.'

On Broad Street, a car horn splits the festive burr.

I force a smile and don't protest when Fraser kisses me again. But my world just tilted.

It was a mistake. It meant nothing.

Don't leave me, Otty.

What am I supposed to believe?

I arrive home in the early hours. Fraser wanted me to stay – and I was tempted – but I need to write this weekend. And all my stuff is at home. And all of this is an excuse because my head is a whirling, undignified mess I need to make sense of.

I can't believe Joe apologised. What made him do that? We've barely spoken outside of work since I found out what he'd told Fraser. When he thought I was leaving he'd offered to put things right, but I never thought he'd do it. The glares I've seen him trading with Fraser across the writers' room seemed to confirm that. I thought I was losing them both.

What made him take that step?

Does it change anything?

The house waits for my answer.

I sit on the sofa in our darkened living room, the otherworldly orange glow from the streetlight outside casting long shadows from the window. The stillness after the frenetic life of the market and the maelstrom of emotions with Fraser is startling. I should feel completely at peace. But I don't.

I have so many questions. And no answers at all.

A rumble of noise sounds above me.

Joe's awake.

I don't even wait to consider going up there. I'm at the top of the stairs in a few strides. There's a light from Joe's room, his door not quite closed. I need to talk to him tonight or I'll never sleep.

Gently, I knock on the door.

No answer.

'Joe?'

There's no reply, but the bed creaks. He's definitely awake. I push the door open.

'Joe? Are you awake?'

He's lying very still, head turned away. His breathing is steady. I don't know if he can hear me but I'm going to say it regardless.

'I just wanted to say thank you. Fraser told me what you said.' I wait for a response but he remains still beneath the sheets. 'It made a difference. It made *all* the difference.'

'I'm glad.' His voice is soft, measured. He doesn't turn to me, but at least I know he's listening.

'Can we go back to how we were, please?' I ask, surprised by the way my voice cracks. 'It's been horrible without you.'

'I'd like that.'

'Okay. Tomorrow back to normal. Another bounce-back, eh? Night, Joe.'

I'm at the door when the sheets rustle behind me. 'Otts?'

I turn. 'Yeah?'

He's propped up on one elbow, looking at me. He looks tired. 'Does this mean you're staying?'

I guess it does. Maybe it will be easier, knowing exactly where we stand.

'Yes, I am.'

The weary smile is a glimpse of the old Joe I've missed. 'Thank you.'

'But you can't hurt me like that again, Joe. Three strikes and you're out.'

'For a cricket fan that's a very American reference.'

'I mean it. You're two down. You can't hurt me again.'

His smile fades. 'I won't.'

As I walk from his room, I feel Joe watching me.

Chapter Fifty

JOE

Blank page.

And that bloody cursor, flashing away. The word-processing equivalent of a boss tapping his pen impatiently during your presentation.

Flash... flash... flash...

Come on... come on... come on!

Little flashy git.

If I could will words onto the page just by staring madly at the screen, my script would be written by now. And it would be brilliant.

Russell is waiting for the draft so we can have our consultation. Now the second season of *Eye, Spy* is almost complete he'll be expecting it. I keep making the right noises when he asks how I'm getting on:

'I'm loving the direction of it...'

'It's coming together...'

'I think you're going to love it...'

'Some tweaks, but yeah, the whole thing's there...'

All lies, pretty much. And it isn't just me – I mean we all do it;

so the irony is that while I'm trotting out those lines, I'm invariably saying them to writers who know it's a load of bollocks, and nodding approvingly when they say it all back to me. But that's the kind of weirdos we are.

I guess what sets us apart from people who tell you they *could write if they wanted to* is that eventually – after many coffees, bowls of cereal, biscuits, gin, dark nights of the soul, social media procrastination and endless moaning – we sit down and do the work.

Which is what I'm trying to do now.

I'm stuck on a line of dialogue one of my protagonists is saying in a scene that's key to the whole show. Seth, a young and ambitious reporter in a twenty-four-hour newsroom, has been caught out for fabricating a story, the ramifications of which are dire. Political unrest in the country and a media hell-bent on dividing the nation mean that Seth's convenient lie spreads like wildfire, inciting riots across the UK, with one person dead already. His colleague, brilliant intern Evie, has uncovered his lie, just as the newsroom is put on security lockdown due to violent clashes outside. The channel has steadfastly stood by the story, but to admit now it was based on a fabrication could put everyone inside in grave danger...

Sounds good, right? Except that's where I'm stuck. I've tried all routes into it and it just refuses to yield.

```
                      SETH
       I said it because I was scared.
```

Well, Seth, you win the prize for Most Obvious Statement. But what were you scared of?

<pre>
                      SETH
       I said it because I was scared.
       I was scared of being found out...
</pre>

Perfectly understandable. *Not* great telly.

<pre>
                      SETH
       I said it because I was scared.
       I was scared of losing my job...
</pre>

That's a real fear – one that might be my own sneaking onto the page as my nerves about this project grow. But it's not enough.

Maybe I should talk to Otty about this.

She's out with Fraser today. It's been almost two months since they got back together but it still hurts that she's with him.

I gaze out of the kitchen window at the wintry landscape beyond. Snow refused to arrive during Christmas and New Year but now, in the last week of February, it's dumped a whole month's worth on Birmingham.

I have Otty back, but it isn't like it was. There's a bank of reserve that borders all our conversations and I know she's put it there to prevent me hurting her again. I wish I could explain it all to her, show her exactly why I acted the way I did. Not just with Fraser, but way before – on the morning after the night we shouldn't have had. Because I haven't been honest with her about that. I said it meant nothing – and I repeated it to Fraser to make him take her back. But that night meant everything to me. Still does.

I said it because I was scared. Because I thought I'd already lost her...

The cursor flashes on my screen.

                    SETH
        I said it because I was scared.

My breath stalls. Reaching for my keyboard, I start to type.

                    SETH
    I said it because I was scared. Because
    I thought I'd already lost you. But it
    wasn't a mistake, Evie. It was what I
                    wanted.

I feel dizzy, possibilities firing through my brain. What would
Evie say to that? I answer my own question:

                    EVIE
        I don't believe you. You said...

                    SETH
    Self-preservation. Load of rubbish. It
    didn't save me at all. You stole my
                    heart.

                    EVIE
    But you said you don't remember...

                    SETH
        I remember everything.
                    (beat)
            I remember you.

And there's the truth.

Every moment. Every touch. Every discovery. It plays in a relentless loop in my mind and has done since that night. I've lied to everyone, but most of all, I've lied to myself.

I stare at the words I've written, that spilled onto the page immediately. The flow I've been seeking is *there* when I'm talking about Otty. I love her. I've been in love with her for a long time. And the screen was where I finally admitted the truth.

Perhaps I am a writer after all.

Bleeding all over the page. Hemingway would be proud.

That's when I know what I have to write about.

Scrap the newsroom and the riots. Find the story worth telling. So Otty becomes Evie and Joe becomes Seth. They share a house in a city suburb. Maybe they work together, too. One night, they make a mistake that shakes everything. And now Seth is in love with Evie.

Chapter Fifty-One

OTTY

'Shh! *Shh!* It's coming on!'

'Turn the sound up, Joe, I can't hear it.'

'It is up.'

'Okay, who has the remote?'

Rona chucks it across the writers' room at me but it veers off course, skilfully plucked from the air by Jake, who raises both hands in triumph as my colleagues cheer.

We've gathered together to watch the first episode air of the drama we birthed in this room. I can hardly believe it.

Russell is here but he isn't *here*. He threw the party for us but he's now holed up in his office, all phones off, listening to Prince albums. It's a ritual of his, Joe says, a superstition that if he doesn't watch the first episode of a show, the gods of television will smile upon it. And Prince is for extra luck.

'Here we go,' Joe whispers to me. 'You ready?'

'I don't know. I can't feel my hands.'

He grins. 'Then you're ready.'

And now on BBC One, a brand-new series for spring. Secrets, lies and spies. Maya Marple and Mac Finan star in the new original drama by Russell Styles… Eye, Spy.'

This is it. Instinctively, we reach out and grab each other's hands, wide-eyed and watching as the opening bars of Michael Price's haunting theme play and the titles roll.

I don't think any of us breathes for the next hour. It's the most surreal feeling to know exactly what a character is about to say before they say it. There are edits, of course, and some of the script isn't in the finished episode, but all of us in the room hear lines we dragged out of thin air as we worked around the clock to create this. Some of the characters are exactly as we imagined, others so different it presents a fresh take on what we wrote. Occasionally an actor will change a word, causing a chorus of *'Ad-Libber!'* to rise from us all. But I love that the cast have made our words work. Their interpretation takes the script to a whole new level. It's nerve-wracking and breathtaking and by the time the last scene arrives, we're a snivelling, whooping, exhausted mess.

'Here's your line, Rona,' Fraser yells.

Wilson, played by the magnificently bearded Rory Wilton, slowly lowers the phone from the call he's just taken and looks straight into camera. 'We've been compromised. Control just confirmed data from our secure systems has been leaked on the Dark Web. There is a mole in this unit.'

The picture fades to black as the theme music soars and the credits roll.

Created by
RUSSELL STYLES
Written by
RONA BASU   JOE CARVER

TOM DAVISON   REECE HART
OTTILIE PERRY   JAKE TAYLOR-ROSS

We fall silent in a reverent guard of honour as we watch our names appear and slowly scroll up the screen. That's the moment all of us dream of when we write drama. Seeing our names in white capitals, gliding over black.

It's perfect.

I close my eyes and let it hold me.

And then, all hell breaks loose.

Mobiles start vibrating, the office phones ring, texts arrive and notifications chime. Suddenly everyone is looking at screens, answering calls and scrolling social media, laughing and yelling and sharing news.

'Top UK trending topic on Twitter!' Fraser says, waving his phone. 'Hashtag EyeSpy and hashtag WhoIsTheMole are number one and two.'

'My mum loved it,' Rona laughs, wiping tears from her eyes. 'Half the street is packed into her house to watch!' She shares a photo of at least forty smiling people crammed into a tiny lounge, all giving thumbs-up signs.

'I'd better get Russell,' Joe smiles as he leans in to kiss my cheek. 'Good work, partner.'

'You too.'

My mobile begins to buzz and I look down to see Dad's number. Squeezing my way past my celebrating colleagues, I hurry out into the brightly lit reception to take the call.

'We all saw it!' Dad yells, sounding as if he may have been watching with a beer or two. 'Bostin, chick! Absolutely cracking.'

'Are you at home? Who's with you?' I ask, picturing Dad's living room filled with family and friends.

'We couldn't get 'em all in at ours, so we're down the cricket club in Moseley. Say hi, you lot!'

I'm shocked to hear an enormous cheer erupting down the line.

'Wave back at them for me,' I say, blinking away tears.

'They'm all here, our Otts. The lads from the Sunday League team, me, Jarv and Steve, Sheila, *Chris*. He has his new girlfriend with him.'

'Oh…' That's news to me.

Dad lowers his voice, which, considering his surroundings, might not be the most effective approach. 'Hates her guts, our Sheila does. But she'll live. Is your Jock there?'

I smile against the phone. 'Fraser's here. So is Joe.'

'Spoiled for choice then, bab! I'll let you go, okay, but – er – we're *proud*, Otts. So proud. You're doing what you should be and that's – well, that's as it should be.'

I never thought I would receive a phone call like that.

I know my dad's proud of me and to hear it means the world. But his parting comment – that's incredible. That tremor in his voice, the small hesitation before he said it, those made it remarkable. *I'm doing what I should be.* I never thought he'd say that.

'Here's the man himself,' Joe says, guiding a very relieved showrunner into the writers' room. I follow them in and join the applause. Russell takes centre stage, the ringmaster accepting the plaudits on behalf of his company. Then he reaches under the writers' table and produces two large bottles of champagne.

'I wasn't sure whether we'd need these, but now I think they *must* be opened.'

Daphne hurries out to find fresh plastic glasses while Fraser wrestles with the corks.

'Speech!' Jake yells.

'Okay, you asked for it. Now I'm presuming episode one was all right, seeing as I was in a very important meeting…' He grins at the laughter this remark receives. 'I just wanted to thank all of you for making this happen. When I was putting this team together, I had little support from my esteemed colleagues in the business. To be frank, they thought I was insane. But we've more than proved them wrong. You guys did that. We're not just a pretty bunch of writers – Fraser excepted, that is – we're a powerhouse of creativity. *Eye, Spy* is just the beginning. So drink up, party on and then get back to writing tomorrow.'

For the next two hours, we celebrate. It feels like I've lived a lifetime in this place when it hasn't even been a year yet. When the festivities naturally wind down and people start to disperse, Joe helps me tidy party detritus from the room.

'That was some evening,' he grins. 'There will be mammoth hangovers in here tomorrow.'

'I think one of them might be mine.'

'Ha, you and me both. Otts, can I ask you something?'

'Of course. Don't make the question too hard, though. I'm not sure my brain can take much more today.'

He rests the black refuse sack on the table and sits down beside it. 'My spec script – I know what I want to write about now.'

'That's great. You'd better get a shift on, though. Time's running out.'

'It's okay. Now I have an idea it's flying.' I can't pin down his expression. 'I wanted to ask, will you read it when it's done?'

335

'I'd love to, but we're not supposed to share them until after the judging.'

'Yeah, sure. I meant after.'

'Of course. How about we swap? On decision day.'

'Sounds good. It's a date – but don't tell Fraser.'

I shake my head. 'You want to be careful with that kind of humour. You know what happened last time.' It still feels strange to joke about it. But at least we don't seem to be joking about *that night* anymore.

'You cracking on to my girl, pal?' Fraser's arm slides around my shoulder. I'm relieved to see his grin when I look up.

Joe looks relieved, too. 'Wouldn't dream of it.'

'That's what I like to hear. So, Miss Ottilie, back to mine or are you chaperoning this Sassenach back?'

Like Dad said, spoiled for choice…

Chapter Fifty-Two

JOE

Overnight viewing figure: 10.4 million. A week later, the consolidated figure for the first episode is nearer 10.6 million. It appears we have a hit on our hands.

Twitter is ablaze with speculation about who the mole in Laura Eye's organisation is – so far every name mentioned is wrong. Good-natured jokes about the show appear and an *Eye, Spy* bingo card is produced by some internet wit, the cause of great hilarity in the writers' room.

'*Laura looks up, Dr Montgomery takes off glasses, Gus hand shot!* These are incredible,' Jake laughs as we gather round his phone. 'Oh man, some people are using this as a drinking game! That's dangerous.'

'There's the idea for the weekend, then,' I say, grinning at Otty, who rolls her eyes at me.

On the side of the planning board Reece is keeping track of the current William Hill betting odds for the identity of the mole. Hot favourite is Laura's boss Charles Wilson at 5-1, followed by Gus at 10-1. It's crazy to think people we've never met are risking actual money on this. I half wondered about having a flutter myself but that's highly illegal, even if it would be fun to clear up.

We're four episodes into the six-week run and our weekly viewing parties have now moved to our house. It's great having everyone round and it's making us even closer as a team. Very few people get to see their words become drama, and sharing the experience with these writers we've worked with for almost a year is something very special.

In the middle of our fun, Daphne hurries in.

'Nobody show Russell today's *Sentinel*, okay?'

Our laughter ebbs. 'Why not?' Tom asks.

Daphne blows out her cheeks. 'Hatchet job.'

The room falls ominously silent. Everyone is on their phones. I watch as, one by one, faces fall. I go to google the article, but I don't have to search for it – as soon as I type *Eye, Spy* it's there. Top result.

'Ugh, *bastard*,' Rona says beside me.

'Don't, whatever you do, read the comments,' Reece says flatly. 'If Russ sees these he'll freak.'

It appears tall-poppy syndrome has kicked in and as usual *The Sentinel* leads the charge. Popularity is a dirty word as far as certain newspaper commentators are concerned – as soon as ordinary, licence-fee paying people are loving a programme, out come the snobbish knives. Because to them, something being popular must automatically mean it's less worthy. I hate that attitude.

'Listen to this,' Otty says, scowling at her phone. *"'Russell Styles' latest offering of bland, set-scene montage is indicative of a worrying trend: patronise your viewer, make them come back for more. It's the fast-food approach to TV: overloading the senses with saccharine storytelling and wholly unnecessary violence, while presenting poorly researched facts as gospel. So the ill-informed man in the street is armed with inaccurate schlock-culture 'facts' to spout down the pub…"* Oh my life, who wrote this?'

'Unsuccessful screenwriter,' Tom suggests, as Rona and Jake agree.

'Oh, here we go,' Reece grimaces. *"Even the writing is cynical. Produced in Styles' controversial US-modelled writers' room, it's writing-by-numbers stuff from a team rumoured to have been selected more for their commissioner tick-box likeability than their writing prowess. A machine, churning out mindlessness for the masses…"*

We stare at him. I know exactly what everyone is thinking.

'Shit. Russell's going to lose it.'

'We just don't tell him?' Jake suggests.

Daphne shakes her head. 'He'll have seen it. Best we can do is hope viewing figures sustain for the last two eps and the talks with the commissioners progress.'

It's one article, in one newspaper renowned for click-bait headlines. Compared with the deluge of love and excitement all over social media and viewing figures we could only have dreamed of, it's a drop in the ocean. But it still stings.

'He's coming!'

Phones are stuffed away, laptops hastily rebooted, heads bowed so that when Russell storms into the room, he finds his charges hard at work and absolutely, definitely *not* reading the article.

He slams the door and chucks a large pile of paper on the table.

'I'm guessing you've seen it,' he growls. 'I've been going over the scripts we've completed for season two and there's stuff we need to change.'

The entire team deflates.

Russell looks up. 'For the record, every single one of you is here purely because of your writing ability. No tick-boxes in this room. We have work to do and no time to do it, so I need you on side and I need you firing on all cylinders, okay? We'll show the bastards.'

It isn't just small changes. Everything is measured, sharpened, overhauled; hours of hard work cut in a single stroke. We're battling time and Russell's increasingly dogged insistence that nothing can be predictable. Twists build on twists, complicated subplots woven into the main thrust of the story. Hidden symbols fans of the show can help push into folklore, red herrings to fox even the most astute viewer. Dead alleys, shock exits, every character weighed and discussed and refined.

Meanwhile Daphne intercepts the daily papers before they reach Russell's desk, while I accompany him on frequent, frantic laps of the eleventh floor as we discuss plot knots and his latest interactions with commissioners. All of us make a pact to distract Russell every time we see him reach for his phone, tag-teaming the mission constantly to keep him away from the inevitable counter-wave of opinion on social media. I think it's this game that saves us: watching each other chuck ourselves between our showrunner and his device at every turn is grimly hilarious.

We have to laugh or else we might never stop crying.

I'm exhausted. Doubt is a writer's biggest nemesis at the best of times, but when every word you write is critiqued it's hard to keep focus. Otty's going through it, too.

'I'm starting to edit what I say when I talk now,' she says one evening, after a stupidly late finish. 'I have to think about every word. I doubt *everything*.'

I know she's strung out. I bought her surprise dinner on JustEat from her beloved Diamond Balti that arrived at home just after we did, and Otty burst into tears on the doorstep in front of a very startled delivery guy. I don't think I've ever seen anyone vault the gate at the end of our path before…

It's 11 p.m. and we've allowed ourselves an hour for food, then we're back to it. Russell isn't happy with one of the storylines that threads through season two. He wants it changed, but our episode is where it's introduced, so we have to rearrange the entire thing. We've already sketched out four possible replacement strands, the wall above the sofa covered in bright lines of Post-it notes to give us an idea of how the restructured episode could run. It feels like a backward step.

'None of these work,' Otty says, hands on hips.

'The second one might…'

'I just think it's too similar to the Gus backstory we did in season one.'

She has a point. Also a near-encyclopaedic knowledge of the series bible, which is a killer skill for this.

I glance at her, my heart swelling with pride. Her brow is furrowed, lips moving gently as she silently reads each note. She is so different from the terrified newbie I met on her first day. She's earned every bit of success she's worked for. She's a better writer than I am, that's for sure. Instinctive, brave, unwilling to let go of stories she believes in.

I think back to lines of my spec script I scribbled this morning while we were having coffee, Seth speaking the words I found watching Otty.

                    SETH (v/o)
        I watch how she sees her world and it
        floors me. Evie finds beauty where I see

dust. I've never met anyone who can do
that before. And the thing that steals
my breath? That she sees something in me
worth watching.

It's helping, pouring it all into the script. If she reads it, will she realise whose story it is? I still can't believe I asked her. But I don't know any other way of finally being honest. I'm not brave enough to say it to her face.

I think I just want her to know. With no expectation that it will lead anywhere. I put her through so much and none of it was deserved. Against the odds, she's still my friend. I have to repay that faith she has in me.

I just hope it's enough.

Chapter Fifty-Three

OTTY

I am so tired.

The script edit still isn't done, although Joe and I have rewritten most of our episode. Every time we take it to Russell, we wait for the inevitable notes, the red lines scrawled through dialogue we've debated hours over.

'No. Not strong enough.'

'Gus needs bite. Viewers won't suspect him otherwise.'

'No, Anya can't know that at this stage. Write it again, twist it…'

No. Not good enough. Do it again… It plays like a mantra in my mind, so that Russell's voice has merged into my own internal critic.

'Hey, it's nearly two thirty. Go to bed.'

I open my eyes, that I don't remember closing, and I blink the blur away to see Joe's big smiley face. 'Sorry… I didn't mean to drop off…'

'You're knackered. It's a wonder you're even functioning.' Joe eases the laptop from my hands, placing it on the coffee table. He returns to me. 'Want help standing up?'

I laugh. 'I'll be all right. Just give me a minute here.'

'Okay. But don't go back to sleep. You pay for a bed, remember?'

'Do I get a discount if I sleep on the sofa instead?' I ask. It's good to smile after hours spent scowling at words that refuse to help you.

'Er yeah, good luck selling our landlord on that,' Joe says, flopping down beside me. 'Eric would sublet your room in seconds.'

We lean our heads back.

'I am so tired.'

'Me too,' Joe says, closing his eyes. 'I keep walking into rooms and forgetting what I went there for.'

'These rewrites are *endless*. I swear if Russell doesn't like the new workaround in our episode I'm giving up and going back to the bike shop.'

'I'd work at Waitrose,' Joe says.

'Waitrose?' I laugh and now he's laughing too.

'Think about it, right: everyone is lovely in Waitrose. They have nice uniforms and sell lots of nice food. No rewrites, no annoying blank pages. What's not to love?'

'Ah, but you don't care about that,' I say. 'I know what the attraction is for you, Joe Carver: it's the apron, isn't it?'

Joe snorts. 'Yeah, that sexy-ass apron…'

'Shameless!'

'You wouldn't say that if I was wearing the apron right now. Think of the *tapes*…' He raises a suggestive eyebrow. I'm too tired to work out if I should join in the joke or not. We collapse into giggles.

'I need to get to bed.'

'Yeah me, too. Want a hand?'

'Go on then.' I stick my arm out.

Joe struggles to his feet, laughing, and yanks me to my feet. I wobble a little and throw my hand out to his shoulder to steady myself. 'Okay? Steady?'

I nod, my laughter subsiding. 'This job is crazy. But I'm glad I'm doing it with you.'

'Me too. We'll get through this, Otts.'

I hope he's right.

Fraser is in the strangest mood when I arrive at Ensign the next morning. He can't keep still, moving from the edge of the writers' room table to a seat, then getting up to pace the room. His smile is as lovely and warm as ever, but his restlessness is at odds with it. Everyone's noticed, surreptitious glances following his dance around the space.

When Russell arrives and collects Joe for their daily eleventh-floor stomp, I leave the script I'm leafing through and take the vacant seat next to Fraser.

'What's up with you?'

'What do you mean?' He tries to feign surprise, but there's too much life going on in those eyes to convince anyone. 'By the way, did I tell you you're gorgeous today?'

He steals a kiss and I let him, glancing back to check if any of our colleagues saw it. But all I see is a room of weary writers, heads uniformly bowed over printed scripts as we double-check the latest round of changes.

'Clever. You've not answered my question, though.'

'I can't here. Come find me when we get a break.'

Voices beyond the writers' room make me scurry back to my seat, Fraser's impossibly lovely smile trained on me as I force my focus back to the pages.

'Hey,' Joe rushes in, dropping into his chair.

'You sound out of breath.'

'Russ walks *really* fast when he's stressed. But…' he lowers his voice, 'today it's *good* stress.'

'What do you mean?'

'Just watch,' he grins, reaching for a script.

What is it with people and secrets today?

I just hope it's good news. Rumours are rife of award nominations for the leading and supporting actors. Of course, we're all hoping for a writing nomination, but it's too fanciful to dwell on. We need season two ready if we get a chance.

'Right, everyone, last round of changes, I promise,' Russell says, ignoring our groans as he strides around the room, handing out stapled sheets.

Really? More? I'm starting to feel like I'm caught in a never-ending loop nobody's bothered to cut.

A copy spins across the laminate desk to land by me. I reach for it. Only two pages, that's more promising.

'Go on, open them,' Russell snaps from the head of the table.

I pull back the cover sheet at the same time as my colleagues. There is a single change, centred in the middle of the page:

```
ONE CHANGE:
WE ARE NOW A
TWO-SEASON SERIES!
```

We're all so knackered it takes a moment to sink in. Then an entire writers' room scream as one, a torrent of hugs and backslaps and excited chatter breaking out. And at its centre, our showrunner, beaming brighter than a lighthouse.

'We're done on the script changes,' he says when we've all

collapsed back into our seats. 'Commissioners love it. So, terrestrial on BBC One and BBC America, simulcast as before. They wanted an option on a third season—' a ripple of delight travels the room, but he raises a hand to temper our expectations, 'which I've declined for the time being. However, I have agreed tentative first refusal when and *if* we are ready. Also Netflix are interested in a multi-series, multi-film deal. Again, early doors on that.' He lifts both hands as if bestowing a blessing. 'This is down to you guys. Thank you for your patience and for not walking out.'

Daphne and Molly arrive with yet more champagne, a questionable choice given that most of us haven't slept for a week and are likely to be comatose after one sip.

Our showrunner raises his glass. 'I think there's really only one toast we can make, given the circumstances. Make sure someone films this, please: I'd like to post it to our social media channels immediately – and tag a certain newspaper, too.' Clearing his throat like a hammy actor about to deliver a speech, he raises his glass: *'Mindless machine, my ass!'*

We laugh and chorus back: *'Mindless machine, my ass!'*

Fraser joins me and Rona as we gather in the fresher air of reception.

'Seriously, I had visions of us being found in that room in ninety years' time,' Rona yawns. 'Just a load of dusty carcasses forgotten by the world, still trying to get through Russell's notes.'

'That'll be your spec script, will it?' Fraser asks.

'Watch it, Langham.' She wags a finger. 'I'm still working out who to bump off. A rude Caledonian script executive might be just what I'm looking for.'

'Make it grisly, Rona.'

She looks at me. 'I like him. I'm getting a top-up. Any takers?'

I hold up my glass, which has hardly been touched.

Rona tuts loudly. 'Lightweights.'

When she's gone, I lean into Fraser, enjoying the way his arm moves around my waist. 'So, you knew about Russell's announcement?'

'No. I found out the same time as you.'

I frown. 'Then what's your news?'

'Let's go to my car.' He takes my hand and we slip out of the room.

We dodge a spring rain shower as we hurry out of West One to the car park. Fraser's Jaguar is warm and welcoming when we get inside.

'So?'

His eyes sparkle as he faces me. 'Okay, you cannot tell a living soul about this—'

'I won't.' I love his excitement. 'Tell me.'

'I've been offered a job.'

The rain thrums more insistently on the car roof. I'm not sure I heard him right. 'What?'

'At Exemplar. They love what we've done on *Eye, Spy*. They want their own writers' room, just like ours. They've asked me to set it up.'

I can't believe I'm hearing this. Exemplar Productions are probably Ensign's biggest competitor. That Fraser even talked to them while working for Russell is bad enough, but I know for a fact they aren't based near Birmingham. 'Where?'

'London! Old stomping ground, calling me back. But it's *huge*, Otty, it's the chance to run my own gig.'

'But Russell needs you here.' All trace of celebration leaves me as I face him.

'Russell is more than capable of running his own outfit. And the team are ambitious, ready to push forward. I got us to a second series; Russell doesn't need me now.'

I stare at him, not sure if this is real or an awful hallucination. 'So, that's it? You just take a job in London and don't tell me?'

Fraser's eyes widen and he takes both my hands. 'No, no, listen. They want you, too. *I* want you,' he laughs, 'in many different ways, but I want you to be my lead writer.'

Hearing this while battered by sleep deprivation, emotionally raw after the green-light news, is not the best. 'I'm not lead writer material, Fraser. I have barely a year's experience in the job.'

'Russell saw your potential. Joe too. Both of them considerably more experienced than you, and yet they talk about you as Ensign's secret weapon.'

'No they don't.'

'Russell does. Do you have any idea how hard it is to win his approval? He's infamous for trusting no one. And yet who was on the planning team for season two? You can do this, Otty. I know you can.'

'But London—'

'Think about it, Otts. Me and you, working together. *Living* together. A new city, a new start. Exemplar are the kind of innovators that catch the market's attention. And that means springboards into who-knows-what. This is a break for both of us.'

'But you're only telling me now?'

'I wanted to wait until the offer was certain.'

'Does Russell know?'

His gaze drops.

How can he do this? When everything else is certain and

sorted? Has he no loyalty at all? To Russell? To his colleagues? To me?

'Tell me what you're thinking, Otty.'

'I… I don't know what to think.'

His hand reaches across to stroke my face, the green-grey pools of his eyes earnest, questioning. 'Come to London with me. We'll start something new. I can do anything if I have you.'

'I need to get out of here.' My hand is on the door handle.

'No, Otty, wait! Think about it, please?'

It's too much. I can't possibly make a decision like that now. Ignoring Fraser's protests, I run through the pelting rain back to West One.

Chapter Fifty-Four

JOE

Something's playing on Otty's mind.

It isn't lack of sleep because we had the day off after we got the green light for *Eye, Spy 2*, and slept side by side on the sofa for much of it. I don't think it's Langham, either. He was round here last night like flipping Captain PDA, all touchy-feely stuff and lingering kisses – and Otty seemed fine with that.

I guess it could be the fallout after such an intense period of work. It's happened to me before. One minute you're working like a dog, forfeiting sleep and generally going bonkers, the next the project's done and you're left hanging in mid-air. It can take a while to reacclimatise. I always think being a writer is a bit like P.T. Flea from *A Bug's Life* and his Flaming Death trick. Invite an audience, set yourself alight, take a few days to heal, and do it all over again.

Otty's laptop is open on the coffee table but I haven't seen her type anything since I got up. I'm tempted to have a peek at her spec script, find out what she's planning. She won't tell me anything about it – which is how we're supposed to do this – but I'd kind of hoped she might make an exception for little old me.

Not that I'm going to ask her today, though. She could use that spoon in her empty cornflake bowl to gouge my eyes out.

She's staring at the television as if she can see straight through it to the wall on the other side, biting at a hangnail on her thumb. There's a tiny crease between her eyebrows that hasn't softened all morning. Even the pink tips of her hair look subdued.

I can't let her stay like this all day.

'Penny for 'em, *laydee*,' I say, in my best Dick Van Dyke cockney voice.

She just blinks ahead, long and slow.

So much for my comedy skills. 'Otts, what's up?'

'I'm fine.'

'If by *fine* you mean giving the telly death-stares then, yeah, you are fine.'

That works. She gives a weary shake of her head and looks at me. 'What do you want?'

'To take you out.'

'Not today.'

'*Yes* today. Have you not checked the fixtures list? Warwickshire are at home at the – stadium thingy.'

'You hate cricket.'

'I like it if you tell me all the proper words.'

Her sigh is heavy, but the prospect of an afternoon spent watching her favourite team causes a sparkle she can't hide. 'Okay.'

As it turns out, we pick a good match to watch. Warwickshire are batting and, to a layman, seem to be pretty handy in that department. I'm impressed by how far they actually hit the ball – on televised matches it never seems that big a distance. We stand to applaud when they score runs and sit when they play, the slowest, Brummiest Mexican wave I've ever seen.

I'll say one thing for cricket: it certainly seems to attract a nicer type of person. Everyone seated around us is pleasant and we get included in bursts of their conversation as if we all rocked up here together. It's nice.

I glance at Otty, who is intently watching the game, elbows on knees.

'Are you going to tell me what's going on?' I ask, handing her a plastic cup filled with tea from the thermos I remembered to bring.

'Are you going to stop asking me about it?'

'Probably not. And cricket's a long old game.'

Otty looks at me. 'I can't tell you. Not yet. But this is lovely, thanks.'

'Nice try, Perry.'

She fiddles with her shoelace. 'I don't know. Do you ever feel like life is just waiting to jump you like a… a… *ninja*?'

'Ah, the infamous Birmingham Life Ninjas.' I nod. 'I've heard the legend.'

'Don't mock me. All of my good words are in my spec script,' Otty says with a rueful grin.

'I'd stick the ninjas in if I were you. Might be the killer touch.'

'I'll bear that in mind.' It's only a tiny laugh, but it's a start. 'I just really like the life I've got now. I like the house and my job and… I suppose you're okay too.'

I roll my eyes, glad that she's attempting humour. 'That's a good thing, isn't it? Especially the me-being-brilliant bit.'

'Yeah, it is. I wish we could press pause when life is just how we like it. Freeze it, right there. So it doesn't change… Ignore me. I'm just tired.'

I watch her for a while as her eyes follow the play on the field. I want so much to talk to her about the script I'm writing – that I finished a draft of in the early hours of this morning. It's solved a lot of the questions I've carried about what happened, but some knots remain. I wish I could discuss it objectively with Otty – if we could critique the story without it being ours, how would we resolve it? I imagine us placing sticky-note lines across the walls of our home, strands of potential resolution that could direct our lives…

'Have you sketched out the options?' I say, surprised that I'm voicing my thoughts.

She turns her head. 'For what?'

'For whatever's on your mind. Like we did for Laura and Gus.'

'I haven't. That doesn't work in real life.'

'Doesn't it?' I see her considering my suggestion. 'It's your life, you should be the one sticking the notes on the wall.'

There's a glimpse of a smile. 'Defeat the Life Ninjas with Post-its?'

'*Ninja vs Sticky Note* has a ring to it.'

She laughs and looks at her match programme. She is so lovely when she laughs. I force my attention back to Warwickshire's players.

'Look, I don't profess to be an expert in life stuff. But I know you should at least get a say – if not in what happens to you, then in what your response is. Okay, example: Laura can't stop Soren targeting her family, but she can choose to lie down or fight. Or walk away.'

'Or keep the things the way they are?'

I nod. 'As I recall, the maintain-status-quo thread was the orange Post-it line.'

She wrinkles her nose. 'You're strange. But that helps, thank you.'

'My pleasure.'

'Have you booked your consultation with Russell yet?'

I resist the surge of nerves. 'Tomorrow afternoon at 4 p.m. You?'

'5 p.m. tomorrow. Want to share a ride in?'

'Deal. You drive, I'll make dinner.'

I'm nervous about tomorrow. My spec script is very different from any writing of mine anyone has seen before. I think it has pace and focus, but Russell's work is very much the big-action, big-story narrative. Will my portrait of two small lives appeal? Seth and Evie's story is epic in the tiny details: heartbeats instead of explosions, the turn of a conversation instead of the twist of a knife.

Too late to worry about that now. This is all I have to show him.

Otty and I arrive at Ensign a little after 3 p.m. and head into the writers' room. Some of our colleagues have opted to come in and work here on their spec scripts, the hangover of the *Eye, Spy* script revision still pulling us back. Rona is working at her brother's café and Reece at the Library of Birmingham at a hot desk overlooking the city. But Tom and Jake are here and they grin at us when we walk in.

'Ready to meet the executioner?' Tom asks.

'Feels like that, doesn't it?' I grimace. 'How did yours go?'

He shrugs. 'Okay, I guess. Lots to think about. So who's up first?'

'Joe is,' Otty says. 'I'm in after.'

'Team O-Joe separated – can the world cope?' Jake laughs. 'It's like *Avengers Endgame* all over again.'

I grimace. 'I reckon Thanos is a bit more reasonable.'

Otty fixes me with a stern look. 'You will be *fine*.'

'So will you.'

She sits and fetches her laptop from her bag. 'Oh, I know I will be.'

I join in the good-natured banter with my friends but my nerves are a tangle of fear. Time seems to be wading slowly through fast-setting concrete and by the time 4 p.m. arrives, I don't know whether I want to throw up, leg it down the eleven flights of stairs to the car park or hide beneath the writers' room table.

I wipe the moisture from my palm on the back of my jeans before I knock Russell's door. I *have* to calm down.

'Well, well, Mr Carver,' he booms, standing up to shake my hand.

Okay, that's unexpected.

We've all emailed our scripts to Russell prior to our consultations, but I've printed out two copies for the meeting. I want to make notes of Russell's suggestions and if I try to type it up I'll lose things. I can think better when I make notes by hand. A little more time to think about the words I'm forming, not bashed out in a frenzy only spell-check can rescue. I hand one to him as I sit.

'Copy in case you need one.'

'No need,' he says, lifting a script from the desk. It is covered in his large, flamboyant handwriting.

Breathe, Carver, breathe.

'You made notes?'

He wears a strange smile and I can't work out if it's a sign of hope or a portent of doom. 'Plenty.'

At least I can't see any red lines…

I settle in my seat as best I can.

'I have to say, I was surprised by your spec.'

'Um, pleasantly?' The last note of my question is practically falsetto.

'You're scared, aren't you?'

'Can you tell?'

'Relax, Joseph. Let's start with the headlines then work through the body, okay?'

'Okay.' *Is that good?*

It's only a spec script. My future career does not hang on Russell liking it. If it doesn't win the Ensign commission, it won't be the end of the world.

Except it's not just a script, is it? It's our story – Otty and Joe, disguised as Evie and Seth. And I'm so stupid because right until this moment it hasn't occurred to me that any criticism of them will feel like an indictment on *us*. I've bled all over this: if Russell hates it, he'll be damning me.

'It's brave. It's tender. It's not the tense thriller I was expecting, but I was engaged, Joe. Truly.'

I can't believe it. 'Oh… Thank you…'

Russell rests his chin on his hands and observes me. 'I'm curious, what made you decide to go down this route? I seem to remember you referencing a locked-room thriller?'

'It wasn't the story I wanted to tell,' I reply, shocked by my own admission.

'Not the one that mattered?'

I nod.

'Hm.' Russell takes this in, watching me. 'How long have we known each other, Joseph? Seven years? More?'

'Eleven now. I was a trainee staff writer on one of your early projects at BBC Drama.'

'I remember. I caught you writing your own stuff when you should have been working on mine.'

I can't help my smile. 'Yeah, sorry about that. I was a dick when I was twenty-three.'

'Aren't we all? Some of us are dicks at fifty.' He laughs. 'Long time, Joe. Last time I got this feeling from your work was on *Southside*. But this script is beyond that.' He sits back. 'Hurts, doesn't it?'

I stare at him.

'Not easy to put it on the page. Big risk.'

Is that a criticism? I can't tell. Russell talking like this about my work is not what I expected and I am utterly out of my depth.

'See, I put my characters through the wringer constantly. Physically, mentally, occasionally even emotionally. I kill off the ones they love; I threaten their own existence. And I get flak for not caring about them, but that's wrong. I do care. But putting it on the page scares the living crap out of me. You know why? Because it's too close to home. Hands up, I'll admit it. So the care is hidden behind twists and shocks and extended car chases.' He stabs my script with his index finger. '*This?* Takes balls bigger than mine to write it.'

Not sure I'll use that as a pull-quote... But it's the biggest compliment.

'So, any advice?'

'Be this brave more often. Although I get the feeling this is a standalone?' I feel like he's looking through to my bones. 'Evie and Seth are great characters. Bit battered by life, bit world-weary, very funny. I feel like I know them.'

This is *not* the time for a blush to appear. I will my skin to behave. 'Thanks.'

'But – your ending…' He grimaces.

'What? What about it?'

'It's too vague. Too ambiguous.'

'I… I was going for ambiguous. Let the viewer decide.'

'They'll hate it, trust me. You need an ending. Doesn't have to be a happy-ever-after or have all the threads tied up. But it needs to be authentic. It has to be right for Evie and Seth.'

'What if I don't know what their ending is?' I ask.

Idiot! What did I say that for?

One side of Russell's mouth lifts. 'Then write the ending you would like.'

I realise I'm holding my breath.

Chapter Fifty-Five

OTTY

Okay, I'm scared now.

Joe looks like he's seen a ghost when he comes back into the writers' room. Of course, he's all jokes and bravado when we look up from our work, but I saw him before. Something Russell said must have really spooked him.

'Was it that bad?' I ask when he sits by me and downs a whole mug of cold coffee without realising it was mine.

'What? No. Just, you know, the whole showing-it-to-someone-for-the-first-time thing: *Here's my brand new baby! It's perfect! Er, its ears could do with pinning back and look at its nose!*'

His dubious-accented comedy voices crack me up – which, coincidentally, is just what I need now my nerves are revving up for my consultation.

'I bet Russell loved it. How were the notes?'

'Insightful.'

I check my watch. Five minutes to go, but I want to be there early. 'I'd better go in, then.'

Joe smiles, but he looks exhausted. 'Look, I might grab a taxi home, get a start on dinner. Is that okay?'

'Fine by me. No point you hanging around here for an hour.'

He smiles. 'You'll be great, Otts. Look at how far you've come since you started here. Russ adores you.'

'No, he doesn't.'

'Yes, he does. What do you think we spend all those circuits of the eleventh floor talking about?'

I love that he's trying to make me feel better. 'Go on. Back to the kitchen with you, wench! Prepare our feast!'

'Certainly, Lady Perry,' he intones, doffing his imaginary cap. 'Now go in there and knock him dead.'

I risk a brief hug before I hurry out of the room.

I'm surprised to find Russell waiting for me at the door of his office. When I make a swift check of my watch, his booming laugh makes me jump.

'Don't worry, I'm early, you're not late. In you come, Ms Perry.'

My nerves swell as I sit opposite him. It isn't that I don't think my spec script will be up to scratch – it's easily the best thing I've written alone. But knowing what I know about Fraser's plan to leave Ensign Media for its biggest rival makes me feel like a traitor. I haven't said I'm going with him, although Fraser's pretty insistent and it is a great opportunity. But knowing that makes me complicit. It isn't my place to tell Russell, but if he asks me straight out, can I lie to him?

'So, we've gone all supernatural,' he says, sliding a copy of my script in front of him. He's made a *lot* of notes on the first page, I notice. 'Talk me through it.'

I pack away my butterflies and beam my brightest. 'I wanted a fresh take on the revenge thriller and I liked the emotional side that Lizzie brings. She literally has nothing to lose because she's already lost the only person that matters.'

'I've got to say, my first thought when I saw the pitch was that this could turn out to be a cosy-crime remake of *Randall and Hopkirk (Deceased)*. But seeing the script, I'm reassured. It's edgy, it's surprisingly violent and unapologetically tense.'

'Thank you.'

'Your protagonist is what fascinates me. Lizzie is loss, isn't she? Loss personified.'

I hadn't thought of it like that, but it thrills me to know he's seen it in my main character. 'I wanted to show the power of grief, but in a different context. So Lizzie discovers her ability to summon the dead only at the point when grief consumes her.'

'And in the true fashion of superheroes, it's an unwanted gift.'

'Exactly!' I'm excited now. I was worried Russell would dismiss my script as too fantastical. 'I was thinking of characters like Dr Bruce Banner and how he battles his ability to become the Hulk. It often comes from pain – like a spider bite for Peter Parker. It's almost as if pain and loss of normal life to some extent is necessary to unlock these gifts.'

'Pain and loss are powerful motivators. Also love.'

He isn't smiling, but I feel like what he just said was done kindly. 'Love can be both.'

He nods. 'I like it, Otty. I think you can bring out Lizzie's battle a lot more. Be braver with it. The whole *with great power comes great responsibility* idea. And her sadness, the hopelessness she ultimately faces.'

'Okay. Thank you.'

'It feels very personal, if you don't mind me saying?'

'In what way?'

He leans back. 'A very recent loss. Or experience of the pain of love.'

Why do I suddenly feel cornered? 'I tried my best to make it authentic.'

Russell's eyebrows rise. 'You succeeded. So what I want to know is, if this moved to a series, would we see redemption for Lizzie?'

A series. I don't think I dared think that far ahead, but what if it happened?

'I don't know,' I begin, willing words to appear as I speak. 'I don't think it's as easy as that. She might find Dan's murderer, and there may be justice in that, but she's still lost him. And the only way she can see him is by facing that loss head-on.'

He's quiet for a while and I wonder if I've just scuppered my chances. Then he stands and I follow.

'Great work, kid. Don't be scared to push this. See where it goes.'

'I will. Thanks, Russell.'

We walk to the door. And I'm struck by how much I've changed. If I'd had a one-to-one meeting with him when I first arrived at Ensign, I would have been too scared to even breathe. Now I've just held my own in our meeting and not given it a second thought.

'You know, when I started working here, I was terrified of you,' I say.

'Me? I'm a pussycat, Otty, you know that.'

I laugh. 'I know it now. I didn't then. Thank you – for taking a punt on me. I had so little experience and I didn't think anyone would give me a chance.'

'I would have been a nutter not to. Talent means everything, as far as I'm concerned, more than experience or contacts.' He seems genuinely moved by what I've said. 'Style you can learn. Polish you can acquire. I'm just glad Joe took you under his wing, helped you find your feet.'

Joe? What's this got to do with Joe? 'He's been very encouraging.'

'I know. I've loved hearing about your progress every time he's reported back.'

'Sorry?'

'I asked him. To help you and keep me posted. He's been doing it ever since.'

We've reached the door of his office now. My mouth has gone dry. Joe's been talking to Russell about me? Behind my back?

What do you think we spend all those circuits of the eleventh floor talking about?

He just joked about it, didn't he?

Russell is chuckling to himself, completely unaware of my growing horror. 'And I have to say, him persuading me to let the two of you write together was a stroke of genius. My rough Brummie diamond and my star writer – killer combination!'

'*Rough…?*'

I've done this on my own, not because Joe held a door open for me.

'In the lack of experience sense. I'm not suggesting all working-class Brummies are rough.'

Working-class. I think back to my application, the sneaky mention I'd made of my background because it seemed to be something people were looking for. I didn't even think that would help my cause, only that it was worth mentioning.

'You know, you should play up on that. The class thing. Commissioners love it right now. Own voices stuff is big. Not that I'd let anyone else have you, mind. You and Joe are Ensign's major weapon.'

'Well, I like to think I'm a good writer and that's what counts,' I say far too defensively given I'm saying it to my boss.

'Of course. And it's been a joy to see Joe shape you into the writer you are.'

Is that what he thinks of me? That I'm a product of Joe Carver?

And then I start to remember things other people told me about Joe in the beginning. Josh warned me Joe was *more involved with Russell than you think…* And Daphne said he had *an agenda…* I'd dismissed them both at the time. But what if they were right?

I feel like all the foundations I've built my trust on are starting to crumble. Russell is leading me out, singing Team O-Joe's praises, but I don't want to hear it anymore.

Did Joe use me? Did he take me on to score points with Russell?

And has everything he's done been for himself?

Chapter Fifty-Six

JOE

I've been thinking about what Russell said and I'm going to do it. I'm going to tell Otty I love her.

When she reads my script on decision day, I'm going to say it.

I know she's with Fraser, but I don't think she's happy. Things have been off with them lately and while she won't tell me what's happened, I'm pretty sure Langham is behind it.

She might guess Seth and Evie are me and her, but even if she does, what I tell her afterwards will leave her in no doubt. I just keep thinking about how it's been between us lately, like we were regaining some old ground. Writing the script has only made me more certain: the reason we bounce back every time is that we *want* to.

But what if she doesn't feel the same? I have no answer for that, except we've survived worse. But my gut is insisting that won't be the case. I don't think it's just me who can't stop thinking about our night.

The sound of her key in the lock makes my heart jump. I stand up from the sofa where I've been sitting. My chest is tight with impatient breath. I don't know what to do with my hands all of a sudden. I train my eyes on the front door, the shaft of streetlight stretching into the hall from the almost dark evening as it opens, her shadow stepping into it.

All I can do is watch. Breathe. Wait.

At first, she doesn't see me; her body in shadow as she unwinds her scarf, shrugs off her jacket. There's a serene measure to her movement, a beautiful ballet performed in the frame of the doorway.

I should say something, but my heart swells into the space where words should be. So I drink in the sight of her – this stunning soul who tipped my world.

Then she turns and the fading light from the window falls across her face.

And everything changes.

Wide streaks of water stain her cheeks. Gone is her smile, stolen by pain. Her brow sets when our eyes meet, wild hazel damnation aimed straight at me. I open my mouth to say something but I don't get the chance.

'I believed you.'

It hangs heavy in the air.

'Otty?'

'I believed you when you said you believed in me. When you told me I was the only person you could work with. When you begged me to stay…' Her voice falters. She swallows hard and stabs at the tears with her sleeve as she nears me. 'Lies, Joe. All of it. You never wanted me. You just wanted to score points with Russell…'

'No…'

'He never believed in me, either. It was all *you*. He hired me to tick a box and then he told you to turn me into the writer he wanted. And you did it, because you wanted to win.'

I can't believe she thinks that's true. 'Where is this coming from?'

'Russell told me. So don't pretend you don't know. All those long walks you took with him, you were reporting on me then, weren't you?'

'Otts, *no*. It wasn't like that…'

Her stare bores into me. 'Deny it, then. Deny you were talking about me.'

What do I say? I can't deny it, even if it wasn't like what she's accusing me of. 'We did, but…'

She blinks and more tears chase the salt-trails. 'Every idea I had, Russell gave you credit for. I've dismissed it for months because I thought it was just his way. And you let him believe it was your influence, not my skill.'

'I never said that, Otty, you have to believe me…' I reach out but she bats my hand away.

'Don't *touch* me! Even that, Joe… Even *that night*…'

'It meant the world to me. I never planned it… Otty, I would never use you.' I'm slipping, panic threatening to overwhelm me. I have to pull this back. 'Just take a moment, okay? Sit down with me and we can—'

She's inches from me now, hurt and fury seething from her body. 'Third strike, Joe. You can't come back from this. You don't get another chance to hurt me.'

Strikes, lies, schemes… What does it all mean? I'm confused by her accusation, shocked by her anger and lost in the tsunami surge engulfing us. This isn't how it was supposed to be. This isn't the ending I wanted…

Frustration balls up within me. 'Three strikes? You keep saying three strikes, but you only accused me of two. I apologised to Fraser for telling him about us, and now this with Russell – which isn't anything like you think. Where's the third?'

Her breath snaps in staccato bursts, her body so close to mine that I can almost feel the shakes that rock her as she struggles for control. 'When you decided sleeping with me was a *joke*.'

I blink.

This isn't happening.

How can she think that? 'I never said it was a joke. It was—'

'You said it was the biggest mistake and you laughed about it.' A sob escapes and her hand flies to her mouth. 'And then you told me I should laugh about it, too.'

The joke.

I suggested it. I said we could do it. We *did* do it, over and over in the weeks following, as we worked a way back from where we'd fallen. I wanted to hold on to what we had, to find a way through it all. Seen from Otty's side, it looks damning. Hell, it all does. I agreed to mentor her to make Russell see me in a good light. I reported back because it kept him happy. And it doesn't matter that every time I fought for him to recognise Otty's own brilliance because she never saw it. How can I defend what she didn't see?

'I never laughed at you.' She's shaking her head but I carry on. I can't let her think I used her. How could I use the woman I love? 'I never used you. I couldn't…' I reach out and catch her hand, hanging on to it when she tries to pull away. 'Listen to me. I love you Otty. I *love* you.'

She looks away. 'No, Joe.'

'And that night that you say you can't remember? *I* remember it.'

'*Stop…*'

They aren't Seth's lines anymore. There's no time to let Otty read the truth I wrote into the script – into our story. This has to

369

be Joe now. I have to tell her the truth. 'I said I didn't but I lied. I remember, Otty. I remember all of it. All of *you*.'

She's pulling away, her sobs no longer contained. 'Please, stop…'

'And I can't stop thinking about it. About us. I've tried and I can't. It wasn't a mistake; it was what I wanted. What *we* wanted.'

Otty closes her eyes. And when they open again, I hardly recognise her.

'I'm leaving.'

The steel is back, her defence raised, shutting me out.

'Did you hear me? I love you.'

'You need to find someone for my room.'

'Otty, *no*…' My hand falls from hers.

'I'm moving in with Fraser. And as soon as the decision is announced for the spec scripts, we'll be leaving for London.'

The air is snatched from me. 'What? Why?'

'Exemplar Productions want us. I'm going to be a lead writer.'

'Does Russell know?'

She blinks. 'I imagine you can tell him all about it next time you take a walk. Make sure you tell him it was your idea. I'd hate him to think it was mine.'

And then she turns her back on me and walks away. Sure, measured steps power her out of the room. And out of my life.

The door slams.

The house falls silent.

It's over.

Chapter Fifty-Seven

OTTY

I don't want to leave Ensign. But Russell never believed in me on my own.

I don't want to leave the house. But there's no room for me now.

I don't want to lose Joe. But I never had him, whatever he says.

Everything I thought I'd achieved, every counted blessing I'd folded into my jar, gone. I was an idiot for ever believing them real.

But Fraser loves me. He's been pressing me for a decision because he can't imagine the next step of his life without me in it. He hasn't used me to gain favour with anyone, or laughed away the nights we've spent together. And he hasn't used *I love you* like a weapon when he was losing a fight.

I thought I knew Joe Carver. But I never did.

I don't drive straight to Fraser's home. I'm not calm enough yet. So I take a circuitous route, skirting the city I love, passing over flyovers and through tunnels, the lights blurred and dancing though my tears. Once again, I'm alone, adrift in the place that holds my heart; once again the city soothes me. I've cried more over Joe than anyone else and it has to stop. I don't want to leave

Birmingham and these streets that are as familiar as the lines on my skin. But Joe is here. And I can't be where he is.

Does he really remember? Or was that another lie?

I push it away. It doesn't matter. I can't take back what was said tonight.

Finally, when I'm ready, I take the road that leads to my new start.

'Otty?' Fraser meets me by the lift, eyes wide when he sees the state of me.

'Can I stay?'

'Yes – you know you can.'

'I'll take the job.' The flash of surprise in his expression bruises me. 'I'll go to London with you. And – can I move here? Until we leave?'

His smile blossoms, his body already enclosing mine. 'Yes. Yes, to all of it. I love you.'

I let his kisses fall and steal my reply.

West One is shrouded in mist when I arrive on decision day. Locking Monty's door, I let my gaze travel up the sleek green glass and steel lines that disappear into billows of white. Whatever happens today, my life will change. I've loved working here, but life pulls me on.

When I reach the entrance, Rona is waiting. Of course she knows – I poured it all out to her in an email yesterday at Fraser's, bruised and aching from the events of the night before. And being a great friend, she doesn't ask to go over it, just wraps me into a hug.

'You don't deserve it, Otty. Joe should be the one leaving. That's all I'm saying. Now come on: let's face our spec script destiny.'

Last night, Fraser and I talked about what we would do if my script wins. The plan would be for me to work remotely for Ensign on a single commission, while we set up the writers' room at Exemplar. He seems to think Russell will be okay with that. In truth, I'm dreading that outcome. But then I'm dreading Russell's reaction to our news.

Fraser is in with Russell, now. He drove in early to do it. The timing isn't great, but I'm glad I'm not the one dropping the bombshell.

'I reckon you're a shoe-in,' Jake says when we join them for coffee. 'I overheard Russell talking about the new direction the first Ensign-Tempest production will have.'

'That could be any of us.'

He gives me a wry smile. 'My pitch was *Killing Eve* meets *Broadchurch*. I'm anything but groundbreaking.'

'Otty.' Rona's hand tightens on my arm. I follow the line of her gaze and see him, edging into the room, looking for someone.

Joe Carver looks like a ghost.

I feel like I've spent days angry with him and I'm tired of it. I stand by everything I said, but I'm not having it brought into this room, not on the last day I'll be here as an Ensign screenwriter. Giving Rona a nod I leave my friends and make my way over.

'Walk with me,' I say, not stopping for his reply.

I hear his steps behind me as we leave the warmth of Ensign's suite and head into the cool stillness of the eleventh floor. When we're far enough away, I stop and turn to him.

'I'm sorry,' he rushes, getting there first. 'For everything. I don't want you to hate me.'

I sigh. 'I don't hate you.'

'But you don't believe me?'

I look at the floor. 'I don't think I can.'

'Read my script? Like we said. Please? It will make sense if you do.' His hand reaches for mine but stops before they meet. Like Lizzie and Dan's hands on the bench in my script... 'It might not change anything, but I want you to see it.'

'They'll be starting soon...'

'Please. I hate that I hurt you.'

I have to look at him then. 'Me too.'

'Are you coming back to the house tonight?'

'Yes. To pack. I'll pay till the end of the month but I'll leave tomorrow.'

Joe releases his breath in a long slow exhale. 'How did we end up here? It was good, wasn't it? Most of the time.'

'I'm sorry it didn't work out. I'll miss... the house. The fun.'

He nods. 'Team O-Joe were pretty spectacular. I'll miss writing with you.'

I'll miss it too. I'll miss so much more. I want to read his script, but I'm scared what I'll see there. I can't give him even a moment's hope. This has to be a clean break, a new start. No looking back. 'So let's go in there as Team O-Joe, not Otty and Joe,' I say. 'Let's be our success.'

His smile is sad.

Slowly, we walk back to the place where it all began.

The warmth of the writers' room wraps around me like a blanket as Joe and I take our seats together. For the time we're here, we are as we've always been: writing partners. Whatever else has happened, we have to celebrate what we've achieved.

'Uh-oh, here we go,' Rona whispers beside me as the door opens and Fraser and Russell walk in. Russell casts a glance over at me and gives a solemn nod. It's done: he knows and I'm now a departing employee. I pull my heart up from the floor, set my smile in place.

'Well, kids, it's been a journey. I want to thank you for your submissions. All of them stunning. The decision has been a monster, as you can imagine. But we can only begin with one. So here goes.'

In my peripheral vision, I can see the rise and fall of Joe's chest as his eyes are trained on our showrunner. My breath is quicker, too. As we wait, I feel the warmth of Joe's little finger encircle mine, holding on. I let it stay.

Russell takes a script from the pile he brought in. The room holds its breath.

'The winning script startled me. It's unlike anything I've produced before. And it's a risk. But the writer's heart beats through the lines, their breath in the pauses. And I would be a fool not to bring it to the screen. The first Ensign-Tempest production will be written by... Joe Carver.'

The tension breaks, applause and cheers filling the room.

And our fingers part.

I look at Joe, who is staring at Russell.

'Congratulations,' I whisper.

'It's not my story...' he begins. But suddenly our colleagues, with their hugs and chatter and backslaps, surround us. I let the tide of bodies get close to Joe as I leave my seat, moving to the head of the writers' table. Fraser kisses my cheek as I hug him.

'Not disappointed?'

'Relieved, actually.' I smile up at him. 'Nothing's in our way.'

'So, Fraser and Otty, abandoning me.' I turn to see Russell walking over. 'Can't say I'm happy you're stealing my secret weapon, Langham. But you're part of the Ensign family and I thank you for all you've done.'

'Appreciate that, Russ.' Fraser smiles. 'Otty, I'll get us coffee.'
I watch him leave.

'Can't believe Team O-Joe will be no more,' Russell says.

'Me neither. I'm sorry, Russell, for the short notice.'

He shrugs. 'It's how this gig works. I was expecting it with *him*. Listen, I many have given you the impression that your success here wasn't down to you.'

I stare at him.

'That wasn't my intention. You shine, Ottilie Perry. All on your own. Whatever you decide to do, there will always be a place for you here. Any time.'

Overwhelmed, I hug him. His shoulders stiffen like a kid resisting a grandparent's kiss, but I think he appreciates the gesture.

When he leaves, I watch the bustle of the writers' room – this space where I chased a dream and found so much more. I'll work out my notice in whatever way Russell wants and then I'll leave it behind: my colleagues, Russell Styles, this room, the building.

And Joe.

Chapter Fifty-Eight

JOE

One last night in our house.

Tomorrow, Otty will pack her car, leave her keys, and walk out of my life for good. And I have no idea what will happen next.

The house is already brighter with her back here, but it's a melancholy joy. In the middle of the living-room floor, a mountain of boxes is growing. Each one covered in bold, bubble-letters in a hand I would know anywhere.

Hunky Hardbacks

Lifesavers

Weepie Treats

Total Classics

Strange But True

Brummie Noir

Sixteen boxes – the only thing she arrived with.

There are cases, too, new things she's acquired while living here. But gathered together it looks too little, too insignificant a pile for the difference its owner has made in this house.

We smile and edge around one another, but our conversation is muted and minimal. I ordered Otty's favourite meal from

Diamond Balti, but neither of us has much appetite, so it sits, forlorn and untouched, on the coffee table.

There is so much I want to say to her. But the time to say it is over.

And the worst thing? When I lie in bed that night, too awake to sleep, the memory of her being there with me refuses to leave. I can't say I wish it hadn't happened, but I wish its ghosts would go.

I left my door open and the lamp on, hoping she might wander in as she's done before. But her door remains closed.

At 4 a.m., I stop trying to sleep and get up. The house is cold and dark, sorrowful, still. I make a drink and sit in the coolness of the kitchen. And that's when I decide: I won't be here when Otty drives away. I'll help her pack, but I can't see her leave. It might end me.

Weariness hits and I fold my arms on the table, resting my head on them. And sleep must sneak in after all because the next thing I know, soft fingers are stroking my shoulder.

'Hey, go back to bed.'

I blink away sleep and wince as my neck cramps. 'Sorry, I must have dropped off.'

Otty smiles. 'You pay for a bed, you know.'

It's a tiny sliver of *Past Us* and it's as welcome as the first light of dawn spilling into the kitchen. 'Don't tell Eric.'

'Coffee?'

I glance at the stone-cold offering beside me. 'Love one, thanks.'

I watch her move around the kitchen, as if this were any other day and not the one I've been dreading. She knows where everything is now, moving instinctively from drawer to cupboard to fridge. If her eyes were closed, I don't think she'd miss a beat.

After she sets two fresh mugs down, I'm surprised when she sits next to me.

'So,' she says, 'this is it. Let's part as friends, okay? We've spent too long fighting.'

I force a smile. 'Friends.' I think of her driving away and put my plan into action. 'I have an early meeting with Russ this morning, so I'm afraid I won't be here to see you off.'

'Oh.' Her gaze slips. 'Okay.'

'I mean, I'll help you pack your car – shift all those boxes for you – but then I have to go. Sorry,' I add, as if that makes up for my total cowardice.

'You don't have to help.'

'I'd like to.' I lift an arm and pat my bicep. 'Besides, these could do with a workout and I can't afford the gym.'

A flash of amusement registers beside me. 'Oh well, in that case, be my guest.'

So we pretend. That breakfast and our kitchen-table chat are like we've always shared, and not the last. But I can't escape the reality – with each ordinary act we're saying goodbye.

Last lull in the conversation as we drink coffee.

Last smile glimpsed.

Last pass in the hall as we prepare for our day.

Otty is as beautiful as she's always been; as she was the first day she sent me a brave smile across the writers' room. I realised far too late what my heart was doing. Today, it hurts to watch her, the defiant smile she wears because we are done fighting. I think she wants to forget too, keep this moment free of the complications we've knotted around ourselves. Just us, in the house that will for ever be changed when she's no longer here.

Last fight.

Last irritation.

Last silence.

When I can put the moment off no longer, I lift the first box from the living-room pile, starting the final chain of events that will pull Otty from my life for good. We don't speak as we carry them to her car, our smiles sad as we pass on the harlequin path. I hate every step. The front door propped open ushers coolness into the house that feels like a growing emptiness. It's blowing away all traces of her, the scent of her, the air around her. When I come home this evening, it will all be gone.

Finally, her car is packed, the space on the living-room rug achingly empty. I can't stay. I want to, but my heart needs to survive this. We meet on the doorstep, where a year ago she gripped my hand like she was scared of letting go.

'So,' she says, her eyes full of me.

'So.'

'I'll miss you. I've loved this.'

'Even the crap bits?'

She laughs but her eyes glisten. 'Even those.'

'Thank you,' I say. It encompasses more than I could express. 'Would you read my script? It won't change anything, but I'd like you to see it.'

'I – can't…'

'Not today, then. But any time. You know where I am. Just turn up and ask to see it. I wouldn't have written it if it weren't for you.'

Her eyes are sad. 'Maybe.'

It's all I can hope for. 'I'd better get going.'

'Yeah.' She swears under her breath and pulls me to her. The warmth of her body is a shock, the fullness of her in my arms the final stab of pain. I hold on tight, my cheek against her head, the scent of her hair filling my lungs. I feel the gentlest shaking of her shoulders and bite my lip to keep my own emotion in check.

'Goodbye, Joe,' she murmurs against my chest.

I love you, the words urge in my mind. *Don't go*. But it's too late. I pull back and look at her.

Last time on my doorstep.

Last time in our house.

Last time we're *us*.

'Bye, Otty.'

And then I walk away, kicking out my pain with every hurried step. I don't stop or try to look back.

It's time to let go.

Chapter Fifty-Nine

OTTY

I watch Joe until he gets in his car and then I hurry inside. I can't watch him drive away.

This is so much harder than I thought it would be.

His door was open all night, light from his room bleeding out onto the landing – a final invitation. I almost accepted. When I woke at 5.30 a.m. I'd made up my mind to go in there and say what I really wanted to. But his bed was empty. I thought he'd gone already but then I found him fast asleep in the kitchen. I sat beside him for a while before I woke him. I needed to remember his face without the dark cloud that has shadowed it since I returned.

It's for the best this way. I don't know why we've kept coming back every time we've hurt each other but I know it doesn't achieve anything, in the end. I'm moving away and starting again: it's the chance to draw a line for good.

I'm sad, though.

I'm sad that it's over.

The house is silent now. I make a slow circuit of the rooms, noting the details I've taken for granted, letting the memories sparked by each space wash over me. I don't try to stop them: when I leave today I'll lay them all alongside my key on the kitchen table and close the door. But just for a while, I want to remember.

I remember all of it, Otty. All of you.

That was the beginning of the end for us, I think. Until then it had been a spark in the air, a possibility we wouldn't explore. When it became real, it changed us. All of the pain I've felt stemmed from that night.

But I can't wish it never happened.

I climb the stairs, laughter and embarrassment, jokes and fury trailing behind me as memories collect in my wake. On the landing, I sidestep the whisper of an awkward dance on the night of my first date with Jas, and skirt the shaky, held breath at the entrance of Joe's room waiting to break the news about Fraser. By the bathroom the revenant of first-morning Joe emerges wearing only a towel; by the entrance to my room the faintest glow of an almost-hug after our first writing session. Doors opened and slammed, mornings greeted and goodnights wished.

And one night where only one door closed us in.

I don't go into Joe's room, though. I can't.

And then there are no more reasons for me to stay. I go back downstairs, find my house key and slide it off my key ring. Blinking back tears, I walk through into the kitchen.

The scent of breakfast still lingers here, fresh as if we'd dashed out together on our way to Ensign. That's how I'll remember it, I decide. We've just hurried away, the house awaiting our sure return. The bright summer sun sparkles now, dust motes spinning in the pools of gold. I always loved the light here. I follow the sunlit path from the window across the kitchen floor, to where it comes to rest on the fridge door.

My breath stalls.

In the natural spotlight, two faces grin at me, their arms flung around one another in wild abandon. Otty and Joe in Purnell's, confident in their own friendship, loving their lives. That's how I want to remember us.

I consider taking it with me, but then a thought occurs. My fingers hover next to the image, heart suddenly loud in the quiet space. I should leave it; walk away. But there's one thing I haven't said yet.

Taking the photograph down, I slide open the drawer nearest the cooker and find a lidless biro that inexplicably still works, despite being in the house for as long as I've lived here. I turn the image over and write a message on the back.

Ten words that tell the truth.

Quickly, I replace the photo on the fridge and the pen in the drawer, leave my key in an open envelope on the kitchen table and hurry out.

On the beautiful tiles of the hall – the first thing I saw when I arrived a year ago – I pause one last time. I reach out and rest my hand against the wall, feeling the history of the house hum beneath my fingers. Lives lived here, chances missed, dreams found. Countless breaths taken, smiles shared, tears shed. We aren't the first and we won't be the last to share our days with this building. There's comfort in that.

'Goodbye, house,' I whisper. 'I love you.'

I open the front door to the bright day outside, pulling it shut behind me. The click of the Yale lock reverberates through my hand. It's done now: I can't ever go back.

My tears fall in silent, uninterrupted tribute as I make my way to Monty. Across the city, Fraser waits for me, already arranging our new life from the home I will now call mine. Joe is my past: Fraser my bright future. Who knows what waits for me in London?

I'm strangely light as I drive away from a road I won't revisit. I've said all I have to now. Nothing else remains.

Chapter Sixty

JOE

> EVIE
>
> How do you know it's right? I have so
> many questions, Seth. So many things we
> can't know…

SETH takes EVIE'S hand and places it
against his heart.

> SETH
> This is all I have to answer them. Trust
> this.

I sit back in my chair and rub my eyes. I've been working on the full script for a week now. I thought the writers' room team would write it with me, but Russell had other ideas.

'This is your story to tell,' he said when I met with him to discuss next steps for *Evie & Seth*. 'Your words, your voice.'

It's what I've dreamed of. My name as creator *and* writer. From the earliest days of my writing ambition, this was the goal. I have the might of Ensign-Tempest Media behind me, a guaranteed green light before I write a single page – I mean, who gets that? It never happens. If the series is a success, it could make my name. I am the luckiest beggar in the business. So why doesn't it feel like a victory?

I'm still hoping Otty might ask to read the spec. I know she's still in the city – Russell agreed she could work out her notice away from the writers' room. He loved her spec, too, and secretly I think he's planning to find someone to take it on for her. I hope he does. Otty deserves that.

Gradually, I'm getting used to having this place to myself again. If it weren't for the small issue of money, I'd be tempted to rent it alone. But needs must: soon Otty will tell Eric that she's moved out and then I'll have to sort it so he doesn't use the opportunity to force me to leave.

I'm refilling the coffee machine when I hear the sharp rap of the front-door knocker. My heart jumps. Is it her? Has she come to ask for the script?

Coolness abandoned, I race to the door, willing Otty to be standing on the doorstep.

'Hey…'

'Have I caught you at a bad time?' The diminutive figure of my landlord peers up at me, amusement playing across his face. 'Or were you expecting somebody else?'

'What? No… I just like answering quickly.' I do my best to style it out – not that it's likely to fool anybody. 'Saves all the waiting around… Sorry, would you like to come in?'

Eric's balding head wrinkles. 'Pleasant though the day is, I think it better we talk inside.'

I trail after him into the living-room, thanking my lucky stars that one of my procrastination methods this week has been deep-cleaning the house. Amazing how enticing a dirty oven can be when you're on a writing deadline… I offer tea, which Eric politely refuses, so we sit down to talk.

'I had a notice of intent from Ottilie,' Eric states carefully. 'She's moving out?'

I nod. 'She already has. But she's paying till the end of the month.'

'So I understand. And—' he lowers his voice as if it might embarrass the walls around us, 'yourself?'

'I'm staying.'

'Hm. Alone?'

I knew this would happen. I fix him with my friendliest smile. 'There will be someone to take the room.'

He wasn't expecting that. His white eyebrows soar like tiny white clouds. 'There will?'

I nod. 'Just finalising details, actually. It will be strange to share with somebody new again, but I'm prepared for it.'

'You're sure? Ottilie seemed like such a lovely young lady and you looked so happy together in this place. It would be completely understandable if you felt you couldn't stay.'

'I have no intention of leaving.'

Eric nods, his smile gone. I know his dream of having a *nice professional couple* has been dashed again. Did he expect Otty and me to fit that bill? 'As you wish. Two housemates in just over a year – one might say, "To lose one housemate, Mr Carver, may be regarded as a misfortune; to lose both looks like carelessness."' He beams and when I don't follow, he reddens. 'Lady Bracknell. *The Importance of Being Earnest*? Forgive me, I know you're a writer and who can resist a bit of Wilde, eh?'

'Not me.' I give him a weak smile. 'I'll send you their details as soon as I can.'

My landlord nods. 'In that case, I'll be going.' He stands and I walk him to the door. 'I'm sorry, Joe. Must be hard to lose someone so lovely.'

I'm left reeling on the doorstep as he leaves.

The smell of coffee drifts into the hall and I follow it, suddenly in need of warmth and comfort. The kitchen echoes as I walk in and I ignore the familiar memory of Otty crashing about in it during her first weeks of living here.

It's too quiet. I need noise.

I hit the button on the DAB radio that lives on the windowsill. The pots of herbs Otty and I bought months ago are wilted and sad beside it. I grab a jug to water them, sticking it under the tap. But as the water floods in, a song on the radio stops me dead.

Otty's favourite song.

She played Tom Walker's *What a Time to Be Alive* album practically on repeat when she lived here, often wearing the T-shirt from his tour to sleep in. It's his storytelling she fell for, she often said, the way he can convey a whole world in a few verses. The song that's playing tells of a young couple in different cities, falling in love and maintaining a relationship despite the distance between them. It's a gentle, intimate song, packed with dreams and defiance, and I can't hear it now without imagining Otty's voice singing along. Taking over the world, step by step.

The memory makes me look at the fridge, at the photo I haven't been able to remove yet. That night at Purnell's seems a lifetime ago now. We look like we could take over the world and not even realise it.

I can't keep it there. It kills me every time I see us.

I stalk over and snatch the photograph from the fridge door, the magnet clattering to the floor. I don't look at *that* Otty and Joe as I kick the pedal on the bin. I don't want to see their faces when they fall.

As my fingers start to let go, my thumb passes across the glossy surface – and hits something. A bump. I grab it back as it starts to slip, moving my fingers over the image and finding more.

Not bumps. *Indentations.*

Writing.

Slowly I turn it over. And the wind is knocked from my sails.

Ten words, written in Otty's exuberant lines and loops:

I remember too.
And it meant the world.
Be happy.

I don't even stop to think. I grab my jacket from the back of the chair, then spot something else on the table that has been there for a week. Stuffing it into my pocket, I run for the door.

The city passes in a blur, my palms damp against the steering wheel. What am I doing? I don't know… But Otty left that message for me to find and it's the truth we missed before. She always maintained she had no memory of that night; that she was drunk, that she didn't know what she was doing. I remember her very much present, every decision, every movement consciously made. I thought she regretted it, that the way she was the next morning was proof that it meant nothing to her.

We've wasted so much time by avoiding the truth. By speaking every word except the ones we should have said.

Now we both know.

The photograph lies on the passenger seat, Otty and Joe gazing up at me with hopeful eyes.

Will it make a difference? Can I change the story?

The traffic grinds to a halt in front of my car in the bright sun and I glance at the dashboard clock.

'Come on!' I yell.

It takes an age until the red brake lights start to disappear down the snaking line of vehicles towards me. I force air into my lungs, my head dizzy with everything. I *have* to see her.

Fraser's apartment building is everything I expect. Glass, stone, steel, regimented greenery confined in stark grey metal. I find a space to park and leave my car, snatching my phone from my back pocket to check the number on the text Rona sent me.

Apartment 10.

I press the buzzer and wait.

'Yes?'

My heart leaps into my throat. 'Fraser, hi, it's Joe Carver.'

'How can I help you?'

'Can I come up?'

'Why?'

'I just need to see Otty for a minute.'

'That's not possible.'

I don't want to be having this conversation on the street. People passing glance at me, the strange man arguing with an intercom. 'Please, mate, if you could just…'

'Otty isn't here.'

I close my eyes. 'When will she be back?'

'Next week, sometime.' I hear a rattle of a sigh against the intercom speaker. 'She's in London, looking at flats.'

'Why aren't you with her?'

'Goodbye, Joe.'

'No – no, wait…' I say, but the call has ended. I stare at the bank of intercom buttons and try to think. It never occurred to me that she wouldn't be there. What do I do now? I can't just drive home.

'Excuse me,' a voice says beside me. An older woman is waiting patiently.

'Yeah, sorry,' I mumble, stepping back.

She beams a swift smile and presses a button. And I just stand there because I don't know what else to do. I could call Otty but what would I say? And would she even answer? She's busy building her new life, far away from here.

But why leave the message if she didn't want it found?

The door lock buzzes and a slight cough sounds. I look up. The lady is holding the door open. 'After you?' she says.

In the lift, I wrangle my thoughts together. This is my only chance. Pulling an envelope and a small stack of orange sticky notes from my pocket, I scribble a note and shove it inside. The lift slows, and the doors part. I see the door for Apartment 10 to my left.

Fraser looks shocked when he opens the door. Jaw tight, brows low. 'I said she isn't here.'

'I know. She forgot something.' I hold out the envelope. 'I just wanted to give it back.'

He pulls the door closed behind him and steps out into the hall. 'Okay.'

I pull the envelope back from his hand just as he's reaching for it. 'And give her a message for me, okay?'

Fraser's eyes register defeat.

I drive slowly home. Otty and Joe watch me from the passenger seat.

It's done now. I have to deal with it, make the most of my life from now on. I won't waste time again.

Chapter Sixty-One

OTTY

I should be excited.

The apartments look great. Any one of them would be okay. London is exciting and enormous, and living there will be an adventure. The CEO and board of Exemplar are beyond excited about the writers' room Fraser and I will create. They've already started advertising for writers. I wonder if there's someone like me, working a day job to pay bills so they can write, who might dare to dream they could work there. I have come so far in just over a year and I've proved I can do this.

So why am I not excited?

I've watched Fraser throw himself into all the arrangements, grinning at me over his phone as he paces the kitchen. He looks like a man who won and his energy is boundless. He is full of plans and dreams, the freest I've ever seen him. And I can't doubt how he feels about me.

Even Dad was excited about my news when I told him. 'London, eh? 'Bout time they had a bit of Brummie class.'

'I'll miss you,' I said.

'We'll miss you right back. Joe too, I shouldn't wonder. But as long as you're happy, bab, that's enough for me.'

I should be happy, shouldn't I?

It's probably nerves. I'm about to make a major step in my career, a sea change in my life. It's bound to be daunting. And today I finished my final assignment for Russell and Ensign. There's a lot to take in.

I throw the stack of apartment details on the bed beside me and lay my head back against the pillow. The bedroom is cool and flooded with early-summer sun, causing the white sheets on the bed to glow. I have everything I need, I remind myself. I have to count my blessings.

Maybe I'll go out into the city for a while, let its vastness comfort me. Being surrounded by something so much bigger than I am will give me perspective – maybe even stop me being so hard on myself.

I roll off the bed and move to the full-length window that looks across the city and down to the street below. Sunlight glints off a car as it pulls away from the pavement, slowly edging into the traffic. It's dark blue, like the deepest hue of a rock pool, the dancing sunlight on its roof reminding me of sparkles skirting seawater eddies.

Dark blue.

I squint against the sun.

The car is almost at the end of the street now, where the adjoining road will either take it left or right to disappear into the city. I move along the window as I follow it: when its tiny indicator flashes and it turns right, it's unmistakable.

Dark blue Volkswagen Golf.

Joe's car.

No, Otty. Get a grip.

I laugh at myself. Now I'm seeing ghosts in Birmingham. It's definitely time to leave. I turn away from the window and stare at the stack of boxes piled up in Fraser's otherwise sparsely furnished bedroom. I feel like I'm cluttering up his space, although he assures me I'm not. I pat a box and try not to think of the words imprisoned in there. It's practical: no point unpacking my books here if we'll be leaving in a few weeks. But a space without them feels wrong.

At least these old friends will be with me when I leave.

I was going to try to sleep, but I'm awake now, my mind too restless to switch off. It wasn't Joe's car, but I'm annoyed I thought it was. I need to sink into the arms of the man who matters now, who is working so hard to establish the foundations we will build our new life upon.

Leaving the bedroom I wander into the large open-plan living space. He's sitting on the armchair near the window, gazing out at the city.

'Hey, you,' I say.

Fraser looks up. 'I thought you were having a rest.'

'I tried. My brain had other ideas.' I walk over to him and kiss his forehead. It furrows beneath my lips. I pull away and look at him. 'Everything okay?'

'Are you happy, Otty?'

'Yes. Of course I am. Are you?'

His eyes are wide when they meet mine. 'I love you. Why wouldn't I be happy?'

There's an edge in his tone that sends a shiver along my shoulders. 'Am I missing something?'

He looks back at the city. 'You had a visitor.'

'Who?'

'He left you this.' He lifts a white envelope from the chair arm. It arcs from his fingers to my hand.

I take it. The sun burns through the window glass. The front is blank, the flap sealed. I pull it open, aware of Fraser's storm-cloud stare on me.

The moment my fingers meet metal, my heart drops.

My key. To Joe's house.

Stuck to the key is a small orange sticky note, covered in Joe's handwriting.

As I recall, the maintain-status-quo thread was the orange Post-it line…

I shake off the memory of his voice and read the note:

Have found someone for the room.
Offering it to them today at 3 p.m.
Joe

Tears well in my eyes. I can't hide them from Fraser – I hear his sigh.

'There was a message, as well.' His voice is heavy with hurt. 'He said you still have something of his. But he doesn't want it back. He said it was yours all along.'

I close my eyes.

Fraser's laugh is cold and soulless. 'I don't think he was talking about his books.'

He knows, doesn't he? Fraser knows what's coming.

'I can't do this,' I say, the pieces finally joining – the cause of my restlessness becoming clear.

'Yeah. I figured that was what you were going to say.'

Gently, I kneel in front of him and place my hand on his. He won't look at me but I know he'll hear me. 'You're wonderful, Fraser...'

'Don't.'

'This is all on me,' I insist, gazing up into his lovely face. 'I can't be everything I want to be to you until I've put this to rest. You deserve someone who loves you completely, with nothing in the way.'

'Maybe you should let me be the judge of that.'

'It would destroy us, eventually. I can't do that to you. I'm so sorry.'

He shakes his head, finally meeting my gaze. But he knows. And I can't lie to him anymore.

'Then go.'

In tears as the lift descends, I look at my watch. 2.30 p.m. It's not enough time, is it? And if Joe's found someone else for my room, would he even consider me?

But I have a key. That has to be a sign.

Monty groans and creaks as I steer him around the city streets. My mind is a whir of shortcuts and alternative routes in case the building Friday-afternoon traffic conspires against me. The dashboard clock reads 2.35 p.m.... 2.40 p.m.... 2.45 p.m....

Temporary lights flick to red when I'm three streets away.

'No! *Change!*' I yell, my knuckles white where I grip the steering wheel.

2.50 p.m....

The oncoming traffic ebbs. A couple of teens dodge in front of the line and walk in a leisurely manner across my path.

2.52 p.m....

Green light.

I speed away, Monty's wheels squeaking like a roadster.

2.55 p.m....

I swing into the street I swore I'd never visit again.

2.57 p.m....

I spot the smallest space at the edge of a row of parked cars. I don't even know if Monty will fit between the last car and the beginning of the double-yellow lines. But I park, open my door and run.

2.59 p.m....

I can see the gate ahead, the harlequin-tiled path beyond, the dark front door. I race along the street towards the house where my life changed. The gate latch sticks when I try to lift it. I wrestle with its many painted layers to free it from the stay, precious seconds lost.

I hurry up the path, my red shoes flashing over the black and white diamonds and the pale stone doorstep I have climbed countless times before. I pull the key and Joe's note from my pocket – then hesitate. This isn't my house – not yet. Using my key feels too presumptuous. Joe has to decide if he'll let me back in.

So instead, I raise my hand to the lion-head door knocker and slam it three times against the black painted wood.

Then I wait.

Breath heavy and quick.

Eyes trained on the door.

I wait...

... And there is no answer.

Heart crashing inside me, I look at my watch.

3.03 p.m.

I'm too late.

I step back onto the harlequin tiles, gazing up at the home I will never call mine again. The Edwardian facade looms dark and empty in my vision as my tears slowly drown it.

I missed him.

I can't go in. I can't go back.

No home, no job. No *Joe*.

Think, Otty!

I turn away, retrace my steps. I have to start again. Regroup. I am not at the beginning – my achievements are still there. I can't go back to work at Ensign-Tempest because Joe is there. But maybe Russell will recommend me to another company. I have his respect now: that's a door I can try. I'll call my dad and move into my old room for a few weeks while I work everything out. It won't be easy, but at the end of the day, we look out for family. Dad loves me, so we can make it work.

I haven't thrown everything away. I've just reached the next point of decision. It hurts, but I can get through it.

As I have done so many times in my life, I push steel into my spine, set my face towards the future, raise my chin. I have not been defeated in the past and I won't be defeated today. It will be hard for a while, but nothing I can't overcome.

I pause and breathe. Let it wash over me.

In the end, I followed my heart. That's all I can ever do.

'Otty?'

I freeze.

The voice sounds behind me – back where the house stands, watching.

I turn – and there he is.

'Joe.'

He doesn't move from the doorstep.

Slowly I hold up the key and the note – like the crumpled card

I'd brandished on the day we met. 'I heard… you were looking for someone…'

He's breathing quickly now. I can see his chest rise and fall.

The words are there, where they always were. I know them by heart.

'I'd like to apply.'

In a moment he's with me, his body warm around mine as my hands frame his face. And Joe's kisses are worth racing across a city for. It's the final scene we didn't dare write, the action we couldn't commit to the page. It's out of time and over deadline with no guarantee of a next season.

But right now, it's perfect.

```
OTTY & JOE kiss. As they do, the note
falls from OTTY's hand, fluttering softly
down to rest on the black and white
tiles of the path. They break apart, JOE
pausing to stroke OTTY's face. Then they
walk together into the house and, kiss-
ing once more, close the door.
                         FADE TO BLACK.
```

END OF SHOW.

Acknowledgements

Written by

MIRANDA DICKINSON

Produced by

HQ, HARPERCOLLINS

Director

MANPREET GREWAL

(editor extraordinaire)

Executive Producer

HANNAH FERGUSON

(ace agent!)

Copy Editor

JON APPLETON

Proofreader

CHARLOTTE ATYEO

Production Team

MELANIE HAYES   LILY CAPEWELL

MELISSA KELLY   HALEMA BEGUM

ANGIE DOBBS   TOM KEANE

Production Design

ANNA SIKORSKA

KATE OAKLEY

Rights and Legal

HARDMAN SWAINSON

Author Support Team

RACHAEL LUCAS   TAMSYN MURRAY

JULIE COHEN   ROWAN COLEMAN

KATE HARRISON   CALLY TAYLOR

KIM CURRAN   A.G. SMITH

THE DREAMERS   THE MINTS

TEAM SPARKLY   WHITES & DICKINSONS

MY FAB SOCIAL MEDIA FOLLOWERS

Location Catering

JIM 'BOB' WHITE

Music

OTTY & JOE THEME inspired by

JUST YOU & I – Tom Walker – *What a Time to Be Alive*

FINAL CHAPTER inspired by

PHOTOGRAPH – Ed Sheeran – *X*

CHAPTER 59 inspired by

NOSTALGIA AND HOPE – Michael Price – *Emotional Cinema*

BACK IN THE WATER – Haevn – *Eyes Closed*

I DON'T WANT TO KNOW – Sigrid – *Raw – EP*

LIFE KEEPS MOVING ON – Ben Rector – *The Walking in Between*

HOLD ON – Olsson (feat. Mapei) – *Hold On (feat. Mapei) – EP*

WHAT IF I - Ben's Brother – *Battling Giants*

YOU ARE THE REASON – Calum Scott – *Only Human (Deluxe)*

WE DON'T TALK ANYMORE – Charlie Puth (feat. Selena Gomez) – *Nine Track Mind*

ALL WE DO – Oh Wonder – *Oh Wonder*

JOSEPHINE – RITUAL (feat. Lisa Hannigan) – *From the City to the Wilderness – EP*

FOREVER – Lewis Capaldi – *Divinely Inspired to a Hellish Extent*

FOOLS – Lauren Aquilina – *Fools – EP*

FLAWS – Olly Murs – *24 HRS (Deluxe)*

With thanks to

All the screenwriters of TV shows and films that I have loved. Your words make magic happen.

You, dear reader, for spending time with my words. I wrote them for you.

My lovely Bob and fabulous Flo – you're the reason for everything. I love you to the moon and back and twice around the stars xx

Written entirely on location in The Black Country, West Midlands. BIRMINGHAM appears as herself.

No writers were harmed in the making of this book.

Turn the page for an extract from the breathtaking and romantic love story from bestselling author Miranda Dickinson, *The Day We Meet Again*…

THE DAY WE MET

14th June 2017

Chapter One

PHOEBE

ALL TRAINS DELAYED, the sign reads.

No, no, *no*! This can't be happening!

I stare up at the departure board in disbelief. Up until twenty minutes ago my train had been listed as ON TIME and I'd allowed myself a glass of champagne at St Pancras' Eurostar bar, a little treat to steady my nerves before the biggest adventure of my life begins.

'Looks like we aren't going anywhere soon,' the woman next to me says, gold chains tinkling on her wrist as she raises her hand for another glass. She doesn't look in a hurry to go anywhere.

But I am.

I arrived at St Pancras two hours early this morning. The guys driving the cleaning trucks were pretty much the only people here when I walked in. They performed a slow, elegant dance around me as I dragged my heavy bag across the shiny station floor. I probably should have had a last lie-in, but my stomach has been a knot of nerves since last night, robbing me of sleep.

I'm not always early, but I was determined to be today to make sure I actually get on the train. I want this adventure more than anything else in my life, but doubts have crept in over the last two weeks, ever since all the tickets were booked and my credit card had taken the strain. Even last night – frustratingly wide awake and watching a film I didn't really care about, after the farewell drinks in our favourite pub in Notting Hill when I was *so* certain I was doing the right thing – I found myself considering shelving the trip. Who jacks in everything and takes off for a year, anyway? Certainly not me: Phoebe Jones, 32 years old and most definitely *not* gap-year material.

It wasn't just *that thing* Gabe said, either. Although it threw me when it happened. After all his bravado inside the pub – the *You won't go through with it, Phoebs, I know you* speech that in his actor's voice rose above the noise and look-at-me-I'm-so-important laughter from the tables around us – the change in him when he found me on the street outside was a shock.

'I'll miss you.'

'You won't, but thanks.'

And then that look – the one that got us into trouble once before, the one that has kept me wondering if it might again. 'Then you don't know me, Phoebs. London won't be the same without you.'

Why did he have to launch that at me, the night before I leave for a whole year?

But the money is spent. The tickets are in my wallet. My bag is packed. And Gabe is *wrong* if he thinks I won't go through with it. I know my friends privately think I'll cave in and come home early. So I got up hours before I needed to this morning, took my bag, closed the door on my old life and posted my keys through the letterbox for my friends and former flatmates to find. And I'm *here*, where Gabe was so certain I wouldn't be.

But now there's a delay and that's dangerous for me. Too much time to think better of my plan. Why is the universe conspiring against me today?

'Having another?' the woman next to me asks. Her new glass of champagne is already half empty. Perhaps she has the right idea. Maybe drinking your way through a delay is the best option.

'I don't think so, thanks,' I reply. I can't stay here, not until I know exactly what kind of delay I'm facing. 'I'm going to find out what's happening.'

The woman shrugs as I leave.

The whole of St Pancras station seems to have darkened, as though a storm cloud has blown in from the entrance and settled in the arcing blue-girdered roof. Beyond the glass the sun shines as brightly as before, the sky a brave blue. But I feel the crackle of tension like approaching thunder.

At the end of the upper concourse near the huge statue of a man and woman embracing, a crowd has gathered. Somewhere in the middle, a harassed station employee in an orange hi-vis gilet is doing his best to fend off the angry mob's questions. And then, without warning, the crowd begins to move. I'm almost knocked over and stagger back to stop myself falling. Being trampled to death is definitely not in the plan today.

The mob swarms around the station employee as he makes for the stairs to the lower concourse. The forward motion of their bodies pushes me backwards until my spine meets something immovable. I gasp. Around me the angry commuters part, a splitting tide of bodies flooding either side of me, their feet stomping inches from mine. Once they pass me they continue their pursuit of their prey as the poor station official flees down the stairs.

I'm shaken, but then I remember: I hit something. *Someone.*

'I'm *so* sorry,' I rush, turning to see the poor unfortunate soul I've slammed into. But my eyes meet the kind, still expression of an iron man in trilby and suit, his billowing mackintosh frozen in time as he gazes up, as though checking the departure boards for his train.

The Betjeman statue.

I'd forgotten he was here. Compared with the huge iron lovers beneath the enormous station clock over the entrance, he's diminutive. I've seen visitors double take when they find him. He's just *there*, standing in the middle of the upper concourse, humble and friendly. The only thing marking him out as a statue and not another train passenger is the ring of slate around his feet, the words of one of his poems carved into it in beautifully elegant script. I've heard station announcements asking commuters to meet people *by the Betjeman statue* when I've been here before and thought nothing of it. But finding him here this morning, when everything has suddenly become so uncertain, is strangely comforting.

'I don't think he minds,' a voice says.

I jump and peer around the statue. 'Sorry?'

Over the statue's right shoulder, a face grins at me. 'Sir John. He won't mind you bumped into him. He's a pretty affable chap.'

Laughter dances in his voice, his green eyes sparkling beneath dark brows and a mess of dark curls. And I instantly feel I know him.

'I can't believe I just apologised to a statue.'

'Happens to us all, sooner or later.' His hand reaches around Sir John's arm. 'Hi, I'm Sam. Sam Mullins. Pleased to meet you.'

I hesitate. After all, this is London and my seven years in the city have taught me strangers are supposed to stay anonymous. But Sam's smile is as warm and inviting as a newly opened doorway on a winter's night and – suddenly – I'm accepting his handshake. His hand is warm around mine.

'Phoebe Jones. Pleased to meet you, too.'

The concourse is eerily empty now; the raging commuters all disappeared to the lower floor chasing the poor man from the train company. It's as if me and Sam-with-the-smiling-eyes-and-laugh-filled-voice are the only people in the world.

Apart from the statue, that is.

'Did you get to hear what the bloke from the station was saying?' I ask, suddenly aware I am still holding Sam's warm hand, and quickly pulling mine away.

'Most of it, before the mob closed in. They've stopped all trains in and out of the station. I haven't heard the Inspector Sands announcement, so I'm guessing it isn't a fire or a bomb threat.'

My stomach twists again. I've only heard the automated announcement used to alert station staff to a possible emergency like a fire or a bomb once before at Euston and I ran from the station like a startled hare then. Given my nerves about my journey, if I'd heard Inspector Sands being mentioned today I would already be halfway to Holborn. 'Did he say how long it was expected to last?'

'Well, I heard four hours, but there were so many people yelling around the chap by then I guess anyone could have said that.'

'*Four hours?*'

'Nightmare, huh? Trust me to pick today to make the longest train journey.'

I blink at him. 'Me too.'

'Oh? Where are you headed?' His eyes widen and he holds up a hand. 'Sorry, you don't have to answer. That was rude of me.'

It's sweet and it makes me smile. 'Paris, actually. To begin with. You?'

'Isle of Mull. Eventually.'

'Oh. Wow. That *is* a journey.'

He shrugs. 'Just a bit. Already had to change it because of the

9

engineering works at Euston, so I'm going from here to Sheffield, then over to Manchester then changing again for Glasgow. Going to stay with two of my old university mates near there for a night or two, to break it up a bit. Then I'll catch a train to Oban, take the ferry to Craignure and then it's a long bus ride to Fionnphort, where I'm staying with a family friend.' He gives a self-conscious laugh. 'More than you wanted to know, probably.'

Although I'll move on from Paris later, Sam's journey sounds epic and exhausting by comparison. And it's strange, but I don't even consider that I've just met him, or question how he can share his entire travel itinerary with me when we don't know each other. Like the heat from his hand that is still tingling on my skin, it feels like the most natural thing. So I forget my nerves, my shock at finding myself here beside the statue, and the looming delay. And instead, I just see Sam.

'How long will all that take?'

'The whole journey? *Hours*. Days, even.' He laughs. 'It's okay. I have several books in my luggage and my music. I'll be fine.'

Novels are one thing I do have, although they are safely packed at the bottom of my bag. Books are the reason I'm here, after all. The Grand Tours across Europe inspired my PhD and have underpinned all my dreams of seeing the places the authors wrote about for myself. My much-loved copy of *A Room with a View* is in my hand luggage and I'm more than happy to hang out with Lucy Honeychurch and George Emerson for the thousandth time, but I'd much rather be on the train heading off already.

What if this delay is a sign? I hate the thought of Gabe being right, but the doubts from last night return, swirling around me, Sam and Sir John Betjeman like ragged ghosts. *There are other ways of pursuing a great adventure*, they call. *You don't have to spend a year away to prove you're spontaneous…* My room at the flat-share is already someone else's but I could persuade one of my friends to let me stay at theirs until I can sort out a new place. I don't really want to go home to Evesham, but I know my parents and brother Will would love having me to stay for a bit. Maybe I should be a bit less intrepid – Cornwall would be nice this time of year, or maybe the Cotswolds? Safer, closer, easier to come home from…

I don't want to doubt this now, not when I'm so close to boarding the train, but I can feel panic rising.

But then, Sam Mullins smiles – and the ground beneath me shifts.

'Look, if you're not going anywhere for a while and neither am I, how about we find a coffee shop to wait in?'

Did I just say that? But in that moment, it feels right. Who says my new, spontaneous self can't start until I board the train for France?

'Yes,' he says, so immediately that his answer dances with the end of my question. 'Great idea.'

As we walk away from the statue of Sir John Betjeman, Sam's fingers lightly brush against my back.

And *that's* when I fall in love.

Chapter Two

SAM

What am I doing?

I hate complications. As a musician I've done my level best over the years to avoid them wherever I can. When band politics have got too much, I've quit. When my brother stopped talking to me, I walked away. When relationships have become too demanding, I've backed out. Simple. Effective. Safe.

And I've been doing okay with that. Mostly. The last four years have been the happiest of my life professionally – playing my fiddle in studio sessions in the winter and spring and joining festival-bound bands in the summer; teaching where I've needed to make up shortfalls; even scoring studio time for my own new-folk project and producing a half-decent EP that, touch wood, will bring in a steady flow of cash on iTunes and Bandcamp. And my new studio venture with Chris that we launched last night finally gives us a chance to make real money. To be fair, I said I'd postpone this trip so close to the launch, but Chris said he wants to get it running smoothly and I'd just be getting in his way. So that complication has been ironed out, without me even trying. Why would I willingly volunteer for one to take its place?

She just looked so lost by the Betjeman statue.

And gorgeous...

I should have been annoyed by this unplanned delay to the journey I've promised myself for years. I've waited so long for the time to be right and then, suddenly, it was. Time to make the journey to find who I am. It was supposed to begin now, not in four hours, or whenever the train system deems it possible. Train delays are the worst, especially for a jobbing musician travelling to gigs across the country and particularly given the shenanigans I've already encountered changing stations for this journey. On any other day I would have been right in the thick of that angry commuter mob, baying for someone's blood.

But I'm not.

And it's all because of Phoebe Jones.

I glance at the large ironwork clock over the coffee concession counter and I'm surprised to see almost an hour has passed already. She was shy at first, but as soon as she suggested we come here she just – *blossomed*. Like watching a water lily unfurl on the other side of the bleached-wood table.

It's beautiful to witness.

'I know a year away is a big step. I mean *enormous* for me. But ever since I first read *A Room with a View* and Mark Twain's *A Tramp Abroad*, I've dreamed of doing this. Paris, Florence, Rome – seeing the places the authors and characters in their books saw. I've saved forever to do it. My parents gave me the last bit of the money I needed when I got my PhD last month.'

'So you're *Dr* Jones?'

I could bask in the way she beams for a long time.

'That sounds so funny, doesn't it? Dr Jones. I like it but it still feels like it should belong to somebody else.'

'A PhD is a huge amount of work, though. You've earned it.'

'I have.' There's a self-conscious laugh she does that's like a flash of sunlight. Blink and you'll miss it. 'I loved every minute of it, though. It was such a surprise to find that from a piece of work.'

'Maybe that's what you're supposed to be doing.'

'How do you mean?'

'Well, like for me, playing and gigging and the studio I've just set up with my friend – none of that's easy. It's all long hours and hard work' – I nod at the concourse beyond the coffee concession window which is packed with stranded passengers – 'and train delays… But I'm energised by it, you know? Because this is what I'm meant to do.'

Phoebe nods but she isn't smiling. 'I hear that all the time. My best friends all seem to have found what they're meant to be doing. Meg's the most amazing event organiser, Osh is a film director and Gabe is an actor. When they talk about what they do, it's like they are describing a piece of themselves; like if you put them under a microscope their job titles would be imprinted on every cell. I haven't found what I should be doing yet. But I think this year I might get closer to working out what I want.'

'Do you write?'

A patter of pink traverses her cheekbones. 'No – well, not unless you count my PhD dissertation. I mean, I love the idea of writing fiction, but I wouldn't know where to begin. Gabe says I'm not personally tormented enough to be a writer. I don't know if that's a good thing or not.'

She isn't wearing a ring – I mean, of course I've checked. But she's mentioned *Gabe* a few times already and I notice her right hand instinctively touches the finger on her left that would have worn one when she says his name. Who is he? A recent flame? An ex? An unrequited love?

'He thinks I can't do this. But I know I can.'

'Why do you care about what he thinks? He sounds like a knob.'

She laughs. The sound is joyous. It surges up from her core, like champagne bubbles. 'Maybe he is. But I've always talked to him about everything. We used to trade awful dating stories when both of us were between dates – it became a game we'd play to make ourselves feel better.' She toys with the teaspoon in the saucer of her almost empty cup. 'So, enough about me. What's taking you to Scotland? Work?'

'No. Well, maybe a little.' I see a fine line form between her brows. That's me sussed. 'I'm going for personal reasons,' I reply. And then, just because it feels like she's the person to say it to, I say more than I have to anyone else. 'I was born on the Island and then my father left home. He played fiddle, too, although he left before I discovered music for myself. I guess I've always wondered, you know? What happened to him.' Suddenly aware I've said too much to be comfortable, I pull back. 'But I plan to hook up with some friends from the circuit while I'm there, too. Relearn the trad stuff.'

'You're a folk musician?'

'New-folk, I guess you'd call it. But I want my next project to be the old tunes I vaguely remember from being a kid on the Island.'

'I thought you had a bit of a Scottish accent.' She blushed. 'I'm sorry, should that be *Hebridean*?'

It's the most hesitantly British thing to say and it's all I can do not to laugh out loud. 'Scottish is fine.'

'So you're going home?'

Home. That's a word I haven't used for a while. With Ma gone and my brother Callum as good as dead, I don't know what I call home any more. The flat I've been sharing with my drummer mate Syd is homely, but is it *home*? Is that what I'll discover in Mull when I return?

'I don't know. Maybe. You?'

I've asked it before I can think better, but here in the too-warm crush of the coffee concession, I realise I want to know the answer. I expect her to sidestep the question, but to my utter surprise, she doesn't.

'Not a home to live in. I want to find out how to be at home with myself.'

Until that moment, everything Phoebe Jones has told me could just have been polite conversation. But this is something else. It's a window, inviting me in. I lean closer, zoning out the clamour and conversation around our small table, not wanting to miss a thing.

'Me too.'

Her eyes hold mine.

'I haven't said that to anyone before.'

'Not even Gabe?'

'Especially not him. He thinks I'm too serious.'

'No!'

'I know, right? I mean, look at us, Sam. We met – what – an hour ago? And all we've done is laugh.'

'You're a very funny lady.'

'Well, thank you for noticing.' Her eyes sparkle as she mirrors my grin. There is so much more going on behind those eyes than she's allowing me to see. I sense it bubbling away, just out of view.

And *that's* when I realise.

Sam Mullins, your timing stinks.

The more we talk, as the minutes become an hour and head towards two, the more the feeling deep within me builds. Phoebe Jones is *perfect*. And I know my own battered heart. I'd sworn I wouldn't fall for anyone again, not after Laura. The pain and injustice I've battled most of the year and the bruises still stinging my soul have all been good enough reasons to avoid falling in love.

Could this be love?

No.

But what if it is?

By now we are wandering the concourse, passing crowds of stranded travellers. Every available bench has been commandeered and people are claiming the floor, too, perched on makeshift seats made from suitcases, holdalls and folded-up coats. It's like a scene from a disaster movie, displaced people caught in limbo, dazed by the experience. Some groups of travellers are even *talking to each other*. In London, that's pretty close to a miracle.

I have to step to the side to avoid a small child who's weaving in and out of the crowd – and when I do my hand brushes against Phoebe's. Startled, she looks up and our eyes meet. The noise around us seems to dim, the pushing bodies becoming a blur as I sink into the deep darkness of Phoebe's stare.

'Do you believe in fate, Phoebe?' The words tumble out before I can stop them.

'I think I do,' she breathes, as her fingers find mine. 'Do you?'

I gaze at her, a hundred thoughts sparkling around us like spinning stars. And suddenly, all that matters is the truth.

'I didn't before today.'

ONE PLACE. MANY STORIES

Bold, innovative and
empowering publishing.

FOLLOW US ON:

@HQStories